REDCLAW

DRAGONKIN

BOOK ONE: WYVERNWOOD

iBooks
Habent Sua Fata Libelli

iBooks
Manhanset House
Dering Harbor, New York 11965

bricktower@aol.com • www.ibooksinc.com

Library of Congress Cataloging-in-Publication Data

Bailey, Robin Wayne
Dragonkin; Wyvernwood
p. cm.

1. Fiction. 2. Fantasy—Dragons. 3 Fantasy—Epic
Fiction, I. Title.

978-1-59687-523-4, Hardcover
978-1-59687-836-5, Trade Paper

Copyright © 2003 by ibooks, inc. and Robin Wayne Bailey
Cover art and interior illustrations
copyright © 2003 by iBooks

Dragonkin is a trademark of iBooks
An original publication of iBooks
An ibooks, inc. Book

Edited by Judy Gittenstein and Steven Roman

Jacket art by Troy Howell
Jacket design by j. vita
Interior design by Gilda Hannah

February 2019

DRAGONKIN

BOOK ONE: WYVERNWOOD

ROBIN WAYNE BAILEY

Illustrated by Troy Howell

For William Edward Foss
on his birthday

For my nieces,
Christine and Allison Chesney

For Diana Bailey,
who counts the stars

For Ron Davis,
who counts the sets and reps

For Jim Degarmo,
who accounts

And for Jim Washek
to let him know how much he counts.

Some say that we are gone—
It is not so.
Some say that we are dead,
Or passed on long ago—
But, no.
In the golden sunset,
Or in the dark of night,
Sometimes in the silver glow
Of full moonlight,
We ride the currents of the stars—
Look and see!
For there we are
On the borderland 'tween
Dusk and dawn—
Dragons all in graceful flight!
Some say that we are gone.
Ah, but others know
It is not so,
That the world still is full of
Wondrous things—
So pause and listen
For the whisper of our wings!

—A Song from
The Great Book of Stormfire

Table of Contents

Prologue

A SOFT, EVENING WIND RUSTLED through the trees on the southern edge of Wyvernwood, shaking the last of the autumn leaves from the black branches and setting the high tops to swaying. In the west, the sunset shone down in beams of red-orange light through the stout trees and gnarly limbs, but its distant, fading warmth could not chase the chill from the air.

Marina lay curled up at the mouth of her cave, watching the dying sun with one eye as she measured the slow approach of night with the other. She felt old and weary and filled with a sense of sadness she didn't understand as she gazed down from her hill and across the ancient forest. It was the coming of winter, she told herself, that was responsible for her mood.

Quick, small footsteps sounded behind her, then suddenly stopped. Marina lifted her silver-scaled head and craned her long neck to look back into her cave, and she smiled gently at the dragon-child that stood there.

"Come closer, Puck, my little one," she urged. And Puck did so, nuzzling down into the crook of her arm as she drew him near and sheltered him under one shining wing. "It's too late to play outside, and it's growing cold. Let's just lie here close together and count the stars as they appear."

Puck folded his arms under his narrow chin and kneaded his claws lightly on his mother's arm. After a few moments, he began to purr, cat-like, as was the manner of all dragon-children. Without lifting his head from her arm, he rolled his eyes skyward, searching. Suddenly, he sang out:

> "I spy! I spy!
> High up in the velvet sky,
> The first star of night I see!
> Now my wish will come to be!"

Marina rolled him over and tickled his stomach. Puck squealed, but made no real effort to escape. Finally, Marina stopped and gazed down upon her dragon-child, and her sadness lifted a little. The sunset shimmered on his golden scales, and in its light he looked like a beautiful little bundle of fire. She loved Puck so.

"Show me your star," she said.

He flipped over and resumed his former position stretched out beside her, his head resting on her arm, as he pointed. "There!" he answered. "Just above those trees. See how it seems to hang on the branches!"

Marina smiled again and drew her long tail up to encircle them both as she studied the star. It was Rono, the eternal dusk-time star, ever bright and ever constant, always the First Star.

"You have sharp eyes, little Puck," she said. "Now tell me your wish, and perhaps I can help it come to pass."

He squirmed against her, flexed the small, leathery stubs of his immature wings, and yawned. "I wish you'd tell me a story," he said. "I love it best when you read to me from Stormfire's Book, or when you tell me tales from the old days."

Marina closed her eyes briefly. *A tale from the old days.* But there were so many stories to tell, so many heroes to remember, so many adventures that needed passing on. She stroked little Puck lightly with one paw.

"A story from the old days, then," she said, her voice little more than a whisper. "When the Age of Dragons was drawing to an end, and Wyvernwood was young and wild and beautiful."

"Wyvernwood was our home then, too?" Puck asked as he gazed out across the darkening forest.

"Our home and our refuge," Marina answered. "Wyvernwood is vast and deep, and all the Dragonkin are gathered here. And the griffins, too, and the basilisks and minotaurs and manticores, and all the creatures that remain from the Ancient Days. But hush now, little Puck, and close your eyes, and listen to the gentle breeze and the rustle of the leaves as they are swept away, and to the soft creep of approaching night, for they are the music that brings my tale to life.

"And if you chance to open your eyes even for a moment, look to Rono above the treetops, and remember what I tell you now—that there are still dreams to dream and stars to be wished upon. Then close your eyes again and let imagination take wing."

Marina sighed as her child relaxed against her, and she felt the soft vibration of his tiny body beneath her protective wing. "I am old," she continued. "Older than you know, my pretty dragon-boy, but I remember Stormfire and the time when dragons and griffins warred in the Wyvernwood skies, and when the humans of Angmar to the north and Degarm in the south made a battleground of our homeland. The Redclaw Fortress did not yet stand, and Undersky had not yet been found.

"The Age of Dragons was not yet quite past, and to Stormfire and his dragon-wife Sabu was born a rare clutch of three eggs from which came the triplets, Harrow, Chan, and Luna."

"The Dragon Sabu," Puck murmured without opening his eyes, "who went insane."

"Do not speak ill of her," Marina chided softly. "For it was all according to prophesy, and all that her children dared and accomplished was for the good of the Dragonkin. As I said, it was long ago, but I will tell the tale as if it were today or yesterday, and your imagination will give shape to my words."

Marina looked at her child, and his eyes were tightly closed as he waited for the story to begin. She experienced a sudden warmth and peace, and the sadness she had earlier felt melted away. Beyond her cave, beyond the edge of the woods, the sunset faded and faded, and the violet night stole closer. Rono no longer shone alone in the sky; a few more stars twinkled, and the glow of the rising moon cast tree-shadows over the earth.

"This is your wish, to hear a tale," she whispered. "And it begins like this. . . ."

1

BUMBLE FLEW FROM ONE TREE TO THE NEXT, his tiny wings a blur of speed, his heart pounding with anger and despair. They were coming with saws and axes, long lines of dirty men with loud voices and thick ropes coiled over their brawny shoulders! Even as he fled, he could hear the powerful *chop, chop, chop* of their efforts resounding through the forest, followed by the terrible crash of the great mahogany tree he'd called home for three summers.

Panting, he paused in the branches of a redwood and looked around. He'd put enough distance between the woodcutters and himself that he could no longer see them, although the relentless pounding of their axes and the rasp of their saws continued to fill the air. Something more immediate caught his attention, however.

At the base of the redwood a wild rose bramble grew. Its blood-red blossoms exuded a delicious and tempting perfume. Bumble wasted no time, but dived straight for the roses. *A hummingbird has to keep up his energy,* he told himself as he dipped his long, needle-like beak between the petals, and drank deeply from its pool of nectar.

"Ummmmm! So good! So sweet!" he exclaimed as he hovered over the bramble. "I must sample another, I simply must!" And he darted to a second blossom. Its nectar was as savory as the first. And, of course, he had to try a third. After that, he landed on a tangle of branches, ignoring the numerous thorns, and patted his bloated little belly as he belched his satisfaction.

"I must remember this delightful smorgasbord!" he said. "I must remember . . . !" He screwed his tiny face up suddenly, and licked the last drop of nectar from his narrow beak as he listened to the saws and axes. "Oh, dear! I remember! I remember!"

He took off again, zipping through the forest at a frantic pace as he cried out for help in a voice that was barely audible over the drone of his wings. "Alert! Alert!" he shouted. "Invaders! Monsters! Gather your women and throw the children overboard! Be calm, but we're all doomed!"

Bumble was a stout little fellow, but excitable and given to confusion. He zigzagged among the trees without direction or destination, screaming his warning until his voice gave out. In no time at all, he grew hungry again, for a hummingbird's appetite was almost endless. He looked around for his next meal, and plunged toward a crop of daisies growing beside a stream.

Hovering over the yellow petals, he thrust his beak forward. "Oh, yes! Oh, rich!" he cried in a paroxysm of joy as he drank his fill. "So many tasty flowers! What a delightful golden treasure I have found!" He flew to an overhanging branch, fluttered his wings before folding them tightly against his body, and then stretched out on his back with his legs straight up in the air.

He felt so full and content as he stared up through the thick, green leaves at the blue sky beyond. Through a gap in the branches, he watched a white cloud slowly change from one shape to another as it drifted past. First, it looked to him like a huge chrysanthemum, so savory and delicious. Then, as the breeze pushed it along, it became an amaryllis. Bumble groaned and licked his beak at the thought; nothing tasted so good as a fresh amaryllis! Well, except an orchid, which is what the cloud resembled next.

Bumble folded his wings over his round belly. Cloud watching was hard work, and he felt famished already. There were still daisies by the stream below he had not sampled. Indeed, as he flipped over to his feet and stretched his wings, he realized that he was in a part of Wyvernwood he'd never explored before. He gazed up and down the stream. On both banks it was bordered with the most delectable selection of wildflowers! The tree in which he found himself might serve him very well as a new home.

Oh, but he had a home in a beautiful mahogany.

Somewhere.

He hopped around on his branch, suddenly nervous and uncertain. There was something he should remember, but hummingbirds were cursed with notoriously bad memories. He glanced toward the daisies, and despite his unease, he couldn't help but admire the way those sweet blossoms reflected in the stream's clear water.

Perhaps a drink of nectar would help him recall what he had forgotten.

But a dark shadow skimmed the tops of the trees, and Bumble instinctively froze. Every taut muscle in his body quivered. When the shadow passed, he waited for long minutes with his eyes squeezed shut, letting the sunlight chase away the chill that had seized him.

"Never a good day when a griffin crosses your path."

Bumble jumped, startled, though the voice was gently feminine. Further downstream, he spied a white unicorn reclining delicately on a bed of moss with her legs folded beneath her. The sunlight flashed on one exposed golden hoof as she batted her blue eyes at him.

He struggled to remember her name before exclaiming, "Miriam! What a wonderful sore for sight eyes you are!"

"Marian," she corrected with a bemused smile. "What are you doing so far from your tree, Bumble, besides gorging that legendary tummy of yours? Even in Wyvernwood there are dangers for those who venture too far from home."

Pushing his chest out, he answered, "I'm not afraid, dear Miriam." He began to strut back and forth as he regarded her. With his shimmering green plumage and the distinctive white band around his throat, and his rapier-like beak, he knew he cut an impressive figure. "In fact," he continued, "it's well-known that I lust for adventure, that I spit at danger, that . . ."

Marian chuckled softly, but Bumble barely noticed as he stopped in middle of his boast. *Danger.* There was something he needed to remember. He strained his tiny brain, and his heart began to race again. Something . . . something!

"Alert! Alert!" he cried in sudden panic as he jumped up and down. "Danger, will . . . !" He beat the tip of one wing against his head, trying to jar his memory. "One if by land! Two if by sea!" He gave a squeal, a single, shrill note that hurt his throat. "In blackest day, in brightest night, I wish I may, I wish I might!"

Marian laughed. "You are a silly creature."

Bumble stopped his pacing and shot her a stern look. "You can say that to me with a straight face and a horn sticking out of your head?" It was rude of him, and he regretted his remark instantly for one should never be rude to a unicorn, yet it jogged a memory. "Miriam! I remember now! There's a herd of Men loose in Wyvernwood!

They're cutting down the trees! They cut down my beloved mahogany!"

"Poor Bumble!" Marian murmured sympathetically. "No wonder you're so addled. It must have fallen on your head!"

"A grievous loss, indeed," Bumble answered, "and it's true I barely escaped with both my wings intact!" He looked around frantically, and his gaze settled on the daisies. He was so hungry! But there wasn't time to eat, because he remembered! He remembered!

"But it's worse than just my poor mahogany, Marian," he continued, at last getting her name right. "Much worse. They've got him! Got him bound in their cruel ropes hand and hoof and horn!" He pointed to her head with one wing. "That's how I remembered, because you have a horn, too! And we've got to do something! Call out the army . . . !"

Marian sprang up from her soft bed of moss, and though the shadows of limbs and leaves dappled her slender flanks, the sunlight flashed brilliantly on the tip of her proud spike. When she interrupted him, her voice was low and angry. "They've got who, you Bumble-bird?"

"My poor home! My poor home!" Bumble moaned, rubbing and wringing his wings as he paced again on his limb. "But Marian! I saw! The Men have captured Chernovog—the Minotaur!"

Marian tossed her mane and crashed a hoof on the ground.

"We have to tell Stormfire!" Bumble said. "Or Sabu, or . . . !"

"There isn't time," Marian answered sharply. "Lead the way, Hummingbird, and see that you fly straight and true. We'll save him ourselves!"

Bumble gulped.

2

GORGANAR GLIDED LOW THROUGH THE AIR, just skimming the tops of Wyvernwood's mighty trees. He took pleasure in the ripping and churning of leaves in his wake, in the rustle of the branches, and he took particular, cruel pleasure in the way the other forest denizens scurried and rushed to hide themselves from his keen eyesight.

As if anything in Wyvernwood could escape a griffin's notice.

He turned his head to left and right to make sure that Gaunt and Morkir were keeping up with him. His heart swelled with a father's pride as he watched his two sons. The sunlight gleamed on their golden pinions and powerful, leonine bodies. Morkir, his youngest, flew with his front paws stretched out before him so that the thick, taut muscles under his yellow hide rippled. Off to the left, Gaunt sailed higher than his father and brother and slightly behind them. He flew with an aloof indifference to the residents of Wyvernwood, even to his father and brother, and his great wings beat the air with a steady rhythm as he kept his gaze trained straight ahead.

It was a beautiful day, a good day to rend and tear and destroy something, a day to remind the world why griffins were the most feared of creatures, and why he was the most feared of griffins. Gorganar flexed his wings, swooped toward a towering pine tree, and snapped the top of it off with a single swipe from his left paw. A pair of nesting swallows flashed out from their home among the branches, flying as fast as they could in the opposite direction, and Gorganar laughed.

"Father!" Morkir called. "Look toward the sea! There's better sport than an old pine tree!"

Gorganar flew up beside Morkir and looked where his youngest directed. Not far off the coastline, crawling on the water at no great speed, was a ship. He noted the white sails and the tall mast with its fluttering red banner, the sleek manner in which the high bow cut the waves, the sailors frantically busy on its decks.

Men out of Angmar! The fools! So close to Wyvernwood! So close to *his* kingdom!

Gorganar called over his shoulder to his older son, Gaunt. "You're flying higher than either of us!" he shouted with a hint of accusation. "Why did you not see this ship before your brother?"

"I did," Gaunt answered calmly. "I also see the tinier boat a hundred yards off its starboard side. It is filled with children who seem to be racing for shore."

Gorganar climbed higher in the sky, the better to see what Gaunt saw. Indeed, a small boat containing five children, two of whom desperately worked a pair of oars, was headed for Wyvernwood.

"Why didn't you alert me to this at once?" Gorganar demanded.

Gaunt merely shrugged and said no more.

"Give the order, Father!" Morkir called. "Let me knock these haughty men and their pathetic vessel into tomorrow's sunset for you. Let me stain the sea with their blood!"

Gorganar turned to his older son with a stern, almost angry look. He was proud of Gaunt, as any father would be, but he didn't understand his first-born, and he didn't like the sullen insolence he sometimes exhibited. It bordered on disrespect. "Your brother is an eager cub," Gorganar said. "But what do you say, Gaunt?"

"You are Gorganar," Gaunt answered coolly. "Of course, you're going to destroy these men. Their fates were sealed the moment they fell under your far-seeing gaze. Why ask my opinion, or even Morkir's?"

A low growl formed in Gorganar's throat. "It is you, Gaunt, who have pronounced their sentences."

"No, Father," Gaunt answered with a barely concealed smirk. "Unlike Morkir, I have nothing to prove. I only yield to the inevitable."

"My brother is a coward," Morkir laughed.

Gorganar watched Gaunt from the corner of his eye to judge what kind of an effect such words would have on his first-born. But Gaunt didn't react at all. Indeed, he gave no indication that he had even heard Morkir's insult. No father liked to see his offspring fight among themselves, but such passivity made his blood boil. He wondered if Morkir was right!

The sailing ship would make a fine target upon which to spend his anger. The men of Angmar had been too bold of late and needed to be taught a lesson. For generations they and all their kind had feared and avoided Wyvernwood. Once, they had considered the forest haunted, evil, a harbor for ancient, nearly forgotten magicks, and the dark legends and tales they told of Wyvernwood had served as well as any wall to keep the Men at bay.

But things had changed. Men were losing their fear of the woods and its residents. Increasingly, they were pushing across the borders, deeper and deeper into Wyvernwood to hunt game and cut the ancient trees.

Gorganar cared nothing about the creatures they killed or the trees they chopped into firewood. But the audacity of their actions—that outraged him!

Faster and faster he flew, beating his massive wings and flexing his claws, working himself into a blood-frenzy. Over the hills and valleys of Wyvernwood he raced, with his two sons keeping pace beside him. White beach flashed beneath, a narrow ribbon of sand that separated the deep green of the forest from the intense blue of the Windy Sea. Then he was over the water.

The sailors on the Angmar ship saw them. "Eagles!" some cried, and others, "Lions! Flying lions!" They pressed against the deck rails in wide-eyed fear, brandishing clubs or swords or pikes. Others found bows and filled the air with a rain of arrows.

Gorganar laughed cruelly as he climbed high above the range of their primitive weapons. Then, folding wings and paws tight against his golden body, he plunged straight downward. With one mighty swipe, just as he had done to the pine tree, he snapped the vessel's mainmast. The ship lurched sideways under the force of the blow. On deck, men screamed as they flung themselves away from the falling timbers, the sail sheeting, and the coils of whipping rope. A handful tumbled over the rails into the sea, others slid bare-bellied over the rough deck, catching hold of anything they could to save themselves.

Behind his father, Gaunt hit the bow hard, and the stern of the ship pitched out of the water. An instant later, Morkir hit the stern in the same manner, snapping the tiller and pitching the bow high. Between the brothers, they made a seesaw of the vessel, and men tumbled like helpless rag dolls. Over the cries of terror came the sound of splitting timbers, and at mid-ship a crack appeared across the breadth of the deck.

Gorganar hit the ship again. On the leeward side, he closed his claws around the rails, while on the starboard side, Morkir did the same. With a furious beating of their wings, they lifted the ship half out of the water. Then the starboard rail tore free in Morkir's grip. Gorganar also let go. The vessel rolled and rocked and threatened to capsize. Yet, by virtue of its engineering it managed to right itself.

"Destroy it!" Gorganar called to his sons. "Sink it! Make them all remember why they fear our forest!"

But Morkir was climbing high into the blue sky and banking on the point of one wing toward the small boat with the five children, who had stopped their frantic rowing to watch the one-sided battle. As Morkir turned toward them, two of the children freed the oars from the oarlocks and rose in the boat to defend themselves.

Morkir screamed a challenge and flexed his claws. Against a son of Gorganar, against any griffin, such little pink herdlings stood no chance. He dove straight for the tiny boat.

Then Gaunt, flying at his swiftest, hit his brother with the force of a battering ram, knocking him from the sky. Morkir struck the water with a stunning impact; the splash created waves that tossed the children's boat and flipped it over.

Between his huge front paws, Gorganar held the shattered mainmast. The surface of the Windy Sea was dotted with men swimming in all directions or clinging to floating debris. But Gaunt's treacherous attack on Morkir had not escaped his notice. He flung the mainmast like a gigantic spear, impaling the Angmar ship through deck and hull. Then with an enraged shout, he turned toward his sons.

Gaunt turned to meet Gorganar with a furious growl that was the equal of his father's. In his eyes was the same glint of steel fearlessness.

Gorganar drew back to strike with a claw that would have ripped his older son's throat out. But in Gaunt's eyes he saw, perhaps for the first time, that they were indeed two of a kind, of the same blood, and he stayed his attack.

"What have you done?" he demanded. "You struck your brother!"

Gaunt met his father's gaze without flinching. "I am not in the mood to make war on such small things as these," he said, tipping a wing toward the five children clinging to the sides of their boat. "Where is the honor in it? Destroy the ship, Father. Destroy its masters, and be satisfied."

"I will not be satisfied!" Morkir shouted, rising from the waves. Streaming water, he flew straight for his brother. Before Gorganar could intercede, Gaunt turned to meet Morkir. The air exploded with feathers and fur. Locked tooth and nail, they tumbled out of control through the sky and fell into the sea with such a splash that the wounded ship gave a loud groan and turned over on its side.

Up from the waves, oblivious to the sinking vessel or the screams of its crew, the two brothers rose. Gorganar raced to separate them. "Stop it!" he called. "Stop it, or I'll break both your fool necks!" He batted them apart with his great paws, but Gaunt and Morkir strained to reach each other.

"I'll kill him for you, Father!" Morkir shouted. "Let me rip his . . . !"

Morkir never finished his threat. Gaunt forgot his brother and their fight and flew higher into the air where he stared toward the west. Beating their wings, hovering above the wreckage of the Angmar ship, Gorganar and Morkir also turned.

A surge of anger filled Gorganar, but along with the anger there was also an old chill of fear.

Beneath the yellow-gold orb of the sun, the sky blazed with red-orange flame. For an instant, it appeared that Wyvernwood itself burned, but it was not the forest. The flames faded, and then blasted forth again, drawing rapidly closer.

"Stormfire and his whelps!" Gorganar shouted to his sons. "So the old fool ventures out of his stronghold at last!"

The flames faded again and resolved into four silhouetted shapes, one larger than the others, which flew with grace and speed. With their keen eyesight, the griffins watched, steeling themselves for war. Gorganar flexed his claws. Morkir drew closer to his father and trembled. Gaunt awaited an order.

Over the white sand beach four dragons came, and over the blue water. Gorganar knew them all, as did his sons.

Harrow, black-scaled and shining as a piece of living onyx.

Chan, all red and gold and yellow, as keen-eyed as any griffin.

Luna, Stormfire's daughter, all ivory and blue-eyed, as fierce as either of her brothers.

And Stormfire himself, the legendary dragon-leader who had gathered all the Dragonkin and the strange creatures of the world, even the griffins, and led them into Wyvernwood and made it a refuge for their kind. He was huge and golden-scaled, impressive in his sleek, almost serpentine power despite his great age. His wingspan was twice that of his triplet children, and more than matched that of Gorganar.

"Take him now, Father!" Morkir urged. "We can truly rule Wyvernwood!"

"They are four to our three," Gaunt noted.

Gorganar growled. He wasn't afraid of the three youngling dragons, but he and Stormfire were old enemies. Dragons and griffins had clashed before over matters involving Men and the safeguarding of Wyvernwood. True, Stormfire had found the forest, gathered the Kin, and led them here, and true he had made it a haven.

But he had thwarted the griffins' natural leadership and tried to pacify them! Gorganar's own father, Argulo, had fought Stormfire for possession of the Stronghold and lost. Neither Argulo nor Gorganar had ever forgotten the humiliation.

"Are they coming to join us in destroying the Angmar ship?" Morkir asked nervously.

Gaunt sneered at his brother. "It's already destroyed, you idiot. And still they come."

Gorganar clenched his paws until he felt his own claws. How he wanted to taste Stormfire's blood! Wyvernwood would grow strong and powerful under a griffin's rule. Why be merely a refuge when you could dominate the world? Some said the Age of Dragons was passing, but did Stormfire have to drag them *all* into obscurity and oblivion?

Still, he knew in his trembling heart that it was not to be. Dragons had the power of fire. Against that, tooth and claw and muscle meant nothing. Argulo had learned that lesson the hard way. Now, Gorganar had his own sons to think about. He would not suffer humiliation before them.

"Turn away," he ordered.

Morkir said nothing, though his anger was palpable. Folding his wings, he plummeted toward the capsized ship, struck its exposed hull with his full fury, and shattered it.

Gaunt lingered with an eye on the small boat and the children who clung to it. It was still a long way from shore, but Stormfire's daughter, the Dragon Luna, was plainly making for it. If he knew dragons at all he was sure she would save them. As for the rest of the sailors, there were few survivors, and Morkir seemed intent on finishing them.

With a shrug, Gaunt followed after his father northward along the coastline, then deep into Wyvernwood toward home.

3

LUNA GLIDED OVER THE BLUE WATER toward the capsized boat and the five man-children. The shore was still too far away for them to swim—if they could swim—and as the rolling waves washed over them, they sputtered and coughed and cried to each other for help. It was plain to her that if she didn't do something they would drown.

Yet, as she swooped over them, one of the boys raised an oar and swung it at her. The effort pushed him under the water, and he surfaced again, screaming and cursing . . . and also oarless. But he'd lost his grip on the side of the boat. He slipped underwater again and bobbed back up. One of the other boys, without surrendering his grip on the boat, stretched out an arm and strained to reach his comrade, but the first boy was too far away.

The other children screamed and tried to propel the boat toward the drowning boy by kicking their feet. The current proved too strong, though, and their uncoordinated efforts only worked against each other. The boat drifted still farther away.

Luna turned gracefully, so low above the water that the tip of one ivory wing cut an arcing wake through the waves. The sunlight glistened through the wall of water her wing flung up, and rainbows suddenly filled the air. Through that shimmering spray, she came racing.

The children clinging to the boat stared wide-eyed as she sped toward them, and their screaming and crying intensified. A little girl shot a look over her shoulder at Morkir, who was smashing the larger sailing ship further out to sea, and when she returned her gaze to Luna, her tearful eyes were filled with horror.

Luna's dragon-heart went out to the man-children as she realized that they feared her as much as they feared the griffin, Morkir.

13

But fear or not, she couldn't let them drown!

The boy that had swung the oar was barely keeping his head above the water. He had found his oar again, and he clung to it with desperation, but it couldn't keep him afloat, and the current was carrying him farther and farther from the small boat.

Luna narrowed her blue eyes against the sun's glare as she turned again. She couldn't just snatch the boy out of the water. He was thin and delicate, and with her strength she might injure him if she gripped him in her claws. Better to win his trust if she could. Time was short, though; the boy was thrashing, his strength failing.

Ignoring the shouts of the other man-children, she flew toward the drowning boy, and with a steady, powerful beating of her wings, she hovered directly above him. Again, he mistook her intention and tried to raise the oar to drive her off. It would have been an amusing gesture, but for the pity and the bravery in it. His tired arms could not swing it without the effort forcing him underwater again.

She gazed down at him. His dark hair was plastered to his face and neck, and his shoulders were sunburned an angry red. He flailed and grasped at the water as he fought to stay afloat. For the first time, she noted the iron bracelets he wore. They were obviously heavy and weighed him down; didn't he have the sense to cast them off?

Once again, the boy lost his grip on the oar, but Luna saw finally how she might save him without causing injury. Dropping low, she caught the paddle end of the oar in one claw and pushed the other end toward the boy. "Take it!" she urged.

The boy stared up at her, then slipped under the water as a swell washed over his head. He arose sputtering, but still he managed to shout, "You speak!"

"Only to those who will listen," she answered crisply. "Now grasp the end of your odd stick and hold tight!"

The boy did as she instructed. Luna turned toward the distant shore and pulled him through the waves. Her gleaming tail streamed out behind her, and her wingtips touched the water with every downbeat as she skimmed the Windy Sea. She flew swiftly, but not so swiftly as to shake her precious passenger loose. In only moments, she dragged him into the shallows and deposited him on the white sand.

"What kind of monster . . . ?" the boy began to say.

Luna soared into the sky and banked again. There were four more man-children to save and little time. As she turned she spied the gray dorsal fins of sharks circling in the vicinity of the wrecked sailing ship. She had to work fast before the children drew their attention.

But she no longer worked alone. Headed for the beach, her brother Chan skimmed above the water just as she had done. Two children, including the little girl, clung tightly to the very tip of his tail as he pulled them through the waves to safety. Despite the seriousness of their rescue effort, Luna laughed. Few dragons of her acquaintance would have permitted such an indignity, but Chan had a soft heart and a good nature.

"Well done, Brother!" she called as they passed each other. "Where's Harrow?"

"Chasing Morkir away!" Chan answered without slowing his flight. "There are still a few Men alive amid that destruction!"

She stared out to sea, toward the pieces of the shattered sailing vessel. It had split completely apart at midships, and Morkir had demolished the stern portion. Amazingly, the bow half, though turned on its side, still remained afloat. Bits and pieces of wood dotted the surface around it—crates, the broken mast, planks and boards. Among those bits of flotsam she spied the struggling shapes of desperate sailors—and still more of those ominous dorsal fins.

A great shadow glided suddenly across the water.

Stormfire!

On mighty wings of golden leather, her father raced above the waves. His claws flashed, sweeping a shark out of the water and into the air. Again he struck, flinging another shark after the first. At the same time, his powerful tail smashed down amid a circle of gray fins, causing a splash that tossed the hungry predators in all directions.

Luna returned her attention to the remaining pair of children. Their plight was now more desperate than ever. As she raced toward them, the boat to which they were clinging pitched at an angle and sank beneath the waves. The children screamed and thrashed. Like the first boy, they were weighed down with heavy iron bracelets. A rolling swell pushed them under. The blond-headed boy bobbed to the surface immediately, and the dark-haired girl a heart-stopping moment later. They reached toward each other and managed to clasp hands as another swell forced them under again.

Luna had no choice now. With the greatest of care and speed, mindful of her strength, she snatched them from beneath the water and lifted them one each in her front claws. Half-drowned, they let out shrieks of fear as she swept the struggling pair into the air, but she hugged them close to her breast and turned once again toward the white sand beach.

Chan was waiting for her. With the sun dancing on his red-gold scales, he looked like a living flame on the glittering shore. His unique coloring spread even to the very tips of his wings, and Luna thought him the most beautiful dragon of them all. Except for herself, of course. She settled on the beach beside him.

"Where are the other three younglings?" she asked as she set the last two children gently down.

The two man-children stared with gaping mouths at Luna and Chan. Then, with barely a glance and a nod to each other, they sped around Luna, leaped over her tail and disappeared into the depths of Wyvernwood.

Chan gave a deep-throated laugh. "There's your answer," he said with a gesture toward the forest. "Without so much as a thank-you or farewell. Now I ask you, Sister, what kind of upbringing does that suggest?"

A tiny, high-pitched voice called from the dark edge of the woods where the afternoon shadows were at their thickest. "Thank you, O monsters!"

Another voice whispered sharply, " Shut up! They'll have us for dinner if they find us!"

Luna and Chan exchanged looks, and both laughed. "Have no fear, little two-legged fish!" Chan called. "Come out, and tell us your names!"

No answer came from the woods.

The steady sound of wings alerted Luna, and she turned back toward the sea. The Dragon Stormfire, shining like the sun itself, flew toward the shore. In one claw he held the end of a long rigging rope. Along its length, men clung with red-eyed mixtures of fear and hope and anger as her father towed them to safety. She counted them. Fourteen alive—out of how many, she wondered?

Stormfire landed beside his children, his hind claws digging deep into the sand. The rope went slack as he relaxed his grip on it, but the men were close enough to wade ashore. By ones and twos they came, some with their arms around each other as the stronger lent support to the weaker. Luna noted that with interest. She knew much about the creatures of Wyvernwood, but little about the race called Men.

"Admirable how they care for each other," Luna whispered to her father.

The dragon leader said nothing.

One of the sailors trudged forward. He was shirtless, thin and muscled, with deep-set blue eyes, and his face was nearly hidden behind a sopping brown beard. His black trousers hung on him in shreds, held around his waist only by a sash of red linen. From the sash, a sword hung still in its scabbard of hard, polished wood. Though he seemed barely able to stand, he rested one hand on the sword's hilt as he stopped before Stormfire.

"I've heard of the great nobility of dragons," the sailor said with a hint of a bow, "but I have never seen your like, nor any of your kind."

"You are Men of Angmar?" Chan asked.

The sailor stared at Chan for a long moment, his mouth open in an expression of surprise. "That's right," he answered finally. Shielding his eyes from the sun's glare, he gazed up at Chan. "My name is Caanan."

Luna liked the sound of Caanan's voice. It had a deep, gracious quality. Not so deep as a dragon's, to be sure, yet she found it charming.

"My father, Stormfire," Chan said, making the introductions, "and my triplet sister, the Dragon Luna. And if I'm not mistaken, I hear our triplet brother approaching."

Except for Caanan, the other men stumbled back into the waves or scattered along the beach. A few, too injured or too weak to move, remained where they rested on the sand, but even they threw up their hands in fear of the black shape that sailed across the sun, banked sharply, and dropped into their midst.

"Our brother," Chan added, "Harrow."

Caanan turned a disapproving eye over the other sailors. "Forgive my fellows," he said. "Their spirits seem to have gone down with their ship."

Harrow paid no attention to the men. He held up his right front claws, revealing the red wetness that stained their tips. "Morkir will think twice before he ventures far from the griffins' valley for a while!" he announced.

"Oh, please!" Luna replied, tilting her head as she frowned at Harrow. "You must have taken a griffin-blow to the head, my brother. Consider that you just used the words *think* and *Morkir* in the same sentence."

Stormfire interrupted his children and, folding his great wings tightly around his massive body, spoke for the first time to Caanan. "How is it," he asked, "that a ship of Angmar sails so close to the coast of Wyvernwood?"

Caanan gazed upward into the golden eyes of the dragon leader. He stood no taller than Stormfire's knee, and yet, unlike the rest of his comrades, he did not quail, nor tremble. "The strong winds blew us off course," he answered with a shrug. "It's true that we usually avoid your shoreline, but this time nature had its way with us. A sailing ship is at the mercy of the winds."

Harrow looked sharply down at the man. "The winds were not that strong."

The Dragon Stormfire turned his head toward his black-scaled son—nothing more—and Harrow fell silent. Still, he glared at the man called Caanan with instant and obvious dislike.

Luna stuck her tongue out at Harrow. She liked Caanan well enough. Indeed, she found his appearance somewhat pleasing.

"The winds were the winds," Stormfire resumed, turning his attention once more to the man before him. "They did not seem to hinder you as you chased the smaller boat."

Caanan forced a smile. "Ah, yes, the children," he said in a softer voice. "A misunderstanding. They had misbehaved and feared they would be punished. Our captain—rest his soul, he's at the bottom of the Windy Sea now, or in the belly of a shark—was a stern and fearsome old man, though gentle in his own way. He wouldn't really have hurt the young ones, but he scared them a little so that they stole a lifeboat and tried to escape."

"Escape," Chan said as he lowered himself onto all four paws and then stretched out until he lay flat on the sand. Eye to eye with Caanan, he winked first one yellow eye, and then the other. "Now there's an interesting word."

"It was a poor choice of words," Caanan admitted. He turned his hands up in a gesture of appeal as he grinned. "But then, how does a child *run away* at sea?" His grin faded, to be replaced with a look of concern as he turned back to Stormfire. "Still, they're our children, and we love them, and we want them back."

"It is most strange," Stormfire answered in a low voice. "I am a father myself, and know something of the ways of children. These younglings you speak of have just been through a terrible ordeal. A griffin attacked them; their boat was overturned; several of them nearly drowned. Still, though they are in the woods just behind us, they do not come running into the arms of their loving parents."

"Of course, they're afraid!" Caanan answered. "Griffins, sharks, dragons! No offense, but they hide from you!" He raised his hands in a gesture of appeal again. "With your permission, we'll go into the woods to get them."

A dark shadow fell over the fourteen sailors as Stormfire unfolded his wings and spread them wide. The meaning of his action was not lost on Caanan, who took several steps rapidly backward.

Luna gasped as she felt the anger radiating from her father. He had made of himself a living barrier between the water's edge and the forest. But why? What had she missed? She glanced at Harrow, but he was as surprised as she was. Chan had not moved, and she could not see his face.

"It isn't wise to lie to dragons!" Stormfire warned. He fixed his gaze on Caanan, and the man took yet another step backward, until he stumbled over one of his own comrades and fell flat on his back. Suddenly fearful, he struggled to free his sword from its scabbard, but some cord held it in place, and trembling fingers couldn't overcome the wet knots.

With a speed that belied his size, Chan slithered over the sand. The other sailors scrambled to get out of his way, but Chan paid them no mind. He only lay his head down again near Caanan's head and regarded him with an unblinking gaze as he smiled.

A dragon's smile can be a terrible thing.

Caanan looked at Chan, then at Stormfire, Luna, and Harrow, and he removed his hand from his sword.

"You and your companions may rest awhile on our shore," the dragon leader declared. "But do not go into wood, and do not be here when morning comes. Follow the coast northward back to Angmar. My son, Harrow, will be watching you until you are clear of Wyvernwood."

"And remember," Chan said with a bemused smirk, "we don't call him *Foul-tempered Harrow* for no reason."

Harrow laughed as his tail lashed back and forth. "If Morkir should be about, I may let him have you."

Caanan sputtered. "But our children . . . !"

The air swirled suddenly, alive with sand that stung the eyes and flesh of the men as Stormfire flexed his wings. Even Caanan, who had seemed so bold before, rolled to his knees and curled into a whimpering ball as he begged for mercy.

"They are not your children!" Stormfire raged. "You would not put manacles and chains on the wrists of your own children! Your own children would not risk sea and drowning merely to escape punishment!" He folded his wings again, and the sand settled down.

The fourteen sailors didn't wait to rest. Confronted with the truth and Stormfire's anger, they scrambled to their feet and ran as swiftly as they could up the beach. Caanan led the fleeing pack, while the injured hobbled after as best they could. None of them looked back.

Luna stared after them with a feeling of confusion and disappointment. "I don't understand, Father," she said. "What did Caanan do to enrage you? What are manacles and chains?"

Stormfire wrapped a wing around her. "You know too little of the ways of Men, my daughter. But there was a reason why the Dragonkin retreated to Wyvernwood, and they are it."

Chan rose to stand on his rear paws again. With a great shiver and ripple, he shook the sand from his scales. "I suppose you want us to gather the younglings," he said to his father.

But the children were not to be found. At first sight of the sailors, they had run deeper and deeper into the gloomy recesses of Wyvernwood.

4

THE DRAGON RONALDO KEPT MOSTLY TO HIMSELF. He
lived alone, and liked it that way, and seldom socialized with the other
inhabitants of Wyvernwood. He made his home far from Stronghold,
in a southern corner of the forest that was known as the Whispering
Hills, in a cave that he had discovered and enlarged and appointed to
suit his own tastes. Rugs woven from various exotic grasses and bark
fibers covered the floors. He had made them himself. The walls were
sealed with a plaster made from mud and pine tree resin to keep his
home dry, and he had painted the interior a pleasant eggshell white.
At the entrance to his cave hung a round door that he had constructed
from the most beautifully striped tiger oak.

But Ronaldo's talents did not stop there.

Ronaldo was an artist.

The walls of his home were covered with paintings and pictures.
Most were landscapes done of his favorite places in Wyvernwood, or
seascapes illustrating the different moods of the Windy Sea at dawn
or at sunset, at peace or during stormy weather. Some were self-por-
traits executed in various art styles, and a few—only a few—were portraits painted on those rare occasions when he invited some
interesting friend or neighbor to pose for him. There were other paintings stacked and forgotten in corners of the cave. Sometimes he gave
one away. Sometimes he just painted over an older piece.

An easel stood near the fireplace, and there was always some work-
in-progress upon it. Paintbrushes and paint pots sat on a table close
by. It wasn't the best light for working, but to a dragon's eyes it was
adequate for touching up, refining lines, or simple color sketching. It
didn't matter to him that only a lucky few people ever saw his work.
His joy came from the painting itself.

Having arisen earlier than usual from his night's rest, he was sitting before his easel on his curled tail and mixing a fresh pot of red ochre. The day before he had found some interesting clay by a stream at the base of a nearby hill. Its deep color had intrigued him, and he had scooped some up. Though he hadn't needed a fire for warmth this time of year, he had built one to dry the clay overnight. He was grinding it to powder and adding the grains to one of his regular red paints when a cautious knock sounded at his door.

At first, he didn't really hear the knock. So faint and timid did it sound that he dismissed it as a trick of hearing, for sometimes there was an echo in his cave, and he had been stirring his paints rather vigorously. But after a moment, the knock sounded again, more persistent and more determined this time.

Ronaldo set down his paint pot and brush. It wasn't that he avoided company or disliked his neighbors, but in the Whispering Hills, the residents generally lived their lives quietly and minded their own business. So it surprised him that someone should be disturbing him so early in the day. On all four paws, he moved to the door. Grasping a polished wooden ring of his own making, he pulled the door open. A similar ring on the outside of the door doubled as a knocker.

A plump minotaur-mother with a young babe in one arm stood nervously at the threshold. Her threadbare blue dress stirred in a slight breeze, as did the strings of the yellow apron she wore around her waist. If her clothes looked worn, though, they were clean, and her brown hair was neatly brushed and her horns polished. She looked up at Ronaldo with wide brown cow-eyes.

"Beatrice!" Ronaldo exclaimed. Beatrice and her children lived on the far side of the same hill in which Ronaldo had built his cave. Like most minotaurs they were private folks and seldom bothered anyone. "What brings you and your fine baby Coniff to my doorstep this bright morning?"

Beatrice rocked Coniff in her arms with an agitated energy, and she seemed to hug him almost too tightly to her breast, though he made no sound of protest inside his blue-and-white checkered blanket.

"It's Chernovog," she blurted. She bit her lip, looked down at her feet, and finally back up at Ronaldo. "It's almost lunchtime. He went out this morning to gather kindling for the cookfire, and hasn't come home. He hasn't answered my calls, and I can't find him anywhere."

"Lunchtime?" Ronaldo gazed up at the sky and experienced a second surprise that morning. Immersed in his work, he'd completely lost track of time. He blinked and licked his lips with a pink, slithery tongue. He returned his attention to Beatrice. "Well, you know teenagers, Beatrice," he said, trying to reassure her with a grin. "Something probably caught his interest, and he's forgotten the hour. I certainly know how that can happen." He winked a large gray eye at her. "His stomach will remind him soon enough to come home."

She nuzzled Baby Coniff with her chin before she looked up again. When she did, Ronaldo at last saw the deep worry in her wide eyes. "I wouldn't be so concerned," she said, "but there were Men in the forest this morning. Granny Scylla told me. She saw them when she was gathering herbs over by Century Hill." She swallowed, shivered, and her voice dropped to a whisper. "They were chopping down trees!"

Ronaldo felt a rush of anger. He'd painted Century Hill; the trees that grew there were ancient, stately. That Men would dare to violate the refuge of the Dragonkin was aggravating enough, but that they would dare to cut those magnificent pines!

Then his anger vanished as he suddenly understood Beatrice's worry. Every time he'd painted Century Hill or the vistas visible from its summit, he'd found young Chernovog there, too, lying on his back in the grass, watching the clouds—*just thinking*, he'd say.

"You take little Coniff back home, Beatrice," Ronaldo said with a gentle calm. "I'd be happy to look for Chernovog for you. He and I have spent more than a few moments chatting on lazy days, and I know a few of his hiding places."

"He's normally a good boy," Beatrice continued as she fought back tears, "but he's growing up, you know, and he misses his father so much!"

Beatrice's husband, Ranock, had perished the past spring, when a lightning strike set their house on fire and the family was sleeping. He had gotten his pregnant wife out of the house and gone back for Chernovog when the roof collapsed on him. He never realized that Chernovog had already escaped through his bedroom window.

Friends and neighbors from all around Whispering Hills and Wyvernwood had pitched in to help Beatrice rebuild her home. She had a child on the way, after all, and a boy to raise on her own.

Ronaldo, admittedly, had not helped as much in that effort as he might have, and looking down at Beatrice and little Coniff he felt some guilt. However, he also genuinely liked young Chernovog.

"I don't know how I can ever repay your kindness," Beatrice said, wiping her eyes with a corner of her apron. "So many people have been so good to me, but I just couldn't bear it if anything happened to Chernovog."

Ronaldo stretched his long neck down until he could look Beatrice eye-to-eye. He patted her shoulder with a massive claw. "There's only one way to ever repay kindness," he said in a gentle voice, "and that's to show kindness to someone else. You pay it forward to the next person in need."

Beatrice forced a weak smile. "I'll remember that, dear Ronaldo," she said. "I promise I will. In fact, Granny Scylla needs some help weeding her flowerbeds and herb garden." She sniffed. "I believe I'll go there now. And if you find Chernovog, you send him right home." Cradling little Coniff even more tightly, she inclined her head and kissed the back of Ronaldo's claw. "And thank you, oh, thank you!"

Ronaldo watched with a good feeling in his heart as Beatrice walked back down the path that led to his door. When she could no longer be seen through the trees that grew at the base of the hill, he retreated inside his cave. Humming to himself in a slightly off-key voice, he sealed his paint pots, washed his brushes, and extinguished the fire in his fireplace. He didn't really expect to be gone very long, but one didn't take chances with an unguarded fire.

He looked around. He was proud of his home; it comforted him. He felt a pang of sadness and sympathy for Beatrice, who had lost so much—her home, her belongings, her husband. He wondered how he would bear such a loss.

It occurred to him, not for the first time, that he had few friends. Neighbors, yes, and even some acquaintances, but few real friends. The fault was his, he knew. He liked his seclusion, his privacy, and he generally found that if he left others alone they left him alone.

Why, then, did it please him that Beatrice had turned to him for help?

He pulled the massive and beautiful tiger oak door securely closed as he left his cave. He craned his long neck upward and sniffed the sweet air and the fragrances of the forest. The sun felt warm on his face.

Sometimes, Chernovog played on Century Hill, but sometimes he also fished along the Blackwater River, or just sat daydreaming for long hours on the cliff at Watcher's Point.

Ronaldo made up his mind to check these places first. It was a beautiful day. Maybe he'd also find some new places worth painting.

He spread his gray wings, and for a moment, he hesitated, half-smiling at himself in a deprecating manner. Gray wings. Gray scales. He wasn't the fairest dragon to ride the air. Maybe that was why he painted—he loved the colors.

With a sigh, he spread his wings again and took to the sky.

* * *

Filled with indignation, Marian stared at the mahogany stump that was all that remained of the tree that Bumble had called home. "The nerve of some people!" she muttered in disgust. "The sheer gall! We don't go marching into their villages, dismantling their homes!"

Bumble fluttered about her head and perched on the tip of her horn. "Homeless!" he cried. "Homeless and hungry! Such a sorry state I'm in!"

Marian's eyes crossed as she looked up at him. "Do you mind?" she said. With a shake of her head, she dislodged him.

His wings a nervous blur, he darted to a high branch in the nearest tree. Then he flew back again and repositioned himself on the cleanly sawed edge of the stump and looked up at her. "So sorry!" he apologized. "That wasn't very gentlemanly of me at all, landing on your horn like that without even asking!"

She sniffed the ground around the stump. The grass was thoroughly trampled, shrubbery was crushed, and many of the nearby trees showed damage, too. "There must have been a lot of them," she said. "So many sweaty smells—my sensitive nose can barely stand the stench."

"If only I could remember how many!" Bumble said, nodding. He bent his slender beak toward the stump and sniffed, too, but all he detected were the odors of the honey-scented forest flowers and the rich pollens that wafted in the air, and they made him so hungry he couldn't think straight. Still, he lifted his head and fluttered his wings to command Marian's attention. "What of poor Chernovog?" he asked.

Marian paced delicately around the stump, sniffing as she went. Sawdust covered everything, and it made her sneeze. "I don't find any minotaur-scent at all," she reported. "Are you quite sure they took him?"

Bumble could restrain himself no longer. He zoomed to the nearest crop of untrammeled wild fuschias and thrust his beak deep into a red bloom. In ecstatic frenzy he drained its nectar. The next blossom looked just as sweet. Why should he deny himself? He shoved his face down among its petals.

"Bumble!"

Marian's shout startled him. His tiny heart hammered in his chest as he flew to the highest limb and stared down at her. A drop of nectar still clung to the end of his beak. He quickly licked it away, then folded his wings behind his back. Unicorns were so excitable. Why had she yelled at him?

She stamped one golden hoof on the grass. "Get back down here, you silly Bumble-bird!"

Bumble sighed. It was best to show patience with such creatures and humor them, especially when they were so much bigger. If only he could remember her name! Was it Marian? Mary Ann? Marlys? Oh well, she had said to get on her back, so in one swooping glide he dropped from his branch and settled on her back just between her shoulders.

With a quick toss of her mane, Marian brushed him off. Caught by surprise, Bumble tumbled through the air and landed in a thick patch of grass. "I remember now!" he said, righting himself and shaking dust from his wings. "Marian, right? Foolish of me to forget. Small brain, you know. All of us hummingbirds. We're all very sharp—very quick, as it were. But no memory, I'm afraid."

He flew back to the stump. It had the familiar smell of *home* about it, but of course it couldn't be his home. No self-respecting humming-bird would make his home in a stump. He looked up with wide, clear eyes at Marian. "Now where were we, my dear?"

It was Marian's turn to sigh. "Think, Bumble, think! Is Chernovog in danger or not? I can't find his scent with all the Man-stink here. If you're sending me on some wild-goose chase . . ."

"Oh, no, no!" Bumble fluffed his tail feathers. "I haven't seen any wild geese in ever so long. They don't come to this part of the forest often, you know. But Chernovog. . . ." He hopped from one leg to the other and tapped his temple with the tip of his right wing. "I seem to know someone by that name, yes, I'm sure I do." He paced across the stump and gazed past a delicious-looking patch of crushed monkey flowers as he strained to remember. Through a gap in the trees, a tall hill rose. "Of course, Chernovog!" He pointed with his left wing. "I saw him just this morning up there!"

"Century Hill," Marian murmured.

Bumble nodded. "I never can remember its name."

Marian sighed again as she regarded the high peak. "I can't believe I'm saying this—but get on my back, Bumble-bird, and hold on tight."

Bumble blinked his eyes and hesitated. "Well, that hardly seems gentlemanly," he said. "If you wish, I can just meet you there."

"Hmmph! You'd get distracted by some daisy and forget," she answered. "It's better that we stick together. And as we go, I want you to repeat everything you remember about Chernovog and the Men who chopped down your tree. Then repeat it again and again so it all stays clear in your mind."

The little hummingbird shrugged. "Well, I'll try," he said as he flew up and perched on her back. Her thick white coat felt so luxurious under his small talons! And Marian smelled wonderfully like wild-flowers. He was sure she must have recently lain in a bed of lemon bottlebrush. "But I have to warn you," he continued. "I'm awfully hungry and may have to stop soon for a nutritious lunch."

"You fly from my back once, and I'll leave you behind," Marian warned as she started toward the distant hill.

Shafts of noontime sunlight streamed down through the trees. On the brightest of days Wyvernwood was always a patchwork of light and shadow. It was a place of warm, wide-open clearings and gray, twi-light glades and canopied thatches, where the leaves and vines inter-wove so thickly as to shut out the sunshine entirely. Light and dimness and dark existed together in the forest.

It was this quality of light that Marian loved most about the forest. She loved the way the sun dappled down through the branches, the way it penetrated the thinner leaves with an almost stained-glass effect. And at night she loved the way the moon silvered those same leaves, the way it frosted the grasses in the clearings and glimmered on the bubbling streams.

While other creatures had their nests and caves, their burrows and houses and shelters, Marian thought of the entire woods as her home. She needed no walls, no ceiling, or floor beneath her hooves. When the breeze stirred her mane, when the rich and earthy smells of the land filled her senses, she felt in tune with the forest, almost an elemental part of it.

Now strangers had come into her home, destroyed property, and if Bumble was right, they had taken something. And though the little hummingbird's memory had more holes than a community of worms, she felt in her heart that on this matter he was right, or at least mostly right. She felt angry and violated.

Marian began to run. Bumble's tiny claws tightened in her hair, and he clung with all his strength. A hedge of lantana appeared in her path. She leaped it without a second thought, grimly chuckling to herself as she felt the hummingbird turn and stare after the lantana's tasty blossoms. But still he held on, and with her gaze fixed on Century Hill, she weaved a highspeed course through a copse of ash trees. Divots of earth flew up from under her hooves. Rabbits scampered out of her way, and squirrels took frantically to the trees.

A wide stream presented no obstacle to Marian. She jumped it with graceful ease, ducking her head to avoid a low-hanging oak branch as she landed on the other side. Zebra butterflies and Monarchs, at play among the wildflowers by the stream's bank, fluttered into the air in a cloud of color as she raced by.

A swiftly gliding shadow passed overhead, but caught up in the excitement of her run and a deep sense of urgency, Marian ignored it. Century Hill lay just ahead. The ground began to rise, and the ash and mahogany and oak trees became pine trees and redwoods whose soaring tops swept the wispy clouds across the sky.

The air ignited suddenly with a shimmering of gossamer wings as she plunged through a colony of locusts. The hill rose at a steeper incline. A rock turned under her hoof. For an instant, she nearly slipped, and Bumble's claws tightened through her coat and down into her hide, but she caught her balance effortlessly.

Without slowing, she sniffed the air. The smell of Men was faint, but definite. Bumble had been right. And with the man-stink she detected another sweeter scent, one she knew as Chernovog's. She raced on, following her nose, and the various scents grew stronger. Soon they would converge, and she would reach the spot where Chernovog and the Men had met.

But before she reached that spot, a new scent touched her delicate nose, and she stopped with such unexpected abruptness that Bumble found himself tumbling over her head, past her horn, and toward the ground.

At the last moment before impact, Bumble spread his wings, saving himself. Back and forth between the limbs of a pair of pine trees he darted, disoriented, confused, half in a panic. Then, turning in mid-flight, he flew straight for Marian and perched on the tip of her golden horn. His small eyes glared into hers.

"Sorry," Marian said. Her gaze went past him.

Bumble slowly turned, and his wings whirred. "Oh, my!" he said.

Marian started up the hill again at a walk. It took only a few moments, though, for her to reach the pinnacle.

A large dragon flexed its wings, then folded them tightly against its gray-scaled body and stretched its neck down until its head was near the ground.

"I saw you coming this way, Marian," the dragon said. "Hello, Bumble."

Marian recalled the shadow that had passed overhead a little before. "Dear Ronaldo!" she replied. "It's so good to see an old friend!"

A smile flashed across his face, but it couldn't conceal the look of concern in his large gray eyes.

5

THE BLACKWATER RIVER CUT RIGHT THROUGH the center of Wyvernwood, flowing on a rough, diagonal course from the north-eastern region of the Imagination Mountains to the Windy Sea. In some places, it carved a swift and treacherous course through the forest, but as it traveled southward, it grew calm.

In the north, at the river's widest and deepest point, lay the Valley of the Eight Winds. It was to this valley that Argulo had led his griffin followers and commanded them to make their homes. In short time they had stripped every tree, every bush and blade of grass to make their gigantic ground-nests, which were as large and deep as any dragon's cave, with many rooms and corridors, but all made of wood and brush and bark.

For a time afterward the valley had looked like a wasteland, a great and gaping wound that had turned brown and ugly, parched by the sun, rutted by rains. But slowly, the wound had begun to heal. Green grass had covered the ugliness, and seedlings had begun to grow into new trees again. Here and there, even a few flowers dared to spread their petals.

But amid the returning beauty there were still the nests. Some stood like sharp, small mountains with logs or sticks jutting out every which way, all packed with mud and leaves and grass. Other, older nests lay like sprawling hideous mounds. These were half-covered on their up-slope sides with the mud and earth that had washed up against them. Grass and molds and lichen, even toadstools and mushrooms in season grew on these.

The largest nest of all belonged to Gorganar. It had belonged to his father, Argulo, before him, but he had enlarged it and enlarged it again. At the north end of the valley, it towered over the other nests, black and stark and awesome in its ugliness. In Gorganar's mind, it stood as a symbol of power to all that looked upon it.

To anyone who was not a griffin, however, it stood as a symbol of cruelty.

Only the faintest light ever seeped into a griffin's nest. It didn't matter; a griffin's eyes were sharper than an eagle's.

Gorganar stalked through the dark corridors of his monstrous home and kicked open the doors to the chamber he called his throne room. With a bitter scowl on his face, he folded his wings tightly against his body and slumped down upon his crude throne. A young serving griffin appeared with a platter of fresh perch from the river, but Gorganar chased him out with a harsh snarl.

Alone, he rested his chin on one paw and closed his eyes. He felt angry with himself. He had run from Stormfire and his cursed hatchlings. There was no denying it. What he had passed off to his own sons as wisdom and the better part of valor, he knew in his private heart had been cowardice. The taste of fear still lingered in his mouth.

Opening one eye, he looked at his paw and knew the humiliation his father must have felt those many years ago. How long since that paw had drawn dragon-blood? When had it *ever* drawn dragon-blood? He extended his claws and stared at them with his one open eye. Even in the darkness he could see that they were clean and white.

Gorganar closed his eye, retracted his claws, and sighed. He felt weary and inexplicably tired.

He had almost slipped into a doze when Gaunt walked into the chamber. His older son also bore a platter. Upon it was a single fish, a fat silver bass so fresh it still smelled of river water. He licked his lips as he realized he had been hasty in dismissing the young servant earlier. His belly rumbled at the sight of Gaunt's offering.

"You are a good son," Gorganar said as he speared the fish with one claw. He held it up and felt its slimy wetness run down his fur-covered paw. An instant later, he swallowed the fish whole. The sound of his belch echoed through the chamber, and he patted his stomach.

Gaunt set the tray aside and curled up on the floor at his father's feet. "I hope the fish pleases you, Father," he said. "You were unusually quiet as we flew home."

Gorganar stretched his wings and then folded them again as he leaned back on his throne once more. He frowned as he studied his son. Why was it that even in Gaunt's most innocent words he always seemed to detect some edge of sarcasm, some barely concealed hint of criticism?

A quartet of basilisks entered the room bearing towels, wash basins, and combs. Their large, round, lidless eyes made them ideal slaves, for they could see as well inside the dark nests as their griffin masters. Two of the reptiles went immediately to Gorganar. With delicate care one began to wash the griffin-leader's paws while the other trimmed and polished the razor-sharp claws.

The second pair of basilisks performed the same service for Gaunt.

Gorganar extended his claws. "Make sure you clean down between them," he warned the lizards. He gave his attention back to his son. Gaunt seemed totally relaxed, almost asleep. The slaves went about their work with no evidence of fear or timidity as they touched him. "You enjoy these grooming sessions too much," he said.

"I can think of no reason not to enjoy them," Gaunt answered without looking at his father.

"Too much of it will make you soft," Gorganar argued. "We griffins are not meant to be pampered. We are meant to be strong and to rule others!"

Gaunt yawned and said nothing.

Gorganar pushed one of the basilisks away and leaned forward. "Do you hear me down there, my son, or are you asleep at my feet?"

With a languid effort, Gaunt stretched his wings and rose to stand. The four basilisks scampered back, clutching their grooming utensils, awaiting orders. "You confuse muscle with strength, Father," he said calmly. "And what have you ever ruled, but a valley full of stick houses and rotting timbers and the few sad creatures that live in it?"

Gorganar shot to his feet with a roar. Then he stumbled back again and caught the stout wooden arms of his throne. The look of rage Gaunt's words had inspired turned suddenly to one of puzzlement as he sat down once more. "There's not a creature in Wyvernwood that doesn't fear me!"

Gaunt yawned again. "Stormfire doesn't fear you."

Gorganar slammed a paw down on the arm of his throne. "Stormfire is old. He won't be around much longer!"

Gaunt shrugged his massive shoulders. "None of the dragons fear you," he continued. "Why should they? They have the power of fire."

Gorganar rose to his feet again, more carefully this time, and spread his impressive wings in a threatening display. What had gotten into Gaunt? His son had never dared to take such a tone with him before! "They're growing weaker," he shouted. "They're all growing weaker!"

"We are all growing weaker," Gaunt corrected. "Take our little basilisk friends here. Once they could kill with a stare. But no more, and we have made them our slaves. And we griffins—we're still strong, indeed. But not as strong as we once were. Once, as with the dragons, we were many. Now we're few. And those few of us are but shadows of what we were in the past."

Gorganar folded his wings and sat back down again. He felt tired, so tired. Why did Gaunt have to choose this time to argue with him? He had been too lenient with his first-born son, and that would have to change. The young upstart was overdue for a lesson in the meaning of strength and power. But that would come later. Right now, he wanted only to sleep.

"The Age of the Dragons is passing," Gorganar mumbled as his head nodded forward onto his chest. He could barely keep his eyes open.

"And you dream of an Age of Griffins," Gaunt sneered. His words were cruel, openly defiant, though he spoke without raising his voice. Indeed, his calm demeanor only emphasized his cruelty. "But your dreams have always been small dreams, Father. You dream of this valley, and sometimes you dream of ruling Wyvernwood. Pathetic!"

Fighting to keep his eyes open, Gorganar lifted his head and glared at his son.

Gaunt paced from one side of the chamber to the other, and his leonine tail began to lash the air as he continued. "You lack scope. You lack ambition. Worst of all, you lack vision. There's an entire world beyond this wretched little river valley, Father. Wyvernwood is only a small corner of it!"

Gorganar lay his head back against his throne, but through his fatigue he found energy enough to laugh at his first-born. "You give yourself away, Gaunt," he scoffed. "It's you who've been dreaming!"

Even in the darkness of the nest, Gaunt's eyes gleamed. He stopped his pacing and stood directly before his father. "Yes," he said.

"You called me pathetic," Gorganar said in a quieter voice as he fixed his gaze on the chamber's distant ceiling. "But you're a fool. Dreams of conquest are always fools' dreams."

Gaunt lunged toward his father and braced himself on the arms of the throne. The basilisks, silent until now, squealed and ran away without waiting for dismissal—all but one, who remained close by and watchful.

The son brought his face close to his father's face. Eye-to-eye, he said, "How would you know, old griffin? What have you conquered? When was the last time you even tried your claws in a true competition?"

The griffin leader gave a roar, but it was a weak and unenthusiastic sound. Gorganar looked up at Gaunt so close above him. There was a light in Gaunt's eyes that reminded him of Stormfire, his old enemy. Except the light was young and vital and merciless.

For the first time, staring at his son, Gorganar saw another griffin— saw him truly!—for what he was. A monster! He cringed down upon his throne, unable to look away, for in his son he saw himself as well. Half lion and half eagle, as some described them. But neither. And more! Hideous creatures!

His weary mind reeled with new insights, and his heart hammered in his chest as he felt Gaunt's breath on his face and the heat of his son's massive body looming over him.

This was what it felt like to be prey!

He roared again, but the sound was little more than an echo of the first. What was wrong with him? He tried to push Gaunt away, yet he could barely lift his paws, and there was a strange tingling all through his limbs, a numbness that he had mistaken for fatigue—but now he knew was something else!

Gaunt gave a low chuckle. At last, his father understood.

"There are still creatures in Wyvernwood that fear you, Father," he admitted with a sly expression. Straightening, Gaunt backed away from Gorganar. In the center of the chamber, he sat back on his haunches and folded his forepaws upon his chest. "And I'm one of them. I can't match your muscle or your sheer power. As I said, though, you've always confused muscle for strength. There are other kinds of strength. Strength of will. Strength of resolve."

"The fish!" Gorganar said. He tried to fix his gaze on his son, but Gaunt wavered like a reflection on water. Whatever was affecting his limbs was beginning to affect his vision.

"Yes, the fish," Gaunt answered. He gestured to the remaining basilisk, which had moved away from the throne and now stood at Gaunt's side. "Struther knows far more about mushrooms than is good for him, I'm afraid. Certainly more than is good for you. He stuffed the fish I brought you with enough Angelhead mushrooms to poison even the strongest griffin. And you gulped it down so quickly you probably never even noticed the taste."

"I tried t' be considerate, Master," Struther said, speaking for the first time as he bowed low. His high-pitched voice dripped with hatred and mockery. "Fer all the good things y' done fer me an all the basilisks, and knowin' as I did how Silver bass was your very favorite."

Gaunt waved a paw, and the little poisoner obediently crept out of the chamber.

"Don't fight it, Father," he continued when the basilisk had left them finally alone. "Struther says it's really quite painless, that you'll just feel weaker and weaker and drift off to sleep." He hesitated, then dropping onto all four paws, he stole closer to Gorganar. "Just sleep, Father, sleep and dream your little dreams."

Barely able to lift his head, Gorganar listened to his son and laughed softly to himself. In a younger day he had stood before his own father as Gaunt stood before him now. Whipping his tail about, flexing wings and claws, making arrogant and threatening displays of power— "Rule!" he had demanded. "Take! Dominate!"

What a foolish cub and a puppy he must have looked to Argulo. He wondered if his father had laughed at him silently as he now laughed at his own son. Gorganar closed his eyes, and it seemed as if his father's spirit was close beside him, that it was leaning closer, that it was whispering to him, and he, Gorganar, recognized the words.

I will tell you a secret that will answer all your questions. On his deathbed, Argulo had beckoned him near, touched his face one last time, then died with tears on his cheeks. Now it was Gorganar's time to weep as he thought of his father.

"What's this?" Gaunt said as he approached Gorganar again. It was clear that his father had no strength left, and that the Angelhead mushrooms were doing rapid work. He watched his father's chest, noted the slowing of his breathing, the feeble flutter of his eyelids. But it was the tears that fascinated him.

Gorganar struggled to raise his head and focus his eyes. He couldn't really find it in himself to blame Gaunt. Still, with his last energy, he lashed out with his right paw, extending his claws. "Something to remember me by," he murmured, going limp on his throne again.

Gaunt screamed with pain and lunged away. He clutched the left side of his neck where hot blood oozed from a trio of cuts and spread through his feathers. Trembling and wary, he watched his father until he assured himself that the wounds were only scratches, no matter how they bled.

A soft laugh came from the throne. Gorganar could no longer see. The veil of death was nearly upon him. He felt cold all over, and he felt Argulo's spirit at his side, touching his paw, whispering.

"I'll tell you a secret," Gorganar repeated the words of his own father. His voice was weak, little more than a whistle of wind through his throat. He wondered if Gaunt would understand. "Why we do not . . ." he hesitated, waiting to see if he could draw one more breath with which to finish. "Why we cannot rule."

The gleam in Gaunt's eyes reignited, and he curled his paw into a bloody fist. "I can rule!" he hissed. "But tell me, dear Father. Tell me your secret, then die and be done with it!"

Tell him, Argulo's spirit whispered.

Gorganar's thoughts wandered. Where was Morkir, his younger son? He would have liked to see Morkir once more, to share the secret with him, too. Morkir was young enough—he might learn from it. He knew Gaunt would not.

"Griffins are cowards."

That was the secret Argulo had shared with him. He had not understood it, and he had tried not to believe it. But in his heart—his monster's heart—he had long known that it was true.

"It's our nature. We are all cowards." He tried once more to lift his head. He wanted to see Gaunt's face, to see if his words had made a mark on his son. But he could not. He couldn't move at all, couldn't even draw breath.

Sleep, Argulo's spirit murmured. *Dream.*

Silence filled the chamber. Gaunt stood at his father's feet, his heart hammering, frightened. For long moments, he watched Gorganar, and then he crept forward and brushed the tip of a claw over the old griffin's knee. When Gorganar didn't move he lifted a paw and let it fall.

It settled with lifeless grace on the throne's wooden arm.

Gaunt's mouth went dry. In the quietness, he found it hard to believe his simple plan had succeeded, and on some subtle level it disappointed him that he felt no sense of elation or triumph. It seemed wrong that so much daring should end in silence!

"Was it this way with you and Grandfather?" Gaunt spoke aloud, his gaze fixed on Gorganar's body. "You never talked about him. Did you covet his nest and scheme to take it from him as I've taken yours?"

Struther cautiously entered the chamber and approached Gaunt. "Is it done?" he whispered.

Unable to take his eyes from his father, Gaunt nodded. "Why are you whispering?" he said, realizing with a cold start that he had just whispered the question. He spun about, displaying his wings, knocking his basilisk accomplice down with an accidental lash of his tail.

The entire chamber seemed suddenly full of whispers.

Struther spoke again as he picked himself up and made a show of brushing dust from his person. "Shoddy treatment, if y' ask me," he grumbled, "for the one what's come t' warn ye that yer brother's just returned."

Gaunt's eyes narrowed at the news. He hadn't given much thought to Morkir. It was an oversight he'd have to correct now. Morkir was too close to Gorganar, more his father's son than he, Gaunt, had ever been, and his propensity for unpredictable violence made him dangerous.

Morkir, too, would have to die.

Struther moved through the darkness to Gorganar's side and nudged the old griffin several times. When he had assured himself that his former master was dead, he leaped high and clicked his heels together, turned a pirouette upon landing again, and chortled. "It's a happy slave," he sang in a low voice, "that lives to dance on his master's grave!"

Gaunt watched Struther's performance with a ruthless leer. Of course the basilisk would also have to die. The vile little lizard knew too much—too much about poisons and too much about what Gaunt had done. Not that Gaunt wasn't grateful for Struther's assistance. But a creature that took that much glee in his master's demise could never be trusted.

Particularly now that Gaunt was the master.

"Interesting," Gaunt whispered as he wrapped himself in his wings. "The first murder leads to the second, and the second to the third." He shivered and turned away. Let Struther dance a brief while longer.

After all, someone should celebrate their success.

6

LIKE ALL LARGE RIVERS, the Blackwater was the parent of numerous other rivers and streams, and the most powerful of these was a river called the Echo Rush. While the Blackwater continued its southward course through Wyvernwood and on through Degarm, the Echo Rush broke away to cut a shorter course to the Windy Sea.

It was a river that had made its mark on the world. Huge chasms and canyons rose up on either side of its sandy banks, and spectacular spires and crags jutted along its shores, all carved by the surging waters of the smaller river.

But that work had been done long ago. Like all things grown old, the Echo Rush had lost much of its strength. It flowed at a slower, more thoughtful pace now, seeming to take its time to admire the beauty it had created in its more energetic days.

Of all the canyons along the Echo Rush, Stronghold was the deepest and the most awesome. Here, the ages of the earth were plainly revealed in the many shaded striations of brown and gray and ochre that painted the walls, in the glittering layers of mica and limestone and granite, all exposed for the eye to see.

It was here, after coming to Wyvernwood, that the Dragonkin had made their home in the many natural caves that honeycombed those walls, and in the forests at the summits of the cliffs.

Some had dispersed throughout the forest, of course, to make new homes for themselves. But many still remained.

Stormfire looked out from the mouth of his cave and let the wind play upon his face. He listened to the sussurus of the water below, and inhaled the fragrances of the forest, which, to him, seemed always sweetest at evening. The canyon was a blaze of color as the sun slowly set. Another day was ending.

On a towering needle of stone at the east end of the canyon sat the last phoenix in the world. Her face was turned toward the sun and her wings were spread wide, as if to catch the fading rays. With her splendid plumage of yellow and orange and red, she looked like a creature of flame as she arched her neck and offered herself to the sun.

Phoebe was older even than Stormfire. It saddened him to look upon her and know that when she was gone, the world would never see her like again. Other creatures had passed entirely from the earth, too. Gone were the manticores and the cicatrices. Perhaps there were a still a few rocs somewhere, but they had not followed him to Wyvernwood. Of the unicorns, he knew only of Marian.

He smiled as he thought of Marian. She was too in love with the forest to come often to Stronghold.

Phoebe rose from her pinnacle and took to the sky in a wide, gliding spiral. Stormfire watched her as she climbed higher and higher. The last sunlight seemed to cling to her like dew, and she sparkled as she sailed away.

"If there were one last drop of magic in the world I would give it to you," Stormfire whispered as, at last, she turned away from the sun and disappeared over the canyon's northern rim.

"Now there's the opening line for a good poem," a voice said behind him. "I'll scribble it down and work on it a bit when I get back to my library. Best not to let Sabu hear such a sentiment, however. It might hurt her feelings. And a dragon with hurt feelings is not a pretty sight."

Stormfire turned back into his cave. Another dragon regarded him from behind a stack of books on an old table. One of the books lay open, and half a page was covered with fresh ink markings. The Dragon Ramoses, still gripping a writing quill in his left hand, sat on his haunches while he rested his blue-scaled chin on one clawed fist. His large golden eyes were both thoughtful and amused.

"I thought you were making my home your library," Stormfire said, nodding toward the pile of books.

"Nonsense!" Ramoses answered. "These are just a few volumes I've brought over for your perusal. When you find time, of course. But as these specifically concern your exploits, the gathering of the Dragonkin, and the journey to Wyvernwood, I thought you'd like the first look at them."

Stormfire shrugged. "You are our chronicler," he said as he laid a hand upon one of the books, "and our best storyteller. Why not read them on the river shore tonight when the moon is high over the canyon, and let everyone come hear your words?"

Ramoses' great eyes narrowed. Slowly, he set aside his writing quill and stoppered his ink jar. That done, he carefully marked the page upon which he'd been writing, then closed the book. Rising, he came around the table and laid one hand on Stormfire's shoulder. "What is troubling you, my old friend?"

Stormfire turned back to stare out the cave entrance. Daylight was nearly gone. On the far wall of the canyon, a long shadow marked the advance of night. "I've had dreams," Stormfire said without looking at Ramoses. "Every night for a while now. Dreams of flying once more beyond the Imagination Mountains."

Ramoses didn't answer immediately. "Then perhaps you should go," he said finally. "See what's out there. A little adventure would rejuvenate you."

Again there was a pause before either spoke. "In the dreams," Stormfire whispered, "I don't come back." He folded his arms upon his huge chest as he watched the shadow inch its way across the canyon wall. "Once I cross the mountains, I just keep flying through a blue sky that never ends, and I never get tired, and I never come back."

Ramoses went back to the table and stared for a long moment at the stack of books. "Have you told Sabu about these dreams?"

"She knows," Stormfire answered. "She's a good wife. She says if I go she'll follow me. She doesn't really understand what I'm talking about."

"I suspect she does," Ramoses said.

They were interrupted when the cave entrance was suddenly filled with the noisy flapping of leathery wings. Harrow's claws found purchase on the stone, and for an instant he stood framed in the fading light.

"Father!" he cried. "I have news! But, you have to come up to the village! Hurry! You won't believe it! You, too, Ramoses!" Then he jumped away from the entrance back into space, spread his wings, and was gone.

Stormfire blinked. "What in the world could make Harrow so excited?" he said, forgetting all talk of dreams as he shot a look at Ramoses.

"He's been gone for two days," his old friend reminded him as he left the table and pointed to the entrance. "More than time enough for an adventure or two when you're that young."

One after the other, heedless of the sheer drop to the river and shore far below, they leaped from the cave. Stormfire's wings glimmered in the very last rays of the setting sun as he climbed out of the shadowed canyon and soared high into the air, with blue Ramoses right behind him.

On the clifftops directly above the dragon's caves, a village had sprung up chiefly populated by Fomorians—a collection of people that were part human and also parts of a wide variety of animals. Among them were also a number of minotaurs and satyrs, who were not really all that different from the Fomorians. There were also several families of bears, squirrels, and red foxes. Even a few of the smaller dragons, choosing not to live in the caves, had made log homes and lived with the others.

In the longest and largest of those log houses lived the Dragon Sabu. Deeply loved by all, the residents of the village had built her home for her when an illness took away her ability to fly.

Canyon, caves, and village—they all made up Stronghold. Everyone got along. Indeed, they depended on each other. They were a community.

They were also, at the moment, a community in an uproar.

Stormfire sailed above the canyon rim. The sight that greeted him caused him to blink again. Residents were rushing from their homes and nests into the village square, which extended right to Sabu's front yard. Above him, a number other dragons, roused from their caves by the shouting, were circling and competing for air space.

In the square with all the other residents surging about them, he spied Sabu and Harrow. Taking note of his father's arrival, Harrow called for the throng to make room, and they did, pressing back to the very edges of the square so that the largest of all dragons should not be crowded.

Stormfire landed carefully, gently, mindful of the smaller creatures. Then, for an instant he stood completely still, stunned by what he saw.

On the ground between Sabu and Harrow lay Morkir. The young griffin's once-golden hide was covered with blood and slash marks. So were the feathers around his throat, and one of his wings looked as if it had been severely twisted near the shoulder. Despite his injuries, he made a stubborn effort to rise to his feet when he saw Stormfire, and when he lifted his head his eyes were filled with blood and pain.

It was obvious that Morkir had been in the fight of his life.

Softhearted Sabu was calling for pails of water and bandages, and such was the respect that the villagers had for her that many were hurrying to respond to her wishes. Not everyone was happy to see a griffin in their village, however, and more than a few had grudges against that kind. A handful of stones or dirt clods flew through the air, pelting Morkir, but the griffin just stood still and tolerated the abuse.

That, in itself, was an amazing thing. Almost as amazing as Harrow suddenly spreading his wings to shelter Morkir from the barrage.

"Stop!" Stormfire's voice rang out over the village like a thunderclap. All eyes turned toward him, and hands that were grasping stones froze in midair, their missiles unlaunched. "All creatures that come to Stronghold in peace may expect that peace returned!" the dragon leader reminded the residents sternly. Then, his golden eyes narrowed to menacing slits as he turned his gaze on their injured guest. "Even you, Morkir."

The young griffin gave a low growl and nodded his head. It was the closest he could come to expressing gratitude.

Harrow folded his wings tightly against his body as he turned to his father. "I followed Canaan and his sailors until they were well on their way toward Angmar's border," he reported. "But as I flew above the place where Skyrunner Creek flows into the Windy Sea, I decided to turn inland and return home."

Sabu knelt down beside their griffin guest with a steaming wet cloth and a pair of Satyrs for assistants. Morkir flinched away and showed his teeth as she reached for one of his bloodstained paws, but Harrow quickly smacked him on the top of the head with the tip of one black wing. "Mind your manners," he warned. "My mother's trying to help you."

"Forgive me," Morkir growled as he cast his gaze toward Sabu's feet and extended his injured paw. "Old animosities are hard to put aside."

"Let's hope that's not true," Sabu answered in a kindly voice as she began to wash away the dried blood on his claws. "There's no animosity in my heart for any hurt creature."

Morkir glanced around the assembly, particularly at Harrow, then back to Sabu. "My heart is filled with animosity," he said. "But your hatchling, a dragon, saved my life, so I will hold no more hatred for Dragonkin."

A general murmur ran through the crowd as they heard Morkir's declaration.

Stormfire turned one eye to his son while he kept the other on Morkir. He wasn't too sure he trusted the griffin so near his dragon-wife. Yet he knew better than to try to tell Sabu what to do. "What does he mean you saved his life?"

Harrow moved to one side as the pair of satyrs and a Fomorian cat-wife went to work washing the blood from Morkir's matted fur and feathers, and bathing his wounds with warm cloths. He noted, though, that not everyone in the crowd had put down their stones. Some were still uncertain about welcoming the griffin among them.

"As I flew near the south end of the Valley of Eight Winds," Harrow explained, "I heard loud griffm-cries and the sounds of fighting in the forest below, so I turned to investigate and found Gaunt on top of Morkir. He was slashing away at his brother."

"A family squabble?" Ramoses called from the cliff edge. "That's not unusual among griffins."

Harrow shook his head. "I saw the look in Gaunt's eyes. He meant to kill Morkir."

"He came very near it," Morkir snarled. "If you hadn't frightened him off by showing up so unexpectedly, I'd be dead now. I've never seen Gaunt so powerful or so crazed."

"Why didn't Gorganar stop Gaunt?" Stormfire asked as he watched Sabu wrap a bandage around Morkir's right front paw. She worked with such care and gentleness, quietly directing the ones who assisted her, completely unafraid of Morkir and his griffin-nature.

Morkir answered in a harsh whisper. "Gorganar is dead."

A gasp went through the crowd. Even Stormfire felt the shock of Morkir's news. Sabu stopped her ministrations and patted the band-aged paw. "You poor child!" she purred. "Your father!"

Morkir looked up at Stormfire. There was no grief in the young griffin's eyes, only a smoldering anger. "I think Gaunt killed him," he continued. "I didn't get very close to Father's body before Gaunt jumped me from the shadows. We nearly destroyed Gorganar's great nest, but my brother is stronger than I realized. When I tried to fly away, he followed and brought me down again." Morkir fell suddenly silent as a shudder passed through him.

"I thought it best to bring him to Stronghold," Harrow told his father. "He couldn't fly, so we walked for a night and a day. Gaunt followed for a little while, and I think he would have finished what he'd started if I hadn't stayed close."

"For better or worse," Ramoses broke in, "the Griffinkin have a new leader."

"For worse!" Morkir growled. "Gaunt is up to something. He's been meeting regularly with Men from Angmar on the northern edge of Wyvernwood. He doesn't know I've followed him."

The residents of Stronghold drew closer. The last of them dropped their stones and began to listen in earnest. "Why?" someone called. And someone else: "That can't be good news!" And still another voice: "What's the purpose of such meetings?"

A sudden rush of wings caused everyone to turn their gaze skyward as a pair of dragons skimmed the treetops, sailed out above the canyon, and banked sharply. The wind of their passage shook the leaves, rustled clothing, and stirred the dust. No one minded. "Chan!" the villagers called in greeting as they waved their arms and jumped up and down. "Luna!" The village square was already crowded, so Chan beat the air and hovered while his sister settled on the cliff edge beside Ramoses.

"Now there's an interesting and unexpected guest!" Chan called down to his father as he regarded Morkir from above.

"We've got more guests coming, too," Luna shouted. She pointed toward the forest with the tip of one ivory wing.

Stormfire cocked an eye toward his daughter. "You found the man-children?"

"It took a little time," she laughed, "but we finally convinced them we weren't going to eat them."

"They've been fed some incredible stories about us," Chan added, echoing her laughter.

One by one, the children emerged from the darkening forest. Three boys and two girls. Bedraggled and dirty and wide-eyed, they gazed at the dragons and all the strange creatures around them, and they moved a little closer together, looking as if they might bolt back into the woods at any moment.

Sabu set aside the towel with which she was cleaning Morkir's wounds and rose to her full height. "Who would dare to chain their hatchlings in such a cruel fashion?" she said with indignation. She motioned to the Fomorian cat-wife that was assisting her with the griffin. "Carola, your husband should just be waking. Please ask him to bring his hammers and strike that hurtful metal from their wrists!"

Carola was half cat and half human. Her green cat-eyes flashed, and with astonishing feline grace she sprang over the heads of the crowd and ran toward a cluster of houses and around a corner. A moment later, she reappeared and took her previous place at Sabu's side.

Her husband stumbled sleepily through his neighbors. The children gasped as they saw him and started to draw away. Like his wife, Gregor was a Fomorian. From the waist down, his body was that of a man, but from the waist up, his form was that of a white-feathered owl. Wings even adorned his shoulders, although they were too small and weak to actually lift him. In one taloned hand, he carried a hammer, and in the other a chisel. His large, round eyes were still full of sleep, for like the bird he so resembled, he was a creature of the nighttime.

The tallest boy stepped cautiously forward. His brown hair hung down across his dirty forehead, and the sleeves of his shirt were ripped at both elbows. When he held out his arms, his manacles rattled. "Can you get these off, please?" he said to Gregor.

Gregor covered his mouth with one hand as he yawned. "Sorry," he muttered, then he yawned again. "I'm just not at my best so early in the evening. Carola barely let me get my pants on!" He bent forward for a doser look at the chains on the boy's wrists. "Oh, my! Iron!" he exclaimed. "I'll bet that chafes!" Straightening, he began to pat his pockets and turn them inside out. "My anvil! Where's my anvil?"

Carola smacked Gregor on the back of the head, an action that elicited chuckles and grins from their neighbors. "Wake up, husband!"

she snapped. "You're not packing an anvil in your pants. Now can you remove those chains, or not?"

"Am I not the best metalsmith in Stronghold?" Gregor's answer could barely be understood by anyone, for he yawned again as he spoke. "Carola, my beautiful dear, send someone to fetch my anvil, and I'll just lie down here and take a nap."

The brown-haired boy lowered his arms and stepped back "I could do with some sleep, myself," he said with quiet disappointment, "but I'd sleep better with my hands free."

Sabu clapped her front paws together for attention. "Gregor, may I suggest that you and Carola lead the man-children to your shop? You can strike off their chains quickly, then be back in your bed and sleep until moonrise." She turned her gaze over the other residents of Stronghold. "And while he does that, perhaps the rest of us can prepare a suitable meal for our guests. I'm sure we're all way past our suppertimes. In fact, I think that a feast is in order!" She knelt down beside Morkir again and returned to the task of cleaning the griffin's many wounds.

"Feast!" someone cried. "Oh yes, by all means!"

"Wine! Food!" one of the satyrs shouted. "Kill the fatted calf, eh?"

A tall minotaur bristled. "Hey, I resent that!"

"Figure of speech!" the satyr grinned. Pulling a flute from a pouch on his hip, he blew a flurry of notes and danced away.

Others produced musical instruments. If the satyrs were masters of the flute, the minotaurs were drummers and percussionists. A trio of Fomorian dog-men disappeared into their homes and returned with harps. In a very short time, the wildest music poured forth.

In an equally short time wooden tables were erected in the square. Sabu and Morkir moved closer to her front door where she and her assistants continued to nurse their unlikely patient while others brought forth platters of cheeses and sliced breads, bowls of apples and pears and wild grapes. A fox-wife contributed a huge pot of vegetable stew. The squirrel families added an astonishing assortment of tasty nuts, and old Bear Byron produced a barrel of the richest, darkest honey anyone could remember seeing.

Chan, tired of hovering over the scene, settled down on the cliff edge beside his sister and Ramoses. Stormfire, ever mindful of his great size when he moved through the village, strode toward them.

"You were gone for two days," he said to Chan and Luna. "I was beginning to worry."

"You worry too much," Ramoses said. "They're no longer hatchlings."

Luna swished her ivory tail. Her blue-eyed gaze was locked on the man-children as Carola and Gregor, accompanied by a small group of interested villagers, led them off to Gregor's shop. "We had quite a time catching them," she admitted. "They're like quick little mice, able to hide under any rock or tree."

"She's right," Chan agreed. "It took some time and effort—not to mention my inestimable charm—to corner them and convince them we meant them no harm." He grinned and winked at his sister.

"Charm?" Luna exclaimed. She folded her paws across her chest and struck an indignant pose. "It was positively embarrassing the way you laid down on the ground and rolled over and put your legs in the air and began to purr for them."

Stormfire and Ramoses, each observing the dragon-children, exchanged looks, then burst out laughing.

Chan laughed, too. "But the tall one did finally come over and scratch my nose," he reminded Luna. "And when the others realized I wasn't going to eat him, they followed. He seems to be their leader. And my nose really did need scratching." He gazed across the village square toward Morkir and Sabu.

Harrow still stood close by, watchful of Morkir's every move.

"For all the fun we had chasing these small ones," Chan continued in a more serious voice, "I'd say it's our brother who's proved himself today. What in the world did he do to Morkir?"

Ramoses raised an eyebrow as he regarded Chan. "He saved his life."

Luna gasped. "What?"

"Are you joking?" Chan said.

"The winds of change are blowing through Wyvernwood," Stormfire told them, "and deep in these old bones I've a feeling the changes are only just beginning."

He stretched his long neck skyward. The moon was just peeking through the branches of the trees in the east, and overhead the stars were winking into brightness. Drawn by the excitement and the music, all the Dragonkin had come out of their caves and homes. The

canyon was filled with dragons and eagles and owls and all sorts of flying creatures.

Even Phoebe had returned to perch nobly on the canyon's far rim.

The party was in full swing. Torches and lanterns were lit as the
night grew darker. The musicians played in a frenzy while in all parts
of the village, neighbors danced and ate and laughed. Swathed in
bandages and his wing in a splint, Morkir lay at Sabu's feet, as unlikely
a sight as Stormfire had ever thought to see. Sabu noticed him and
smiled, and her smile warmed his heart.

The five man-children, freed from their shackles and their faces
washed, wandered about in a close-knit group, still obviously nervous
and half-afraid, until they found the tables with the platters and
mounds of food. Then, their eyes grew big, and they fell to stuffing
their hungry mouths. A stern look from the tallest one, however, cautioned them to slow down and exercise some manners.

"A poem, Ramoses!" someone shouted. "Give us a poem!" And
others took up the cry. "Give us a poem!"

Ramoses pursed his dragon-lips and curled his claws against his
chest. With a loud sigh, he opened his wings wide, then folded them
again, cleared his throat, and began.

> "In a land where the trees grow tall,
> Where dragons fly in a sun-painted morning . . ."

A muted hush spread through the village as others began to draw
close and listen. The music changed as the players picked up the mood
of Ramoses' poem.

> "Where an eagle rises to catch the first wind of dawn
> There rests my heart
> Where rivers flow between banks
> That drip with ice and snowmelt,
> Where the waters fall beside crumbling fountains,
> There rests my heart.
> There rests my heart.
> Where the night warms me in a blanket of stars,
> Where the dark forest whispers lullabies
> With familiar, half-remembered voices,
> There rests my heart.

In an Age that seems like a distant dream,
There rests my heart."

Ramoses lowered his head. A last strain of music from one of the harps sounded, then faded away. The entire village had grown quiet, and for a moment, nothing could be heard but the breeze and the rushing of the river in the canyon below.

7

RONALDO AND MARIAN CONFERRED QUIETLY while Bumble, half-starved by their long journey, darted back and forth between a patch of trumpet honeysuckle and a crop of luscious red coral bells. The little hummingbird's ecstatic moans as he engorged himself might have been a source of amusement to his companions, if not for the seriousness of the decision that confronted them.

For two days they had traveled together. Marian's nose and Ronaldo's sharp eyes had led them along a faint trail of mingled scents and broken branches southward to a bend in the Blackwater River. On the evening of the first day, on the muddy bank the trail had ended, but in the mud they had found the footprints of many men, and signs of boats that had been dragged ashore and launched again, as well as evidence of considerable industry.

"I believe we've stumbled upon a small logging operation," Ronaldo had said. "They must be towing the trees they cut down river."

"Logging operation, my left hoof!" Marian had answered. "Wyvernwood has been invaded! Why would mere loggers be so interested in Chernovog?"

Bumble, in a fit of agitation, had flown circles around Marian's golden horn. "Invaded! Yes! To arms! To arms!" he cried. "Why, oh why, with so many trees, would they chop down my home? Millions for defense, I say, but not one cent for tribute!"

After a brief rest, they had continued southward, following the course of the river, and on the evening of the second day, as the sun sank low through the branches of the trees, they found themselves at another bend in the Blackwater, and at the very edge of Wyvernwood.

Ronaldo ignored Bumble's moans and groans as he stared across the river into Degarm. He thought of his warm cave and his paints and the softly colorful way the sun set in the Whispering Hills. He missed those things suddenly, and he shivered inside a little as he wondered when he would see them again.

But he also thought of Beatrice and little Coniff, and he knew what he must do.

"I have never been so far south," he said as much to himself as to Marian. "I've never thought of myself as an adventurer."

Marian regarded him with a strange light in her eyes. Without saying anything, she gazed back over her shoulder into Wyvern-wood. Then she turned once more to stare toward Degarm. "I followed the Dragon Stormfire to this forest," she said, "because I was the last of my kind, and I was lonely, and with the changing of the Ages the world was becoming a hostile place." She shifted her gaze and smiled as she watched Bumble feeding at the coral bells. "That was a hundred years or more ago, Ronaldo. Maybe longer. In truth, I've lost count of the years. Wyvernwood was to be our refuge from the race of Man, and I've been content to wander safe within its borders."

Ronaldo thought how small and delicate and noble Marian looked, and he made up his mind to paint her someday. It would be a challenge to capture her rare qualities in ordinary pigment, but if he succeeded, she would be his masterpiece.

Suddenly, he didn't want her to cross the river. "I'll find Chernovog," he said. "You don't have to come with me. Stay here safe in the forest."

Marian shook her head. "You don't understand, my dear," she said. "You were born in Wyvernwood, and you've lived your entire life here. But I'm old, older even than Stormfire, and I know things. There's no safety anymore, and there's no refuge." She looked once more toward Degarm as she dipped her front hooves into the water.

"But Marian!" Ronaldo argued. "If anything should happen to you . . . !"

The hummingbird flew three swift circles around Marian's horn and, perching on the very tip, pushed out his fat belly. "No harm to Molly Ann will come," he declared, fluffing his feathers proudly. "Nor to the Dragon Ronaldo! Not while Bumble is in command! Charge!" He fluttered down to land on Marian's ear and whispered, "Tell me again, soldier, where are we going?"

"Tell me again," Ronaldo sighed with a roll of his dragon eyes, "why he's still with us?"

"I said I know *things*," Marian answered with a chuckle. "I didn't say I know *everything*. But even the smallest creatures have a purpose, and if the Bumble-bird wants to come along, I won't chase him away."

"But he's so little," Ronaldo grumbled.

Marian started across the river, wading at first, with Bumble perched once more on her horn. "Have you ever been stung by a wasp?" she asked as she began to swim. "Or bitten by a spider? They're little, too." The fading sunlight sparkled on the waves as the water parted around her. She swam with grace and power, her head held high, and her golden horn shining. "But then," she called back with a hint of laughter, "from your perspective, great dragon, everything is little."

Ronaldo sighed again. "Point taken."

Stepping out from under the trees, he spread his wings and took to the sky. The wind felt wonderful on his face. Flexing his muscles, he lashed the air with his tail, climbing and arcing backward in a great loop. For an instant, all of Wyvernwood spread out below him, green and dark and mysterious, full of shadows. Then the river flashed below, and the forest was behind him.

His heart pounded with fear—but also with excitement!

Marian's hooves found purchase on the muddy bottom, and she waded ashore. For a long moment, she stood with her nose close to the ground, shivering and wet and afraid. She'd tried to be brave in front of Ronaldo—but it had been an act. The air smelled foreign, less sweet than the air of Wyvernwood, and she felt cold in a way she had never felt cold before.

Bumble walked down the length of her horn until he was so close to her eyes that strands of her forelock tickled his wings. "Does Maryanne cry?" he asked.

Marian listened to the rush of Ronaldo's wings as the dragon crossed the river and sailed into Degarm. *From one world into quite another*, she thought, wondering if he felt the transition as sharply as she did. "I'm not crying," she lied to Bumble. "I'm just . . ." she hesitated, then slowly lifted her head. "I'm just remembering."

"Remembering?" Bumble asked, puzzled.

She couldn't explain her feelings to the little hummingbird. She wasn't sure she understood them, herself. Leaving the safety and peace of Wyvernwood had unlocked a part of her heart that she had neglected for a very long time. Faces and names of long-ago friends, places that no longer existed, memories that she had neatly folded and tucked away and forgotten all flooded back upon her again.

Turning, she stared back into Wyvernwood. She had hidden from the world there and been happy amid its ancient trees and sweet flowers, its brooks and streams and rivers. But by the simple act of leaving it, of crossing the Blackwater and setting hoof on the soil of Degarm, she realized something else.

She had also hidden from herself.

"I'm remembering," she said at last to Bumble, "things that I've seen and places I've been." Sniffing, she stretched her neck toward the sky, and the familiar scent of Wyvernwood seemed to blow across the river to her. "Most of all, my tiny Bumble-bird, I remember what I once was, and I remember what I am now."

"I'm sure that all makes tasty sense," Bumble said. "But not having much of a memory, I can't be sure. What good are memories? They have no flavor, no texture, no sweetness."

Marian gave a soft laugh. "Oh, you're wrong, little one. Some memories can be quite sweet. Others can be very bitter. Still others can be quite salty, but we shouldn't talk about those in polite company."

Bumble paced the length of her horn until he stood at the tip again. "I do remember one thing always," he said, turning back to face her. "I remember that I'm glad I'm not a butterfly. I met one once. A very fine fellow, but he had no brain at all!"

"Then he was a natural politician," Marian replied.

The sun was nearly gone. Its fading rays touched the river's surface and turned the water blood red. Once more, the rising breeze carried the scent of Wyvernwood to her nostrils. Closing her eyes, she breathed deeply of it, savored it, and made up her mind to hold on to the memory of that smell.

Then she turned her nose toward Degarm and put Wyvernwood out of her mind.

"Do you remember who we're looking for?" she said, making conversation with Bumble as she started walking along the bank. There were no tracks at the place where she and her companions had crossed the river, nor any sign of a landing, so she followed the direction of the current.

"Wait! Don't tell me! I can see his face as clear as day," Bumble answered. He rubbed his chin with one wingtip and his belly with the other. "Except it's almost night now, isn't it? The minotaur boy. Are we stopping for supper?"

Marian laughed again. "It's always food with you, isn't it?" she said. "Aren't you in the least concerned about leaving the forest you've always called home?"

Bumble fluttered into the air and landed again on top of her head, his tiny feet grasping the hairs of her mane and forelock. "Home is where Bumble's heart is," he sang. A barely visible blur, he flew high up into the air and returned to perch on her ear. Leaning down, he looked inside. "Hmmm, deep and dark! A nice place to make my nest!"

Without slowing her pace, Marian shook her head. Her tossing mane caught Bumble off-guard, and he tumbled three times, beak over feet, before spreading his wings and flitting off to the safety of a patch of cattail reeds by the river's edge. A moment later, he flew back and hovered near Marian's nose.

"Still friends?" he asked with tiny hummingbird tears in his eyes. "Friends are homeless Bumble's last comfort!" His voice rose to a wail. "Me is woe without friends!"

"Woe is me," Marian corrected. "I didn't mean to knock you off so suddenly, you silly creature, but that tickled! A unicorn's ears are particularly sensitive, you know."

Bumble's tears ceased immediately, and he landed on Marian's nose again. "Mary-em is ticklish?"

The unicorn slowed, then stopped. A hummingbird's face was small, and its expression was often hard to read. But there was an upturn in the corners of Bumble's lips and a gleam in his eyes that suggested mischief.

"No, I am not ticklish," Marian answered archly. "I just misspoke, that's all."

"Marian is ticklish!" Without warning, Bumble flew into the sky. Performing a somersault, he straightened and plunged toward Marian's head. For the briefest moment, he seemed to disappear, so swift was his flight. The unicorn tried to turn her head away, but there was a sudden sharp buzzing and vibrating in her right ear.

"You bumble-bird!" Marian cried. "Stop that!"

But before she'd finished her sentence, Bumble flew over her head and perched in her other ear. Tiny talons grasped her earlobe, and tiny wings whirred ever so lightly inside her ear. The sound was almost as maddening as the touch! Marian reared up on her hind legs and tossed her mane, but before she could sweep him aside, Bumble flew off, cartwheeled in the air, and targeted her left ear a second time. Again came the feathery brush of rapid wings, and with it came delicate, musical laughter!

Marian bucked and kicked at the air, shook her head, tossed her long mane—and squealed. Bumble tickled her ears, then brushed his wings over the very tip of her nose, and that tickled, too. "Good fun!" he cried.

"You little pest!" Marian shouted. She broke into a gallop, but the hummingbird easily kept up with her, passed her, came back and circled her nose. She spun, tearing up divots of earth and grass with her hooves—and he was in her right ear again. "Okay, okay! I'll beg! Please, Bumble, stop!"

He tickled her nose again as he teased her. "Say the magic word!"

Marian rolled on the ground, but still the little bird found her nose again, and her left ear. Worse, he found a new spot on the inside of her front thigh! She sprang to her feet, breathless, gasping. "What—what's the magic word?"

Bumble ceased his torment and hovered in the air directly in front of her. His eyes sparkled with mirth. He flew a few paces to the right suddenly, then a few paces to the left, back and forth, until he stopped and hovered before her again. "I forgot!" he shouted. He was in her ear once more, and his wings made that frantic buzzing and brushing.

Marian thought her mane would stand on end if it didn't stop—and suddenly it did stop. Bumble whispered in her ear. "I'm only a hummingbird."

Marian stood still. "Get up on my horn, Bumble, where I can see you."

With a blur of speed, Bumble obeyed. Perching on the tip, he looked down at Marian. The pulse in his red-banded throat throbbed as the last of the sun shimmered on his dark green feathers.

Through her sensitive horn, Marian could feel the vibration of a valiant heart racing in Bumble's small body. He looked proud and timid at the same time as he folded his wings and hung his head until he touched her with the tip of his needle-like beak.

"I'm sorry," he said without looking up. "Marian looked so sad. I wanted only to make Marian laugh."

The unicorn stared at the hummingbird, seeing him as if for the first time. "You got my name right," she said. "Twice. It's I who should apologize, Bumble. I've been condescending and rude, and I *was* feeling a bit sad." She hesitated. "No, not sad. I was afraid."

Bumble fluttered his wings. "Don't be afraid, Marian," he answered, getting her name right a third time in a row. "I'll protect you." He looked very serious as he wrapped his wings around his white belly. "Are you as hungry as I am?"

Marian laughed. "Let's watch the end of the sunset together," she suggested, turning toward the west, moving with deliberate care so as not to startle or dislodge Bumble. "Then we'll find you a rich crop of rosemary or woolly bluecurls. Even in the dark my ticklish nose can find those!"

Bumble danced. "Nose...those! You are a poet like the Dragon Ramoses!"

"There are few poets like Ramoses," she answered, "and no better storytellers. But hush now, and watch. There's so much to learn from simple, quiet moments. So much the world has to teach us if we listen. And I haven't listened, really listened, for a long time."

The sun had already slipped below the rim of the world, but its weakening rays still lit the western sky and ignited the band of low clouds that followed it. The river, living up to its name, had turned black and glassy. It seemed to run away from the light as it flowed eastward. Moment by moment, the light dimmed, and stars like unpolished diamonds began to appear as a rising breeze ushered in the darkness of night.

"Now that was worthy of one of Ramoses verses," Marian sighed as the last trace of sunlight faded.

Bumble held his stomach. "What did Marian learn?" he asked.

Marian smiled to herself. "Sometimes it takes a while for the lessons to sink in."

Her fear was gone; so was the embarrassment she'd felt for being afraid. She turned her mind to immediate tasks—finding food for Bumble, as she'd promised; finding Chernovog; and finding Ronaldo. Where had that dragon flown off to?

"It's very dark," Bumble murmured, his gaze sweeping the sky. "Owls and falcons and hawks—oh, my."

"Ride on top of my head if you like," Marian offered. "They won't see you between my ears."

Bumble bravely kept his place, though he also kept careful watch.

Marian kept watch, too, but her gaze was on the ground. The darkness was no hindrance to her sharp eyesight and keen sense of smell. At an easy pace, she followed the riverbank in the hope that Chernovog's captors had come ashore somewhere and that she might pick up their tracks or their scents.

Many were the times she had observed young Chernovog fishing by the Blackwater. He was a lonely and unhappy young minotaur with a habit of talking to himself as he hunched over his pole and stared into the water. From behind a bush or a copse of trees she had sometimes eavesdropped, unseen, to his private conversations, but she had never revealed herself or spoken to him.

She regretted that. Who knew better than she, who was the last of her unicorn kind, what it meant to be lonely? Yet, she had kept herself hidden when she might have reached out to him, when he might have needed a kind word or a friend.

Her nose twitched. "There's lousewort ahead," she whispered.

"Lousewort! My very favorite!" Bumble cried, taking to the air. "Very different from lemon grass, is lousewort! Different from fuschia, too, and ocatillo, or red-hot poker, or honeysuckle, or. . . ." His tiny litany faded as, all fear of predators forgotten, he disappeared in the night.

Marian paused to drink from the river. The moon, rising low in the east, reflected on the surface, and the water lightly rippled as her mane spilled forward and brushed across its face. She waited for the ripples to subside, and then she bent and drank again, pressing her lips to the lips of the moon. It was a silly, romantic thing to do, but there was no one to see her. She kissed the moon again.

Then there was another face beneath the moon's reflection—a face with a cruel and hungry glare. Marian leaped back as a sudden, violent splash threw water into her eyes. Powerful jaws crashed shut, catching nothing but some strands of her mane. She jerked free and danced back another step, slipping in some treacherous mud.

On short, ugly legs the alligator lunged at her, snapping its jaws as it scrambled onto the bank.

"I'd love to stay and talk," Marian said, her heart racing as she pranced backward. "But I can tell you're not my type."

"Kiss me, baby, like you did the moon," the alligator answered as it slithered after her. It showed sharp, white teeth as it grinned. "I might turn into a prince."

Marian laughed, continuing to back away as the creature followed. "That old line only works for frogs," she shot back. "I've been around, and I've met your kind. Lizards and reptiles! Always trying to rush a girl!"

The alligator stopped and arched up on its front legs, indignant. "Please!" it said. "I am not a reptile!" Lifting the point of its snout proudly, it informed her in an offended tone, "I am an amphibian!"

"I'll do my drinking elsewhere from now on," Marian replied.

Still, the alligator persisted, its claws digging in the grass as it came after her. "I'd love to have you for supper!"

Marian turned her back as she walked away. "I'll bet you say that to all the girls," she laughed, "and no doubt to the boys, as well."

"But I love you!" the alligator called after her.

Marian trotted a few paces down the shore, chuckling to herself. When a soft splash told her that the alligator had given up, she paused and stared back. The moon still floated on the river, and as the ripples rolled across its face, it seemed to laugh at her.

The smell of lousewort on a random breeze drew her attention and reminded her of Bumble. She'd just had a lesson—not all the dangers in the night could be easily seen, and the little hummingbird was alone. Concerned, she hurried in the direction her nose indicated.

"Marian!" Bumble hailed her as she reached the patch of lousewort. The fragrant blossoms, bright red in the daylight, hung black and half-closed in the night. Nevertheless, Bumble made his rapid way from one to the next, sampling them all. "Delicious!" he cried. "A culinary treasure!" He sputtered and backed away from a bloom whose petals were starting to shrivel. "Not fresh!"

Marian shook her head as she watched. "Bumble, you glutton! You're belly's all distended! You're so fat you probably can't even fly up to my horn!"

Quick as thought he darted upward and took his now familiar perch. "Wanna bet? Five to one, and jokers wild! All on the red, let it ride!"

Marian stared at the hummingbird. "You're not stuffed. You're stiff!"

Grinning, Bumble saluted her with a wingtip. "Genuine one-hundred proof nectar—and smooth!" He pitched a little to the side, then balanced himself again. "They don't call it lousewort for nothing!"

With that, he toppled sideways and fell off her horn. Marian gasped as he hit the ground, and she knelt down beside him. "Bumble-bird, are you all right? Bumble?"

Bumble's only answer was a tiny snore.

Sighing, Marian folded her legs beneath her and lay down on the grass. There was nothing else to do, and though she hated to admit it she was weary. She nibbled a few of the flowers. They really didn't taste bad!

There was another thing she hated to admit.

Degarm was not Wyvernwood. She could gaze across the Blackwater and even in the darkness still see the lovely forest she had long called home. But this land beyond the river had a beauty all its own, a rolling and wide-open loveliness. Under the moonlight, its low grassy hills shimmered with dew, and the stars, no longer mere unpolished diamonds, sparkled brightly in a sprawling sky.

There is magic here, Marian thought to herself. She listened to the purl of the water, inhaled the perfume of the flowers, and turned her gaze southward. *At least, a kind of magic.*

She didn't know how long she lay on her bed of grass, letting her thoughts wander where they would, remembering things and places from long ago, from before Stormfire and Wyvernwood. She didn't resist the memories now, nor did they make her sad.

They made her smile.

She lay like that, remembering and smiling, watching over Bumble, until the sound of heavy wings brought her back to the present. She gazed upward, alert. A huge, gray shape eclipsed the stars as it glided low along the riverbank and settled on the ground nearby.

"So you've finally decided to come back," Marian said without getting up. With the tip of her horn, she indicated the hummingbird still sleeping beside her. "We had a little party in your absence."

"I decided to scout ahead," Ronaldo told her.

"Nice of you to explain your plan after the fact," Marian answered tartly. "It's not like we worried about you or missed you."

Ronaldo bowed his head, then looked up again, plainly excited. "I guess I did get a little carried away," he apologized. "But there's a village up the river. And beyond that, lots of villages! Some men actually tried to chase me!"

Marian flashed him a look of concern, but stayed where she was, her neck stretched protectively over Bumble's unconscious form. "What did you do?"

Ronaldo grinned. "This!"

Raising his gray head and spreading his wings wide, he blew a blast of red fire that lit up the landscape.

8

IN STRONGHOLD, THE FEASTING AND CELEBRATION continued through the night and into the early hours of morning. When the last of the food was consumed and the last barrel of wine emptied, the residents began to drift off toward their homes and their beds. A few musicians, caught up in the spirit of their sounds, played on with their eyes half-closed and their heads nodding to the beat, while a few last Fomorian dancers encouraged and inspired them.

Stormfire retired to his cave in the cliff face of the canyon, and Ramoses slipped away to his bed. One by one, the rest of the Dragonkin excused themselves and flew away. Sabu, after saying her goodnights and goodbyes, took Morkir into her longhouse and made a pallet for him by her hearth.

The triplets were the last dragons to go. Harrow, then Luna, took off into the night, each to their own beds. Only Chan lingered when the others were gone. He enjoyed the music and the dancing, and tapped his tail to the beat of the drums, and he loved chatting with the Fomorians and the satyrs and the foxes and the bears. Finally, however, even he began to yawn. Stretching his wings, he paid lavish compliments to each of the musicians by name, then said his goodnights. The remaining partiers waved and called after him as he flew away to his own cave.

In the center of the village, the bonfire burned down until it was only a crackling pile of red-glowing coals. The torches burned out. The lanterns were extinguished and carried home by their owners. Only the bright moonlight lit the scene.

The last dancers finally wearied. Still, a small group of musicians played on, too caught up in the music to quit. One of the minotaurs finally nodded off and passed out over his drum. His friends laughed and shook him awake again, but the glazed look in his eyes said that he was finished for the night, and so the rest, packing up their instruments and congratulating each other on fine performances, carried their comrade to bed.

Gaunt watched it all from the shadows at the edge of the forest. When no one remained awake in the village, when even the red-glowing coals of the bonfire had burned down to a dull smolder, he crept out from his hiding place under the trees.

Rising on his hind legs, he looked around. His keen eyes spied no movement at all. He sniffed and made a disgusted face. The smoke from the fire, the lingering odors of pies and cookies and honey, the sweat from the musicians and dancers—the village offered a cacophony of stenches that confused and confounded his nose. His ears, though, almost as sharp as his eyes, detected no sounds other than the soft hissing and popping of the coals and the snoring of random sleepers.

Without turning, he made a signal with his right paw.

From under the trees, a score of sour-faced griffins stole silently forward and spread out behind their leader. Four more came behind those, and the other griffins parted to make room for them. Unlike the rest, those four walked on their rear legs. With their front paws they carried between them a giant log, a newly cut tree that had been stripped of its branches. Once it had been a mighty tree, old and thick, and such was its weight that even the four griffins with their formidable strength strained together to manage it.

Gaunt signaled again. All the griffins stopped. Alone, he strode to the center of the village until he stood beside the bed of coals. Again he looked carefully around. Despite the smoke, he picked up the familiar scent of his brother, Morkir. He glared toward Sabu's longhouse, but kept his place. He would deal with Morkir another time.

A soft sigh caught his attention. He shot a glance toward the far side of the village and the canyon rim, and silently cursed. Nearly invisible, even to his eyes, were two Fomorian creatures. They sat perfectly still, side-by-side, at the rim. One, a cat-faced female, pressed her lips to the beak of an owl-headed male who sat with his arm around her shoulders. Their gazes seemed fixed on the point where the sunrise was pushing its first pinkish rays above the eastern horizon.

Well, let them be the first to fall before the new King of Wyvernwood!

Gaunt thrust both arms into the air. All the griffins but the four carrying the huge log let out savage roars. Half his force spread their wings and took to the air above the village. The other half scattered among the houses and shops. Those in the air ripped open rooftops, while the ground troops knocked down doors and smashed walls.

At the edge of the canyon rim, Carola and Gregor sprang up to find Gaunt right behind them. Carola screamed as the griffin leader's claws locked about her throat. Without a thought, he brushed Gregor over the side with one wingtip. The owl-man gave a terrified shriek as he tumbled head over heels toward the river below.

Throughout the village startled and frightened residents awoke from their beds and ran into the streets as their homes were destroyed around them. Roofs crashed inward and boards splintered as the griffins used their incredible strength to destroy Stronghold.

Sabu let out a cry as her roof was torn away. Spying her in her bed, the griffin who had done the deed, extended his claws and dived downward for her. What a glorious opportunity to kill the wife of Stormfire! Sabu raised one wing to protect herself, but before the griffin could strike, Morkir leaped to her defense. The two griffins crashed through the wall in one vicious, fur-flying ball.

Gaunt lifted Carola off her feet and held her at arm's length with one paw. "What a fine little pet slave you'll make!" he said. With his other paw, he signaled to the four griffins carrying the tree. "Hurry, you fools!"

Obediently, the four ran forward on their hind legs only, the tree between them, until they stood on the canyon rim. Peering over the edge, Gaunt positioned them where he wanted them. "Be ready!" he ordered.

Chaos reigned in the village. So savage was the attack that in only a few moments half the dwellings were flattened. Terrified screams filled the night, along with a chorus of savage growls and howls.

"That'll wake old Stormfire!" Gaunt laughed to his men. A fox leaped out of the darkness and closed his teeth on one of Gaunt's ankles. With a snarl and a shake of his leg, Gaunt flung the brave creature away.

From the far side of the canyon, a young dragon emerged. With a blast of fire, she rose into the night and raced across the chasm. A pair of griffins rose to meet her, flanking her on either side. From a second cave, another dragon appeared and looked around with large, sleep-filled eyes.

"The Dragon Diana!" Gaunt called as he watched the female roast the hindquarters of the nearest griffin. With a sweep of one powerful wing, she sent him spinning through the air. "Ignore her!" he ordered the four with the tree when he saw that their attention was fixed on the aerial fight above. "Stand fast!"

Then came a new cry, a sound so angry and so ancient that Gaunt felt it through the earth beneath his paws. His heart quailed with sudden dread. Yet he forced himself to lean even further over the edge of the canyon to look downward. His grip tightened around Carola's throat as he dangled her over the rim. Her screams and struggling meant nothing to him. But this moment meant everything! "Be ready!" Gaunt shouted again.

Great Stormfire thrust his golden head out of his cave. Gaunt watched, frantic with anticipation, as that long, sinuous neck stretched forth.

"Now!" Gaunt ordered. "Now!"

The four griffins, all their muscles bulging, raised the tree until it hung like a downward-pointing spear and let it go.

Stormfire spread his wings and prepared to leap into the sky. Too late, he heard an unexpected rush of air and twisted his neck to look upward, but there was no avoiding the huge blunt trunk. It struck him in the back like a massive battering ram, knocked him from his cave before he could take flight, broke his left wing as it pitched sideways after the first impact.

"Now I'm truly king!" Gaunt shouted as he watched Stormfire fall to the shore below. "No creature can stand against me!"

Carola stared in horror as the unthinkable unfolded before her eyes. Then, with a scream of pure outrage and hatred, no more fear in her, she struck at Gaunt, raking her cat-claws across the Griffin's left eye.

It was Gaunt's turn to scream. Flinging Carola away, he clutched at his face. Blood poured from under his paws and streamed down his feathered throat and chest. Lancets of pain shot through him as he staggered. Only his four griffins kept him from following Stormfire to the river below. They dragged him back as he writhed in torment.

"My eye!" he cried. "My eye!"

"Retreat!" one of the griffins shouted. "Retreat! Our leader is wounded!"

With two of his griffins supporting him, Gaunt turned and started away from the canyon rim. He could barely see through the pain and the blood, and his mind reeled. He had achieved his goal. Stormfire was dead, and Stronghold lay in ruins. But at what price? Blind in one eye, and his handsome face destroyed!

"You're not getting off that easy, monster!"

A pink-skinned man-boy rose up unexpectedly from behind a pile of rubble that had once been a house. Without warning, he lunged forward with a sharply pointed pole. Perhaps it had been a drapery rod once or an awning support. No matter, it was a weapon in the boy's hands, and it slipped between Gaunt's ribs with a soft sluicing sound.

"Aaauughhh!" Gaunt fell to his knees. "Kill him!" he ordered, ripping the makeshift spear from his side as the boy turned and ran.

A blast of fire from overhead interrupted them. Gaunt twisted his head and saw Harrow, Chan, and Luna directly above the village. Ramoses was also there, and the young warrior, Diana. They didn't dare actually direct their fire at the ground for fear of burning the residents of Stronghold, but their dragon claws were every bit as sharp as any griffin's.

Nor were they the only foes the griffins had to deal with. Once over their initial shock, the creatures of Stronghold were fighting back. Unable to fly, Sabu waded vengefully among the griffins, with a large brown bear fighting at her side. Foxes harried the heels of his troops. Even squirrels threw nuts with annoying accuracy. "Retreat!" came a griffin voice. "Run!"

Two of the four griffins, abandoning their leader, spread their wings and took to the air immediately. The remaining two caught Gaunt by his front legs, and helped him across the square toward the shelter of the woods.

But as he crossed the square, he spied his brother by the bonfire's coal-bed. Morkir stood over another griffin that he had pinned down under his paws. His bandages were red, and the splint on his wing hung shattered and bloodied, but not all the blood was his own.

"We'll meet again, Brother!" Morkir promised, "and you'll remember that this was the dawn of your destruction!"

Gaunt shivered as he regarded his younger brother, but he didn't say anything. He let his aides hustle him into the trees and deep into the forest. Leaves and branches slapped him in the face, and every step brought torture to the wound in his side. Only a mere few of his followers remained to protect him. The others, cowards all, had deserted him and flown away, thinking only of their own worthless hides.

"I am king!" Gaunt shouted to the trees. "I am King!"

"Shut up!" snapped the griffin supporting his right arm.

Gaunt jerked free. "How dare you!" he demanded, even as he stumbled and fell flat on the ground. He clutched his side, and blood poured under his paw. His breath came in short, ragged gasps. "I am Gaunt, your king!"

The aides pulled him roughly to his feet again and got him moving. "You can be king when we get you home," said one.

"That's *if* we get you home," said the other. "Right now, we're all rats in a trap, and the cats breathing on our necks breathe fire. So shut up!"

Gaunt tried to focus his one good eye on the griffin who spoke disrespectfully, but it was so hard to see! Through the mist of pain that obscured his vision, the creature looked astonishingly like his father. But that couldn't be, for Gorganar was dead!

"I've done what you couldn't do, Father!" Gaunt shouted. He began to laugh. "I've killed the greatest dragon of them all!"

One of the griffins clapped a paw tightly over Gaunt's mouth to silence him. All eyes turned fearfully upward as three dragons, Stormfire's hatchlings, skimmed the thick tops of the trees. "They're searching for us," hissed one of his aides, "and we don't have a bunch of weak Fomorians and minotaurs to shield us from their flame now!"

A measure of sanity returned to Gaunt as he watched the triplets through the branches. He wanted to laugh again, but managed instead to remain silent and still until the three were past and out of sight. Only then did he allow himself a quiet chuckle.

"They're heading for the Valley of Eight Winds," some griffin whispered.

"Let them," Gaunt answered. "They won't find us."

"If they don't," said another griffin, "Morkir surely will."

Gaunt peered around again, trying to identify the last speaker through the fog in his one good eye. There was a dangerous tone in those words, a veiled anger that verged on rebellion. If not dealt with, such an attitude might spread among the ranks.

"There's no room in my kingdom for cowards," Gaunt said. "Any of you that hold fear in your heart had better leave before I get my vision back, or after that I'll teach you the true meaning of fear."

The griffins began to move again. Unless they decided to brave the skies and risk being seen, it was going to be a long, slow walk home, and Gaunt wasn't at all sure he could fly. From time to time, he shot a nervous look at the griffin on his right side. He was just another griffin to Gaunt, steadfast and loyal to his king

Except, when the morning light struck him just right, he was also Gorganar.

Fatigued and half-crazed from blood-loss, Gaunt began to mutter. *Go away, Father, he said. I don't need you. I don't need Morkir, either. I have other allies. Do you hear me?*

If anyone heard him, no one gave an answer.

Harrow, Chan, and Luna searched the forest for the remains of Gaunt's griffin force as they flew northward, but the woods were tricky in the weird darkness and half-light of approaching dawn. They skimmed the tops of the trees, hoping for some sign of their enemies on the ground, but that created its own problems, for the wind from their wings caused the branches to sway and shiver and the already twisted shadows to dance in confusing patterns.

None of the triplets spoke of their father as they flew. Each grieved privately, each grim, knowing that with Stormfire gone, their entire world had just changed. By searching for the murderers, they set aside the pain they felt, at least for a little while.

If they needed proof of that change, they found it when their meandering search took them to the Blackwater River. Three long, wooden ships filled with Men from Angmar, painted black and propelled by banks of oars, glided down that deep current. No ship would have dared such a thing before. The Blackwater ran right through the Valley of Eight Winds, and neither Gorganar, nor any previous griffin leader, would ever have allowed Men to penetrate so far into Wyvernwood.

"We should turn them back," Chan said as they passed the vessels.

"I'm only interested in Gaunt," Harrow answered.

"They see us," Luna said, eyeing the Men closely. "They cower in their ships and brandish their weapons. But they don't turn back."

"I'm only interested in Gaunt," Harrow repeated.

And as the sun rose higher in the morning sky, they flew on.

They reached the Valley of Eight Winds without seeing a single griffin. The black nests that rose on the riverbanks and the hillsides were abandoned. The triplets circled the valley, eyes keen for any movement. Harrow finally perched on the very top of Gorganar's great monstrosity of a nest, his dark eyes full of anger and disappointment. Luna landed next on the riverbank and deliberately toppled a smaller next with a twitch of her tail. Chan remained in the air, circling and watchful.

"Come out!" Harrow called. "If anyone at all is here, come out!"

There was no one to respond. All the nests were empty, deserted.

Harrow rose once more into the air and circled Gorganar's river-spanning nest. "I will not let this abomination stand!" he declared. With his great black wings beating the air, he breathed a stream of flame, then a second, and a third.

The old wood caught fire quickly.

"Why should a griffin village stand," Luna said, "when griffins have destroyed the village at Stronghold?"

Exhaling a fiery breath, she set fire to the nearest nest, then to another and another. The eight winds that gave the valley its name fanned the flames, carried them to other nests until not a single one remained that was not burning.

"Now you've wreaked your vengeance on some hapless dwellings," Chan said with quiet disapproval when his brother and sister rejoined him in the air. "And we can't go home until it's all burned out."

"Why not?" Harrow demanded as he surveyed the flames with pride.

Chan shook his head. He loved his brother, but sometimes Harrow was too impulsive. Luna could be as bad, always following Harrow's example. "Would you have the entire forest burn? This is our work, brother and sister, and now we must see it through to the end."

"But, Father . . . !" Luna hung her head and began to cry. "It'll be days before it all burns out!"

Harrow glared at Chan, but he knew that Chan was right. Then, he grinned. "I've been a fool, brother," he said, "but with your help I think we can satisfy my need to smash something, and still get home quickly."

Harrow spread his wings wide and dived straight for Gorganar's flaming nest. Fire was no threat to his black scales. He tore into the structure with his claws, pushed at it with all his strength, and toppled a burning section of it into the river below. Smoke and steam rose up in a billowing hot cloud.

Chan nodded his head and launched himself at another section of the nest. Again, burning logs and chunks of wood fell into the river. Again and again, the two brothers struck, and Luna added her own considerable might to the task. Always they pushed and smashed their sections so that the pieces fell into the river.

"It's working!" Chan called as the water began to flow around the barricade they were building.

"Well," Harrow said with a grin, "so it is."

Little by little, the water began to spread over the valley floor, rising higher and higher until the largest nests, those closest to the river, were toppled and engulfed by the flood. The smaller nests above the water's reach were less of a problem. Those would burn quickly.

"We'll be home by nightfall," Luna said as the three landed side by side and studied their work. They were each exhausted, but also eager to be home. "I wonder where the Griffinkin have gone?" she added.

"I'm sure we'll find out." Chan folded his wings around himself and turned away. It was his turn to cry.

9

AS DAWN BROKE OVER THE RUINS OF STRONGHOLD, Ramoses rallied a troop of dragons, eagles, owls, and ravens. "Carry the news throughout Wyvernwood," he told them, "to every corner of the forest, from the shores of the Windy Sea to the slopes of the Imagination Mountains. All must know." His old voice turned dark and grim. "And if any other settlement or village suffered a similar attack, we must know that, too."

For much of the early morning, the residents of Stronghold wandered about in shock, consoling each other and rummaging through the destruction to salvage what they could of their belongings. Entire homes lay flattened. Others leaned at precarious angles with shattered walls or missing rooftops. Hardly a dwelling remained that was safe for occupancy.

"What are we to do?" wailed the fox-wife, Sarah, as she curled into her husband's arms before the wreckage of their smashed cottage.

Next door, on the doorstep of her roofless home, Carola received at least one consolation when the Dragon Diana, carrying Gregor gently in her claws, set the owl-man down before her.

"Gregor!" Carola cried out as she threw her arms around him. Pent-up tears suddenly streamed down her cat-face. "I thought you were dead!"

Gregor, too, began to cry as he embraced his wife and drew her tight against him. "It seems that although my wings are too small to lift me," he explained, "they're just enough if you push me off a cliff."

In the square, Bear Byron tossed down a bag of tools and called together a group of bachelor satyrs and two of the strongest minotaurs. "Ye've got no immediate families to worry 'bout," he rumbled, "an' poor Sabu, what we all love, she's got no home an' no husband now.

We can't do nothin' 'bout the one, but I say it's the least we can do to fix the other."

The satyrs and minotaurs agreed, and they got to work.

"We can help."

Bear Byron turned around with a hammer in his hand, and his eyes widened at sight of the five pink man-children. "Hank o' me hair, boy," he said to the tallest one that had spoken, "ye must think we've no manners at all the way we keep forgettin' ye." He extended a big paw. "Now here ye be offerin' to pitch in with our troubles. What might yer names all be?"

The tall boy hesitated as he stared at the large paw with its sharp bear claws, but then he reached out and shook it. "I'm Jake," he said. He gestured to the two girls next. "Ariel and Pear."

Ariel and Pear smiled. Pear, the youngest of the five brushed back a stray lock of blond hair as she made a small curtsy. "Pleased to make your acquaintance, Mr. Bear," she said in a shy voice.

Jake introduced the remaining pair of boys. "And Trevor and Markam."

With lopsided grins, Trevor and Markam stepped forward and shook the bear's paw.

"Look like ye be twins!" Bear Byron said as he gazed from one boy to the next. "Same hair black as night, and same black eyes."

"My brother and I are pretty strong," Trevor said with a serious look. "We can help you clear some of this damage."

"I'm pretty strong, too," Ariel said with an indignant glare at Trevor.

Jake also put on a serious expression. "Look, this is a little awkward," he said as his face reddened. "Heck, it's completely weird. You're all monsters to us. You're supposed to be scary and dangerous. Our parents tell stories about you and this forest I wouldn't repeat to you now. But you . . ." He hesitated again as he searched for the appropriate word. "You *people* rescued us and then broke our chains, and you fed us . . ."

"And you've been nothing but nice to us!" Ariel interjected.

Markam nodded. "We're not going to forget that. So we're willing to do whatever we can to help."

Bear Byron brushed a big tear from the corner of his eye as he beamed at the man-children. "It does me good to hear such a generous offer," he answered, "an' to tell ye the truth, my little friends, one or two o' us has heard some might' terrible tales about a monster called Man. Maybe 'fore all this is over we can learn somethin' 'bout each other." He winked as he handed his hammer to Jake and pointed toward Sabu's longhouse. "Now there's a lot o' work 'head o' us."

But all work stopped, and all eyes turned skyward as Phoebe, the last phoenix, suddenly sailed down the canyon. Clutched tightly in her talons she carried a collection of dead wood and brush from the forest. She deposited her cache on the top of the tallest, easternmost spire, the place from which she had made it her habit to watch the sunset each evening.

A pair of silver-scaled dragons flew behind her. They, too, carried loads of brush and wood in their claws, and they added their collection to Phoebe's. While Phoebe flew back into the forest, the pair remained, circling the spire like guardians.

"What are they doing?" a young squirrel asked. "Is it a nest?"

The young squirrel's father, his right foreleg wrapped in a fresh bandage, shook his head as he put an arm around his son. "Not a nest," he explained. "It's a pyre. A pyre for a great hero."

A family of wolves caused a stir when they strode suddenly into the village. The wolf-wife carried a cauldron filled with delicious-smelling stew, and the arms of their two children were filled with loaves of fresh-baked bread. Over his back, the wolf-father carried his bag of tools.

"Everyone who's heard the news," the wolf-father announced when Bear Byron stepped forward to shake paws, "they're all coining."

It was true. A few moments later, a group of minotaurs from a nearby part of the forest called CrackWood arrived with more tools and sacks of nails and bundles of raw lumber born on their broad shoulders. Next came a family of Wyrms from Grendelton to the west. They were cousins to the Dragons and actually true Dragonkin, but smaller and wingless. They brought a wagon loaded with food and still more tools.

"Where is Sabu?" asked the Wyrm-wife, Betha, when Bear Byron greeted them. Her large gray eyes were wet with tears that ran down her red-scaled face.

Bear Byron also began to weep again, and he at wiped his eyes. He hadn't planned it, and didn't feel qualified for it, but he seemed to have become the official greeter and organizer as more and more help arrived. "They've taken her down to the river beach to be wit' Stormfire."

Betha turned to the other Wyrms. "I'm going to find my way down to Sabu to be with her and express our sympathies. All of you make yourselves useful, and I don't want to hear of any laxity!"

They were interrupted by the sound of wings from the western edge of the forest and by a shrill screeching. Bear Byron put a paw to his mouth. "Hank o' my hair!" he muttered, "I don't believe it!"

"Oh, my heart!" Betha caught her husband's arm. "I didn't know there were any harpies left in the world!"

Amid exclamations and cries of surprise, three harpies flew into Stronghold. The noon sun shone on their black feathered bodies and large, powerful wings, and their silver talons shimmered. Their faces, vaguely manlike, were hideous and strangely beautiful at the same time, and streamers of black hair trailed on the wind as they flew.

One only had to look at them to know they were old, older than the dragons, older than any of the creatures in Wyvernwood.

Everyone made room as Ramoses strode to the center of the ruined village. With his wings tightly folded, he bowed his head. "Oh, most welcome, long-lost sisters!" he said. Then he turned to one in particular. "Most welcome, indeed, Electra. I can't tell you how it pleases me to know that you live!"

Electra placed a kiss on Ramoses' lowered head. "From the peaks of the Imagination Mountains we've come," she said. "We've kept watch over Wyvernwood since Stormfire led the Great Retreat. Our hearts are saddened, Ramoses."

Phoebe sailed down the canyon again with another load of wood, which she deposited atop the spire at the end of the canyon.

"But my heart is pleased," Electra continued with a weak smile as she observed the phoenix, "to see that our most ancient sister still is with us!"

"We've all been too separate and too long apart," Ramoses told her. "It shouldn't take something like this to bring us together."

They were interrupted as a beautiful singing arose from the edges of the forest. The song had no words, and yet it conveyed the heart-rending grief of hundreds of unseen voices. It was more than mere vocalization, and it was more than mere harmony. It touched the minds and hearts of every listener.

"The banshees are here," Ramoses noted with a sigh. "More of our kindred who have been too long apart."

The song soared over the canyon, echoing between its immense walls. The leaves of the trees shivered with the force of it, and everyone paused to listen. It was dirge and paean and requiem, sad, yet uplifting, seeming to surround Stronghold. Wyvernwood had never heard its like.

Harrow, Chan, and Luna, flying side-by-side and wingtip-to-wingtip, flew overhead and descended into the canyon to join their mother on the beach below. She was not alone as she kept watch over Stormfire's body. Betha stood beside her, as did the young Dragon Diana. Morkir stood on her right side, looking grim and humbled, and at the edge of the shore, a host of Mermen and Merwomen from their island of Thursis just off Wyvernwood's southern coast also kept silent company.

The Merfolk, with seaweed from the Windy Sea and from the river bottom, had woven the shroud that covered Stormfire. They continued to weave as the morning and the afternoon progressed. In the deep green pattern could be seen the shapes of dragons and Wyrms, of griffins, of minotaurs and satyrs. Phoebe was represented, as were bears and foxes and wolves. As the harpies arrived, they were added, as were the banshees and all manner of forest creatures. The shroud they wove was a guest book of sorts, documenting the presence of those who came to pay their respects.

"Someone is missing," Chan noted as he studied the shroud. "Someone important."

Harrow's eyes were hard and gleaming as onyx. His anger at Gaunt had still not fully abated, but as he bent near the shroud, he realized at once whom it was that Chan meant. "Miriam," he said.

Luna began to weep soft tears as she turned to Sabu. "Please, Mother, ask the Merfolk to include her, anyway. Word must not have reached her. I'm sure she'd be here if she knew."

Sabu consented, and the Merfolk resumed their work.

The pile of wood atop Phoebe's spire continued to grow. The last Phoenix worked meticulously and with patient care, making trip after trip to the forest and back. Indeed, the pile began to resemble a great nest, high on the rounded sides with a center bedded with softer grasses. In the cycle of life and death, it seemed an entirely fitting resting place for a noble creature, and for the first time in Wyvernwood's history, the spire began to acquire a name—Stormfire's point.

Throughout the day, Sabu stood watch in silence. Unable to fly on her own, some of the Dragonkin had helped her navigate a narrow path from the clifftop to the beach so she could be beside her husband. But she had shed no tears, nor said a word to anyone. Like a black-scaled statue, she remained unmoving on the white sand, nodding whenever someone spoke to her or shaking her head only, and many began to worry that her spirit might soon follow her husband's.

Ramoses flew down from the village above and spoke softly in Sabu's ear. What he said could not be heard by any except her, and she slowly nodded. Turning to the triplets, he beckoned with a blue claw.

"There are words I must say to you in private," he explained in a grim voice. "Follow me to my cave. There's room enough there for all of us, and no one will disturb us." Spreading his wings, he took to the sky and flew eastward, low between the canyon walls.

Luna protested. "But, Father . . . !"

"Mother . . ." said Harrow.

Chan fixed his gaze on Ramoses and prepared to follow. "We can do nothing for Father now," he said. "Nor, I think, for Mother, but Ramoses would not call us away at this solemn moment without good reason. I want to hear what he has to say." With a whispered promise to his mother to return, he flew after the old dragon.

The Dragon Ramoses had been given the largest and driest cave in the canyon with the consent of all Stronghold's residents, not because of his status as Stormfire's friend or because of his considerable age, but because within it he stored and maintained the great library of the Dragonkin. Aside from his bed, which lay off in a darkened side chamber, and his writing table, a few chairs, and a few lanterns, there was little else but shelf upon shelf of books and scrolls, parchments and tablets within it.

The high, vaulted ceiling and the floor had been polished smooth by Stronghold's craftsmen, and covered with thick carpets, and a cleverly designed fireplace whose chimney rose up through the cliff itself kept the library warm during the chilly months. A narrow stairway carved into the cliff face allowed visitors and students access whenever they wished. Although it was generally considered polite to ask Ramoses for permission to visit, the old dragon always scoffed at the notion, insisting that the library was open to all at any hour of the day or night, that the urge or need to read superseded any other concern.

Entering his cave, Ramoses paused to look back. His home was almost directly across from the spire where Phoebe was building the great nest, and he felt a deep pang in his heart as he watched her deposit a load of brush and depart again. *I've lived too long, that I should see the death of my dearest friend*, he thought to himself.

Circling outside the library's entrance, Chan waited for the old dragon to clear the way. Recovering himself, Ramoses muttered an apology that no one else could hear and moved deeper into the cave. Even now, as he looked around the shelves, he found a measure of comfort among the many books and writings.

Chan landed on the cave rim, folded his wings tightly, and followed Ramoses inside. In only a moment, Luna joined them. Lastly came Harrow with a hint of a scowl upon his face. Of the three triplets, he was the least interested in Ramoses' books, and the library had never been his favorite place.

"Now, what's so urgent that you take us from our parents' sides?" Harrow demanded.

"The world is changing, my young hatchlings," Ramoses told them. "Have you given any thought to your places in it?"

The triplets gazed blankly back at him. It was clear that they hadn't. "What are you getting at?" Chan asked. Shifting his position to a deeper corner of the library, he curled up on his tail.

"I have," Harrow answered crisply, his dark eyes narrowing. "My place is standing over Gaunt's body when my claws rip his eagle-head from his lion-shoulders."

"I think you'll have to get in line behind Morkir for that place," Chan replied.

Luna ignored both her brothers and leaned closer to Ramoses. "We're Stormfire's children," she said in an uncertain voice. "Are you suggesting that, with father gone, we have some sort of leadership responsibility?"

"That remains to be seen," Ramoses answered. Turning, he reached up to the highest shelf, pulled a book down, and placed it on his writing table. Its leather-bound edges were thick with dust, but the leaves were still clean and white, showing no sign of age, as he opened the volume to a marked page.

"That's dragon-hide!" Harrow exclaimed as he bent closer to examine the page.

"Bleached, stretched, and pressed flat and trimmed," Ramoses nodded. "From one of your father's own sloughings." He squeezed his eyes shut and opened them again. "This is the *Great Book of Stormfire*. Few know of it; fewer still have actually seen it."

Harrow seized the book and riffled its pages. "Some of them are blank!" he said.

"Because I haven't finished it," Ramoses answered, taking the book back and replacing it on the table. "I've been writing it for years, but it contains his wisdom, his words, things he said that I thought worth preserving." He tapped one claw on the page he had marked. "And there's a message of sorts for the three of you."

"What kind of message would Father leave in the pages of a book?" Luna asked.

"One he couldn't deliver himself," came Chan's answer.

Ramoses turned to Chan.

"Stormfire knew his time was ending just as surely as he knew the Age of Dragons was ending and giving way to the Age of Man. He led us along with the fantastic creatures of the world, creatures he considered all to be Dragonkin, to this forest. Wyvernwood, he named it, and it was to be our home and our refuge."

Harrow interrupted. "We know all this," he said. "It's ancient history."

Ramoses raised one eyebrow and folded his arms across his chest as he answered sarcastically, "Then perhaps, my smart young hatchling, you also know that Wyvernwood was not to be our last home, that your father envisioned another and final refuge someplace far from this one, far from the ravages that Man inevitably brought wherever he went?"

Chan rose with sharp interest. "Another home? Leave Wyvernwood?"

"You can't be serious," Luna gasped.

"I believe your father was quite serious," Ramoses answered, thumping his claw on the open page again. "As the Age of Dragons began to pass and magic began to fade from the world, Stormfire made certain preparations. He stored the last of his own personal magic inside three objects, which he hid as he gathered the fantastic creatures from all corners of the world."

"Why?" Chan asked.

"I ask each of you to read this book for yourselves," he said. "Your father believed that a small amount of magic could be contained and kept from fading, and that by doing so, the Age of Dragons might be extended and all of us given a bit more time to live when the Age of Man was upon us." He paused and pushed the book toward Chan. "But he also believed that those same objects would one day point us to the new refuge that he envisioned, a place he called *Undersky*."

"What are these objects?" Harrow asked. His anger, at least for the moment, seemed finally to have subsided, and he was as curious as Chan or Luna. "Where are they hidden?"

At last, Ramoses turned back to Harrow, and there was a satisfied look upon his face. "He gave each one a name," the old dragon informed them. "He called the first one *the Glass Dragon*. The second he called *the Diamond Dragon*. And the third, he called *the Heart of All Dragons*." He shrugged. "As for where they are hidden—I believe it's up to you to learn that. And when you've done so, then you'll know even among yourselves which of you is most suited to taking your father's place as leader of the Dragonkin."

The triplets stared at Ramoses and at each other. For the first time in their lives, none of them could think of anything to say.

Outside, the song of the Banshees took on a new quality, and beyond the cave entrance, the light seemed to have dimmed and the sky grown darker. A strange stillness hung in the air, and even the sounds of industry from the village above had stopped.

Ramoses moved past the triplets toward the entrance. "It can't be later than mid-afternoon," he said in a puzzled tone. Then, peering out from the opening, he exclaimed, "By the first egg!" Without another word, he spread his wings and flew.

Harrow hurried after Ramoses, and like the old dragon, stared up at the sky and gasped. "An eclipse!" he called back to his brother and sister. "There's an eclipse!"

They all fled the library, spread their wings and sailed outward. Along the rim of the canyon, Fomorians and satyrs and minotaurs, wolves and bears and man-children were all lined up shoulder to shoulder with their gazes trained toward the darkening sky. A cadre of dragons and eagles flew in circles around Stormfire's Point while other birds flew nervously from one canyon wall to the next and back again.

On the beach below, Sabu spoke for the first time all day. "There's still a thimbleful of magic left in this world," she said, smiling at the ring of fire that appeared around the solar disk. "This is my husband's time!"

The Merfolk were prepared. Taking ropes they had woven along with the shroud, they tied Stormfire's legs and slipped another beneath his neck, and still another beneath his body. Sabu called to her children. "And you, also, Ramoses. Diana, you also. And one other! Come! Carry him!"

At Sabu's command, the triplets, Ramoses, Diana, and an emerald dragon named Fleer took the ends of the ropes and lifted Stormfire's shroud-covered form, and wings beating powerfully, bore him to the nest that Phoebe had prepared. With a gentleness born of deep love, they lowered him into it.

On the rim of the canyon, at the edge of the village, torches were lit and passed from hand to hand until every man, woman, and child held one. Unlit torches were thrown down onto the beach, as well, and those were lit with the merest dragon breath.

The banshees' song rose, more beautiful and magical than ever before.

"Someone call Phoebe," Sabu asked. "My voice isn't strong enough at this moment."

Moments later, the last Phoenix appeared before the wife of Storm-fire. "Of all the creatures in the world, dearest Phoebe," Sabu said softly, "my husband thought you the rarest and most beautiful. Not because he loved me less, and I have never felt jealousy toward you." She held out her torch to Phoebe. "Take my fire, Phoebe. I can't fly, and can't light my husband's pyre. Please, do it for me."

Phoebe wept as she accepted Sabu's torch. Spreading her wings, rising on magnificent plumage, she soared toward Stormfire's Point. For a long moment, she hovered over the great nest as if to say good-bye. Then she dropped Sabu's torch and turned away.

The other Dragons and eagles fell away from the nest to make room for Stormfire's children. Harrow, Chan, and Luna positioned themselves around their father, and each exhaled a fiery breath. The wood and brush crackled. Flames shot up toward the burning ring that marked the place where the sun should have been.

One by one, the other winged creatures leaped into the sky and dropped their torches on the dragon-leader's funeral pyre. Electra and the harpies were among the first, then Morkir, then the eagles. When all of them had dropped their torches, they flew back to the cliffs and to the river's shore and carried the torches of the Merfolk and the citizens of Stronghold, and the torches of all the visitors and those who had come to help, and they dropped them also onto the pyre.

In the deep and unnatural darkness, a beautiful light burned, and at the center of that light was the Soul of an Age.

10

NIGHT ON THE OPEN GRASSLANDS OF DEGARM proved surprisingly chilly, much cooler than in the sheltering environment of
Wyvernwood. A sharp wind whistled constantly over the hills,
rustling the grasses, bending the few slender trees that dotted the stark
landscape, and raising white-capped ripples on the surface of the
Blackwater River. Shortly after moonrise, dark clouds began a steady
advance across the sky from the west. One by one, the stars
disappeared.

Ronaldo watched a distant flicker of lightning dance across the hilltops. To him, the minute flashes of red-orange fire behind the black
clouds were a source of wonder and beauty, but he felt Marian stir
nervously against his body. He curled up around her, drawing his tail
closer to protect her from the wind.

Buried deep in Marian's mane, Bumble shivered and fluffed his
feathers until he looked like a plump, round ball with his head tucked
under one wing. Every now and then, he poked up and waved his
beak at the clouds or at a flicker of lightning, or at the swift shadow
of a nocturnal bird passing overhead.

"Owls and falcons and hawks—oh, my!" he grumbled
drunkenly. Though the hummingbird had awakened at last, he had
yet to shake off the full influence of the lousewort. "Too exposed! Too
exposed! Oh, my aching head!"

Ronaldo smiled to himself. Bumble hadn't mentioned food or flowers or hunger for over an hour now.

A harsh crackle and a bright flash drew his attention back to the
sky as a jagged red bolt stabbed at a black hillock. For an instant, the
air tingled. Then a deep, rumbling thunder shook the darkness, and a
stinging rain began to fall.

Ronaldo spread his left wing over his comrades to keep them dry.
The rain didn't bother him; it simply rolled off his leathery gray scales.
He batted his eyes against the heavy droplets and continued to watch
the growing storm. He'd never watched one from such open country
before, and never realized that lightning contained so many vibrant
colors, not just orange and red-orange, but yellow, too, and sometimes
blue, and even green.

And the way each bolt lit the clouds—it was wonderful! He began
to see such shapes in the brief flashes—a horse's head here, and there
a dragon, and there one of the ships of Man floating on the storm! It
was as if the lightning were hammering and chiseling colossal works
of art from black chunks of the sky, itself!

Marian stirred again beside him as she peeked out from under his
wing to look around.

"I've never seen anything so beautiful!" he exclaimed, raising his
wing a little so that she could stand and still remain dry. "And I
thought the storms over the Windy Sea were something!"

Her golden eyes ignited briefly as they reflected the dazzle of a lightning bolt. "It's a dangerous beauty," she reminded him.

"Keep our heads down!" Bumble shouted from somewhere under
Marian's mane. "Chernovog! Chernovog!"

"Yes, Bumble-bird," Marian agreed. "It was a bolt of lightning that
struck Chernovog's house and started the fire that killed Ranock."
She fell silent for a moment, then sighed.

"I saw a bolt of lightning knock a dragon from the sky once," she
continued. "The Dragon Navigator, they called him, because he had
a pair of the most peculiar ivory birthmarks on each of his emerald
wings."

"Birthmarks?" Ronaldo said.

"Yes, each in the shape of a compass rose." She sighed again. "But
it was a long time ago, Ronaldo, when the world was still full of magic.
Before you were born. Before Stormfire led us all into Wyvernwood."
She shook her head, and stopped talking.

Ronaldo encouraged her. He enjoyed Marian's company, and liked
the musical quality of her voice. And with the thunder and lightning
and rain keeping them awake, the night seemed made for stories.
"What happened to Navigator? It sounds like you know him well."

Marian seemed reluctant to answer. Her voice dropped to a whisper. "There was a war."

Ronaldo looked down curiously. He wasn't sure he'd actually heard right. "A what?"

"A war," she repeated again in a whisper. "One shouldn't say it too loudly or too often. There's a spirit behind all wars that can be conjured and brought forth with too much talk."

Bumble thrust his head up. "To arms! To arms! From the halls of . . . !"

"Shut up, Bumble," Marian cautioned, and the little hummingbird disappeared beneath her mane again with a pouty look. She pranced in place suddenly, lifting one hoof and then the other.

"You're agitated," Ronaldo observed. "I didn't mean to upset you."

"It's not your fault," Marian answered. "Leaving the forest has just brought back a lot of memories, some pleasant and others not so pleasant." She ceased her prancing and became still again as she watched the rain and lightning. "Against all good sense, Navigator and some other dragons chose sides in this war. One night, despite a storm every bit as terrible as this one, he agreed to carry a message to some allies in another camp." She shivered as she paused and swallowed. "I happened to be watching from a hill nearby when a bolt of lightning struck him in mid-air. I saw him fall."

Ronaldo heard the sorrow in her words and curled his tail a little more closely about her. She was small and delicate. Well, not that small, actually, compared to many other creatures, but to him she was small, and it hurt him to see her sad.

"I'm sorry I made you remember," he said.

She nuzzled the side of her face against him. "No, Ronaldo," she answered. "No matter how sad it makes you, it's a good thing to remember old friends. Otherwise, you might forget them entirely, and nothing would be more sad than that."

"You amaze me, Marian," Ronaldo said. "How did you acquire such wisdom?"

A violent bolt turned the landscape blood red for an instant. To his surprise, Marian laughed. Then she answered smartly, "I found a coupon and sent off for it."

Ronaldo didn't understand, but he laughed with her.

When Marian grew quiet again and settled back down to rest, he began to think about her story and about the Dragon Navigator with compass rose birthmarks. It would make an exciting illustration, he thought to himself as he watched another bolt of lightning stab at the hilltops, strike a young tree, and split its slender trunk. The resulting crackle and boom of thunder shook the ground.

He closed his eyes and tried to imagine war. It was a simple enough word, not all that unpleasant on the tongue. Why then did Marian seem to dread it so? He repeated it to himself, and then remembered her caution not to say it too loudly or too often.

He had not realized it before, living alone in his cave in Whispering Hills, painting his landscapes and his occasional portraits. He had thought himself a sensitive and intelligent dragon. But there were a great many things he didn't understand about the world.

The storm continued its westward advance, taking the thunder and lightning with it as it rolled toward the Windy Sea. Only a thin, cold drizzle lingered, then even that ceased.

Beneath his wing, Marian was quiet, and Bumble's tiny snores could be heard once more. Ronaldo breathed a deep, satisfied breath, inhaling the fragrance of the wet grass and the clean air. Overhead, a weak moon tinted the edges of a bank of clouds as it tried to break through, and low on the horizon, a single bright star glimmered. He watched it with a strange sense of contentment.

> *I spy! I spy!*
> *High up in the velvet sky,*
> *The first star of night I see!*
> *Now my wish will come to be!*

The old nursery rhyme made him smile. It wasn't really the first star he'd seen that night, only the first one since the storm's passing. He made a wish anyway, remembering to frame it in the form of a four-line poem the way all wishes had to be made if one really wanted them to come true.

> *Under brilliant stars I sleep,*
> *Beneath a sky so black and deep;*
> *Through the dark and still of night,*
> *Keep us safe 'til morning light.*

What silliness, he thought as he closed his eyes again. Wishes were for children, who believed in such things. He was a grown dragon, after all.

Still, he wished he'd brought his paints.

* * *

The rising sun and Marian's singing woke Ronaldo. For a few minutes, he listened with closed eyes, pretending still to be asleep, for fear that she might stop if she knew he wasn't. The words were in some language unknown to him, but the melody was light, and her voice sweet and clear.

At last, he opened his eyes, and the sight that greeted him brought a smile of instant delight. As she sang, Marian pranced and scampered along the bank of the river. Yet, she didn't play alone. A host of butterflies surrounded her. They followed her every movement, her darting changes of direction. And such an assortment of butterflies! There were monarchs and yellow sulphurs, red admirals and white peacocks, marblewings and swallowtails, painted ladies and common buckeyes, and more. Even a few of their moth cousins—lunas and polyphemus moths—joined in the fun.

The morning was alive with the colorful creatures, and they all danced to the tune Marian sang. Some, taking a moment's rest, landed to fan their wings on her horn or in her mane, or on her rump only to spring into the air again and resume their places in the incredible choreography.

Abruptly, Marian stopped and sneezed. The butterflies scattered, as if blown in all directions by the force of her sneeze, then returned to flutter around her at a more respectful distance.

"I'm allergic to the powder on their wings," Marian said, looking back over her shoulder at Ronaldo.

"You knew I was awake?" the gray dragon asked with some surprise.

"They told me," she said, indicating the bright cloud around her. "There are thousands of facets in a single butterfly's eye, so not much escapes their notice."

Ronaldo grinned. "Especially not a dragon playing possum?"

"Not even a possum playing dragon," Marian replied. Turning back to the butterflies, she bent one knee and made a deep bow to them.

"Fly away, fly away!" she sang. "May the wind be ever at your wings and spider webs never block your paths!" Then she spoke again, and her words were in the same language as the song she had sung.

Ronaldo's eyes snapped wide. "You speak butterfly!"

"You don't?" Marian laughed as her insect friends flew upward in a dense funnel-shaped formation, then broke away each to pursue their separate occupations. For a brief moment, the sunlight caught their wings at a particular angle, and the sky sparkled with vibrant hues.

Ronaldo rose to stand and stretch his wings. "Were all unicorns like you, Marian?"

She laughed again as she walked toward him. "Are all dragons like you, Ronaldo?" Rising up on her hind legs, she skipped a few steps and tossed her mane. "Of course not. We're all butterflies in our own ways, each unique and each gifted with our own special beauty."

"They certainly are beautiful," Ronaldo interrupted, "and so are you, Marian, more than any other creature in Wyvernwood, and that's the truth." He looked nervously askance, taking in the last few lingering butterflies as he shrugged. "Me, I'm just gray."

"Just gray," Marian scoffed. "And that's why you live apart from the other dragons, isn't it? They're golden and silver, green as emeralds and red as rubies, or they shine like ivory or glitter like onyx. But you, you're just gray." Folding her legs, she lay down on the grass and regarded him with one blue eye. "You're an amusing kind of fool, Ronaldo, but still a fool."

"You don't understand what it's like to be ugly when all your brothers and sisters are so beautiful," Ronaldo answered in an uneasy voice. "Have you seen Stormfire? He shines like the sun when . . ."

"Open your eyes, Ronaldo!" Marian shot back. "Look, you're an artist. I've seen some of your paintings, and you're really quite excellent. But is a beautiful painting just a matter of bright color?"

Ronaldo pursed his lips and frowned, "Well . . ."

"Of course it isn't," Marian continued. "There's composition to consider, and technique and style, even theme and message. You're not so different from one of your paintings, Gray Dragon. Beauty doesn't depend on just color, alone. Do you understand what I'm saying?"

Ronaldo forced a grin. "I don't speak butterfly," he quipped.

"Chernovog has the same problem, you know," she told him. "That's why he spends so much time alone fishing or wandering in the woods. He thinks he's an awkward, ugly little minotaur, and he's embarrassed by the way he looks."

"That's ridiculous!" Ronaldo said. "He's as handsome as they come!" He stopped suddenly, staring at Marian. Then he turned his gaze across the river toward Wyvernwood.

"What are you thinking?" Marian asked with a suspicious smile.

After a long moment, Ronaldo answered. "I'm thinking that it's been too long since I visited Stronghold."

"Well, what do you know," Marian said, dancing back. "You *do* speak butterfly!"

"Perhaps a little," he admitted grudgingly. "But speaking of Chernovog, shouldn't we be moving on? Where's Bumble?"

"Finding his breakfast, of course," Marian answered. "But I warned him to avoid any more patches of lousewort or any other flowers with a similar effect. If he can't hold his nectar, we'll have to leave him behind."

"Agreed," said Ronaldo. "This new land we've ventured into fascinates me, but we can't forget that it's full of woodcutters and kidnappers. We need to locate Chernovog as quickly as possible and return him to his mother, and I think that village I found yesterday is the best place to start." He raised his head high, twisted his long neck, and looked all around. "But we're still missing the third member of our erstwhile fellowship."

"I told him to stay close to the river, so he shouldn't be far away." Marian began to walk eastward by the water, calling Bumble's name as she went.

"You're assuming he'll remember what you told him," Ronaldo said, rolling his eyes as he started after her.

Moments later the slight hum of rapid wings touched Ronaldo's ears. A greenish blur circled his Dragon's nose twice, causing him to sneeze before it plunged toward Marian and flew a ring around her horn. It darted toward the water, made an abrupt turn, flew back to Ronaldo, barely avoided bouncing off the dragon's gray chest, and materialized on Marian's forelock right between her ears.

"It better not be lousewort," Marian warned in a low voice.

"Sunflowers! Yummy, yummy sunflowers!" Bumble sang. "Yellow, pretty, big, and sweet! Yummy sunflowers, good to eat! This will never come to pass: a sunflower feast without the gas!"

With that, the little hummingbird broke wind.

Marian gritted her teeth as she spoke. "You are so lucky there's a strong breeze blowing, or I'd show you something else that would never come to pass, like a hummingbird flying with my hoof up its . . . !"

Ronaldo gave out with a full-bellied laugh and fanned the air with his wings in mock-horror as mirthful tears ran down his face. He didn't envy Marian—it was her head, after all—and he knew he really shouldn't laugh. But the harder he tried to stop, the funnier it all became.

Marian glared. Then the gleam in her eyes turned mischievous. "Bumble, dear," she said with false sweetness, "for the rest of the day, I want you to ride on Ronaldo's head. Do you understand?" She tossed her mane, shaking the little hummingbird free.

Obediently, Bumble took up a new perch between Ronaldo's ears. "Sunflowers! Yummy, yummy sunflowers!" he sang.

Still, Ronaldo couldn't stop laughing. "Oh, now wait!" he protested. "Not fair!"

Marian lifted her nose high and put on a smug expression as she trotted off along the riverbank. "Yummy, yummy sunflowers!" she sang over her shoulder.

"Hey, she knows my song!" Bumble cried in Ronaldo's ear. "Song-thief! Song-thief!" He lowered his voice to a conspiratorial whisper as he stuck his head right next to the dragon's eardrum. "Should we tell the song-thief about the Men lying in wait?"

Ronaldo stopped laughing. "Men?" he said. "Lying in wait?"

"Many Men," Bumble affirmed. "A whole herd, all sneaky mean-looking in the grass."

"Marian!" Ronaldo called in alarm.

Mistaking his tone, Marian only laughed harder and broke into a run.

"How far away are these Men?" Ronaldo demanded of Bumble.

"Not far! Not far!" Bumble answered, growing excited again. "Throw a stone—crack some bone! Through the sunflowers, one by one and two by two! They came for me, and they come for you!"

"Marian!" Ronaldo called again, but the unicorn was far down the riverbank, almost out of sight. "Hold on, or follow!" he warned Bumble. Spreading his wings, he leaped into the sky. For a brief moment, the ground pinwheeled beneath him as he banked on one wingtip and gave chase. Her speed in the open country astonished him, and as if sensing his pursuit, she increased her pace.

She thought they were playing a game!

Swift though she was, Ronaldo was swifter. With a fearful determination, he overtook her and surged past. The grass rippled, and the few trees bent in the wake of his passage. Ahead, his sharp eyes spied a veritable forest of yellow sunflowers. Dazzling and sweet on tall green stalks, they blanketed the plain and the hillsides, and even from his altitude he could smell their perfume.

Something swished through the air beneath him, so small and fleet that he failed to get a good look at it. But below, a herd of Men sprang up suddenly from the high grass. Yelling and screaming, they pointed their tiny weapons his way. A black cloud of arrows rose upward, none sailing high enough to reach him. Another round followed the first.

Ronaldo glanced over his shoulder. Marian, witnessing the attack, had stopped short by the riverbank, and for a moment, he thought her safe. But suddenly she raced forward again, trumpeting a challenge, her horn lowered.

His heart hammered at the sight. The arrows were no real threat to him, but he feared for Marian. She lacked his scales, nor could she fly above the danger. Brave she was, but not invulnerable!

Ronaldo faced forward again and exhaled a powerful blast of fire. Without slowing, he sailed through the heart of his own inferno, and the flames crackled around the edges of his gray wings. Then he dived earthward, straight for the position of his attackers. Their yells took on a sharper note of fear. Some ran back to hide in the sunflower forest. Others raised their weapons again and fired more arrows. With a mighty downbeat of his wings, Ronaldo knocked the shafts from the air as soon as they took flight.

He had no desire to harm the Men, or to damage the lovely sunflowers, but he wouldn't risk them hurting Marian, and she was rapidly closing the distance. Directing his fiery breath skyward, he blew another blast. "Fear me," he shouted in his deepest, scariest voice, "and run!"

To his great relief, they threw down their weapons and did just that. Back into the sunflower forest they ran, disappearing among the tall stalks and thick leaves, until only the violent shaking of the golden petals marked their panic-driven retreat. Ronaldo climbed high and blew another breath to make sure they continued running.

When he at last landed, Marian was waiting for him.

"Fear me and run?" she said. Her tone was sarcastic.

"I was improvising," he answered with a shrug. "Where's Bumble?"

"Still on top of your head," Marian noted.

Hearing his name, the little hummingbird fluttered down to perch on Marian's horn. His tiny eyes were glazed, and the tips of his feathers looked singed.

Ronaldo remembered flying through his own flames and forced an apologetic smile. "Oops."

Marian shook her head and started toward the edge of the sunflowers. "Boys have all the fun," she muttered.

But something caught Ronaldo's attention. The sunflowers didn't have the same golden shimmer, and their green leaves seemed darker than before. "Wait," he said, and the unicorn stopped.

He looked around. All the colors seemed subtly wrong. The flowers were less bright; the river took on a muddy shade; the grass acquired a strange blue tint. More, a peculiar stillness hung in the air where earlier there had been a nice breeze. Stranger yet, insects in the grass and flowers and in the trees across the river began to chirp and sing in the middle of the day!

He glanced at the sun.

A piece of it was gone!

Marian noted the direction of his gaze and his sudden silence. "An eclipse," she said quietly.

Ronaldo wrapped his wings around himself as he watched the darkening solar disk, but the sudden cold he felt had nothing to do with the fading of the sunlight, nor could he explain the rushing sense of sadness. He turned toward Wyvernwood on the other side of the river.

It seemed so far away now.

11

LEANING ON A CRUDELY MADE CRUTCH, Gaunt stared outward with his one good eye from the highest parapet of his new fortress. The black patch that covered the left side of his face and the socket where that eye had been itched and collected sweat, which stung his wound, but despite the irritation he wore a wicked smile.

At last the griffins had a stronghold of their own! No more living in filthy nests that stank of wood-rot and fungus. Never again would he share his bed with maggots and vermin. He had a room now, a real room! Lots of rooms! And a feather mattress on which to sleep, and windows from which to smell the fresh air.

He slammed his paw down on the parapet's hard, mortared stone wall, ignoring the pain it caused in his bandaged side. His wicked grin turned cruel.

He had a throne room, too, and a real throne as befitted the undisputed King of the griffins. Luxuries were his, as well, and wealth— gold and silver and jewels, all bright and glittering and his!

All it had cost him was a father and a brother, and that was no price at all. Certainly other monarchs had paid as much. He gazed down at the green forest below. To the south, the east, and the west, lay Wyvernwood. With Stormfire out of the way, it would soon be his domain. No one lived who could oppose him, and once his injuries were finally healed, he would take what belonged to him.

He turned toward the north. Three more towers just like the one on which he stood rose above the high-walled courtyard and the complex of moss-and-ivy-covered buildings below. He studied the newly patched rooftops and the restored structures with a careful gaze. On each of the other towers a trio of griffins stood watch. Their eagles' heads were helmeted and they carried bronze-tipped spears.

A steady line of Men moved through the central gate. On their backs they bore bags of weapons, swords, spears, pieces of armor all shaped and fashioned for wear by Gaunt's griffin forces. They brought other supplies, too, tools and nails and hammers for further construction, bags of food for the workmen and artisans. And most importantly, they brought barrels of coins and jewels to add to the tribute already delivered.

"Now you are lord of all you survey," said a voice behind him. "Are you pleased, your Majesty?"

Turning, Gaunt focused his one good eye on the dark-haired man rising up through the parapet's open trap door. The fellow wore a smirk on his tanned face that Gaunt found irritating, but then, Gaunt found almost everything about Men to be irritating. Still, they had gold and wealth and skills that he found useful, and he appreciated their capacity for guile and deceit and treachery.

"Your people have done a fine job of rebuilding this old ruin, Canaan," Gaunt answered. "Just make my treasury room is filled to the ceiling by the end of day."

"Angmar keeps its bargains, my friend," Canaan answered. "As long as the Blackwater River remains open, your treasury will never be empty." He rubbed his stubbled chin as he leaned on the parapet and gazed at the workmen busy down below. "I must admit, however, I had my doubts about our arrangement when you destroyed my ship."

"I took no part in that action, as you well know," Gaunt answered. "My father and brother were to blame, and they have been dealt with."

Canaan nodded as he carefully removed the scarlet gloves he wore and placed them on the parapet wall. "And we've already launched three ships down the river. With another force closing in from the sea, Degarm will never know what hit them."

"I'm unconcerned with your war," Gaunt interrupted.

Canaan flashed that irritating smirk again. "You wouldn't be if you understood the kind of wealth Degarm possesses. If you had a clue, you'd be making your own invasion plans instead of hiding out here on Angmar's borderland dealing with shady characters like me."

Gaunt leveled a cold eye on Canaan, but kept his own council. It wasn't the first time he'd heard that smug tone of superiority from Canaan, his workers, or his predecessors. He'd tolerated it all the months while his fortress was being rebuilt and restored and while his coffers were being filled, through all the secret meetings behind Gorganar's back, from one foreman to the next. Canaan was only the latest in a long and arrogant line of Men he'd had to deal with.

But he had this fortress now, and it was only a start. He scrutinized the buildings again, the high, moss-covered walls and the main gate, the stout grace of the four towers. "Did this place ever have a name?" he asked Canaan.

"If it did," Canaan answered, picking up his gloves and slapping them against his palm, "no one remembers it. Truthfully, no one remembers even who built it. The ruins were older than the kingdom of Angmar. They've always stood here among the foothills on the edge of the forest, and no one's ever taken up permanent residence." Putting his back to the parapet wall, he leaned back on his elbows and stared up at the sky. "There's a legend, you know, that this place is haunted."

Gaunt was not one to let a human frighten him with a story. "It may be," he answered. "There are older things in Wyvernwood than dragons and griffins. But they'd do well to find another haunt, because Redclaw is mine."

Canaan raised an eyebrow. "Redclaw?"

"The four towers," Gaunt said, gesturing with a wingtip. "They rise like a griffin's talons, smooth and strong and gleaming. This fortress is a symbol of the grasp I will soon extend over Wyvernwood and all its creatures." He looked aside momentarily. *Nor will I stop at this pathetic forest*, he thought to himself. *Angmar, Degarm, and the world itself will all fit nicely in my paw.*

"Redclaw it is then," Canaan said, as if his agreement was of the least importance. "With our military might and your natural strength, Angmar and the Griffinkin will make fine allies."

Gaunt closed his eyes and for a moment entertained himself with the idea of seizing Canaan, lifting him high, and throwing him from the tower. He could then make slaves of the rest of the workmen still inside the fortress. With Redclaw complete and Gorganar and Stormfire dead he wasn't really sure what further need he had for Angmar.

"Allies, yes," he said, resisting the impulse. He laid a huge paw on Canaan's shoulder as he looked the man in the eye and wondered if he sensed how close to death he had just come. "And friends."

A sudden wind rustled Gaunt's feathers, and he spread his wings to fly. He'd had enough of Canaan's company. But a deep pain lanced through his right side, causing him to cringe and reminding him of the bandage that wrapped his chest. He sagged heavily on his crutch and let go a loud sigh.

"You're bleeding again," Canaan observed, and Gaunt scowled because he couldn't tell whether the note of concern in the man's voice was genuine or not. He suspected not, and as he clutched his wound he considered again how much pleasure it would give him to heave Canaan over the parapet.

"Leave me!" he growled. "Get off my rooftop before this pain drives me to a rash act!"

"Let me send for a healer" Canaan offered. "My people have skills with herbalism and surgery you haven't . . . !"

Gaunt let out a roar. Casting his crutch aside with a noisy clatter, he reared up on his hind legs and displayed his wings again. Too late, Canaan stumbled back a step, but Gaunt seized him by an arm and a leg and raised him over his eagle's head. The man kicked and struggled helplessly, and his terrified screams rang across the fortress's grounds. For an instant, all work stopped, and every eye, whether griffin or man, looked upward with desperate anticipation.

Then, an instant before launching Canaan into the air, Gaunt relented and set him back down on the tower rooftop. Why, he wasn't sure, but as quickly as the anger had come upon him, it had left again, and only the aching fire in his side remained. He touched the wound, and a rich, red wetness matted the fur of his paw. "I'm not myself today," he said in a quiet voice. It was the closest he could come to an apology.

Cowered down against the parapet wall, Canaan stared at Gaunt with wide, fear-filled eyes. "You broke my arm!" he cried as he hugged the injured limb to his chest.

Gaunt barely heard. He felt a strange weakness and disorientation. Looking outward from the tower's great height actually made him dizzy. Turning away from the wall and from Canaan, he limped toward the trap door that led down inside the fortress. "Don't be such a baby," he told Canaan over his shoulder as he descended the first stairs. "Your people have great skills with herbalism and surgery."

The stairs spiraled down, round and round, one cold stone step after another. Yet, every so often, a torch burned in a sconce on the wall, and the bright yellow flame danced with a flickering beauty, casting pools of warm, amber radiance that filled Gaunt with a satisfying joy. Despite his pain, he paused to admire the light, to hold up a paw and feel the heat radiance it gave off.

Fire!

It was the one thing no griffin had dared possess before. The nests that had made their homes were too vulnerable to fire. In all the Valley of Eight Winds there hadn't been a single torch or lantern or candle. Even outdoor fires were forbidden for fear of the destruction a single stray spark could bring. In all his life, Gaunt had never curled up before a fireplace and enjoyed a story or a song by the crackling light, nor had he ever warmed himself by a hearth-fire on a winter night. nor dried his feathers on a gray and rainy day.

The nests had been dark, always dank and smelly, and without the simplest amenities. With no light, there had been no interest in art, no need for the rugs or tapestries that now adorned his throne room in Redclaw. What good to own a precious jewel or a golden goblet when there was no light to give it shine or glitter?

But in Redclaw, in his new fortress of stone and brick, fire posed no danger. Torches lit the stairways, and lanterns lit the halls, and in the great rooms fireplaces were kept ever burning. Gaunt hated the darkness, and so he had forbidden it in Redclaw the way his father and grandfather had forbidden fire in the Valley of Eight Winds.

As he reached the bottom of the tower stair another griffin approached. In one paw he carried a long spear, and Gaunt recognized him as one of the griffins that had helped him attack and escape from Stronghold. "Greetings, Minhep," he hailed his follower. "It pleases me that you answered my summons. This tower above my throne room is your Watch now. Choose those you would have serve under your command and assign them shifts. None of the four towers are ever to be unguarded, but this one above all must be kept secure."

Minhep bent his right knee and touched his beak to the floor at Gaunt's feet. Rising again, he asked, "And what is it that your Majesty fears might be strong enough to attack us this far at the northern edge of Wyvernwood?"

Growling, Gaunt raised the back of his hand, but stayed his blow. "You risk much with your derisive tone," he warned Minhep. "And yet I respect you for it. I'll have no cowards around me, so speak your mind, Minhep, even if it tries my patience."

"You haven't answered my question," Minhep snarled. "What is it we're keeping watch for? Do you expect Stormfire's hatchlings to find us here?"

Gaunt wrapped his wings around himself and rubbed his chin. "Inevitably, word will spread that the Griffinkin have resettled here," he grumbled. "More and more of Angmar's ships will soon sail down the river as they conduct their war with Degarm, and we'll soon begin to take the slaves we need from Wyvernwood's population. We have to be strong and alert, Minhep. Not just for retaliation from Stronghold. We have an *ally* at our back now."

Minhep grinned. "You load the word with such love and trust."

Gaunt held out his paws and shrugged. "What can I say? I'm ruled by my tender heart." He glanced back up the way he had come. "By the way, when you take your post you're likely to find my new pet Man hurrying down the staircase. If he doesn't show you proper deference and get out of your way quickly enough, feel free to break his other arm."

"Something so weak and pink?" Minhep sneered as he moved past Gaunt and began the long climb to the tower rooftop. "I can't imagine anything that would give me less satisfaction."

Gaunt glared at Minhep's back. That griffin would bear watching. While the insolence in his tone was admirable, it was also suspicious. In fact, it bordered on treasonous. It wouldn't do for Minhep's attitude to spread among the other griffins. He drew a deep breath, holding his side against the accompanying pain as he realized he would have to keep a much closer eye on all those around him from now on.

There was no one he could trust.

It was strange to feel so alone, he reflected as he headed for his throne room and pushed open the large pair of doors. A warm fire burned in the fireplace within, but there was no one inside, no friend, no follower, no servant. Perhaps he had been too quick to dispatch Struther. The little basilisk had sometimes been good company in a bootlicking, subservient sort of way. Of course, it was impossible to trust a poisoner.

Impossible to trust anyone, he thought again. Impossible to confide fully in anyone.

The fireplace popped and crackled, and the flames danced, yet it seemed to lack the warmth Gaunt had anticipated. His ominous shadow stalked across the stone floor and up the side of the far wall as he strode to his throne. Deep in thought, he ran his paw over the richly padded blue velvet seat, and then recoiled from the red smear of blood his touch left on the fabric. For a long, numbing moment he stared at the crude stain. It was only blood from his wound, he told himself, not a symbol of anything. Yet, he was a being given to seeing things in terms of symbol and portent, and there was no denying that there was blood on his hands and blood on his throne in more than just a literal way.

Ripping a tapestry from the wall behind his throne, he pressed the cloth to his side to absorb any further blood loss. Then, with his wings folded tightly, he curled up on the velvet seat, rested his head on his crossed paws, and stared into the empty corners.

He wasn't sure how long he lay like that, alone with his thoughts, listening to the unsettling silence, wondering where everyone was, and it was with a genuine sense of relief when Minhep flung open the doors and rushed inside. His eyes were wide with excitement, and his golden muscles rippled as his claws raked the floor.

"Welcome!" Gaunt called, glad for the distraction of company.

"The sun!" Minhep cried. "Something's happening to the sun! The light is dying, and a vast darkness is falling all across the forest!"

Gaunt felt his heart shrivel inside his chest. He rose from his seat and took half a step toward Minhep, then quailed and sank back onto the bloodstained seat. Everything was symbol and portent! Everything!

"Save us!" Minhep shouted.

Gaunt could manage no more than a fearful whisper. "What do you expect me to do?"

Minhep stared, then flung down the spear he carried and rushed from the throne room again, leaving Gaunt alone.

The sun—gone! All that remained was darkness!

The fireplace hissed. A wood chip popped and threw sparks that bounced and skittered over the stone floor before fading out in tiny puffs of smoke. It was a dangerous, unfriendly fire, Gaunt thought suddenly.

And yet, it was also light.

Rising from his throne, the King of the Griffins crept closer to the fireplace. The radiant heat seared his flesh, particularly the wound in his side, as he paced in a slow circle three times and curled up before the hearth. Still, he shivered from a cold he didn't understand.

He thought of Morkir, and wished that his brother was here with him, but he was alone with only his shadow for company, his huge, black shadow that regarded him eye-to-eye like a predator.

12

RONALDO GLIDED ON WARM AIR CURRENTS, following the course of the Blackwater River eastward toward the coast of the Windy Sea while Marian raced across the landscape below. He watched her lithe, white form as she plunged forward along the river-bank, ever sure-footed and graceful, her mane and tail flying as she chased his shadow. Though he ventured ahead, watchful for any threat or danger, he never let her out of his sight.

The sun was once again a normal disk in the afternoon sky. From the edge of the field of yellow sunflowers, Bumble and Marian and he had watched the gradual blackening and cooling of the heavens and the awe-inspiring emergence of the bright stars in the middle of the day. Never had he experienced such a beautiful and fearsome sight! His heart still beat with excitement when he remembered how that fiery ring had hung in the darkness and how the air had turned so strange and still.

Marian leaped a narrow ravine. For a breath-taking instant, she seemed to fly through the air, then her hooves crashed down, throwing showers of dirt and grass as she sped on. A flash of green marked where Bumble clung at the base of her horn. The little hummingbird hadn't left her company, not for snack nor dinner, since the sun performed its miracle.

Not far ahead, Ronaldo spied a farmhouse near the bank of the river. Putting on a burst of speed, he surged forward and circled the neatly built wooden home twice. A man and a man-wife appeared in the doorway, their arms fearfully around each other as they stared upward. A man-child thrust its head up between them, and a dog lunged out and began to bark.

On the ground, Marian cut a wide course around the farmhouse. The couple with their child watched open-mouthed as she raced along the outer perimeter of their yard while their dog howled and did its best to look fierce and made a show of tearing back and forth at the edge of the front porch without ever quite launching into pursuit of the unicorn. A split-log fence marked the border between the yard and the field beyond. Without slowing her pace, seemingly without any effort at all, Marian flexed her muscles and jumped it.

Leaving the farm behind, Ronaldo flew past Marian again and skimmed low over the field. In the grasses ahead and among a copse of trees, he finally spied what he'd been watching for—the men who had shot their arrows at him earlier. They lay on their bellies among the deeper grasses, or cowered among the knotted roots at the bases of the denser trunks, or peeked over the muddy edge of a gully. A few still had their weapons, but none dared draw a bead on him.

He feared for Marian, though. She had no wings to fly above their missiles, nor did she see the men lying in her path. In only moments she would pass right through their midst! He turned toward the largest group of men, those who hid among the trees. The wind of his passing ripped leaves away, and he lashed his tail across the highest branches, snapping them. Screaming and shouting, the men sprang up without firing their weapons, ran for the gully, and leaped in with their comrades. Some of the men lying in the grasses jumped to their feet, only to be blown over again.

Marian's laughter rang sharply over the land as she ran among the panicked creatures. One of the men, finding his feet, threw down his bow and ran with a high-pitched shriek when he saw her coming toward him. She lowered her horn, aiming the golden tip at his plump buttocks, and gave him chase. At the last moment, she turned aside, her laughter unceasing as the unfortunate fellow dived headfirst into a ravine.

Ronaldo laughed, too, and just for the fun of it blew a blast of fire high into the sky.

Marian's voice reached him from below as she ran. "Show off!" she called. "Grandstander!"

He only laughed harder. "I haven't tried to stick my horn up some poor man's backside!"

"Jealous, too!" she shouted back. "You don't have a beautiful horn like mine!"

"Oh, you hide it well, my delectable Maid Marian!" Ronaldo teased as he flew above her. "But it's you who are jealous! It is pinion envy—you don't have my wings!"

The sun sparkled briefly on a flash of green plumage as Bumble sprang into the air. "Jealous you both are!" he cried, as caught up in the excitement as his comrades. "But of me—but of me! My bill is as slender and graceful and sharp-pointed as Marian's horn! Pity the back-side of the man that incurs my wrath!" With a burst of speed, he darted up and perched in Ronaldo's ear. "And my wings are the swiftest of any flying creature! Where is there a match anywhere for Bumble the Mighty? I am the best parts of you both!"

"Truly, I'm humbled in your presence, Little One," Ronaldo answered, giving a shake of his head to dislodge Bumble from his ear. "It's not the Age of Man at all that's upon us, but the Age of the Hummingbird!"

"It may be as he says," Marian laughed. "He certainly has your ability to blow hot air!"

Ronaldo glanced over his shoulder. The men were hauling themselves out of the ditches and ravines, twenty or perhaps thirty of the dirtiest and muddiest fellows he'd ever seen. Now that he and Marian and Bumble were past, they rose and beat their chests and shook their fists and flung handfuls of mud that had no chance of coming close.

Not one fired an arrow, though.

The Age of Man. Ronaldo shook his head again and wondered, *What did that mean?* What was so important about Man that dragons and all the fabulous creatures of the world should step aside for him? He was neither particularly beautiful, nor particularly strong, nor particularly brave, and even a hummingbird had more charm! He thought about circling back for another look at the bedraggled band of—what was the word they sometimes used for themselves?

Humans.

Woodcutters and kidnappers, Marian had called them, and to that he supposed he should add *would-be murderers,* for certainly they had tried to kill him with their arrows. Suddenly, as he thought about that, his mood of merriment melted away, and a darker concern took its place.

He had assumed he would find Chernovog alive, but as he began to consider the actions of the men he had encountered so far, their violence and their aggression, he wondered if that was a reasonable expectation. His heart hammered, no longer with excitement, but with a growing anger, and he increased his pace.

Farms and houses began to dot the landscape. Small fishing boats floated along the riverbanks. Flying at his swiftest speed, Ronaldo made it a point to circle each one. In this manner he announced his coming, tipping his wings toward the stunned humans who looked up from their fields or their yards or their fishing traps, sometimes blasting fire toward the clouds overhead.

In the distance, the spires of the village he had glimpsed the day before began to rise in the bright blue afternoon sky. White stone and sharply slanting rooftops leafed with gold-plating glittered and shimmered with the waves of heat they reflected, and stained glass windows shot rays of colored light in all directions.

In the evening twilight of the day before, and under the slate gray sky with a storm approaching, he had not thought it so impressive. Or maybe his attitude had been affected on that first near-visit by the fact that men had also chased him off with arrows. But despite his anger and the grimness of his purpose, his artist's eye couldn't deny that this village of Man was the most incredible sight he had ever seen.

Well, perhaps next to Marian. She pursued him tirelessly, leaping or weaving around all obstacles, never seeming to slow, never losing her footing. The men she passed fell away from her, or shut themselves inside their homes to stare from their windows. Some rose to stand in their boats so they could watch her go by, and others peered out from the lofts of their barns.

They wore looks on their faces that Ronaldo found hard to explain. Fear, but also wonder. Panic, but also awe. From safe distances or from behind their doors, they raised on tiptoes and crowded against each other for better views.

The farms and homes increased in number, as did the spires of the taller buildings. Suddenly, the blue of the Windy Sea appeared beyond the tallest spires, and a moment later, Ronaldo sailed above the village's heart. The air filled with the sounds of bells, deep-toned and high-toned, and all pitches in between. The air fairly shivered on his wings with the vibrations of their chiming.

"It's a greeting!" he called out in surprise. But Marian was nowhere close by to hear. For a moment, he felt a surge of fear as he failed to spot her. He had flown too far ahead! Something terrible had befallen her! But then, as he flew around the tallest and centermost spire, he spied her racing boldly through the narrow streets below between rows and rows of humans who cheered and hailed her and waved their arms as she ran by.

A huge circle paved with flagstones ringed the tallest spire. As if drawn by the gigantic golden bell ringing within the slender structure, men and women and children rushed and spread small rugs and threw themselves down on their knees and bowed their heads repeatedly to the ground. A line of old men dressed in simple white gowns and bearing gnarly staves emerged from the spire to join the rest, but they thrust their staves at the sky and called to him.

"Dragon! Dragon! Dragon!" And the entire assembly took up the chant.

Suddenly, at one of the gates into the circle, the humans leaped up and threw themselves aside to make a path for Marian. "Hmmmph! *Dragon*, indeed!" She said, her hooves flinging sparks from the paving stones as she stopped before the old men. "Sure, sure, he cuts a scary figure, what with all that noisy fire-breathing and big, leathery wings. But what am I? Yesterday's lunch?"

"You . . . ! You can talk!" one of the old men gasped.

"You're a female!" another exclaimed as he leaned on his staff for a closer look.

Marian rolled her eyes. "Obviously this village is a place of higher learning."

Yet another one of the old men stepped closer. "Village, madam?" he said quietly. "You've come to the city of Karlass, and we are its priest-governors." He indicated the other white-clad elders.

"Do tell," she answered, unimpressed. Glancing up at Ronaldo overhead, she continued, "May I suggest we make room for my companion? We have an important matter to discuss regarding a missing child, and really, his disposition isn't nearly as sweet and gentle as mine."

A green blur circled Marian's horn, and an instant later Bumble took his perch on the tip. With one quick look at the priest-governors, he sprang into the air again. "Woodcutters and kidnappers!" he cried, his wings thrumming.

"Calm down, Bumble-bird," Marian urged as the priest-governors began to usher the crowd back. When a space of sufficient size was cleared, Ronaldo settled carefully to the ground and folded his wings. "The Dragon Ronaldo," Marian said, by way of introduction. "I'm Marian, and our miniscule-but-ferocious companion is called Bumble."

A young girl skipped forward with a wreath of red columbine and quince, which she extended to Marian. "Welcome, most welcome, oh wondrous creature!" she sang, her young face bright and smiling and without a trace of the fear that showed on the faces of so many adults.

"Food!" Bumble cried. "Take out!" He dived headfirst into the blossoms. Startled, the little girl squealed and threw up her hands as she jumped back. The wreath sailed upward and settled around Marian's horn. Targeting the columbine, the hummingbird plunged in again.

"I said *ferocious*, Bumble," Marian snapped, "not *voracious!*"

Bumble lifted his beak from the blooms only long enough to answer. "I'm ferociously hungry!"

Marian tossed her head. The wreath flew into the air, but this time when it came down again it settled around her neck. Bumble fluttered after it and plunged back into his meal as if he hadn't been interrupted at all.

With a sigh, the unicorn turned to the little girl. "Your flowers are a lovely gift and very thoughtful," she said. "Please don't be frightened. Bumble's just impetuous."

The little girl smiled again and curtsied. "I'm not frightened," she answered. "He just surprised me!"

"Your bird is quite amusing." One of the elders stepped forward and bowed first to Marian, and then to Ronaldo, then waved a hand to dismiss the little girl. "My name is Depayne. Consider me the spokesman for the priest-governors of Karlass. May I say that we consider it an omen of great auspice that you should appear to us from the shadow of the sun."

Ronaldo looked at Marian with a raised eyebrow.

"He means the eclipse," Marian translated.

The dragon raised his other eyebrow as he looked back to Depayne. He'd never seen such an *old* man before. The lines and wrinkles on the aged face fascinated him, as did the straight, silver hair that hung to his waist. "Technically," Ronaldo said, "The sun and its shadow were in the east. We came from the west, following the course of the Blackwater River."

Depayne inclined his head and executed another short bow. "I am not wise enough to trade philosophies with you," he answered. "Generations have passed since we last saw your kind in our skies. So we ring the bells to herald your return, and we declare a holiday in Karlass to honor you."

Ronaldo stretched his neck down until his head was on the same level with Depayne and he could look the priest-governor in the eye. "It's a strange kind of greeting when your people fire arrows at us one moment and then declare a holiday the next."

Depayne clutched at his heart and stumbled back a step, visibly paler. "Someone shot at you?" His expression darkened; he raised his staff and slammed the butt of it down on the ground. "It must have been those bumpkins in the outlying villages and farms! I assure you, Great Dragon—" he gestured toward the other priest-governors "—none of us would ever have authorized such disrespectful actions! We hold sacred the stories and tales our ancestors told of the Dragonkin! If you wish, we'll hunt down your attackers . . . !"

Ronaldo shook his head and drew himself erect again. "No need for that," he answered. "Let's just consider it a misunderstanding. But as you hold us in such regard, perhaps you can help us. We seek a group of men, woodcutters and loggers, who ventured across the river and deep into Wyvernwood."

Bumble darted up from the wreath of flowers. "Chernovog!" he sang. "I remember! Chernovog!" He curled the tip of one wing into a semblance of a fist and shook it at Depayne. "Give us Chernovog, you dog of a man, or the dragon will spit fire on your shoes!" With that, he flashed three times around Depayne's head, then dived back into his dinner.

The dragon lowered his head again, this time to glare at Marian. "Why is it you've never mentioned his diplomatic skills?"

Marian looked askance. "Why are you asking me," she said. "I thought he was with you? I'm not the hummingbird's keeper, you know!"

His face expressionless, Depayne looked from Ronaldo to Marian, and then to each of his fellow priests. A couple of them chuckled softly and hid grins behind cupped hands. Then Depayne sputtered; his stony countenance broke, and he burst out with a belly-shaking laugh. He extended an open hand toward Ronaldo. "I'm afraid," he gasped, his face turning deep red, "that your bird has me at a disadvantage! Dragons and unicorns, and birds—oh, my! Yes, these I know. Or at least I've read about." He extended the same open hand toward Marian. "But what, pray enlighten me, is a Chernovog?"

"I'm afraid, too," Ronaldo answered in a crisp tone. "Chernovog is a child. A minotaur child, son of Beatrice and Ranock. Your wood-cutters came deep into the Whispering Hills where we all live, and they took the boy!"

"My home, too!" Bumble cried. His tiny belly at last full, he abandoned the wreath and perched on Marian's horn; "They took my home!"

Depayne's brows pinched together, and his wrinkled face purpled like a raisin. "Our woodcutters?" he replied archly. "That's not possible. The people of Karlass don't venture to the other side of the river. It's forbidden!"

One of the other priest-governors leaned forward. "The punishment is quite severe," he said as he stroked his beard.

"The evidence was clear," Marian said in a more reasonable voice. "Two small boat-loads of men entered our forest. We found the marks of their hulls on the riverbank and the place from which they launched their logs."

Depayne frowned and clutched his staff until his old knuckles turned white. "Perhaps they came ashore somewhere else," he offered. "As I indicated before, many of the outlying farmers live by their own rules. If you'll give us time, I'll send men into the countryside immediately to find these loggers and search for your minotaur-child."

"Such a kidnapping would be unforgivable," the second priest added with a sad expression. He laid a hand on the shoulder of his leader. "Depayne, please. This courtyard is large enough to accommodate our dragon guest. Let us give it over for his comfort and for the unicorn's while we seek the perpetrators!"

All the priest-governors agreed, and an enthusiastic cheer went up from the crowd of onlookers.

"So be it!" Depayne shouted, raising his arms to draw attention. "Let all able-bodied men hearing my voice disperse into the country-side. Ask at every home and farmhouse in every village. Find the child who is half man and half bull, and find the ones that took him! Waste no time!"

"I love a man of action," Marian whispered.

Ronaldo's ears were sharp enough to hear. "I've never seen a man of action," he whispered back. "Or any man at all so close as these."

All around him a great stirring ran through the crowd as grown men hurried to carry out Depayne's command. Fully a third of those assembled rushed for the gates that let into the courtyard. Some of the women went also, but others began to chant and dance. A number of them produced tambourines and small drums and chipolis, and in no time at all a gorgeously musical rhythm filled the air. It charged Ronaldo's blood and excited him. Never had he heard anything like it!

"Let us show you how we celebrate holidays for honored guests," Depayne shouted over the music. "Truly, your coming on this special day bespeaks the return of magic to the world!"

Ronaldo gazed down at Depayne and his fellow priests. He still was not sure what to make of them. Perhaps it was because he'd had so little experience with men, but he couldn't seem to judge their expressions or the subtleties in their words. One moment, he mistrusted them, and the next he wondered if it wasn't a mistake that the Dragonkin kept so apart.

"We are not so different from you," he said. "We live quiet lives, and we care about our children."

"Not so different?" Bumble flew up and, perching on Ronaldo's nose, pressed his wings to either side of his head. "You call this noise living quietly? I can't hear myself think! Not that I do much thinking!"

"Fresh flowers, Bumble," Ronaldo pointed out as lines of young boys and girls filed into the courtyard, their arms filled with large bouquets.

Bumble groaned. "Oh, I'm a sucker for foreign food!"

Ronaldo grinned as Bumble took off. Curling his tail, mindful of the humans pressed so close around him, he sat back on his haunches and rested his spine against the tall structure at the courtyard's center. Most of the priest-governors excused themselves. Some went back into the spire from which they had emerged. Others mingled with the celebrants while still others exited the courtyard through the gates and vanished.

The dancing and music-making continued. The courtyard became a colorful swirl of skirts and shawls and scarves and veils. Different groups of dancers broke off into new rhythms. Some began to compete with each other. Ronaldo watched it all, fascinated. He tapped his right foot to one rhythm and the tip of his tail to another.

Older men and women carried in baskets of bread and rolls, loaves of cheeses, and boxes of fruit. Around the edges of the courtyard they spread blankets upon which they set out platters of steamed fish and trays of hard-boiled eggs. There were cabbages and carrots and turnips, too, and still more food.

Marian wandered among the celebrants. They wanted to touch her, to stroke her fine white coat or run their fingers along the smooth length of her golden horn. She tolerated it in good humor, speaking with some, sometimes singing along on the refrain of a song. They seemed to adore her and the little hummingbird that appeared off and on in her mane or on her forelock.

As the afternoon passed and evening quickly gave way to night, torches and lanterns were brought. Some of the men began to return, and a few gathered around Ronaldo's feet as if to demonstrate to the rest that they weren't intimidated by his great size. One began to ask him about life in Wyvernwood, and another about dragon mating habits.

"What do you do for a living?" one called to him. "You know, with your time?"

Ronaldo thought for a moment. "I'm an artist," he answered finally. "A painter."

The men slapped their knees and laughed as if he had told an outrageous joke. Only Depayne's sudden re-emergence from the spire silenced them. As one, they looked at the priest-governor's stern face, then bowed and drifted away. Depayne folded his arms across his white robe and took a position near Ronaldo's left foot.

"Why do they seem to fear you?" the dragon asked in a quiet voice.

Depayne cast his gaze upward and regarded his fabulous guest with one narrowed eye. "Don't confuse fear for respect," he answered. "We priest-governors serve the people of Karlass. We see that their needs are met and that the laws are obeyed."

Ronaldo stretched his neck down, lowering his head for a better look at Depayne. He thought he had learned much through an afternoon's observations, but this single man puzzled and troubled him, and he found he couldn't resolve his many conflicting impressions. "But who makes the laws?"

Depayne pursed his lips and looked away again. "Our laws are handed down to us from our ancestors and from the founders of Karlass and of Degarm, itself. We priest-governors merely see that the laws are applied fairly and evenly to all, and that they are remembered and preserved and respected."

Ronaldo blinked his large eyes as he continued to observe Depayne. Among men, he noted that the leader of the priest-governors was taller than most. His hair was also longer and more purely silver in color than any other man Ronaldo had seen. So was his face more deeply wrinkled. His gaze seemed constantly to sweep around, never settling for long on anyone or anything, always studying and watching.

Marian turned away from a nearby group of dancers and sidled up to Ronaldo.

"Where's Bumble?" the dragon asked in a soft voice.

"Under my mane—quite fat and very asleep, I think." She faced Depayne, and for a moment her blue eyes flashed with the reflected light of a torch. "What Ronaldo really wants to know," she said, revealing that she had been listening to their conversation, "is who made you priest-governor instead of that man by the gate or that woman with her fingers in the steamed fish."

Depayne looked at her strangely for a moment and then smirked. "They are just fisher-folk," he answered.

Marian looked up at Ronaldo, and it startled him to see the sadness in her eyes. She was older than he, much older, and she had dealt with men before. What was it that she understood about Depayne and he did not? What had he just missed?

"And I am just a unicorn," Marian said, wandering away again, "and he is just a dragon."

"Marian, stay a while!" Ronaldo called. There were things he suddenly wanted to ask her, insights he knew she could give about Depayne and the people of Karlass, about all the new sights he was experiencing.

But Marian shook her head as she walked on. "There are many things to learn from fisher-folk," she said over her shoulder.

Ronaldo ached to stretch his wings. He'd been sitting in the same position for too long. His legs were cramped and his tail half-numb. The bright stars hung over the courtyard like jewels, and he could smell the breeze sweeping inland from the Windy Sea. The city no longer seemed like the most incredible sight in the world to him. It felt small and narrow, and he felt penned by its high walls and buildings.

Then, Marian caught his attention again. She had stopped in mid-step and stood with her nose high, her nostrils flaring. Without warning, she spun lithely about, startling a group of dancers and causing them to flee.

Again, the torchlight filled her eyes. "Fire," she said.

Ronaldo rose to his feet. He didn't have her keen sense of smell, and the wind was blowing in a strong, westward direction. But there was just the hint of smoke on it! Stretching himself to his full height, he could see over the wall that surrounded the courtyard. A dull, red glow lit the distant sky.

And then, a brighter glow lit the eastern sky, and a cloud of white smoke blew across the wall. A handful of men rushed through the several gates, calling in loud and desperate voices. A pair of them spied Depayne at Ronaldo's side, and they threw themselves down before the priest-governor.

"We're under attack!" one of them exclaimed. "Ships from Angmar under cover of night. Half the harbor is on fire!"

"No! It's the farms and fields to the west of the city that burn!" cried the other. "Three ships sailing down the Blackwater River! Must be a hundred men! They're burning everything!"

"From the sea and by the river?" Depayne looked stunned by the news. Then his face blackened with anger. He shook a fist at Ronaldo. "Angmar sails ships through the heart of Wyvernwood? They wouldn't dare do such a thing on their own!"

Ronaldo was no less stunned. He looked to Marian. Bumble stood awake and alert on the tip of her horn. "It's not possible!" he protested. "Angmar would have to sail through the Valley of Eight Winds! Right under Gorganar's own nest!"

Depayne kicked savagely at the two men on the ground. "Get up!" he ordered. "Rally our defenses!" He waved his arms and shouted. "Everyone! To the docks! To the harbor! Fight for Karlass and Degarm!" He spun back around to Ronaldo. "I knew it was no accident or trick of chance that you came here today! You're in league with them!"

"You're wrong!" Ronaldo shouted. Over the wall, he could plainly see the flames in the harbor. He had to see more! Springing into the air, he spread his wings and swept away from the courtyard. Chaos reigned in the city streets. Men and women ran shrieking, their arms filled with children or with their belongings. In the harbor, a score of ships were on fire; their masts and rigging made a fiery lacework against the starlit darkness. Ronaldo flew above the burning vessels, feeling the heat on his underbelly, on his wings.

Among the burning ships were other craft moving at full speed under sails as black as the night itself. From these craft, storms of burning arrows flew, and where those arrows landed, more fire sprang up. On the docks, fisheries and warehouses began to burn. The wind carried the sparks even further inland. Smoke rolled in like a choking fog.

Ronaldo banked sharply. Flying toward the city again, he saw that, indeed, three more craft were making rapid course down the Blackwater. He could barely believe his eyes, and he cried out in anguish. These ships, too, were raining fire on everything within reach of their arrows. They were using the Blackwater to launch destruction and death! They had sailed through Wyvernwood—and no one had stopped them!

A red rage seized him, an anger like none he had ever felt before. He charged through the air toward the first of the three ships. His gray shape worked to his advantage, and in the blackness he was nearly upon the vessel before its crew even noticed. With one fiery blast, he ignited its furled sails, its masts and rigging. The hardened wood fairly exploded with the heat of his breath. Screaming, the panicked crew flung themselves over the side and swam for shore.

The crews of the second and third vessel were no less terrified to find themselves confronting a dragon. They filled the air over the river with arrows, but Ronaldo's powerful wings beat the tiny, sparkling shafts down. Some fell into the water, but others fell to the decks. More screams, and the river churned with the shapes of frantically swimming men. Ronaldo gave them mere moments to get away before he blasted streams of fire at both ships.

When he had made floating bonfires of all three vessels, he banked again for the courtyard where he had left Marian and Bumble. His heart hammered, and dragon-tears blinded him. Now that it was done, the magnitude of his action caused him horror. But greater was his horror that Angmar had sailed through Wyvernwood—through the refuge of the Dragonkin!

How could that be?

He swooped over the courtyard and found still more horror. The gates had been shut, and men had ropes around Marian's neck and legs. She fought them off, but still more ropes sailed through the air, ensnaring her.

Tangled in the folds of his once-white robe, Depayne thrashed on the ground, beat at his head, and waved his arms in the air as he screamed curses and begged uselessly for aid. Several of his fellow priest-governors tried to help him to his feet, but each time he made to rise, he jerked back suddenly, as if struck, and fell thrashing again.

Ronaldo exhaled a blast of fire into the sky, and for an instant the courtyard lit up as brightly as day. Throwing down their ropes, most of the men ran to the walls and struggled to open the gates again and escape into the city. "Dragon!" they cried in wide-eyed fear. "The dragon!"

With space suddenly cleared, Ronaldo landed beside Marian. The priest-governors, abandoning their leader, fled back inside the spire and slammed the door. "What's wrong with Depayne?" Ronaldo asked as Marian tried to shake off the ropes.

"Bumble," she answered. "Minuscule-but-ferocious Bumble."

Ronaldo stared, and finally in the darkness he saw the nearly invisible green blur that struck the priest-governor again and again in the ears, in the eyes, in the nose. Everytime Depayne tried to rise, the little hummingbird hit him again.

"He ordered those men to kill me," Marian continued in a disgusted voice.

The priest-governor beat the air furiously in an effort to ward off Bumble. "Spies!" he shouted, managing to make it to his knees before the hummingbird knocked him sideways again. "Allies of our enemy! My city is burning!"

In the spire, someone opened a window. A candlestick came flying out and bounced off Ronaldo's shoulder. Next came a chair, then a plate, and a goblet. An entire cake followed. Higher up, another window opened. A clock came flying from that and struck him on the edge of his right wing. A rain of objects followed. None of them posed a serious danger to the dragon, but there were his friends to think about.

"Forgive me, Marian," he said abruptly. "I'll try to be gentle!" Bending, he closed his claws around her body, and before she could consent or protest, he took to the air. "Follow me, Bumble!" he shouted.

Before he even had the words out, Bumble's wings hummed in his ear. "Follow?" the hummingbird laughed. "Bumble is the leader!"

Ronaldo blinked tears away as he gazed groundward. Half of Karlass seemed to be on fire, and smoke embroiled the rest of the city. He recalled how beautiful it had seemed by day. Now, it was a place of terror.

"You tried to tell me about war, Marian," he reminded her as he flew southward away from Karlass. Though he carried her with utmost care, he could feel the unicorn's rapid breathing, the drumming of her heart. "Is this what you meant?"

Marian seemed barely able to speak as she stared at the flames. "This is only the whisper of war," she answered, "the merest murmur of the great shout to come."

13

CHAN LOOKED UP FROM THE *BOOK OF STORMFIRE* and rubbed his eyes with the back of a paw. He'd been reading for hours by the light of a pair of lanterns. That was enough to strain even a dragon's eyesight. He sighed as he marked his page with a ribbon and leaned back.

Ramoses' desk was piled high around Chan. The old, blue dragon had been kind enough to turn his cave over to Chan for the afternoon while Chan read and studied. Ramoses assisted when he could, pulling down cross-referenced volumes, answering questions. Officially, Ramoses had composed six volumes of the *Book of Stormfire*, but for each volume he'd assembled companion volumes containing copious notes, comments, observations, corrections, maps, drawings, and more.

Chan rubbed his eyes again and leaned away from the desk as a dragon's dark silhouette appeared at the mouth of the cave. "Thank you, Ramoses," he said, his voice soft and weary. "In the space of these few hours I've learned more about my father than I ever knew."

"And I, about all the Dragonkin," the newcomer answered. "But I'm not Ramoses, my Brother."

Chan really had been reading much too long by poor lighting. He squinted, forcing his eyes to focus until the form matched the voice. It hadn't been a silhouette in the cave entrance at all, but black-scaled Harrow. His brother paused before the desk and shook his head over the stacks of books. Then he picked up a volume, cracked it open at random, and ran a claw lightly along a page.

"Ramoses said you were here all day yesterday and late into the night," Chan commented, watching his brother curiously. Harrow had only rarely emerged from his cave in the days since their father's funeral and only then to fly off alone into the forest without a word to anyone. When his brother didn't respond, he tried again. "What are you reading?"

"A poem," Harrow answered in a sullen whisper. He passed the book over to Chan and turned away from the desk toward the shelves of other books. "I always thought of Ramoses as our poet."

The page blurred before Chan's eyes until he blinked and rubbed them yet again. He bent closer to the desk to let the light from the two lanterns fall more fully upon the ink markings, and read the clear, artful handwriting of Ramoses:

> *There will come years of fear*
> *When I long for your nourishment,*
> *For your sustenance,*
> *When the world weeps falling leaves*
> *For time that passes by,*
> *But you hold me, embolden me,*
> *Show me beauty in the deep autumn colors,*
> *Myself in the frosty shimmer,*
> *Youth and time resolve into mystery,*
> *And I know peace.*

Chan closed the book and gently put it back on top of the stack. He rubbed his eyes yet again, but this time it had nothing to do with the light or with eyestrain. Harrow's back was still turned to him as he pretended to study the shelves, and the lamplight glittered on the scales of his muscled back, on the smoothly black leather of his wings. "You're taking this harder than I expected," he said.

"How are we supposed to know if Father really wrote any of that?" Harrow snapped without turning around. "Maybe Ramoses made it all up."

Chan shook his head as he leaned forward. "Ramoses wouldn't do that."

Harrow spun around and accidentally brushed a stack of books from the desk with a wingtip. The books fell, pages fluttering, and Chan made a grab to save them, but in his haste he only knocked over another stack, and that cascaded into a third stack. Books scattered everywhere. For a moment, both brothers just stared. Then Chan bent down and started to gather them again.

"I know it's Father," Chan said with soft conviction. "You know it, too. You can hear his voice in every word you read."

"Why didn't he share any of this with us?" Harrow bent down to help his brother, and together they rebuilt the piles on the desk. "He never recited poetry, never told us any of these stories, nor talked much about all this history. Not in this kind of detail!"

"Maybe he tried," Chan answered. "Maybe we just weren't ready to listen." He set the last book back on the desk, but his claw lingered on the leather cover that was made of his father's own golden skin. His eyes burned, and finally he could no longer stop the tears he'd been holding back. "I'm a fool," he murmured, looking to Harrow. "I said I heard his voice in every word." He picked up the book and held it out. "It's because he's telling us now, Brother. He's telling us now! All the poetry and stories and history are recorded here. These books are for us. He's talking to us through them!"

"And I'm supposed to listen now because he'd dead?" Harrow glared as he seized the book from his brother and slammed it back on the desk with the others. "I don't want a book, Chan! I want my father back!"

The flapping of wings interrupted them, and the Dragon Diana appeared in the cave entrance. Her cobalt scales shimmered as she stood framed by the sunlight. She hesitated as she looked from one brother to the next. "My father sent me," she said with some embarrassment. "He hopes you'll speak with him on the shore below. He says it's important." She leaped back into the air again, spread her wings, and left them alone.

"With Ramoses, it's always important," Harrow said bitterly. "She's her father's daughter."

"Just as you're Stormfire's son," Chan answered. "You have his temper, you know."

Harrow shot him a look. "Father never had a temper."

Chan smiled faintly and looked down at the book he'd been reading. He fingered the ribbon he'd marked his place with. He'd only set the book aside because Harrow seemed to need company. He didn't really want to stop reading yet. Some of the things he'd learned in the last few hours troubled him. "Have you wondered why Mother can't fly," he asked suddenly. "Everybody says it was an *illness*, but they never say what?"

"She's old," Harrow answered with a note of annoyance.

"No older than Stormfire," Chan countered. "Or Ramoses." He held up the book he'd been reading. "It was us, Brother. These writings don't say so exactly, but I can put two and two together. So can you. You read these same words yesterday."

Harrow waved a claw dismissively. "You've got fire on the brain!"

"It was us!" Chan insisted. "You, me, and Luna. No dragon-wife had ever produced triplet eggs before, Harrow. Never! There had been twins, but never triplets. It wasn't supposed to be possible. But Sabu did!"

Harrow's wings snapped wide. The leathery, ridged edges struck the ceiling forcefully, knocked stone from one of the walls, spilled books from one of the shelves. His presence seemed to expand until he blocked all light from the cave's entrance, and his eyes turned baleful. "What are you saying, Chan?" he shouted. "It's not enough that we allowed Gaunt to sneak in here and murder our father—but we're to blame for what's wrong with Mother, too?"

Chan stared at his brother as his own anger grew. "What did you really do in here all day yesterday?" he demanded sarcastically. "Sit in the dark and feel sorry for yourself? That's how you spent the past days and nights in your own cave, wasn't it? I thought you were reading Father's books!"

"Ramoses' books!" Harrow raged, sweeping the volumes from the desk again. Pages fluttered as they scattered across the floor. One of the lanterns toppled, oil splashed, and a blue flame sprang up on the edge of a book cover. "He wrote them! They're not my father's books!"

Chan put the flame out with his foot before it could grow and do any real damage. There was no extinguishing the fire in his eyes, though. He snapped his own wings forward, striking Harrow in the chest and pushing him backward. "If you damage one more book or knock one more from its shelf," he said, his voice low and full of menace, "I'll hurl your sorry tail into the river below." Leaning across the desk and steadying the remaining lantern, he stretched his neck until he was nose to nose with his brother. "And if you ever cause another fire in here, I swear I'll make you regret it."

"Is this what it's come to?"

Startled, Chan looked up as Luna screamed at them from the entrance. He hadn't noticed her arrival, nor he was sure, had Harrow. Her eyes brimmed with tears, and she trembled as she glared at them.

"All we've lost isn't enough?" she continued. "You have to shatter the bond between us by fighting and threatening to kill each other? I'm ashamed of you! The last coals haven't burned out yet on the funeral pyre, and this is how you honor Stormfire's memory?" She beat her wings in a display of anger and agitation. "Everyone in Stronghold is scared to death that Gaunt will come back. They're looking to us for leadership! What if they saw you now?" She sprang back into the air and wheeled away. As she departed, she called out again, "I can't believe I ever looked up to either of you!"

Harrow turned to Chan. His anger melted into a look of amusement. "She's always been a little high-strung, hasn't she?"

Chan sighed. He'd anticipated a quiet afternoon of reading and some time alone with his thoughts. "Ramoses should install a revolving door on this place," he said, feeling foolish.

"Any door at all would be an improvement," Harrow agreed with a lopsided grin. "It's a sorry state of affairs when two brothers can't have an argument without the rest of the family jumping into the middle of it." With his wings tightly folded, he eased past Chan and began picking up the books on the floor and stacking them on the desk again. "I'm sorry about the lantern," he added. "It was an accident."

Chan nodded as he bent to help his brother.

"You were right," Harrow said in a quieter voice as he held up one of the books and let his gaze linger on it. "I tried to read a few of these, but mostly I just sat here and felt sorry for myself. I wasn't thinking of you, or Luna, or Sabu, or any of the villagers." He placed the book with the others and began to gather the pieces of the broken lantern. "I feel like there's a huge void inside me where Stormfire used to be, and the only thing filling that void is a growing rage!"

Chan's throat went dry. He knew he should say something, but he couldn't think of the right words. He felt the same blind anger and trembled as black waves of it swept over him especially when he tried to sleep, and the dreams he dreamed were terrible. But he knew if he gave into it, that anger would change him, reshape and mold him into something he didn't want to be—something he feared.

"At night," he confessed in a whisper, "just before I fall asleep, I taste Gaunt's blood in my mouth."

Harrow placed the pieces of the lantern carefully on the desk. With no more to do, he slipped toward the mouth of the cave. Chan, still with a load of books between his front paws, watched his brother linger at the rim and look slowly back over his shoulder. The expression on Harrow's face sent a chill up his spine.

"That's good to know," he said, and spreading his black wings, he flew away.

Alone, Chan neatly arranged and rearranged the stacks of books again. He left the pieces of the broken lantern where Harrow had placed them. Ramoses would certainly re-use the wick and various other bits, and there was still a small quantity of oil that hadn't splashed out of the reservoir.

He placed one book particularly in the center of the desk away from the others so that it would lie in plain sight. The old blue dragon would not be happy about the scorch marks on one of his volumes, but Chan made up his mind to take the blame for the damage. He placed a paw on the cover, thankful that it hadn't been worse, and that he had moved quickly enough to save it. Then, recognizing the book, he opened it once more and found the poem he had just read.

There will come years of fear.

How could Harrow not understand? Stormfire's voice spoke loud and clear from every word on the page! When he read them, it was as if his father were in the room right beside him. They were bound in his skin. They *felt* like his father; they had his texture. When he raised the volume to his nostrils, through the odor of scorched paper and spilled oil there came another, dearer and more intense. They smelled like his father!

Reluctantly and with loving gentleness, he set the book down, but still his paw lingered upon it, and he squeezed his eyes shut. Suddenly, the cave seemed filled with echoes of Stormfire's voice, fragments of words and moments of laughter, all reverberating from the walls, the floor and the ceiling.

And then, silence.

Chan opened his eyes and brushed back a tear as he looked around at the shelves. Not all the books were Stormfire's, nor even about Stormfire. But this library was a shrine to his father as surely as Stormfire's Point was a shrine. Here was his father's wisdom, his memories, and his essence.

Here was Stormfire's ghost.

Through the years he knew he would come here often. He was just as certain that Harrow would not. All Harrow felt was the loss. All he heard was the anger rushing to fill him up. He hated Gaunt, and he hated the world for taking away their father. But more than anyone or anything else, Harrow hated himself for letting it happen.

Chan walked to the mouth of the cave and stared outward, unable to believe the day was so bright when he felt mired in so much darkness. But the sun was high in a cloudless, blue sky, and the Echo Rush below sparkled between the canyon walls.

On the beach, he spied Ramoses and his daughter, Diana, and Luna with them. He remembered Diana's invitation. Ramoses wanted to talk. But a burst of laughter and loud applause from the village above caught his attention. Curious, he leaped away from the cave mouth and flew upward to the clifftop.

The villagers had worked hard the past several days to clear away the debris and destruction from the unexpected attack and to repair their homes. Gaunt and his griffins had flattened half the buildings in Stronghold. The surviving structures had been converted to shelters for families while workmen salvaged lumber and nails and began the rebuilding process. Some of the surviving shops had been transformed into kitchens where teams of satyr-wives and fox-wives labored to keep everyone fed. A spirit of cooperation and shared tragedy had brought the villagers closer together than they had ever been before.

So it both surprised and gladdened Chan to hear another outburst of laughter as he rose over the canyon rim. The work had come to a halt. Workers and children were all gathered in the square outside Sabu's damaged longhouse. Sabu, herself, and Morkir at her side were among them. Chan circled high to get a view, wondering what event had drawn them all together in the middle of the afternoon.

At the very center of the square stood the man-child called Jake. He was shirtless, and his skin glistened with sweat under the hot sun. With a sudden burst of energy, he ran half the length of the square, and then cartwheeled and threw himself into an astonishing series of back-flips. The crowd gasped and fell back to give him room, but he stopped well within the circle and flung out his arms with a smile, and the villagers responded with wild applause.

But the show was far from over. Trevor and Markham, the twins, appeared at the east end of the square. Side by side, every step perfectly synchronized, they ran forward, then launched into a complex pattern of handsprings, twists and back-flips, ending on their knees right before Jake and flinging out their arms to accept their applause.

Next, Ariel made her flamboyant entrance with an explosive series of twisting back-flips. Someone had given or loaned her a pair of brown trousers and a white blouse that she had tied up under her small breasts, and she'd braided her hair back tightly and wound colorful ribbons into it. With seemingly effortless grace, she bounded across the square. Closer and closer to the boys she drew, without slowing, her momentum building. Someone in the crowd cried a warning. A general gasp went up.

Ariel proved to be well named. Just as it seemed she would run into Trevor and Markham, who were still on their knees, she sprang over them in a breath-taking, high double back flip, landing on Jake's broad shoulders. He caught her ankles to anchor her as she flung out her arms.

Enthusiastic applause rose up from the crowd.

Then Trevor, Markham, and Ariel put fingers to their lips, asking for silence, and though it took a moment for their audience to understand, an expectant hush fell over the square. Chan wheeled about for a better view, wishing he could land, but not wanting to cause a distraction at a critical moment. Even from the air he found the performance enthralling.

Pear, the youngest of the man-children, stepped into the square. She looked very dignified and serious as she struck a pose. She'd found small red trousers and a white blouse like Ariel's, but she'd bound her bright blond hair back with matching red ribbons and also tied ribbons around her arms. Drawing a deep breath, she ran forward. Incredibly swift and lithe, she cartwheeled and back-flipped, gaining speed with every movement. At the far end of the square, Trevor and Markham joined hands. "Here!" they shouted together.

Twice more, little Pear back-flipped. On the last flip, her feet landed perfectly on the twins' joined hands. With practiced ease, they tossed her high. Executing one more flip, she landed on Ariel's shoulders. Flashing a dazzling smile, she flung out her arms.

The crowd screamed with delight, and their applause became thunderous. Pear jumped down into the arms of Trevor and Markham.

Ariel jumped down to be caught by Jake. Forming a line, the three boys tumbled back to the east end of the square, performing the same precise routine side by side. Ariel followed them with a graceful series of front walkovers. Pear skipped after Ariel, but at the middle of the square, broke into a run. Ariel spun about with cupped hands and caught Pear's foot as the little girl leaped. Pear flipped through the air, landing with her hands on her hips and ran at Ariel again. Again, Ariel flipped her back, and Pear landed with a frustrated look. Again she ran at Ariel.

This time, as Ariel prepared to repel Pear, Trevor and Markham caught her arms and pulled her away. With choreographed precision, Jake took her place, and when Pear leaped he caught her, wrapping her in one arm, shaking a finger under her nose as he carried her off.

The bit of comedy provoked peals of laughter from the villagers. For a moment, the children dashed into Sabu's longhouse, but Ariel quickly emerged again. In one hand she carried a baton about as long as her arm to which she had affixed a long ribbon. She waved it about her head and around her body, creating intricate shapes and patterns as she paraded around the edges of the gathering.

Chan took the opportunity to land beside the longhouse. Some of the crowd turned to call greetings, but most eyes remained on Ariel. Moving toward the center of the square, she suddenly tossed the baton and streamer high into the air. The moment it left her hand, he performed a graceful forward walkover, straightening just in time to catch the baton again and sweep the ribbon around her head. She smiled as the crowd applauded.

Again, she threw the baton, this time in a wide, high arc toward the other end of the square. As it flew, she cartwheeled and back-flipped after it. At the end of her last flip, she straightened, extending her hand immediately, expecting to catch the descending baton. But the crowd exploded with laughter, and Ariel stared gape-mouthed as her baton went sailing away toward the canyon in the talons of an eagle.

"That'll really anger Ariel," said a voice near Chan's foot. "She can't stand being upstaged."

He looked down to see Jake beside him. The man-child idly twirled a wooden staff as he watched the eagle fly away. "He'll bring it back," Chan assured him. "Skymarin is kind of an oddity around here. Eagles aren't known for their senses of humor."

Even as he spoke, the eagle wheeled about and dropped the baton. Ariel's hand shot out and caught it, and she smiled and bowed as if it had all been a planned part of her act. She tumbled back toward the longhouse, performing all her flips and walkovers on one hand as she swept the streamer about with the other. Her routine complete, she turned once again to accept her applause. Then she skulked inside, fuming.

"How about a hand-up?" Jake said to Chan. "The audience will love it."

Chan shrugged. "What do you want me to do?"

"Just scoop me up and toss me over their heads," Jake answered, giving the dragon a wink. "Not too high or too far, mind you. You're not a professional."

Chan grinned. He liked these man-children, and he particularly liked Jake. He hadn't forgotten how the boy had risked his life and wounded Gaunt, nor how he had stepped forward to offer his help after the attack. Bending low, he extended his paw.

"Break a leg," Jake said as he stepped up and grasped his staff in both hands.

"I'd rather you didn't," Chan answered. He rose carefully, afraid of injuring the man-child. He didn't have to toss him. Jake sprang off his palm, leaping forward, and flipping over his staff. He hit the ground, rolled once to absorb his momentum, and rose again. The staff became a blur as he spun it over his head, through his legs, on either side of his body. Right-handed or left-handed, on one foot or two, sometimes executing the most intricate flips over it and around it, Jake controlled the staff as if it were part of him.

Suddenly, he threw the staff high. Trevor and Markham ran out of the crowd and leaped, each catching one end of the staff as it came down, and flipping over it before they landed. Amid applause, Jake left the square and came back to Chan.

"Thanks," he said as he wiped his face with the back of an arm. "I couldn't have gotten enough height on my own to go over all their heads."

"Your skills are very impressive," Chan said, leaning down so that he and Jake were face to face.

Jake's smile turned shy. He wiped his face again. "Everyone was working so hard, and they're still so upset about your father," he said softly. "I figured a little entertainment might be in order."

Chan tilted his head as he studied the man-child with renewed interest. "Perceptive and a natural leader, too," he commented. "And yet we found you fleeing an Angmar ship in chains. What did you do before you came to Wyvernwood, young Jake?"

"We were carnival acrobats," he answered proudly. "The best in Degarm. We traveled all over the country. We even performed for the king!" His voice broke off, and for a moment he looked down at his feet. When he looked up again, there was a flash of controlled anger in his eyes. "That's where Angmar's ambassador saw us. He tried to buy us from the carnival, but our owner wouldn't sell, so a few days later, he kidnapped us."

Chan felt a moment of shock, but not at the kidnapping. "Your owner?"

Jake shrugged and looked at his feet again. "Sure," he answered. "We're all orphans. Old Micah—he's our owner—took us all in and trained us. He fed us well, too, and treated us okay. At least, as long as we performed well and drew in the crowds." He hesitated before continuing. "It could get bad sometimes if we didn't, particularly for Ariel and Pear." His voice dropped almost to a whisper. "I guess that's why we're in no hurry to go home. We like it here."

Chan glanced past the heads of the villagers. In the center of the square, Trevor and Markham were putting on quite an exhibition. Pulling Bear Byron, Gregor, and Carola from the audience, they each made a short run and somersaulted over the three. Then Trevor pulled a fourth from the crowd, a satyr named Spike, and they somersaulted over all four. Next, Markham beckoned to Morkir. The griffin gave a surly growl.

"Go on!" Sabu urged, giving the bandaged griffin a nudge. "You'll heal faster if you learn to play nice with others!"

The crowd laughed. Then, to Chan's surprise, the griffin walked into the square and joined the line.

"You'll have to crouch down a little," Markham said, giving the griffin a pat. "We're going for distance here, not height."

"I don't want to intimidate you," Morkir answered with a deep-throated snarl, "but if you land on me, I'll eat you."

Markham gave a big smile. "I don't want to intimidate you, either," he answered loud enough for everyone to hear. "But my record at this is four people. You're number five."

Trevor waved his hand enthusiastically, his face beaming. "Mine's five!" he called. Then he bit the tip of a finger and put on a nervous look. "Of course, I only made five once."

The audience laughed in response as Morkir crouched very low, and the boys took their places.

Chan bent down to eye-level with Jake again. "You've lightened everyone's spirits," he said quietly. "You've made them laugh when they didn't have much to laugh about. Now I want to know—is there something I can do for you?"

Jake looked thoughtful. Then he bit his lip and his face lit up. "I'm on next. Watch this! I'll be right back!"

The man-child pushed through the crowd to the edge of the square, and Chan stood up again. Out in the center, Bear Byron, Gregor, Carola with her eyes squeezed shut, Spike, and Morkir all stood shoulder-to-shoulder. Trevor gave a loud yell and ran at them. Then, it was Bear Byron's turn to yell, but Trevor sailed through the air, somersaulted over all five, and landed right beside Morkir.

The crowd squealed and applauded, then immediately fell silent as Trevor fell into place shoulder-to-shoulder with Morkir.

"What are you doing?" the griffin demanded.

Markham was already running at them, wide-eyed and screaming at the top of his lungs. Bear Byron covered his head with his hairy paws. Carola opened her eyes and squeezed them tight again. "Look out!" Trevor cried. "He'll never make it!"

Markham jumped, somersaulted, and landed neatly beside his twin. "It's a new record!" he shouted. He shoved close against Trevor.

Jake was already making his run. With phenomenal speed, he approached the line of seven. The audience gave a collective gasp. Trevor and Markham had somersaulted, and they expected the same from Jake. But at the last moment, he cartwheeled, twisted, and back-flipped through the air, sailing high above the heads of all seven. Rolling as he hit the ground, he sprang up, back-flipped again, and finished with one more back-flip without touching the ground.

A chorus of cheers went up from the villagers. Sabu banged her front paws together, leading the applause. Chan grinned from one dragon-ear to the other, then broke out into belly-shaking laughter as he glanced toward the rim of the canyon where Ramoses, Diana, and Luna stood at a safe distance beating their wings and thumping the ground with their tails. The noise from the village had reached them down on the shore of the Echo Rush.

Or they'd come to see what was keeping him.

Chan sighed. Ramoses would have to wait. Right now, his interest lay with a slave boy who'd dared to strike his father's murderer and who'd brought joy to all the residents of Stronghold at a time when they needed it most. He watched with a surprising sense of pride as Fomorians, minotaurs, satyrs, bears and foxes, all surged around the three boys to clap their backs and shake their hands. Ariel and Pear emerged from the longhouse also to be swept up by the crowd. Bear Byron lifted Pear onto his shoulder as she squealed and giggled and waved her small hands.

Sabu moved closer to Chan. "What is that strange light in your eyes, my son?" she asked, touching her paw to his.

Chan looked at his mother, then looked at the man-children and the villagers thronging around them. "I don't know," he answered. He wanted to laugh and cry at the same time, and he was also finding it hard to breathe. "Something amazing just happened here, Mother. I don't understand it—but I can feel it!"

Sabu stretched out her neck and planted a soft kiss on his cheek. Startled, he turned and looked at her again. She hadn't done that in years!

"You just found out you can still laugh," she whispered, "when you didn't think you ever would again. A little bit of grief just melted away for all of us."

He felt her paw against his. A kiss. A touch. When had he last experienced these? It was the nature of dragons that, as soon as they were old enough, they found their own caves or made them. Caverns large enough to hold entire dragon families were rare. So while rabbits and foxes and squirrels shared burrows, and minotaurs and satyrs built homes of wood or stone, that was not the way of dragons. "I've missed you," he told his mother.

"I've always been here," she answered with a smile.

The crowd began to disperse. Some began to sing as they returned to the work of rebuilding Stronghold. A group of children ran into the square and threw themselves upon the ground in awkward attempts at somersaults and cartwheels.

Jake, with Morkir beside him, approached Chan. Morkir went to his now-familiar place at Sabu's side while Jake looked nervous and drew a line in the dust with his toe. Chan bent down so that they were eye to eye once more.

"Just ask," he urged.

Jake swallowed and finally looked up. "What I just did," he said. "We call it flying. But it's not really flying. When Luna rescued Ariel and Trevor from the sea, she picked them up and carried them." He looked suddenly embarrassed and looked away. Then he found his courage again. "Would you carry me that way? Really high? I want to see the world from up there the way you do!"

Chan straightened and looked down at Jake. He rubbed his chin as he considered what the man-child had asked. Jake was fearless and agile with incredible strength and a superb sense of balance. "No, I won't carry you," he said firmly, leaning down to face the boy again. "Not the way Luna carried Ariel and Trevor." He closed one eye and blinked the other. "Let's see how brave you are. Go ask Bear Byron for a rope."

Jake tilted his head and frowned, not understanding. Then, his jaw dropped. He spun around and ran to find the Bear. Grinning, Chan watched him go.

"You can't be considering what I think you're considering," Morkir grumbled.

"You don't know me well enough to read my mind," Chan answered.

Sabu touched his hand again. "No dragon has ever allowed such a thing," she reminded him.

"Why not?" Chan interrupted, brooking no argument even from his mother. "What's the harm? Certainly my dignity and the dignity of the Dragonkin can survive it. And I won't let anything happen to him."

Jake returned with Bear Byron, who carried a large coil of rope over one shoulder. "Our young star here says ye be wantin' me rope. There's a lot o' work that needs to be done with it, but if it's important, I'm happy to lend it."

"I think it's important," Chan answered, leaning down again. "Byron, would you toss it over my neck, please, and tie it close to my wings. Make it tight." He looked from Bear Byron to Jake. "Then wrap several lengths around his waist and leave him the some extra to hold onto."

"Ye mean, like reins?" Bear Byron looked appalled at the idea. He closed his grip around his rope and took a step back. "You're goin' to let him ride ye?"

"I just saw you carrying little Pear on your shoulders," Chan said reasonably. "Are you any less a bear for that?"

Bear Byron stopped and put a paw thoughtfully to his lips. Reluctantly, he unshouldered the coil of rope. "Last time I took a look at m'self," he said uncertainly, "I wasn't exactly one o' the noblest, most majestic creatures in the world, an' nobody never ever named an age after me, an' I'm pretty sure I wasn't one o' the great Stormfire's children." He looked from Sabu to Chan, then glanced at the dragons on the canyon rim that were watching from a distance, their faces curious. "But if it's what ye want!"

The coils of rope sailed through the air and over Chan's neck. He bent still lower so Bear Byron could reach up and tie the necessary knots.

"Now help him up," Chan told the bear.

Morkir snarled. "Throw a couple of saddlebags on him, while you're at it."

Chan smiled faintly. "Don't make me break your other wing," he said in a sweet voice. "Mother doesn't like it when I abuse her houseguests." He sighed and gave a shrug, adding, "Or her lapdogs."

Sabu put on a smile of her own as, unseen, she smacked Chan's rump with her tail.

With an assist from Bear Byron, Jake straddled Chan's neck and settled himself as comfortably as he could. With the bear directing, he wrapped the extra rope several times about his waist and tied neat half hitches. Bear Byron looped the extra rope once more around Chan's neck and passed the ends up to Jake.

"Take care not to choke him," Morkir instructed, his voice less than sincere.

Chan didn't bother to respond. He'd traded enough barbs with the griffin. Besides, he actually felt sorry for Morkir. His entire world had been turned upside down. After years of hating dragons, it was Harrow who had saved him and Sabu who had tended his wounds, and it was the citizenry of Stronghold that had taken him in. Conversely, it was a griffin—and his own brother, at that—who had murdered his father and tried to kill him.

Indeed, Chan saw much in Morkir to sympathize with. They had both lost a great deal.

"Hold tight," he told Jake. "If you get scared or don't like it, say so. There's no way you can fall."

Jake only nodded, though Chan felt his grip on the rope tighten and his knees squeeze against his neck. Chan turned slowly, carefully and walked toward the canyon rim. He could have just sprung into the air, but he didn't want to startle Jake with, what for him, would be a sudden, rough motion.

Luna shook her head in disapproval as he reached the rim. "If you could see how silly you look!"

Chan didn't care, nor did he take much note as the villagers began to gather around again to watch a man-child ride a dragon. Trevor and Markham, Ariel and Pear broke through the growing crowd.

"Me next!" Pear cried. Ariel clapped a hand over the little girl's mouth and held her back.

Chan posed on the edge of the canyon. The afternoon view was spectacular. It seemed almost new and fresh again, as if he were seeing it for the first time. It excited him, and his heart beat faster! Perhaps inspired by the children's grace, he spread his wings slowly, feeling the currents of air play upon them. "Hold tight," he said again. Arching his back, he leaned forward, farther and farther, slowly, until he fell into space.

Jake screamed once, but the fall didn't last long. Chan swooped upward, rising above the canyon again, wheeling over the village. The world seemed to turn beneath, and the villagers waved and cheered.

The next sound from Jake was a long, joyful laugh. Chan turned out over the canyon again and followed the sparkling water of the Echo Rush. The canyon walls loomed on either side of them as he dipped low and sent up a spray of water with the tip of his tail. Then he began to climb, higher and higher. Wyvernwood spread out below them, green and lush and wild. Still higher he climbed, turning south-ward away from the canyon and Stronghold.

As the land rushed past beneath them, he looked back over his shoulder. Jake wore a sublime expression as he leaned forward into the wind. His dark hair whipped straight back, and his trousers' legs fluttered, but he showed no fear at all.

Then, taking the ends of the rope in one hand, Jake stretched out his arm and pointed.

They were no longer alone in the sky. From the southeast, another dragon raced toward them at a desperate speed. A moment more, and the sunlight shimmered on emerald scales. Chan turned on a course to meet the newcomer, increasing his own speed.

"Chan!" the emerald dragon called as they intercepted each other. He wheeled about and beat his wings to hover. Chan also turned, and they resumed flight side by side back toward Stronghold.

"Fleer!" Chan called in greeting "Where have you been?"

Fleer stared at Jake, but if the sight of a man-child riding Chan's back surprised him, he hid it well. "I went searching for my brother," he answered. "I grew worried when Ronaldo didn't show up for Storm-fire's funeral."

There was more than a note of worry in Fleer's voice, and he looked tired. "Did you find him?" Chan shouted over the wind.

The emerald dragon shook his head. "No," he answered. "But I learned terrible things, Chan! Angmar burned one of Degarm's cities!"

Jake shifted suddenly on Chan's back. "Which one?" he called.

Fleer ignored the boy. "But worse! For some reason, they blame the Dragonkin! Their army has already crossed the river and entered Wyvernwood!"

14

WHEN MORNING DAWNED, Marian stared toward the thin veils of smoke that still rose from distant Karlass. Her head swirled with confusion and uncertainty. In Ronaldo's secure grip she'd seen the fires from the air as they'd escaped the city and the people running through the streets. She'd never forget the sight of the docks and the waterfront in flames, nor the burning ships tossing wildly on their anchor chains like panicked animals desperate to break free.

With Bumble clinging to her mane, Ronaldo had carried her away from the fires and turmoil, past the surrounding villages and farms, following the jagged cliffs of the coastline. With the bright moon behind them, they chased their shadows. The only sounds were the rush of the wind and the steady beat of leathery wings.

Only when the moonlight revealed a small forest did Ronaldo finally settle to the ground. Without a word, he crept away among the trees, leaving Marian and Bumble watching the orange glow that lit the northern horizon. Marian called after him once, but there was something in the way he hung his head and dragged his tail as he disappeared into the gloom that caused her to fall silent.

When he was out of sight, she turned back toward the glow of burning Karlass. The firelight pulsed and flickered, reflecting on the roiling clouds of smoke with an effect that was almost as beautiful as it was terrible. For a moment it seemed that she could smell the smoke despite the distance, but with a half-hearted smile she realized that what she detected were the fumes clinging to her hide and mane.

All through the night she had stood alone watching the glow. She didn't remember when Bumble had left her, but the forest wasn't large, and she was sure he was safe. She thought of the citizens of Karlass, especially the dancers and the musicians, and wondered if they were also safe. Some of them had been kind to her, and the ones that had tried to rope her, she forgave, knowing they were driven by fear.

As the sun began to rise over the Windy Sea, Marian finally turned her back to the drifting smoke. The damp ground felt spongy beneath her hooves as she walked into the forest, and the sweet smells of moss and pine filled her nostrils. Shafts of morning light filtered down through the thick branches, spotlighting patches of flowers, rain-washed stones, a nervous squirrel perched on an old log, and the trees were alive with birds all singing to greet the sunrise.

It wasn't Wyvernwood, but it wasn't a bad little forest.

She followed a trail of broken branches and crushed shrubbery. Ronaldo's scent lingered on the grass and leaves, and his footprints became more visible as the morning brightened. When she came to a stream, deep marks on the muddy banks indicated his passage. With her front hooves in the water, she paused to drink.

The soft hum of Bumble's wings alerted her, but before she could look up, he landed on her horn.

"Ronaldo makes rain with his eyes," he said in a worried voice. "I followed him, Marian, but he won't talk to Bumble! Are we not friends anymore?"

Marian blinked her blue eyes at the little hummingbird. "Of course we're all still friends," she assured him. "Ronaldo saw something in Karlass that he's not ready to talk about. He just needs a little time."

"No!" Bumble shook his head and fluttered his wings. "He needs a little paint!"

Marian waded further into the stream to wash the mud from her hooves and to look for a more grassy patch of land to step out upon. "What are you talking about?" she said as Bumble buzzed around her head. "What would he do with paint now?"

"How should I know?" Settling on a low branch, Bumble shrugged his wings. "But he's gathered piles of red berries and blue berries and loads of clay and charcoal and other stuff. He crushes it and mixes it with his tears! Now, I'm only a small-brained hummingbird, but even I know that falls under the category of plain weird behavior!" He leaned forward so far on his branch that it seemed he would fall off, but his tiny feet kept a firm grip as he whispered, "Do you suppose he's been in the lousewort?"

Marian gave a gentle laugh at the suggestion. Then she sniffed the air. Indeed, there was a patch of the flower close by. "No, Bumblebird, and you'd better not get into it, either." She felt a small pinch on her left ankle and looked down to see a fat gray crawfish clinging to her fetlock.

"Do you mind?" she said.

The crawfish turned its round black eyes up to look at her and responded with a burst of bubbles.

"How rude!" Marian kicked her left leg high, sending the offensive crawfish tumbling far up on the bank. With a disdainful toss of her mane, she stepped out of the stream onto soft grass. "Lead the way, Bumble," she said, "before I forget I'm a lady!"

"Way? Which way?" Bumble looked from left to right and back to Marian. "Where are we going? And just what is a *road*, anyway?"

A creepy sensation passed through Marian, and she stopped in midstep. "Bumble, where did you hear that word?"

"On the far edge of the forest," he answered, pointing to the west with one wingtip. "That way. I think. Men in colorful wagons were talking in loud voices. They mentioned *the road from Karlass to Jiwashek*. It sounded important. I've been repeating it over and over so I wouldn't forget."

The far edge of the forest wasn't really that far, and with Bumble's speed, he could have traversed the entire woodland several times. Undoubtedly, his unending quest for flowers and food had already taken him to places neither she, nor Ronaldo, had yet seen. As she thought about that, she shook her legs to dry them, and lashed her tail back and forth as well, for it had gotten wet in the stream, too. Ronaldo seemed to want some time alone, and she was possessed with a sudden curiosity.

"Bumble," she said slowly, "show me where you saw these wagons."

The hummingbird darted to the tip of her horn, encircled her head, and perched on another limb. "Oh certainly!" he exclaimed. "Why don't you ask something easy, like where the lousewort or the coral flowers are, or which is better, honeysuckle or fuchsia?" Frowning, rubbing his chin with one foot, he looked around. Then, he licked the tip of one wing and held it up to the wind. "By the pricking of my thumbs!" he cried as he flew away.

Marian scowled. "You don't have thumbs, you Bumble-bird!"

She started after him at a gallop, weaving around tree trunks, ducking low branches, charging through brambles and bushes. Rabbits dodged out of her way. Squirrels scampered into the trees and chattered angrily at her. Crouched on a large rock, a hungry bobcat watched her go by and decided to wait for easier prey.

Bumble was no more than a green blur that sometimes disappeared against the leaves. With so many obstacles and so much natural camouflage, Marian found it difficult to keep up with him, and she wondered if he'd forgotten she was following. Then abruptly he appeared on a branch directly in front of her and made a trumpeting sound with his beak. "They're coming down the home stretch! It's Bumble by a head!" he cried triumphantly. "Bumble wins! And the unicorn barely stumbles across the finish line!"

Marian glowered up at him. "Have you ever heard of hummingbird pie?" she asked. "The recipe will fascinate you."

Bumble gulped and gazed back at her with a horrified look. "Right through there," he said, pointing toward a gap in the trees. "That's where Bumble saw the wagons. Six of them, all painted so bright they made my eyes ache and my head dizzy, and pulled by the stupidest looking bunch of oxen you can imagine. Don't bake me, please!"

Marian chuckled softly as she stepped between the trees and stuck her nose over a wild hedge that marked the forest's boundary. She realized immediately what had drawn Bumble to this spot. The hedge, which was nearly as tall as her shoulders, was mostly a tangled crop of wooley blue-curls. The rich perfume from the blue and purple blossoms almost made her faint as she eased her way through them.

For long moments, Marian stared at the road from the edge of the forest, and then cautiously she left the hedge behind and walked the twenty paces until she stood in the middle of it. She looked first to the north where the faintest curtain of smoke still hung in the sky. Then she turned and looked south.

Man's road.

It was only a narrow ribbon of dust and mud, worn down by boots and bare feet, rutted by carts and wagon wheels over the course of who knew how many years. At one end lay Karlass, or the ruins of Karlass. She felt a pang of sadness as she thought about that. At the other end, beyond a distant range of hills, was some strange new place called Jiwashek. She turned the name over in her mind. It had a pleasing sound.

Yet, the road smelled of danger. All roads did, because only man made them. She put her nose close to the earth and sniffed. Then, she sniffed again. The scents were odd, many and mingled.

Bumble hummed through the air and perched on her horn. His beak dripped with the nectar of wooley bluecurls. He paced the length of her horn as she looked up. Then he hopped down to the road. His tiny feet barely left a mark in the dust. He fluttered from one side of the road to the other, landed in the grass, fluttered back to the center of the road, then up onto Marian's horn again.

"Chernovog," he said quietly.

Marian stared at the little hummingbird until her blue eyes crossed. His sense of smell was keen enough to detect and identify a specific flower from a considerable distance. She sniffed the dust again, then sniffed the grass as Bumble had done. "Chernovog's a minotaur," she said doubtfully. "Part boy, but also part bull. Are you sure you're not picking up the scent of those oxen?"

Bumble fluttered down to stand in the middle of the road again, and he faced toward Jiwashek. "Chernovog," he answered stubbornly.

Marian hesitated. Could she trust the little hummingbird to remember Chernovog's scent? Yet again she sniffed the road again and looked at him. He returned her gaze with a firmness and resolve she'd never seen in him. There was no confusion in his eyes, no mirth, not even excitement.

"Chernovog," he said with certainty.

Marian's heart leaped. Maybe she did smell Chernovog after all among all the mingled scents! Bumble believed he did, and how could she doubt him? Rearing up, she tossed her mane and crashed her hooves on the road. Bumble darted into the air and hovered before her.

"You believe me?" he asked.

She laughed as she answered. "I believe *in* you!"

Bumble suddenly looked less sure of himself. "If I'm wrong, I'm pie filling."

Marian softened her voice as she offered her horn to her friend. "You haven't been wrong about anything yet," she said. "You just need to have more faith in yourself. You're Bumble the Mighty. Remember?"

He gave her a puzzled look. "No."

She sighed, torn between the urge to laugh and the urge to scold, and realizing neither was appropriate. As she sometimes had before, she envied Satyrs and Minotaurs and Fomorians for the ability to embrace, to put their arms around each other and express affection, to offer assurance, to show love. All she could do for Bumble was let him ride on her horn.

It seemed so little.

There was no more time to ponder such matters. A vibration in the road interrupted her thoughts and she spun about so quickly that Bumble lost his balance and tumbled away. In an instant, he righted himself and settled once more on her head between her ears, his tiny feet gripping with all his strength.

"To arms! To arms!" Bumble cried. "Men! Madmen!"

The morning sunlight glinted on helmets, shields, and weapons. "Soldiers," Marian corrected. "Not much difference."

She plunged into the woods without pausing to count their numbers, but she feared she was too late. They were many, and she knew they had seen her. The soldiers broke into a run. Spreading out as they reached the forest, they charged into the foliage at different points. From behind a tree, she watched them hack at the brambles and tangles with their swords. One of them saw her.

"There it is! The priest-governors have offered a large reward for it!"

A pair of them came running in her direction. A thicket blocked their course. One leaped it adroitly. The other caught his foot as he jumped; his sword went flying, and he fell flat in the bushes

Bumble laughed in Marian's ear. "Men can't catch us! Men can't catch us!"

"Never underestimate their persistence," Marian warned as she turned and ran deeper into the forest. "Or their perversity." No sooner were the words out of her mouth than another soldier appeared from under a fat old pine tree and ran screaming at her. "She's mine!" he called, brandishing his sword. "She's all mine!"

"He's mine!" Bumble cried, launching himself at her attacker.

The soldier never saw what hit him. One moment he was running full speed at Marian. Then his head snapped back, and he stopped cold in his tracks clutching his right cheek and staring at a tiny streak of blood on his palm. A green blur circled his head. With a cry, the soldier grabbed for his left ear. "Ow!" He slapped at the back of his neck. "Oh!" He waved his hands in front of his eyes. "Wasps!" he shouted. "Hornets!" Spinning about, the soldier slipped on the grass.

"Two down!" Marian shouted, laughing. But not far off, another pair of soldiers was sneaking through the brush with determined looks on their faces. One of them carried a coil of rope. It wasn't really much of a threat in such a dense forest, but the last unicorn found herself caught up in the spirit of the chase. She was having fun! Rearing on her hind legs, she bellowed a challenge and took off again.

Forsaking stealth, the pair ran after her. A third soldier joined them. With a crashing and snapping of twigs and branches, they gave manic pursuit. Marian leaped a tall bramble. The three dived through it, earning scratches and scrapes. Ducking under a pine tree, Marian caught the lowest branch in her jaws and bent it back as she hid behind its ancient trunk. As the three followed, she let the branch go. "Duck!" she yelled. The branch whipped around, sweeping all three off their feet.

"Five down!" Landing on her horn, Bumble thrust out his chest and paraded back and forth. "Go, team, go! Give us a W! Give us an I! Give us an M-P-S!"

Marian rolled her eyes up at the hummingbird. "What in the world is that?"

Shrugging his small shoulders, Bumble stuck his tongue out and blew a rude noise at the soldiers. "I don't know," he answered, "but I overheard it in the city, and it started a lively fight."

An arrow thunked into the pine tree's trunk, barely missing Marian. Startled, she shot a look over her shoulder, spying the archer on a rock out-cropping. Already, he had a second shaft fitted to the string ready to fire, but before he could draw his bow, a sharp growl caused him to drop his arrow and spin around.

Crouching on a higher rock directly above the archer, a bobcat rose to its feet and growled again. The sun flashed on its teeth, and its eyes gleamed as they fastened on its prey. Powerful muscles bunched beneath a golden hide. Sharp talons scratched on stone.

For an instant, the startled archer stood as if frozen. Then, flinging his bow aside, he let out a high-pitched scream and jumped to the ground. His trembling knees failed him. Haplessly, he fell into a thorn patch. Scratched and cut and squealing in panic, he fought to his feet and broke free. With his sleeves and leggings in tatters, he ran back toward the road.

Stretching out on the rock, the bobcat crossed its front paws and rested its chin on them. He wore a definite grin on his face as he winked at Marian. "We haven't seen your kind in these woods in ages, my lady," he said. "Run where you will. We won't let these pesky mice annoy you." Casting his gaze over the forest, he opened his mouth wide and roared again. In answer, three more bobcats appeared on the rock behind him, and a fourth leaped up onto the rock where the archer had stood. Their tails lashed back and forth as they regarded the unicorn, and crossing their paws, they bowed their heads low.

"I'll admit I was rather enjoying the exercise," Marian answered as she bent her right front leg and returned their honor. "I hope you won't hurt them."

The bobcat leader rose to his feet with an amused smile. "If that's your wish, Beautiful One. They really don't make for good eating, anyway. Always too thin and bony, and cracking their armor open can be so hard on the teeth." He eyed Bumble on the tip of her horn and winked again. "Now, on the other hand, a fat hummingbird between two thick slices of bread. . ."

Bumble shrieked. "Pies! Sandwiches! Everyone wants to eat Bumble!" Darting to a high branch, he stared down at Marian with a pouty look.

The bobcats chuckled and exchanged glances. "Too small," one said. "Hardly a mouthful," said another. And still a third, "Never cared for the taste."

Not far away, four soldiers crawled slowly closer on their knees and elbows. They pushed their weapons and shields before them as they made their way, brushing aside limbs, slithering around saplings, easing over and around a fallen tree trunk and an old stump, doing their best to move quietly.

"They really have to be the noisiest creatures ever born," the bobcat leader said with a shake of his head. "I don't think they've seen us, yet. Watch."

"Don't hurt them, please," Marian reminded.

The bobcat leader gestured with one paw. In response, his four comrades pounced through the air, stretching out and arching their backs with feline grace, their tails almost rigidly straight behind them. They hit the ground right in front of the soldiers. Nose to nose with them, they roared with a power that shook the leaves.

Terrified, the soldiers screamed and leaped to their feet. One fell over the stump as he tried to run away. Another stumbled over him. "Demons! Ghosts!" cried one of the four. "These woods are haunted!"

Others scattered through the woods took up the cry. "Demons!" With great commotion, men popped up from under bushes and from behind trees. Stumbling and leaping, often falling, they ran for the safety of the open space beyond the forest's boundary. Strips of clothing hung like flowers on brambles and thickets as they made their desperate escapes. Abandoned weapons littered the ground.

One of the bobcats returned, dragging a round and brightly polished shield. "I thought I'd use it for a feeding dish," he said.

The bobcat leader raised one paw and snapped a pair of claws. Instantly, the others gathered around him. He blinked his green eyes at Marian. "My name is Elvis," he said. "And my pryde is always at your service."

Marian bent her right leg and bowed again as she introduced Bumble and herself. "We're seeking a friend," she explained. "Bumble saw some wagons going by and thinks he detected his scent."

On his overhead perch, Bumble folded his wings and looked stern. "Thinks?"

One of the bobcats leaned closer to Elvis. "The Carnival Fantastica passed by while the sky was still dark very early this morning."

Elvis frowned and snarled deep in his throat. "That's bad news," he said to Marian. "The Carnival Fantastica is owned by a man called Malleus, a sorcerer of great power. If your friend is in his clutches, I fear for him—and I fear for you if you attempt rescue."

Marian laughed. "Surely you know there are no more sorcerers!"

Elvis arched his back and gave a wide, toothy yawn. "Surely you know there are folks who say the same about unicorns." Crossing his paws once more, he bowed. "Beware, Marian." With that, he turned and sprang from his rock, and his pryde followed him. In less than a heartbeat, they vanished into the forest.

A cold chill ran down Marian's spine as she considered Elvis's warning. Was it possible there was still magic in the world? She didn't
believe it. It just couldn't be true! What would a bobcat that had
probably never left these small woods in his entire life know of such
things? Yet, he had spoken with such certainty, and his whiskered face
had looked so grim.

"Bumble," she said with a tremor in her voice, "let's go find
Ronaldo."

Bumble fluttered down and settled on her head. "Bake me, boil me,
stew me, flash-fry me!" he grumbled. "Everyone wants to eat me! But
when does Bumble eat? All this fun has made me hungry!"

"You can dip your beak in something on the way," she told him.
"Now fly, Bumble-bird!" Wings humming, her tiny friend swooped
between the trees. Marian galloped after him as she had done before.
His course led her back to the stream where she had washed her
hooves, but then he swerved in a new direction, leading her across a
sunlit pasture and around a small pond that buzzed with dragonflies
and grasshoppers.

Once across the pasture, the forest closed around them again, thick-
er and darker than before. The branches of trees were covered with
canopies of interlacing vines and moss. Little sunlight penetrated, so
there was less brush and foliage to block her way.

She began to feel strangely alone, as well. Except for Bumble, she
saw no other creature. No birds sang in the trees. No squirrels scampered out of her way. Where were the rabbits she had seen before?
Where were the foxes and deer that would love a place like this? She
grew uneasy and unconsciously slowed her pace. The smell of age per-
meated the very ground. Yet, she told herself, *this forest couldn't be so
old!*

"This way! This way!" Bumble called. "Not far!"

She looked quickly around for some indication that Ronaldo had
passed this way—Dragons traveling on the ground tended to leave
trails—but she saw no sign or track. Trusting Bumble, she set aside
her misgivings and increased her pace again.

As she ran, she began to listen to the rhythm her hooves beat on
the soft earth, and the sound startled her. *Malleus, Malleus,
Malleus!* The name pounded deeper into her brain with every hoof

fall. No matter how she tried to drive it from her mind, it persisted.

Marian tried to remember when she had last tasted fear.

Abruptly, sunlight lanced down through the trees. In those pale beams of illumination the air sparkled. A flurry of movement caused her to look up. Birds with colorful plumage glided from one warm shaft to the next, all headed in the same direction she was going. Off to her left, a brown bear rose up on his rear legs to watch her pass.

"Slowly now," Bumble advised, landing on the tip of her horn again. "Ronaldo's cave is very near."

Marian stopped and looked around. The trees were tall and old, majestic. Where the sun penetrated, patches of purple sweet williams and wild red poppies grew. There was little breeze, yet the air bore a slight salt tang, and she thought that she could hear the soft rush of the Windy Sea nearby.

At Bumble's urging, she began to walk, but she didn't go far before she stopped again. Marian gasped.

A wall of earth and limestone rose up from the forest floor. Long, moss-filled cracks lined its stony surface. Hearty roots and small trees pushed out from it, while from above, thick, leafy vines snaked down. All the shadows of the forest seemed to gather around the wall, and gloom clung to it like a black shroud.

But more amazing were the numbers of creatures that sat or reclined before the wall. Squirrels and rabbits, foxes and wolves and deer, bears and bobcats and birds, raccoons and beavers all sat in friendly proximity. A sense of hush and expectation hung over them, and a spirit of reverence.

Bumble flew ahead, reached a cluster of vines and disappeared through it. Taking note of his arrival, a fox looked back over its shoulder. It rose to its feet and turned to face her. Sudden tears began to seep from its eyes. Its voice was only a whisper.

"Unicorn!"

The others turned to look. Some rubbed their eyes as if unable to believe what they saw. Others clapped paws to their mouths. A few, like the fox, began to weep. A plump rabbit hopped carefully forward and reached out a soft-furred paw to touch her knee. The whisper rose like a gentle wind through dry leaves.

Unicorn! Unicorn!

Marian walked slowly forward. Behind the vines where Bumble had disappeared, she at last perceived a cave—no, a cavern to judge by the size of the concealed opening. But while a few shrank back to observe her from a distance, most of the strange congregation pressed around her. She felt their paws on her sides, her back and throat, her legs, fleeting touches that carried no threat and brought no harm, but nevertheless made her uneasy.

"Is she real?"

"Welcome, welcome!"

"Where have you been?"

"She must be with the dragon!"

They whispered as if they were afraid to raise a noise or cause a disturbance, and one by one, after they touched her they stepped back, parting to give her a clear path. As she moved toward the cavern, she studied their furry, upturned faces. Such wonder in their eyes! Such an explosion of hope! They looked at her as if they'd found a treasure that was lost.

But she wasn't a treasure.

She was just Marian.

Trembling and discomfited by the attention, she kept silent. Finally reaching the curtain of vines, she pushed through, and alone again she took a relieved breath. "Oh, by all the horns of my ancestors!" she exclaimed as her eyes adjusted to the gloom.

The cavern was immense. Stalagmites and stalactites of raw crystal grew up from the floor and depended from the ceiling. Phosphorescent minerals blazed in shades of soft yellow and green, deep blue and purple. Her voice echoed in unseen recesses, and when the echo finally died, she heard the soft chittering of bats high overhead.

From far back in the cavern, from another chamber perhaps, came the flickering glow of firelight. Gathering her courage, she started toward it. Her hooves rang on the stone floor. She stopped suddenly as a huge shadow eclipsed the fireglow. Then, reassuring herself that the shadow was Ronaldo's, she called his name and got no answer.

Bumble landed on her head. "Ronaldo won't speak," he told her.

Yet, over the squeaking of the bats, she heard a soft sound—*crying*.

Marian continued on, deeper and deeper into the cavern. Indeed, there was another chamber at the back of the first, and still another beyond that. There was no guessing how far into the earth this cavern extended. Perhaps Ronaldo knew. Dragons had a sense for caves and holes in the earth.

But as she expected, she found the gray dragon in the second chamber. He had gathered wood and built a fire to make light by which to work, and he had worked unceasingly at a furious pace. On one stone wall, using the coal of burned wood, he had drawn a scene, and with the juices of berries and the stains of various plants and muds, he had begun a masterpiece!

"Ronaldo, what have you done?" Marian murmured. She gazed slowly upward from the floor to the ceiling, feeling her chest tighten and her mouth go dry.

Never had she seen a work so magnificent and yet so terrible as the mural Ronaldo labored before. There memorialized upon the wall— the destruction of Karlass! By his skilled hand, Marian witnessed what she hadn't seen herself—the attacking ships of Angmar, the night sky full of flaming arrows, the burning of Degarm's ships and the fires in the harbor, the spreading of the flames to the city, all in intricate and heart-rending detail.

Ronaldo seemed completely unaware of her presence. On one arm, he balanced a palate that once had been a piece of bark. Other pieces of bark lay scattered around the floor, each with a different daub of color on it. His brush was tightly braided grass around a reed core. How could he work with such crude tools?

She dodged his huge tail as he turned unexpectedly and reached for another piece of bark with another color. The glazed look in his eyes frightened her. His pupils had dilated to huge ovals that glimmered with firelight, and yet there was something more there—something dark and obsessive and painful.

With utmost care, barely daring to breathe, she moved around Ronaldo to see more of his great mural. As she did, she realized why the congregation outside the cavern was so quiet. They knew what the dragon was doing, and if they didn't understand, at least they appreciated. *Oh, my dear Ronaldo,* she thought, *what did you see that's possessed you so?*

The fire at the far end of the chamber generated waves of heat that shimmered on the limestone walls and lent the mural a strange semblance of motion and life. As she crept closer to the fire, her shadow began to climb the wall. It seemed an intrusion and wrong, and she backed up again.

Her shadow slipped back toward the floor like a curtain falling to reveal a piece of the mural she hadn't yet studied. Marian squeezed her eyes shut, but it was too late. Opening them again, she stared at Ronaldo's representation of himself, huge and monstrous and ugly. It took her a moment more to grasp the meaning of the three ships engulfed in his fiery breath. Tears ran down her face and dripped on the floor.

Bumble walked the length of her horn. "Ronaldo won't speak," he repeated.

Marian sniffed and, by an act of will, ceased her crying. "No, Bumble," she whispered. "He *is* speaking. He's speaking in the only way he can right now."

15

"FLY ON TO STRONGHOLD!" Chan called to emerald Fleer. His heart beat furiously, and his anger threatened to boil over. "Bring every dragon, and tell them to be swift! It's one thing to be attacked by Griffins; quite another to be invaded by men from outside our forest!"

Fleer gyred in a tight circle above Chan. His green eyes shone with anguish, and his voice was uncertain. "What are you going to do?" he called back. "You shouldn't face them alone, Chan! They have weapons! Come back with me!"

Jake gripped Chan's neck firmly with his knees as he leaned toward Fleer and raised a fist. "He's not alone!" he shouted in answer.

Fleer beat his wings and hovered again. "Your man-child is brave," he said, thrashing his tail back and forth in the air. "But bravery won't protect him from an arrow!"

Chan spread his wings wider, caught a rising wind current, and veered away from Fleer. "He'll be safe enough with me," he answered as he turned his nose southward. "I have to see for myself what's going on and stop it if possible!"

From the corner of his eye, Chan saw the sun flash on Fleer's scales as the Dragon dipped a wing and headed for Stronghold. Fleer was one of the fastest of the Dragonkin, and one of Wyvernwood's most loyal sons. He could be counted on to carry out Chan's command.

Even as he thought the word, it startled him. *Command.* Why should he be giving orders? Luna had said that others would be looking to the Children of Stormfire for leadership, and Ramoses had intimated the same thing. But Harrow was the First-born. Or at least the First-hatched. Harrow was strong, decisive. His black brother was better suited to take Stormfire's place if anyone was.

Yet Fleer had responded as if it were perfectly natural to follow his instructions.

"I'm *not* a child!" Jake shouted over the wind, though Fleer was already too far away to hear. His fist slammed down against Chan's scales. "And get this through your head, dragon—I don't need your protection! I can take care of myself!"

Chan barely heard Jake. It was a long flight to the border with Degarm, and driven by a sense of urgency, he redoubled his speed, pushing himself to the utmost. The hills and valleys of the forest rolled beneath, and his heart swelled. He loved Wyvernwood. It was the only home he'd ever known, and he'd never ventured beyond its borders. All his kin lived among its trees, all his friends, and all those he cared about.

Maybe Jake didn't need protecting—but they did.

He remembered Stormfire standing tall on the shore of the Windy Sea only a few days ago as he barred the Angmar sailors from the forest. Stormfire had always guarded Wyvernwood. His legend alone had been enough to keep most men at bay, and the Dragonkin had lived at peace, free from fear under the shadow of his golden wing.

A chill passed through Chan. Those days were gone. Once word of Stormfire's death spread beyond the borders, trouble would be inevitable. In ancient days, Angmar and Degarm both had claimed Wyvernwood as their own. With his father gone, one nation or both was bound to test the mettle of a new leader.

Was that what this incursion was about?

It didn't seem the logical answer. How could word have spread so quickly to both Angmar and Degarm? Yet, on the same day as Stormfire's death he had seen Angmar's ships on the Blackwater River with his own eyes. Now Fleer brought this report about Degarm. It perplexed and disturbed him, and it boded nothing good for Wyvernwood.

Driven by a rage like none she'd ever known, Luna raced above Wyvernwood's rolling landscape in pursuit of her brother, Chan. Behind her came the Dragon Diana, and farther behind, Ramoses. With Ramoses, or hot on his blue tail, came a host of others—the Dragon Paraclion, whose silver scales reflected the sunlight with a blinding intensity as he flew; ruby-scaled Tiamat, whose temper always bore watching; the orphan Snowsong, and still there were others— Kaos, Maximor, Starfinder, Samina, and more. Seldom had such a gathering of the Dragonkin been seen in the skies over Wyvernwood, or any other land. Only a few remained behind—Fleer, exhausted from his swift flight; Sabu, who couldn't fly at all; the youngest and oldest who couldn't keep up.

And Harrow, who could not be found.

Luna scowled and cursed her firstborn brother. She had always looked up to Harrow and respected his strength, but where was he now when Wyvernwood needed him? As surely as her father had left the world, some spirit of madness had moved in to take his place. What was Chan thinking, flying into danger with a man-child tied to his back? And what was she thinking, leading the Dragonkin into a possible battle?

What did she know of leadership? Hearing Fleer's story and fearing for gentle Chan, she'd simply taken to the skies in a panic, without a word to anyone. She felt a deep gratitude that Diana had chased after her, but the two of them had been friends as long as she could remember. That so many other dragons had also followed without hesitation or question filled her with a strange sense of pride. Even old Ramoses, whom she feared would soon fall behind.

I'm a fool to feel any such pride, she told herself as she raced south-ward. *It's not that they're following me. They fly to defend Wyvernwood!* As if to prove her point, Diana surged suddenly ahead. Yet, abruptly Diana craned her neck backward, and realizing that she had left Luna's side, she slowed and waited for her friend to catch up.

"My thoughts were wandering!" Diana called over the rushing wind. "I didn't mean to break away and pass you! Why did you slacken the pace?"

Luna's eyes narrowed as she realized she had, indeed, slowed her flight. Paraclion and Tiamat were right behind her now, and Snow-song was closing fast. She fought to set aside her self-doubts and gave in once more to her anger. It didn't matter why the Dragonkin fol-lowed. It only mattered that they did. Side by side with Diana, she plunged on through the blue sky, her heart and her wings beating with renewed fury, and her claws flexing. "Ahead of me or behind," she answered in a grim voice. "That's unimportant. Just find Chan and protect our forest."

As they flew above Marrow Lake, one of the largest lakes in Wyvernwood, a family of satyrs fishing on the north bank waved and called after them. An eagle rose from the trees and joined their ranks, his feathers dancing in the wind and his keen eyes sparkling with determination as he strove to keep up.

"A heart like yours mustn't burst trying to match our speed!" Luna shouted to the eagle. "Now drop away and spread this word—defend the forest!"

But the eagle raced on a little farther. "I know you, Luna, daughter of Stormfire!" he screeched.

"And I know you, Aquilla, father of Skymarin!" she answered. "Farewell now!"

Aquilla dipped a wing and veered away. Luna watched as he folded his great, white-tipped wings and plummeted toward the trees and the lakeshore below. Yet another eagle rose up to meet him, and a host of other birds, as well, and they held congregation above the tossing waters.

Then Marrow Lake was behind the Dragonkin, and Luna focused her attention ahead once more. Tiamat surged up on her left wing now and matched her speed. His wings beat in a powerful, synchro-nous rhythm with hers, and for a brief moment each looked aside at the other, and their gazes met. His eyes struck her—they were hard and dangerous eyes.

He reminded her of Harrow.

Stubbornly, she pushed all thought of her first-born brother from her mind. She didn't know where he was, and wishing wouldn't change that.

Tiamat exhaled a cloud of fire and sailed through the heart of it. For an instant, flames clung to the tips and edges of his wings, then flickered out. Against the blue sky his scarlet body stood out like a streak of blood, like a gash in the heavens.

Luna looked away, vaguely aware of the growing fatigue in her muscles and wings. Long distances usually offered no real challenge to her, but never had she flown so far at such relentless speed. She thought of Fleer with a new admiration. She hadn't thanked him for his effort, nor said anything at all to him. She would remedy that when she returned to Stronghold.

A column of smoke rising from some trees on a nearby hill caught her eye, and her heart leaped with excitement and fear.

"Just a cabin down there. It's chimney smoke." Diana informed her. Sometimes her cobalt friend had an uncanny habit of anticipating her thoughts.

Luna breathed a sigh of relief. "Maybe you should drop back and see how your father is doing, Diana," she suggested.

Diana blinked her eyes as she met Luna's gaze. "I'm keeping an eye on him," she answered. "He's old, but he's stronger than you think, and he loves Wyvernwood too much to stay behind."

A flock of geese flying north toward Marrow Lake broke formation and scattered desperately as the dragons flew toward them. With noisy honking, they veered and dived and climbed to get out of the way. But they were too slow. Caught in the wind-wake from Luna, Diana, Tiamat and Paraclion, the hapless birds went spinning and tumbling. Feathers and tufts of down filled the air like shrapnel.

"Maniacs!" an old gander squawked as the four went by. "Think you own the whole sky?"

Luna didn't try to answer or apologize. She was already well past. But she turned her head to watch as the geese recovered themselves and resumed their formation only to abandon it again and fly for the ground as they spotted the rest of the Dragonkin following.

"Where's Snowsong?" Luna asked with sudden concern.

"Back with the rest," Diana answered. "I've been watching the others, and I think some are beginning to tire. They're unused to this pace, but none have turned back."

Luna squeezed her eyes shut and tried to think what she should do. Her first and deepest instinct was to fly as swiftly as she could to Chan's side. She'd just lost her father; she couldn't bear the thought of one of her brothers facing unknown danger alone. At the same time, her reason told her that if they were truly facing war with Degarm, then there was more than just Chan to think about—all Wyvernwood might be at stake.

Opening her eyes again, she called to the ruby dragon on her left. "Tiamat!"

Tiamat turned his head and gazed at Luna with an intense and questioning look as, with sinuous grace, he dipped his right wing slightly and maneuvered closer to her. Side by side, they continued to fly, their wingtips almost brushing.

Luna tried to look away. Tiamat's scales shone too brightly, and his eyes were too full of a dark and unsettling fire. She knew so little of him, and suddenly wondered how she could have ignored him for so long. Yet, didn't he make that easy? He lived alone at the easternmost end of Stronghold, not in the canyon itself, but nearby in a hillside cave of his own making where he kept to himself.

Tiamat's mouth curled in a strange and subtle smile, and Luna became acutely aware of the way his gaze lingered upon her. It made her uncomfortable, and she purposely folded her wings and glided for a brief span of heartbeats. When she opened them again, she made sure that the tempo of Tiamat's wings didn't match hers quite so precisely.

"I swear I heard my name," Tiamat said, his smile spreading into a not-so-subtle grin.

Diana shook her head as she flew and rolled her eyes. "I think you heard the wind whistling between her ears," she said.

Luna glared at Diana, then looked again to the red dragon. "Tiamat, will you please drop back and tell the others we'll meet in the Whispering Hills? That's where Fleer said he went looking for his brother, Ronaldo. They should come as quickly as they can, but fly at their own speeds so that none are exhausted."

Tiamat tapped his ruby chest with his claws in irritation, and he closed one eye to regard her with a single, smoldering orb. "If you're asking me," he grumbled in a low voice that was barely audible over the rushing wind, "then my answer is no, I won't." Without missing a wing-stroke, he turned his head a little farther to regard her with both eyes wide open, steady and brazen. "I like the view up here at your side. But if you're *telling* me as Stormfire's daughter and as our leader . . ."

Luna interrupted him, her voice firm and clear, her eyes as steady as his own. "I don't apologize for saying *please*, Tiamat," she answered him. "Neither do I repeat myself twice." She craned her neck over one shoulder. Paraclion still flew close behind. She called his name.

Tiamat angled his wings and rolled sharply away. Carving a tight arc in the sky, he turned back to carry her message to the rest of the Dragonkin.

The sun flashed on silver scales as Paraclion took Tiamat's place at her side. "Did you need something, Luna?" he asked.

Luna gave Paraclion a brief glance. He flew with the same grace, power, and speed as Tiamat, and the light in his silver eyes bore no hint or trace of darkness. "No," she said, looking straight ahead toward the forested hills that rose in the distance.

The Dragon Diana dipped a wing and flew a little closer to Luna. "If I have wings I'm a fairy," she whispered in a mocking voice. "I think you're starting to enjoy this!"

"You're wrong," Luna answered. She beat her wings faster, finding new energy, leaving both Diana and Paraclion behind.

Diana was wrong, she told herself again. How could one find enjoyment in danger that was knocking at the door? It didn't bear thinking about.

But as she surged ahead, she smiled a close smile that even she didn't yet understand.

Watching the forest, alert for any movement or sign of trouble, Chan circled the Whispering Hills. There was no true village in the area. The residents lived scattered lives in their own cottages and cabins or caves, burrows, or nests. They were a quiet, polite folk that valued solitude and simplicity. He had come here a few times with his brother and sister, or with Stormfire. That memory threatened to bring a tear to his eye, but he blinked it away. It was a long time ago. But he remembered that everyone had made him feel welcome and treated him well.

How tragic it would be if this peaceful land were the first to suffer the cruelty of war?

Abruptly, he spied a hill he thought he knew and, spilling air from his wings, he dropped lower until he flew just above the treetops. A great round wooden door sealed the entrance to a half-remembered cave, and noting the white stones and the flowers that lined the path up to it, Chan smiled to himself. It had been a long time since he'd seen the Dragon Ronaldo.

Stormfire had brought him here when Chan wasn't long out of the nest, with Harrow and Luna, to meet the finest artist in Wyvernwood. His father had regarded it almost as a pilgrimage for them. *Never forget,* he told his children. But of course they did forget, as children always do. Or at least, they pushed it to the back of their minds.

Gently folding his massive pinions, Chan settled to the ground at the foot of the flower-lined path.

"What's this place?" Jake asked. Sitting straighter, he raised his arms over his head and stretched. His bones and joints cracked and popped.

Chan bent down close to the earth and sawed at the coiled rope around his neck with one sharp claw. "A studio," he said quietly, remembering the paintings he'd seen within and those he'd seen on rare occasions since. "A gallery. A museum. A temple. A place where the muses make their home." He severed the last coil and felt the rope slacken.

Jake felt it, too, and rapidly began to untangle himself from his bonds. "Why couldn't it just be a bathroom?" he muttered. Sliding to the ground, he ran back into a thick copse of trees. He hadn't taken the time to untie all the knots around his waist, and lengths of rope went slithering and bouncing behind him.

Chan smiled at the sight. Then he started up the pathway, careful not to damage the flowers or disturb the walkway stones with a misplaced foot or with his tail. Fleer had said he couldn't find Ronaldo, but a polite knock on the door couldn't hurt. Perhaps the master artist had returned home.

But when he knocked, no one answered. He lingered for a moment, hoping for a delayed response while he admired the door's fine, tiger oak surface. The elegant wood held a vibrant shimmer. It seemed almost alive as the fading sun streamed down and the shadows of the leaves shivered and stirred upon it. Chan smiled to himself again. Not even such a simple thing as a door could be plain when Ronaldo made it.

When it was clear to him that Ronaldo was not at home, Chan turned slowly. He began to notice details. The flowers by the pathway had not been watered recently. And though there were footprints and scuffmarks on the grass beside the path, none of them looked very fresh. With growing concern, he put one paw on the door and considered pushing it open to see what he might see, but such an invasion of privacy went against his nature.

"Hello! Oh, hello! Hello!"

A plump minotaur-mother came hurrying around the side of the hill. She waved with one arm to Chan, while with her other she carried her baby wrapped snugly in a blanket and clutched to her breast. Behind her came another, older minotaur-woman with gray eyes and gray hair streaming down her back in a long braid, and she leaned heavily on a gnarled hickory cane as she walked.

The minotaur-mother turned a distraught face up to Chan as she stopped before him. "Have you come with news about my son?" she asked.

Chan leaned closer down and shook his head. The minotaur-mother's bovine face was lined with worry and the marks of old tears. It was plain that she'd lost hair recently from stress and lack of sleep. "I'm afraid I know nothing of your son," he said. "I hoped to find the Dragon Ronaldo home. We've come to learn the truth of certain reports . . ." The older Minotaur raised her cane and shook it at Chan. "Degarm!" she cried, her voice shrill and cracked. "The crow and ravens brought us the warnings yesterday! But I won't leave my home, big fellow, and you can't make me!"

The minotaur-mother reached out and pushed the hickory cane down. "Hush, Granny!" she said. "No one's going to make us leave our homes! Where would we go?" She looked back to Chan. "Forgive our manners," she begged. "We saw the emerald dragon yesterday, but couldn't get around the hill fast enough before he took off again. We were afraid we were going to miss you, too." She made a brief curtsey and tried to smile. "I'm Beatrice." She indicated her companion with the cane. "This is Granny Scylla." She looked quizzically up again. "You said *we?*"

Chan looked down the hill just as Jake emerged from the copse of trees. He'd managed to shed most of the ropes, and his hands were busy with his pants and belt.

Beatrice blushed and shielded her eyes as she looked away. Granny Scylla let out a shriek that flushed birds from every tree on the hill. "They're here! They're here!" she shouted, brandishing her cane again as she glared at Jake. "Come one step closer, and I'll brain every last one of you! Go back to your side of the river, you pink-skinned vermin!"

"Feisty, isn't she?" Chan said, as Beatrice snatched Granny Scylla's cane and tried to calm her down.

"She's got every right to be," Beatrice said with an exasperated sigh. Granny Scylla fell into a sullen sulk and never took her eye from Jake as he walked up the pathway. "A week ago, my son, Chernovog, disappeared when some men were seen chopping trees in the hills close by. Ronaldo went looking for him, and he's disappeared, too. Now there's an armed force less than a day away. A lot of our neighbors to the south have already cleared out." Her large brown eyes blazed suddenly with a fierce resolve. "But Granny's old; she's lived her all her life. And I've got a baby and a missing offspring. Neither of us are going anywhere!"

"I hope I'm not the cause of some trouble," Jake said, putting on his friendliest grin as he reached the top of the path.

Chan made quick introductions, for the moment omitting the fact that Jake came from Degarm.

Beatrice took one close look at him, and her attitude instantly changed. "You poor man-child!" she exclaimed. "You're sun-burned and wind-burned, too! You're red all over!"

Jake looked at Chan, and his grin widened. "Well, not *all* over," he said. "Only down to my waist. I didn't have a shirt."

Beatrice gripped her baby in both arms and shook him lightly up and down against her bosoms, but her attention was all on another child. "We'll fix that!" she said. "Both of you come around the hill to my cottage. I've got salve for those burns, and more shirts than I know what to do with. My late husband would be pleased to see one of them put to good use! And there's food, too! You must be starving!"

Chan rose to his full height. "I'd appreciate it . . ." He stopped and reconsidered his words. He'd been about to ask the Minotaurs to watch after Jake, but he realized that would be a mistake. He looked down at Jake, and resumed as if he hadn't paused at all. ". . . Jake, if you'd stay here and guard our new friends while I learn more about the invaders."

Jake frowned. "I'd rather go with you."

Chan demurred. "You left the ropes at the bottom of the hill," he pointed out, "and there's no one to secure you in place right now."

Jake didn't raise his voice, but he argued. "I don't need to be tied to your back like a sack of flour," he answered. "You're leaving me behind."

Chan cut him off with a stern look. "I'm not leaving you behind," he said. "I'm giving you a job. Will you do your part?"

Jake looked stubborn, then nodded and let Beatrice take his arm. "If you see my son or Ronaldo," she said, biting her lip.

"I'll keep an eye out," Chan assured her.

Dusk was settling over the forest. The last rays of the sun were fading swiftly and dark clouds were gathering. Chan spread his wings and, soaring above the trees, caught a laggard sunbeam and rose like a red-orange flame against the gloom.

The hills and the forest rolled past like a darkening ocean as he flew southward. The gathering night offered no obstacle to his vision. Flying high for the broadest field of view, sometimes skimming low, he scoured the woods for some sign of Degarm's army. Half a day away, the crows and ravens had told Beatrice. For him, that was no distance at all.

A part of him hoped that it was all some mistake, some rumor grown out of proportion. A missing boy . . . some loggers seen in the woods at the same time . . . under the right circumstances, from such seeds a grander story might grow. Rumor gives way to fear, which becomes hysteria, which spawns . . . something worse.

But Wyvernwood was his home. More, it was a refuge for so many others, and no chances could be taken. With a firm-set jaw, he continued his search, and in his heart, he began to believe that rumor might really be fact, after all.

The woods were too quiet, too still. Except for the rustling of the breeze through the leaves and the trickle of an occasional stream, he detected no motion. He saw no wolves, no deer, no foraging bears. No owls or nighthawks flew among the branches. Not even bats. An unnatural hush hung over everything south of the Whispering Hills. Either all the locals had evacuated the area or they were too afraid to venture from their homes and burrows.

A round, copper moon rose low on the eastern horizon. Its light lent a ruddy glimmer to the leaves and cast a chiaroscuro webwork across everything. Chan's distorted shadow kept him company as he began to crisscross patches of the forest. It was all he could do sometimes to keep from talking to it. The winking stars dared him to look up, but he feared he might miss something.

A dim flicker far ahead caught his attention.

Then it's not a rumor, Chan told his shadow as together they turned eastward toward a distant hill that served as a marker when he lost sight of the small gleam. But his shadow didn't answer; it slipped behind him

Suddenly, he spied the glimmer again. Not one, but two! No, three! He flew higher, gyring upward in the night to see what he could see. A ring of small fires. Campfires! Around each fire a cluster of men sat wrapped in blankets and shivering—but not with cold. They watched the trees and the forest depths with wide, nervous eyes as they hugged their knees and kept their weapons close and murmured in low voices.

Six small fires in a small clearing surrounded by forest, and five men huddled by each fire. Mindful of his shadow and the moon's position, Chan descended for a closer look. The weapons he saw, while dangerous, were crude, hand-made. Their helmets looked like old cook-pots, and the few shields he saw in the firelight were metal scraps. Only the bows and arrows looked dangerous.

Thirty Men—and he could smell their fear.

Fear of the darkness. Fear of the forest. Fear of all the things that lived in Wyvernwood.

This was the great army of Degarm?

He knew he shouldn't scoff. Thirty frightened men, even with crude weapons, could cause a lot of harm. He thought of his father and what Gaunt had done with a newly cut log.

A barely controlled outrage filled him. These men of Degarm didn't belong in Wyvernwood!

Chan swooped low across the small clearing. The wind of his swift passing set their tiny campfires to flickering and sputtering and ripped the blankets from their shoulders. Their startled outcries encouraged Chan as he climbed above the clearing again. Turning his face to the black, starlit sky he spread his wings and announced himself with blast of fire.

The outcries turned to screams. The soldiers grabbed for their weapons. Arrow hissed past Chan. A few struck him and bounced harmlessly off his scales. He directed another blast of fire skyward and rose up to frame himself against the brief inferno.

A handful of soldiers ran into the trees and kept going. Some dared to remain. Cowering behind shields, they brandished knives and spears. Another volley of arrows flew upward. Chan swatted them away with one wing and descended into the clearing.

"Go home!" he roared. "Leave Wyvernwood!" With a lash of his tail, he sent the group of archers tumbling.

The sight of an angry dragon in their midst was too much for the soldiers. Turning toward Degarm, they ran with all their fear-driven strength. Chan stamped on each of their campfires, grinding them into the dirt to extinguish them, then rose into the sky and exhaled a cloud of white-hot fire.

Then to his left and higher in the sky, another blast of fire lit the darkness, followed by another and another. Even Chan caught his breath as he witnessed the incredible garden of red and orange flowers blossoming in the star-flecked night.

On the ground, some of Degarm's soldiers froze in mid-step to stare through the trees while others merely looked back over their shoulders and continued running.

With help on the way, Chan settled down in the clearing once more and folded his wings. Within moments, the sky filled with Dragonkin. Luna glided above him, beat her wings furiously to hover, and then touched down to the ground. Diana and Paraclion circled them and flew on.

"It looks like you've won the day, Brother," Luna said proudly. She stretched out her long neck and rubbed her cheek against his. "You've routed Degarm's army all by yourself."

"It's night," Chan pointed out, "and it wasn't very much of an army." He felt weary suddenly, as if a great weight had fallen on his shoulders, and wrapping himself more tightly in his wings, he stared into the depths of the black forest. He thought of how it had appeared to him from the air, without the usual residents and creatures that belonged here. It had felt empty, lonely.

The screams of Degarm's soldiers still drifted back to him, and the sky still lit up with the fiery breaths of his Dragonkin. The woods were no longer empty. Why, then, did he still feel so lonely?

He looked back to his sister. The moon, no longer copper colored, but bright and effulgent, shone down on her ivory form. Bathed in its light, she glowed. "Tell the others, Luna," he said. "Don't harm them. But drive them from our forest. We'll fly all night if we must, or stalk the woods on foot, but herd every last one of them back across the river. Snatch them up, if you must, and drop them in the drink"

Luna looked at him strangely for a moment. She seemed to hesitate, and he wondered what thoughts were racing through her mind. Then she drew herself erect, displayed her wings, and smiled. "We'll make sure they never come back!" she told him. With a powerful leap, she beat her wings and soared away.

"Oh, they'll be back," Chan murmured to himself. *They'll be back.*

16

ALONE IN REDCLAW'S MAIN HALL, Gaunt lounged on the new throne his Angmar allies had made for him. Curled up with his head resting on his forepaws, he luxuriated in the texture of the plush blue velvet cushions. They required cleaning daily, of course, because even he had to admit he shed worse than a common house cat. But no matter—that's what servants were for.

Stretching, he sat slowly up on his haunches and practiced yet again the formal pose he assumed to greet guests and subjects. Proper appearances required diligence and rehearsal. Image, for a king, was everything. A pity his father had never understood that.

The throne's spacious, extra-wide construction and low back accommodated his wings nicely in this position, and as he had so many times, he ran his paws over the carved teakwood arms, admiring the sparkle of the numerous emeralds and rubies set into the polished golden wood. How thoughtful of the craftsmen to so carefully match the color of the wood to the shade of his own fur.

Still, he gave a sigh and, careful of his bandaged side, he reclined on the cushions again. Resting his chin on one bejeweled arm while draping his lionine tail over the other, he dangled his left arm down to the floor and idly scraped his claws over the tiles. The ever-burning fire in the great fireplace flickered and danced, but it had seized to impress him. He glanced toward the banner hanging above it with it its white field and red talon blazon. Only days old, it no longer stirred him. Most disappointing of all, no matter how much time he spent in his throne room magnificently posed on his throne no one came to see him. No one of any importance, anyway.

Being king had proved so far to be surprisingly boring.

As he dragged his claws back and forth on the floor, he thought of edicts he could issue, orders he should give, rules he needed to dictate. But he couldn't get excited about that stuff, and that disturbed him a little. If he couldn't get excited about edicts, orders, and rules, what kind of a politician could he be?

His eyes narrowed, and he scraped a single claw across the tile with such intensity that a long high-pitched noise vibrated right through his bones, stabbed his ears, and shivered through the room.

Only one thing excited him. For days he'd lain on his velvet cushions and considered and schemed. All his long moments alone had not been wasted. In the silence and solitude, his genius had merely found time to exert itself.

He needed slaves.

Not servants, not subjects, not followers—slaves.

The problem, of course, was getting them without alerting the meddlesome dragons at Stronghold. He wasn't ready yet to risk another confrontation with them—particularly Stormfire's annoying hatchlings. The speed and ruthlessness with which they'd destroyed the old griffin nests had surprised even him. No matter, though, soon enough, their time would come. His genius was working on that, too.

A short knock sounded, and without waiting for an invitation, the throne room's great oaken doors pushed open. Minhep strode into the room, making a wide display of his wings as he approached. Gaunt knew his lieutenant did it only out of mockery and to remind Gaunt of the side wound that kept the Griffin leader earthbound. With a subtle leer, Gaunt dragged his claw across the floor again.

Minhep staggered back, folding his wings tightly as he reared up and clutched his ears. "Stop it!" he cried. "Stop that griding racket before my ears begin to bleed!"

Gaunt smirked. "You lack culture and refinement, Minhep," Gaunt said in a taunting voice. He made the screeching sound again. "This is music!"

Minhep settled back down on all fours and regarded the King of Griffinkin with narrowed eyes. "Yeah? Well, call me back when your music lesson is over." He spun about and started for the door, then stopped and turned back with a sneer on his face. "Oh, and I may lack refinement, but you now lack a claw." Lifting his head in disdain, he started for the door again.

Even as Gaunt lifted his left paw up to his one good eye, he felt the first shock of pain. A thin red trickle of blood began to ooze into his fur. Sitting up, he shot a glance at the floor and spied his missing claw stuck in the joint between two of the stone tiles. "Yow!" he shouted, throwing back his head as he grasped his injured limb. In his pain, he forgot himself, and a deeper shock stabbed through his right side. He clutched at his bandage.

"Turn and face me!" Gaunt roared before Minhep could exit.

Minhep stopped, but without turning he shook his head and held up a paw. "No, really!" he said, shaking all over. "I'd better not! Please, don't ask me!"

Gaunt roared again and lurched to his feet. "Turn!"

Minhep turned and regarded his king with falsely calm composure, but his gaze lingered a moment too long on the bandage, the black eye patch, and the bloody paw with only three claws where four should have been. His stoic demeanor crumbled, and he laughed, softly at first, then losing all control. Clutching his sides, he sagged sideways on the floor, kicked at the air with all four legs, and howled. Gales of griffin laughter shook the throne room. Even his tail banged and thumped on the tiles.

Shaking with anger, Gaunt clenched his good right paw into a fist. Slowly, he crept toward Minhep. His lieutenant saw him, and struggled to his feet, but tears of mirth ran down his furred face, and he clutched his belly as another uncontrollable fit seized him. Stumbling back from Gaunt, he tried desperately to regain his composure.

"You're laughing at me," Gaunt said in a dangerous tone as he squinted at Minhep with his good right eye.

Minhep drew himself to rigid attention and made a show of wiping the grin from his face with the back of one paw. "No, my lord," he answered. "I would never laugh at you."

"That's good," Gaunt told him. "I'm really very sensitive about that sort of thing, and my feelings are easily hurt when I think others are making fun of me."

A thin string of spittle dripped from Minhep's beak. He wiped it away with a quick swipe. "I understand," he said, trying to sound sympathetic. "It's an insecurity issue. I'm feeling a little insecure, myself, right now."

"Hmmm." Gaunt paced a circle around Minhep, sniffing him, looking him up and down. Coming around to face his lieutenant again, he leaned close until they were beak to beak. Carefully, he adjusted his black eye patch. "Tell me, my loyal friend, what do you think we should do about this insecurity?" He held up his right paw. Unlike his injured left, there were still four strong talons on that paw.

Minhep did his best to stare straight ahead, but his gaze rolled subtly toward the door as if he were measuring the distance to it. "I really don't know, my lord." His voice dropped to little more than a murmur. "Perhaps if I return to my post and meditate on it, I'll come up with an solution."

Gaunt took a moment to mull that over. Screwing his face up in thought, he adjusted his eye patch again, then rubbed the feathers on his chin. Finally, he nodded. "Yes, perhaps that would be best." He patted Minhep's shoulder with his uninjured paw. "You've shown considerable wisdom in the past, not to mention heroism, saving my life and all that." He turned Minhep toward the door and walked with him.

Minhep breathed a nervous sigh of relief. "I apologize for my untimely laughter," he said, pausing just inside the threshold. "I've been deeply concerned about all your wounds. It was really unfortunate that just as I was leaving your throne room I happened to remember a joke one of the guards told me . . ."

"Think nothing of it." Gaunt held the door wide for Minhep and inclined his head with a sympathetic smile. "These are times of stress for all of us. What's a bit of mirth between friends like us, eh?"

Minhep, looking more relieved by the moment, nodded agreement. "Thank you, my lord!" He bowed low. "Thank you, my *king!*"

Gaunt patted Minhep's shoulder one more time. "Back to your post now, and hold your head high. And sometime, you must tell me that joke."

Minhep grinned. "With pleasure, Majesty, with pleasure!"

With an unwavering smile, Gaunt watched Minhep as he lifted his head with newfound pride and confidence. Grinning, his lieutenant thrust his chest out and turn to exit the throne room. However as he walked away, Gaunt's smile abruptly vanished. His good eye gleamed with malice and locked on the tip of Minhep's tufted tail, which, unlike the rest of Minhep, had not yet made it across the threshold.

Gaunt slammed the door with all his griffin strength. The great oaken door rattled on its hinges, and the doorframe shook. A thin shower of dust spilled from the lintel above.

Minhep's scream echoed through Redclaw's halls and corridors.

With a cold chuckle, Gaunt returned to his velvet-cushioned throne. *Bootlicking sychophant*, he thought. *I should twist Minhep's wings off and have him hurled from the parapets.* He walked a tight circle on the soft velvet, seeming to pursue his own tail in slow motion, then curled up and rested his chin on his folded paws. *If only some other griffin had saved my life!* He sighed again. Sometimes, he was just too softhearted for his own good, but there was nothing to do about it now. He growled low in his throat and, closing his good eye, made up his mind to take a nap.

He dreamed of slaves and how to get them. Freed from waking concerns, his genius always emerged in his dreams. He would start with families in the northernmost parts of the forest. Bears, foxes, satyrs at first—he would demand one healthy son or daughter from each family. If the families objected or told anyone, he'd kill their child. And if the child objected to enslavement, he'd kill their families.

He smiled in his sleep, pleased with his plan. How could it not work? Fear was on his side. Terror was his friend. With a thin tongue, he licked his beak. Soon Redclaw would be full of good cooks to feed him, groomers to curry his feathers and comb the knots from his fur, sweepers to clean the halls, and moppers to scrub away the bloody paw-prints he'd just made on his throne room floor.

With a loud snore, he turned his mind away from that part of his dream.

With this new contingent of slaves, he might even free the few basilisks he'd brought with him from the valley. He no longer trusted the basilisks. They were too small and sneaky, and he disliked the way they regarded him with their huge, round eyes. They were his father's conquest, anyway, and he didn't need any reminders of Gorganar in his new fortress. Or maybe he wouldn't free them. He dreamed of hurling Minhep from Redclaw's highest tower, and sending the basilisks after him one by one.

A knock at the door awakened him from his wonderful dream. Gaunt cracked one eye open. It took him a moment to remember he couldn't open the other. With a scowl, he checked his patch to make sure it was in place. Then he held up his left paw. At least, in his sleep, that had stopped bleeding. "Come in!" he growled.

Minhep and another griffin pushed open both of the great doors and took up positions on either side. Gaunt struggled for a moment to remember the second griffin's name, but he remembered it as *Callus*. Neither cast even the barest glance toward their king, but Minhep announced, "The ambassador from Angmar!"

It pleased Gaunt to note the tightly wrapped bandage on his lieutenant's tail. Then, realizing the importance of the announcement, Gaunt sat quickly upright, adopting the formal posture he had practiced in anticipation of this moment, resting his front paws with precise care on the arms of the throne, turning his head to show off his fine and noble profile. All his previous thoughts of boredom dissolved! At last a dignitary from another land had come to pay respects!

A tall figure strode forward. He was clad from head to foot in elaborate silken robes and wrapped in a shimmering, forest-green cloak, and his head and face were concealed beneath a voluminous green hood. The long cloak and flowing sleeves of green hid his hands. The long hems of his garments covered all but the toes of his black boots. With downcast eyes, the figure approached and stopped before the throne.

"Greetings from His Majesty Kilrain, King of Angmar and the Northern Lands, to Gaunt, Son of Gorganar, Son of Argulo, King of the Griffinkin and Master of the Fortress Redclaw, Slayer of the Dragon Stormfire, friend and ally." A black-gloved hand appeared from one of the sleeves, and without looking up Angmar's ambassador pulled a scroll of papers from his belt. He extended these to Gaunt. "My Letters of Appointment," he said quietly, "and also personal letters of congratulation to you from Kilrain, himself."

Gaunt accepted the scroll and placed it with great care upon his lap. What did papers matter to him? He couldn't read the scrawls and marks that Man called writing. For that matter, he couldn't read anything at all. Perhaps he should soon find a slave to teach him. As he gazed at the figure in green silk, it occurred to him that reading and writing might come in handy for a leader.

"You're welcome here, Ambassador," Gaunt said in his most kingly voice. He placed a paw on the scrolls as he continued. "I'll read these at leisure, but let me first give command to have rooms prepared for you." He waved at Minhep and Callus. The two bowed without a word and departed, shoulder-to-shoulder, closing the doors behind them. "Now then," Gaunt said in convivial tones when he was alone with the ambassador. "Give me a name to call you by, and let us become friends."

The gloved hand disappeared back inside the sleeve and under the cloak. "But your Majesty, you already know me."

Gaunt leaned back on his throne, unsure that he'd heard correctly. Then, he regarded the ambassador with a suspicious glare. With the great doors closed and the two of them in private the man's tone had changed subtly. It bore a hint of mockery, of disdain that raised Gaunt's hackles.

The black-gloved hand appeared again. It pushed back the sleeve on the other arm to expose another black-gloved hand, but also a white-bandaged splint.

Gaunt hissed. "Canaan!"

Canaan lifted his head and pushed back the concealing hood. "Ambassador Canaan now," he replied with quiet reserve.

"What trickery is this?" Gaunt hurled the scrolled papers at Canaan's feet. "How is it that a low-life lackey and military errand boy like you comes to me in these rich garments and presents himself as Angmar's ambassador?"

With one hand, Canaan unlaced his expensive cloak, and with a flourish draped it over his shoulder. "To be frank," he answered with a shrug, "no one else would take the job. I didn't want it, myself, but because of my previous experience with you, I was ordered to take it."

"On pain of death, I'll bet!" Gaunt sneered.

Canaan shrugged again. "Well, yes, there was some threat of pain," he acknowledged, "but there was also the promise of a healthy salary increase and vast new authority. Neither of which should be sneezed at by a low-life errand boy."

Gaunt raged inside. He had expected someone *important*, a real dignitary, and Angmar had sent him a common soldier in a fancy dress. It insulted him! Less than a week ago he'd broken this man's arm and sent him running for home. "I think I'll break your other arm!" he said, rising from his velvet cushions.

Canaan stood his ground and looked unconcerned. "Did I mention *vast new authority*?" he said. "I'm Kilrain's representative now. And if you need that explained to you, for all practical purposes, it means I *am* Kilrain while I'm at Redclaw." His gaze turned hard and dark. He extended his good arm toward the Griffin King, as if daring him. "Touch me again, monster. I can't take back this rebuilt fortress, but I can cancel your services and end any further shipments of gold to your coffers."

Gaunt reached to seize the offered arm, but thought better of it. Still, he leaned forward, counting on his size and strength, his sharp teeth and talons to intimidate the soft, pink thing before him. "Maybe I have enough gold already," he growled.

Canaan laughed, then turned his hard gaze on Gaunt again. "Your kind never has enough gold."

The two regarded each other with open hostility for a long, tense moment. Then Gaunt settled back on his throne and ran his hand over the teakwood arms. He played idly with the inset emeralds and rubies as he considered their luster, their fire, and gradually his anger cooled.

"I suppose if Kilrain named a dog for his ambassador, I'd be obligated to recognize it," Gaunt said with an exaggerated sigh. "At least I shouldn't have to lay down papers for you."

"It would appear you did just that," Canaan answered with a sigh of his own. He bent to recover the scattered Letters of Appointment Gaunt had thrown at his feet. Assembling them into a scroll again, he tucked them once more into his belt, and straightened. "Now let us become friends, as you said, and discuss the Blackwater River."

Gaunt frowned and waved a paw. He had little regard for Canaan, but in truth he had little regard for any man, so what difference did it make who served as ambassador as long as he had Redclaw and the wealth continued to flow. "What is there to discuss?" he asked. "Gorganar is dead, and the nests are destroyed. I've kept my bargain and opened the river to your ships."

"For the moment," Canaan replied. "It's your job now, my Griffin King, to make sure that it stays open. With the Blackwater River under our control, we'll be able to strike at Degarm from the north as well as the east." He paused to remove his gloves, taking special care with the fingers of his broken arm. When the gloves were tucked neatly under his belt with the scroll, he put on a thoughtful expression and continued. "Preliminary reports from Karlass are . . . well, interesting. But they indicate that our surprise attack on the city destroyed much of Degarm's fleet and most of the shipbuilding facilities there. That's a crippling blow, and we have to be quick to press our advantage."

"Spare me all these boring details," Gaunt said with a yawn. "I prefer to leave it to your accountants to tally the losses and gains. What I really want to hear are the reasons behind your war."

Canaan inclined his head and cocked an eyebrow as he regarded Gaunt on the teakwood throne. He looked bemused and, at the same time, a little sad. "My monster friend, wars are never about reasons—only pretexts." Rubbing the splint on his right arm, he looked around the throne room. "You really must get some more chairs in here, Gaunt. Either that, or arrange a more comfortable space for conversation."

Gaunt snarled. Despite Canaan's new robes and new authority, the Griffin King still found little to like about the man. "You dodge the question," he said.

"Technically, you didn't ask a question." Canaan studied the small patches of blood on the floor and paced slowly beside them as if he were playing connect-the-dots. "Angmar and Degarm cling to animosities that reach back into antiquity," he explained. "There are various accusations and charges, but they're only stories, and no one seems to agree on the specifics. An ancient Angmar king once kidnapped Degarm's queen. Or seduced her away from her husband. The two sides fought a lengthy war with no clear victor. Then sometime later, Degarm sacked several of our coastal towns, taking women, gold, and anything else they could lay hands on. And over the years, our pirates have raided their ships, and their pirates have raided our ships. It never really ends, and hard feelings just continue to fester."

He shrugged. "They've even fought for ownership of this forest, although Stormfire and the coming of the Dragonkin pretty well settled that disagreement for them." He came at last to Gaunt's bloody claw, which still lay on the floor near the throne. With a curious half-grin, he picked it up and examined it. It was as long as any of his fingers. He tossed it aside. "All that matters is that periodically we fight. It's a matter of practicality. When war is declared, taxes get raised. Then more taxes get raised, and the leaders on both sides accrue power and they get very rich."

Gaunt snarled again and glared at Canaan with his one good eye. "This is the logic of Men?" he said. "It makes no sense at all."

Canaan rolled his eyes toward the ceiling. "Of course it makes sense," he replied, sounding like a teacher lecturing a particularly slow student. "Just think about it. By killing the Dragon Stormfire, haven't you declared war on the Dragonkin? Haven't you profited handsomely as a result? You have this fine fortress now, and that throne, and you call yourself a king—King of the Griffinkin. Aren't your coffers full of gold and jewels?"

Gaunt leaned back on his velvet cushions, and winced as a small jolt of pain stabbed through the wound in his side. It quickly passed. He put a paw to it, checking to see if it was bleeding again, but when his paw came away clean, he put it from his mind and considered the cynical wisdom in Canaan's words.

"It isn't always smart to speak so much truth," Gaunt said at last.

Canaan drew his gloves from his belt and made a show of pulling them on. "There's no love between us, griffin," he said bluntly. "Nor friendship, nor trust, nor even respect." He fixed Gaunt with a hard, dark-eyed look as he touched the scrolled Letters of Authority. "If we are to work together, let us at least have truth." Throwing his green silk cloak about his shoulders with a flourish, he turned on his heel and walked from the hall.

You know, and I know, Gaunt thought coldly as he watched Canaan's back, *that truth is the last thing we'll have between us.* Canaan was right about many things, but about one thing he was wrong. The Griffin King had found in their conversation a measure of respect for the man, after all—but it was a dangerous respect.

Angmar's new ambassador would bear careful watching.

Gaunt stretched and gave a mighty yawn. Stepping down from his throne, he tried with experimental caution to raise his wings. Pain lanced through the muscles of his right side. He checked his bandage again and still he found no blood. The wound was healing, though slowly.

He thought of the pink-skinned man-child who had caused him this hurt, and he curled his uninjured paw into a fist. There was one more matter to deal with. *In time,* he swore, *in time.* Any child with the courage and ability to lay low the King of the Griffinkin could not be allowed to reach adulthood.

And there was Morkir. His brother must be dealt with, too, and the sooner the better.

He rubbed his paws and licked his lips. *So much to do—so much to do!* It seemed a king's work was never done!

With a new spring in his step, he strode through the great doors and into the corridor beyond. To the west side of the throne room's entrance, a spiral staircase curled steeply upward through the center of Redclaw's tallest tower, leading to numerous rooms and chambers and ultimately to the parapet at its top. Gaunt paced to the foot of the stone steps. "Minhep!" he called in his loudest voice. "Minhep! Get your tail down here!"

Minhep descended with Callus close behind him. Gaunt wondered, was it suspicion in their golden eyes, or just nervousness he saw on their faces? He beckoned and led them through the corridor, past the throne room, and out into Redclaw's main courtyard. He didn't really care so long as they feared and obeyed him. He gazed up at each of the four towers, observing the griffin guards on the parapets. More griffins stood watch along the walls as well, while a pair constantly circled the fortress from the air.

"I need slaves," he said over his shoulder to Minhep. He explained his plan. One member from any family. And make sure you issue the threats as I spoke them to you to insure their cooperation and silence. Choose five of our strongest flyers to accompany you. Six griffins should be enough to intimidate anyone."

"Will you be leading us, your Majesty?" Minhep asked with false sincerity.

Gaunt turned toward his lieutenant. Minhep stood a few paces away at rigid attention, but with his bandaged tail carefully curled over his back. His eyes were wide and questioning as he waited for an answer from his leader.

But Gaunt didn't like the challenging tone in Minhep's voice. Ignoring his wounds, he lunged at Minhep, and with a snarl he drew back a paw and knocked him to the ground. "You dare too much!" he said, holding Minhep down with his injured paw while the talons of his good paw closed on his lieutenant's throat. "You know I can't fly yet."

Minhep's gaze was anxious, yet strangely lacked fear. "You won't kill me like this," he whispered. "You'll feed me a poisoned fish first."

In a rage, Gaunt raised his good claw to strike, then froze. Slowly, he looked down and saw Minhep's talons pressed against his exposed belly, sharp and ready to rip.

"Besides," Minhep continued, "you enjoy having me around to abuse."

Gaunt released his lieutenant and backed cautiously away. "Do you think there's a shortage of candidates for that?"

"Not at all," Minhep replied as he rose to his feet and shook the dust from his wings. "But every master has his favorites."

Gaunt glanced coldly past Minhep at Callus, who had stayed out of the fray. "Carry out your orders," he said finally. Minhep bowed, and displaying his great wings to further taunt the Griffin King, he sprang into the air and flew toward the guards on the wall where they had gathered to watch the brief confrontation. From that group, Minhep chose five to follow him into the forest.

The King of the Griffins smiled to himself as he watched his six soldiers glide away. The other guards on the wall averted their eyes from him and returned to their posts. Gaunt gave those griffins no more thought. He continued to gaze into the blue sky in the direction the six had gone, and as he did so he touched his soft belly and remembered the slight, sharp pressure of Minhep's claws.

He licked his beak and gave an appreciative nod.

Now there was a griffin he could respect.

17

FOR THE REST OF THE DAY AND INTO THE EVENING,
Ronaldo worked at a feverish pace. When his fire burned low, a family
of bears gathered armloads of wood and brush and kindling to fuel it,
insuring him light by which to work. In groups of two and three, squirrels and rabbits crept in side by side with foxes and wolves and bobcats
to witness the dragon at work. They came silently and left the
same way,

Marian watched anxiously as the mural evolved. Ronaldo still
hadn't said a word. He seemed oblivious to her and everyone, as if he
worked in a trance unaware of anything but his paints and his painting. He left the cavern only once for more water and plants to mix
fresh pigments. Beneath a darkening sky with the first stars winking
into view, she accompanied him, and half the crowd outside followed
at a discreet distance while the other half waited.

They're protecting us, Marian realized as she noted the neat, silent
ranks of wolves on her right flank. Bobcats and foxes moved with
equal stealth on the left flank, sliding with noiseless grace through
the brush and among the trees. Bears brought up the rear while squirrels and birds moved among the trees and high branches like watchful
scouts. *The rest are guarding the painting!*

They returned to the cavern to find the fire renewed yet again.
Marian murmured a few words of thanks to the pair of brown bears
tending the flames, but Ronaldo only returned to his work. Marian
folded her legs and settled down on hard floor to watch, but her troubled mind had long since lost any interest in the composition.

When Ronaldo finished his last brush stroke, he set aside his palate
and brush and stood back. The crackling of the flames made the only
sound in the cavern. Then with heart-rending sadness the dragon

began to cry. Turning away from his mural, he gathered his brushes and what remained of his paints, all his improvised supplies, and fed them to the fire.

Marian called his name twice, hoping that with his work completed he might finally respond. Still, he said nothing, and she wondered if he even heard. With nothing more to do, he shambled to the far side of the chamber. There he sank down against the wall, folded his wings about himself like a cloak and curled his tail around his feet.

Weeping, he fixed his gaze on the painting, but it was clear to Marian that what he was really seeing was the destruction of Karlass over and over again in his mind.

She felt like weeping, herself, as she rose to her feet. "Ronaldo?" she said again, hoping to stir some response. Mindful of her horn, she nudged the dragon with her nose, but all her efforts were useless. After a while, she moved over by the fire. The flames felt warm on her hide, but they did little to comfort her.

Marian became aware of the passage of time. Outside, the moon must already be high among the treetops. She turned toward Ronaldo again. His eyes blinked, and she felt a surge of hope that perhaps he was awakening again to the real world. She paced across the cavern floor to his side.

"Please talk to me, Ronaldo," she begged.

But it was useless. The dragon didn't move, didn't answer, didn't even look at her. His gaze remained locked on the mural.

A masterwork it might be, but for all its beauty, she began to hate the painting. She paced back and forth, no longer able to look at it, nor could she continue to watch Ronaldo in his torpor. She trembled as she worried and considered. She tossed her mane as her agitation increased. She felt angry with herself, with Degarm, and Angmar, and race of Men in general, even at Ronaldo.

Then, her anger faded. Marian became calm again and reached the decision that in her heart she knew was the only right one.

One last time she turned to Ronaldo and stood before him. She kept her voice soft, soothing, wishing and hoping that he would respond, knowing that he wouldn't. "My dear dragon," she said, "Bumble and I have to leave. All the bears and wolves and bobcats, and all the new friends we've made here will take good care of you, and they'll all watch over you."

She nuzzled against him, but he didn't look back. "I don't know if you're even listening to me," she continued. "I don't want to leave you, but you'll be safe here. For the first time we have a real idea of where Chernovog is being taken, and he's just a boy, Ronaldo. Barely more than a child. I have to go on. I have to try to rescue him."

Ronaldo's gaze remained fixed on the mural, his mind imprisoned by the tragedy he had witnessed and in which he had played a part. The bears that had tended his fire appeared again with new armloads of wood, and she beckoned them closer. "Stay with him," she pleaded. "Tell the others. Talk to him, and never leave him alone."

She walked a few paces away, her hoof-steps echoing in the quiet cavern, and then she looked back. It broke her heart to leave him, but she had no other choice. "When you awaken, Ronaldo," she said, "go home. Go back to Wyvernwood and to the peace of your cave in the Whispering Hills and to your work. Paint many more wonderful paintings."

A fat gray rabbit brushed up against her fetlock, and she looked down. "Take care of him," she told the rabbit. "He's more special than he knows." The rabbit twitched its nose and laid its long ears back. "We tell a story in these parts," he replied. His voice was low and hushed. "Everything that's good in the world springs from a dragon's heart." He gazed toward the mural and fell silent for a moment, then in a whisper he added, "You have our word, milady."

Marian feared that if she looked back at Ronaldo again she wouldn't be able to leave, so thanking the rabbit, she walked from the chamber and across the outer section of the cavern and out into the night. She felt like she was betraying Ronaldo by leaving him behind, but again she told herself there really was no choice.

A black wolf with his tail curled tightly over his back walked up to her, and though his eyes burned redly, they held no menace. "Is it true that he's finished the painting?" he asked. A family of forest mice scampered closer, and an owl settled on a limb directly above her head.

"It's not a painting," she told them gently. "It's a masterpiece. And yes, he's finished." She glanced at all the assembled creatures. "It belongs to all of you now. It's part of your forest."

A small blur barely visible in the night flew around her head and landed on her horn. "Then off we go once more for Chernovog!" Bumble sang. His breath smelled of hollyhocks and larkspur, and his little belly was roundly bloated. Folding one wing over his stomach and extending the other, he struck a dramatic pose and turned to his audience. "When last we saw the hero, Bumble, and his faithful side-kicks, Marian and Ronaldo . . . !"

"Hush, little bird," Marian said. Then, softening her voice, she added, "The hero Bumble will have to be heroic with only one side-kick now."

Bumble looked at her for a long moment, and his heart beat so rap-idly inside his small body that Marian could feel the vibration through her horn. "Ronaldo still is not well?" he asked.

"Our new friends here will take good care of him," Marian explained. "You and I have to be brave now. It's time to turn our thoughts to find-ing Chernovog and returning him safely to his mother."

"But . . ." Bumble paced the length of Marian's horn. The small black dots of his eyes gleamed with hummingbird tears as he regarded her. 'When shall we three meet again?"

Marian had no answer. It was all she could do to hold back her own tears. She had deep doubts about the wisdom of her decision, not because she feared to proceed alone, but because leaving the gray drag-on just seemed so hard. But she swallowed and licked her lips and said her goodbyes to the creatures gathered around her.

With Bumble clinging to the tip of her horn, she turned her nose to the west and started away from the cavern. With grim expressions, half of the wolves silently took up positions at her side. Bobcats and foxes followed closely behind. Owls and nighthawks and bats provided an aerial escort. Marian allowed an inward smile. Perhaps she felt a little less lonely for their company. Certainly she was grateful for their careful guidance through the dark woods.

When they reached the western edge of the forest, she found a familiar friend waiting. Stretched out in languid fashion on the lowest limb of one of the last trees, the bobcat named Elvis blinked his shin-ing eyes at her. "So, milady, you are leaving us?"

Marian nodded. "I won't forget your kindness, nor any of the friends we've made here."

In one fluid motion, Elvis rose to his feet and leaped down to the ground. He seemed smaller in the darkness as he stood before her, but his sharp white teeth gleamed in the moonlight as he spoke. "Then, I'll walk with you just a while," he said. Turning, he led her away from the last trees across a short, clear space of grass, and to the road that stretched from Karlass to Jiwashek.

The creatures that made up her escort lingered in the shadows, under bushes, and in high branches. Marian felt their gazes on her as she walked away just as she felt the joy and the sadness in their hearts. They wanted her to stay, though they knew she had to go. She glanced back over her shoulder once as she walked across the clearing, and when she stood in the middle of the road, she looked back once more.

"You still don't grasp what you represent to them," Elvis said. "They will watch you until you're down the road and out of sight. And then some of them will continue to watch and wait in the hope that you'll come back."

Marian tilted her head as she looked at Elvis. A beautiful green fire burned in his eyes, and he purred with an almost musical sound. How different he seemed now from the dangerous beast she had first seen on a rock menacing a soldier. "Maybe I understand a little," she answered in a soft voice. "There isn't a drop of magic left in the world, my friend, and yet we wish there were. We long for it, and we hope, or sometimes we dream that maybe over the next hill, or in the next valley, or on some high mountain-top there's still just a little bit left— if we could just find it."

Elvis shook his head and gazed back at the dozens of pairs of eyes that shone from the trees and foliage. "With all due respect, milady, you don't understand at all." He swished his golden tail and took a few steps down the road toward Jiwashek before he turned back to her and sighed. "But it's no matter now. You're determined to find your missing friend, so go quickly under the protection of night." He closed one eye and regarded her with a single staring orb. "And when you meet Malleus, say again that there is no magic left."

Bumble darted from Marian's horn and flew a swift circle around Elvis, then settled on her head again. His small talons grasped her forelock tightly. "Why does Bobcat Elvis sound so bitter?" he asked.

"It's not bitterness you hear, little bird," the bobcat answered. "It's fear. I'm afraid for you both."

"Then fear not!" the hummingbird cried. "Bumble is a hero! Bumble will protect Marian and rescue Chernovog, and then I'll come back to celebrate victory with more of your delicious larkspur!"

Elvis put on an indulgent smile as he bent his front legs and made a polite bow. "We should all have such a companion," he said to Marian. "May luck fill your hoof-steps." With that, he bounded back across the clearing and disappeared among the trees.

A soft wind blew across Marian's back. It stirred her mane and tail and teased the finer hair on her face as it whispered over the flat grassland. The ground glowed with the moon's milky light. At the edge of the black woods, one of the wolves began a mournful howl, and the others took it up.

Marian gazed at the moon and the cloudless sky, then down the dark road to Jiwashek. "Bumble," she whispered, "can you still pick up Chernovog's scent?"

Bumble fluttered down to the road and paced back and forth in the dust. "Very faint," he told Marian. "Faint as a marigold's perfume. Faint as yesterday's starlight."

Marian smiled at her tiny companion. "For a hummingbird who couldn't remember my name a few days ago, you're developing quite a way with words."

He flew into the air again and resumed his perch on the tip of her horn. "For a unicorn, you're developing quite a way with humming-birds," he answered as he stared toward the forest. "Bumble misses Ronaldo. What will become of him?"

Marian listened to the gentle sutures of the wind and the howl of the wolves. For just a moment, she closed her eyes and wondered what it was like for Bumble to forget things so easily. There were memories she wished she could forget sometimes, but this small forest and its dear inhabitants she wanted very much to remember.

"Ronaldo needs time to heal," Marian said, answering Bumble. "You have to understand that he's an artist, a creator of beauty. Even the fire that he breathes is a beautiful thing. But for the first time in his life, he used his fire to destroy."

"Those ships in his mural," Bumble said. "Ships of Angmar on the river where they shouldn't have been."

Marian nodded, marveling again at the little hummingbird. "He may have taken some lives when he burned those ships. That's a trauma from which one doesn't quickly recover."

"Farewell, Gray Dragon." Bumble turned toward the forest again and saluted with one wing. "Rest easy until your stalwart friends return to guide you home."

The last unicorn began walking down the long road in the darkness. The wolves sang louder as if to let her know they were still with her, in spirit at least, while overhead owls and nighthawks circled and tipped their wings to say good-bye.

But Marian could bear no more good-byes. Though she grieved for Ronaldo, there was nothing more she could do for him. She shut him out of her thoughts, if not out of her heart. "Get on my back, Bumble-bird," she said, feeling the wind in her mane again, "and hold on with all your strength. I don't have dragon wings, but I can fly in my own way."

When Marian felt Bumble's talons grip her hide just below her withers, she broke into a gallop. The forest disappeared in the darkness, and the wolf-song echoed behind them and faded away. They were alone again with nothing but the land and a creamy moon, the wind, and their shadows. Marian ran, leaving behind her guilt and her sense of betrayal. Her mane flew wildly, and her silken tail streamed. She cast off the heaviness in her heart and rejoiced in her speed as she raced along the road.

When the forest was far behind them the road curved gently to the east and became a coastal path that ran along high cliff tops. The Windy Sea shimmered, stretching to the distant horizon, seemingly to the end of the world. The moon's brightness couldn't conceal the splendor of the stars in the black heavens. Rivaling the moon for beauty, they speckled the water with their light.

Without slackening her pace, she admired the panorama. The air smelled crisp and fresh, thick with the salt of the sea. But far beyond the coast, barely visible on the sparkling water, she spied the outlines of a dozen ships sailing northward. Pale lanterns swung and tossed in their prows and along their decks. By their sleek lines and banks of oars, she recognized them as warships. On their way to Karlass, perhaps, or more likely to Angmar.

The moon sank lower and lower in the west, and the road curved away from the sea. The flat landscape began to roll with low hills that rose up on either side. Marian continued to run. She could run all night without tiring and into the next day. The road marked her way, and the waning moon and the stars lit her coarse. She paused for nothing, and no obstacle slowed her.

Finally, near the last hour of darkness when the moon was gone and the bright morning star shone down to herald the approach of dawn, two dark towers loomed in the south. Square and tall, they rose like pillars to support the sky. Between them and around them the rooftops of lesser buildings were also visible.

Marian left the road to climb a nearby hill. From its grassy summit she gained a better view of the city called Jiwashek. It was twice as large as Karlass, she guessed, and a stout wall of massive blocks encircled its core. The city didn't stop at the wall, however. Homes and shops and warehouses sprawled over the land outside its boundary and up into the farther hills.

Beyond it, stretched a glimmering bay. She could see the docks and wharves that sat upon the water, and beyond them the bobbing ships at anchor. Marian gasped at the sight. Warships and merchant craft and fishing vessels too numerous to count! Tiny specks of light moved along the docks and the ship decks. Men, she assumed, with torches and lanterns in hand up early to prepare for the day's work.

"Bumble," Marian said, and the little hummingbird flew up from her back to settle on her horn. "If we returned to the road would you still be able to pick up Chernovog's scent?"

Bumble fluttered his wings and shook his tail. "Lemongrass to the right of us; honeysuckle to the left. Salt-air everywhere, and too many phew-smells, fish guts, slops. This sensitive nose has curled up and put itself away for the night!"

Marian knew what he meant. The wind blowing in from the sea carried the stench of Jiwashek with it. To a forest-dweller, nothing smelled quite so bad as an over-crowded city like the one below. She wouldn't be able to depend on her nose, nor Bumble's either, to locate the young minotaur. She would have to go into the city and look for him.

That, of course, presented her with another problem. "How does the last unicorn in the world pass unnoticed in the domain of Man?"

"Marian cannot," Bumble answered. The black dots of his eyes sparkled suddenly. He walked out to the very tip of her horn and struck a pose. "This is a job for . . . Bumble-bird! Up, up, and away!"

"Bumble, no! Wait!"

With a whir of tiny wings, he vanished in the remaining darkness. Marian reared in frustration, tossed her mane, and stamped the ground. Then, casting caution to the winds, she raced down the hill and after her fearless hummingbird companion.

Bumble laughed as he flew toward the city. Marian was fast, indeed, but he was faster! And for once his diminutive size gave him an advantage that neither Marian nor Ronaldo could claim. Who would notice a tiny hummingbird? He could comb the city, search the streets, peek in the windows, even peek in their outhouses, and no one would realize he was there!

"Have no fear! Bumble's here!" he cried as he flew. "Hold on, Chernovog!"

He reached the first homes and buildings. Most of them were still dark, but he darted at top speed to each one and sniffed. The distinctive smells of Man were pervasive. He paused at a window, lingered at a door, landed on a brick chimney and got a nose full of smoke. Dizzy from the fumes, he fell backward and tumbled head over tail-feathers halfway down the roof before he caught his balance and took to the air again.

As he continued on from house to house and from shop to shop, he began to notice a confusion of roads all criss-crossing one another. With no light and no markers, he couldn't tell them apart. Landing once more on the edge of a rooftop gutter, he looked around. His heart was beating even faster than usual, and he trembled, fearing he'd become lost. So many of Man's buildings looked the same to him, especially in the pre-morning gloom. What was he to do?

Then, glancing up, he observed the two tall towers that loomed over the city. He could navigate by those! No matter where he flew, those structures would always be visible. He gave a cheer, congratulating himself for his cleverness, and prepared to continue his search.

A large, black shape lunged at him. Bumble got just a glimpse of wild green eyes and gleaming teeth as he sprang away from the gutter. Sharp claws raked the air where he'd just been, and a disappointed feline growl followed.

Safe in the air, Bumble dared to turn to face the most miserable-looking cat he'd ever seen. Mange had claimed most of the poor creature's hair, and what remained was matted in knots and clumps. Its ribs showed through its thinly muscled sides, suggesting that it hadn't eaten well in a long time, and one ear had been half-chewed away, no doubt in some fight.

The cat licked its lips as it stared at Bumble. "Forgive me, little birdie," it purred. "In my hunger, I thought you were a roof-mouse as you sat there on the gutter. There's no moonlight, and my eyesight isn't what it used to be."

Bumble's wings hummed and blurred as he hovered above the cat. Despite the cat's polite words, he didn't trust the look he saw in those coldly shining eyes, nor did he believe the offered excuse. Even in the darkness, what self-respecting cat would mistake his dashing silhouette for that of a roof-mouse!

The cat sat back on its haunches and brushed its whiskers delicately with one paw. "I can tell you're a long way from home," he said. "A stranger, perhaps, without family or friends in these parts?" It closed one green-glowing eye and studied Bumble with the other. "I could be your friend."

"Friend?" Bumble replied, thinking of Chernovog. "Bumble is looking for a friend!"

"Then look no further, my sweet bite of poultry," the cat opened both its eyes again. Looking askance, it tongued the tip of one paw and washed a spot behind its ruined ear. "I think we can become very close."

Bumble darted to a point higher on the roof and folded his wings as he settled down on the wooden shingles. Maybe this strange night-prowler had information he could use. "Do you know Chernovog?"

The cat shrugged its bony shoulders as it crouched languidly down on all fours and moved a subtle step toward Bumble. "Maybe if you hum a few bars," it said. "But come closer, my little gulp of dark meat so that I can hear better. As you can see, one of my ears isn't what it used to be."

"Bumble must find Chernovog!" the little hummingbird insisted. The cat didn't seem to understand! But if the cat didn't know Chernovog, maybe he'd know . . . Oh, what was it! He shook his head in frustration and pounded on it with one wing as he tried to jar loose a memory. Curse his tiny hummingbird's brain! He squeezed his eyes shut for a moment, trying to concentrate.

"Carnival Fantastica!" he shouted, snapping his eyes open again.

The cat was closer to him by half, but it arched its back suddenly, and laid his ears flat against its head. "What do you know of the carnival, my little drumstick?" it hissed as it dragged the claws of one paw along one of the shingles, making three deep scratches in the wood.

"There is Chernovog!" Bumble explained, growing excited. "I think! Bumble followed his scent, but now Bumble's nose is curdled from all the bad smells!"

The cat lifted one leg and sniffed its armpit. "I could use a bath," it admitted. "Maybe I'll give myself one after dinner. Right now, I'm so hungry I could eat a rubber duck." Sinking down onto its belly, it took another small step toward Bumble, and its voice became even more silken. "Why not come home with me?" it said. "Even by daylight, the Carnival is dark and dangerous and full of monsters you've never seen. That's no place for a tender fellow like you. And if that doesn't scare you, my little condiment, then think about this—the carnival's owner is a wizard."

Bumble leaped into the sky. "Then I'm off to see the wizard!"

The cat sprang after Bumble, swiping with its claws as it attempted to knock him out of the air. But Bumble had anticipated a second attack. He dodged, and the cat fell back to the roof. With a frantic growling and scraping it slid down the roof's steep slope. Only at the edge of the gutter, did its claws find purchase. The cat dangled above a long drop.

"Come baaaaack!" it cried, nervously swishing its tail as it stared toward the ground. "What about our friendship, my little niblet? I was just getting to know you!"

Bumble hovered over the cat. "Tell me where will Bumble find this wizard and his dark carnival?" he demanded. "Have you seen them?"

The cat looked up at Bumble, then down at the ground. Its claws carved deep grooves in the wooden gutter as it held on with all its strength. "Look for them in the center square between the two towers," the cat whined. "Malleus has already pitched his tents! But the show doesn't open until noon! Now help me, my delectable little messmate, for I am too weak from hunger to pull myself up!"

Bumble grinned. He might not have much of a memory, but he still recalled how the cat had licked its lips just before it sprang at him. Now he made a show of flicking his own narrow, thread-like tongue over the tip of his beak as he gauged the distance to the ground.

"I think we should end this relationship on a high note," he said. Diving, he speared the cat's right paw.

With a feline wail, the cat let go of the gutter and fell. Every sparse hair on its body stood straight out as it scratched at empty space, thrashed, twisted, then twisted again, and landed neatly on its feet. With wide, frightened eyes it looked up again and swallowed as if it was unable to believe it had survived the drop.

"You little monster!" it shouted. Rising on its hind legs, it shook a paw at Bumble. "You belong in the carnival with all the other monsters! Go on, then! And don't come crawling back to me when you need a friend again! And stay off my roof!"

Bumble laughed as he flew away. Because he was small and didn't have much of a brain, everyone thought he was also a fool. But Bumble was nobody's fool. He set his gaze on the two towers. No need now to fly from house to house sniffing at windows and doors and chimneys. Chernovog would not be found in houses and shops. He should have remembered that.

The carnival—that was where he'd find Chernovog.

The dark and dangerous carnival.

He gulped as he flew onward. He wasn't really afraid, but something about that name—*Carnival Fantastica*! It sent a shiver through him. And suddenly, he felt so tired! His belly rumbled and grumbled. He was hungry, too! When was the last time he'd eaten? He couldn't remember. Marian had run along the road almost all night with him clinging to her back. Had he eaten even once on that long journey? No! He vaguely recalled the smell of lemongrass and hollyhocks on the hill outside the city. Or was it honeysuckle and fuschia? No matter, he hadn't eaten then, either, but raced away eagerly to search for his friend.

His flying became erratic. He felt weak. He felt faint. His wings became heavier and heavier. He sniffed the air, hoping for a garden's rich perfume or a flowerbed, even a potted pansy, or a begonia on someone's windowsill, but through the stench of the city he detected nothing so delicate, nothing so nourishing.

Unable to fly in a straight line, he zigged and zagged, then spiraled lower and lower. His vision blurred, and he could barely lift his wings. He glanced at the two towers, rising above the city, so close and yet suddenly so far away. Exhausted, he crashed to the ground.

For a long moment, Bumble lay unmoving in the dirt. A thought flashed through his mind, and he wondered if the cat had tried to follow him. Cats were sneaky creatures. He tried to get up, but only managed to twitch his tail-feathers a little and to flutter his wings, and then he lay still again.

Unable to even lift his head, he directed his gaze at the ponderous gates that rose before him. Despair filled his tiny heart, and he gave a sob. He'd made it right up to the city's main entrance before falling right in the middle of the road from Karlass to Jiwashek, and with his nose so close to the earth—right in the very dirt—he could finally smell the scent of Chernovog.

"Bumble is so sorry!" he murmured as he wept soft tears of failure.

A shadow fell over him. The cat, he thought hopelessly, or some unseeing pedestrian about to step on him, or a wagon about to run him over. He would never be able to move in time to save himself.

"Heroes shouldn't cry," Marian whispered.

Vines of honeysuckle blossoms fell all around him. Startled, Bumble found the strength to twitch one wing and flip himself over on his back. He gazed up at the last unicorn. A few petals still clung to the corners of her mouth. The lush fragrance of the blossoms threatened to overwhelmed him, yet, hungry as he was, he just stared at Marian. The morning star twinkled above her head, and a host of fainter ones surrounded her. Framed in the last moments of night, she glowed!

"Drink, my friend," Marian urged. "The blossoms won't stay fresh for very long."

Bumble pressed his face to the nearest flower and drained its nectar. "You shouldn't have come," he told Marian as his strength returned. "Men will see you!"

Standing protectively over him, she shook her head. "Sooner or later, you have to stop hiding," she answered. "I should have remembered that back on the hilltop, but a moment of fear got the better of me."

"But what if they won't let us in?" he persisted. "What if they won't open the gates?

Her blue eyes flashed. "Then you'll fly over their walls," she said. "And I'll kick the gates down."

Bumble shoved his beak into another blossom, then looked up at her. "You really are my friend," he said, "and I'm not just saying that so I can eat you."

Marian started to laugh, but fell abruptly silent. The light in her eyes sharpened as she backed up a single step and lifted her head.

Great metal gears began to grind. Chains clanked and rattled. Iron hinges in need of grease groaned and wooden joints strained.

Bumble looked up from his refreshment with wide eyes.

The gates of Jiwashek slowly swung open.

18

TRANQUILLITY TOR WAS THE HIGHEST PEAK in the Imagination Mountains. Nothing grew on its harsh, rocky slopes, not a tree,
nor any blade of grass at all. In Fall and Winter, snow and ice covered
it. In Spring and summer it rose stark and bare and lifeless above all
the other mountains.

Yet, despite this seeming ugliness, there were qualities to the tor that
made it worthy of its name. From its pinnacle, one could sometimes
look down at the clouds for a change, instead of up at them. And here,
the sky when it was clear possessed a blueness that couldn't be found
anywhere else. At such a height, the wind was not often still, but when
it was, a careful listener could almost hear the world turning.

Harrow had never been to Tranquillity Tor before, or to any of the
mountains in the Imagination Range, but he'd read accounts of this
high place recorded in Stormfire's books, and they had filled him with
a need to see it for himself. His father had called it a perfect place for
meditation. Harrow agreed with that assessment. Isolated and beautiful in a raw way, it inspired a thoughtful state.

Alone on this pinnacle that Stormfire had held so dear, he thought
about his father. In fact, he couldn't stop thinking about his father.
The contents of the books in Ramoses library haunted him, for they
revealed a different Stormfire, a father that seemed almost a stranger
to him. Stormfire the philosopher and prophet. Stormfire the poet.
Had the leader of the Dragonkin deliberately hidden these aspects of
himself from his children? Or had Harrow been so self-involved and
immature that he'd simply never paid attention?

Such questions stung his heart. Maybe he'd just never taken the
time to get to know his parent. The possibility caused him deeper
pain than any he'd ever known.

Though the sun shone brightly in the azure sky, the air was crisp and cold. Wrapped in his wings, Harrow watched the wisps of cottony clouds that drifted past the mountain peak and tried to find some sense of peace. Far below a pair of eagles glided side by side, dipping and climbing in carefree flight as they rode the wind currents. Like graceful dancers in perfect choreography they skipped across the updrafts and downdrafts, inseparable, linked by some bond of friendship, perhaps, or love—or brotherhood.

He regretted his fight with Chan. In time, he hoped he could find the words to apologize. It hadn't been that long ago that he and his brother, and dear Luna, also, had sailed the skies like those eagles, side by side, together. The longer he observed the eagles, the more he missed his siblings.

They would be worried about him by now. Three days had passed since he'd fled from Stronghold without a word to anyone. At first, he'd flown aimlessly. Then, blinded by his anger, he'd scoured parts of the forest for some sign of Gaunt and his Griffin followers, flying as far east as the Windy Sea and ultimately as far west as these Imagination Mountains where he found himself now. He wanted nothing so much as to find his father's murderer, but wherever Gaunt had gone, he'd covered his tracks well.

The hunt wasn't over, though. Wyvernwood was large and deep, and Harrow was only resting.

The eagles swooped lower, then plummeted through a narrow mountain pass and out of sight. What would Stormfire have made of that, Harrow wondered? Would he have found something significant in the flight of raptors? Would he have composed some ruminative poem to hide away with the rest in Ramoses' library?

More questions he had no answers for.

Yet, one thing he had learned by coming to Tranquillity Tor. He knew, or thought he knew, why his father had held this place so dear. Harrow gazed down, and Wyvernwood spread out before him, lush and vast and mysterious. For all his young life the forest had been his world, and he had never ventured from it, nor even dreamed of doing so.

Tranquillity Tor had changed that. He had only to turn his head to the west to see that the world was larger than he had ever imagined. The Windy Sea had marked the edge of his world, and Angmar and

Degarm had been little more than borders to him. The forest had been everything—womb, cradle, playground, home.

He looked beyond the Imagination Mountains now, and for the first time he felt an aching longing to know what was out there. More forests, to be sure. Perhaps more seas. Other lands and distant places!

From those distant places the Dragonkin had come, from all corners of the world and from many nations. Stormfire—his father—had called them, gathered and guided them to the Great Refuge, the place of safety, to Wyvernwood, which became his protectorate, his Stronghold against the advances of the creature called Man.

Harrow squeezed his claws into fists as he stared westward and felt the chill wind on his face. Someday, he would fly beyond these mountains and seek those lands from which the Dragonkin had come. Wyvernwood was no longer big enough to hold him. Its green beauty was all illusion and lie. His father had thought it a place of safety, but his father had been wrong.

There was no safe place anywhere in the world.

And if Wyvernwood was not a safe place, then there was no reason to hide in it.

Snapping his black wings wide, he exhaled an angry blast of fire. His thoughts were heretical—and yet he knew they were true. The great Stormfire, savior and leader of the Dragonkin, had been wrong!

He covered his head beneath his wings and clenched his eyes shut. For a long while he sat trembling with the strength of his realization. He wanted to weep, but there was no point in tears. He remembered his father's voice, his gentle touch, flying for the first time at Stormfire's side, sitting with him in the village while the Satyrs and Fomorians sang and played music, all the countless moments they had spent together.

And yet, he knew his father so little.

Uncovering his head, he gazed out upon the world with newly opened eyes. Perhaps in every child's life, he thought, there came a similar moment of realization when he discovered that a parent was not infallible after all.

Harrow could forgive Stormfire for being less than perfect.

He could not forgive Gaunt for taking him away too soon.

Turning toward Wyvernwood again, he blew another blast of fire that turned the nearest clouds orange. His hind claws dug deep grooves in the rock. Nurturing his anger, he spread his wings and soared away from Tranquillity Tor.

Somewhere below, in some dark hole or hidden canyon or forgotten valley, Gaunt was hiding in Wyvernwood with his followers. Harrow had already criss-crossed much of the forest, but there were still places he hadn't looked. Up north, particularly, where the coasts of the Windy Sea turned rocky, and along the borders with Angmar where it was dangerous for all the Dragonkin. He doubted the cowardly Gaunt had the courage to hide so close to the shadow of Man, but Harrow would look anyway.

Gaunt the Usurper.

Gaunt the Murderer.

Down through the clouds he flew, following the slopes of the mountains to the mouth of the pass where the eagles had disappeared. Through this pass and others like it, the Dragonkin had come hundreds of years ago on their legendary exodus from the outer lands. Harrow pushed the thought aside and flew faster. He'd had enough history for the day.

In the southern skies where the mountains joined the forest, he spied Electra and her Harpy sisters watching him, but they made no effort to intercept him, nor did he wave or acknowledge their presence, and soon they were out of sight. Their appearance assured him, however, that Gaunt was not hiding in the western mountains.

The bright sun filled the woods with shadows, and Harrow slowed his flight, skimming the treetops as he peered into the dark recesses. Even under his sharp gaze, Wyvernwood clung to its secrets. In a clearing, he settled down to earth and folded his wings tightly against his body. A dense section of forest defied aerial reconnaissance, but he refused to pass it by. Dropping to all fours and hugging the ground, he slithered into the brush.

An eerie gloom closed about him. The leafy canopy blocked most of the sunlight, and what light did penetrate possessed the green tint of the leaves it passed through. No breeze penetrated at all; the air was warm and still. A pair of damselflies frolicking among the trees caught Harrow's attention. Turing in their direction, he crawled a short distance through the foliage, peering over bushes, dragging his tail behind. The damselflies separated, darted through the trees, and came back together again above a narrow, lazy stream.

A fifteen-point buck, drinking from the stream, looked up and regarded him with a calm gaze. "Come forth, my overgrown nematode, and join me in a little riparian refreshment. Though no more than a runnel or a rivulet, the stream is cool and as pure as a doe on her first date."

Harrow raised higher on his front legs and opened his wings ever so slightly in the dense brush. "I'm no worm," he informed the buck, "nor even a Wyrm. I seek the mad Griffin, Gaunt."

The buck spat as it fixed Harrow with a hard gaze. "Would that his blood incarnedined these antlers!" he said. "I know a hawk from a hedgehog, Son of Stormfire, and I know you." He hung his head until his antlers brushed the stream's surface. After a quiet moment, he added solemnly, "I grieve for your sire."

"Your heart is as big as your words," Harrow replied. "Have you seen or heard anything of griffins in these parts?"

"The nocturnal efflations of an ant cannot escape my hearing," the buck answered with unabashed pride. "The passing of a griffin through these woods would be thunder to my sensitive ears. As were your maneuvers, I might add." He gazed down at the stream again. Harrow's eyes narrowed. Was he mistaken, or was this deer admiring his own reflection?

The buck looked up again. "There is, however, a rumor, no more than a whisper really, carried by sparrows and finches."

"Tell me," Harrow said.

The buck frowned. "Well, I can't be sure," he demurred. "I'm not exactly on close terms with such avians. An irritating habit of landing in my antlers and soiling my handsome head with their defecations has too often come between us. Still, I hear them muttering among themselves in the branches and when they come to the stream to drink and bathe."

Vain creature, Harrow thought as the buck again paused to glance at its reflection. *I can understand the little birds' behavior.* "This rumor," he pressed.

"You can't trust finches," the buck continued, looking up. "They breathe prevarications and slanders the way you and I breathe air. Sparrows are only slightly less mendacious."

Harrow thumped his tail on the ground to show his impatience. Then he forced a smile. *A dragon's smile can be a terrible thing*, his father used to say.

The buck's eyes snapped wide, and it began to tremble. "Well, I don't speak Finch very well," he said in a more subdued tone. "They do that funny thing with their *r*'s, and their conjugations have more exceptions than rules, if you know what I mean. But they mention a place somewhere in the north. They call it *Redclaw*. Or maybe it's *Ledcraw*. It's so difficult to be sure. But it seems to refer to something between the Windy *Me* and the *River* Blackwater."

Harrow closed his eyes and nodded slowly as he considered the buck's information. In the north—between the Windy Sea and the Blackwater. It was rugged country up there. A small army could hide in the ravines and gorges and hills.

"Of course, it's only a rumor," the buck added. "I'd hate to send you off on a wild goose chase. Wild geese are almost as unreliable as finches and sparrows."

Harrow wasted no more time. Without bothering to thank the buck, he rose on his hind legs to his full height. Branches cracked and broke. Leaves rained down as the canopy tore open, and sunlight flooded the glade. The buck jumped away from the stream, spun about, and vanished into the woods. It was almost a rule of the Dragonkin: *do no damage to the forest*. But Harrow didn't care. For the first time he had an idea where Gaunt was hiding. Nothing would stand in his way now. Rising above the trees, he spread his black wings and leaped into the sky.

The sun beat hotly on his back by the time he reached the Blackwater River. Turning northward, following its course in reverse, he flew to the Valley of Eight Winds. The hillsides were scorched with the charred remains of the griffin nests, but the river waters had receded back into their natural banks. He circled above the wreckage of Gorganar's monstrous castle. Pieces of it had washed downstream, but larger sections lay piled on the shore.

Only a deliberate effort could have done that. With his sister, he'd destroyed Gorganar's nest, then dammed the Blackwater and caused it to flood the burning valley. Yet someone had undone the blockage and set the river free again. Only a Griffin's strength or a Dragon's determination could have managed that so quickly, and he was sure no dragon had done the deed.

Still, he wondered, why would it matter to Gaunt or any of the Griffinkin if the river were open if they no longer lived on its shores?

With a roar of frustration, Harrow turned away from the valley. *Somewhere in the north*, the buck had said, *between the Windy Sea and the Blackwater River*. That still left a lot of ground to cover and a lot of potential hiding places. Without some further clue, he could still search for days.

He swept his gaze around the sky and over the forest below. A narrow chasm almost hidden from sight by tall pine trees drew his attention. He glided from one end of it to the other, finding nothing. Disappointed, he left it behind.

But disappointment faded when he observed a thin column of white smoke rising above the distant trees and diffusing on the wind. Tipping his right wing, he turned and headed straight for it. He knew it was nothing more than chimney smoke, an indication of some hermit or farmer residing in an isolated corner of the forest. Wyvernwood was full of such. But still, he felt it worth investigating.

He found a cottage, small and neatly kept, nestled among soaring redwoods. Space had been cleared for a yard with flowerbeds of chrysanthemums, marigolds, and roses. Taldng care to damage none of it, Harrow settled gently down to earth. The smoke that curled up from the chimney bore the odors of herbs and potatoes, all the ingredients of a rich, vegetable stew, and he wondered if he'd arrived in the middle of someone's dinner.

Yet, no one came out to greet him, and he found that puzzling. It wasn't every day that a Dragon landed in your front yard, and something his size wasn't easy to miss, no matter how tasty and interesting the dinner might be. He called out a greeting, but though the front door and several of the windows were open, no response came back. Stretching out his long neck, he peered inside.

A low fire crackled in the fireplace, and a black pot dangling over the flames bubbled merrily. Nearby, the table was set with dishes and spoons, but there was no sign of the occupants.

He called out again. This time, he heard a sound he didn't like, a low groan from behind the cottage. He heard the groan again, and immediately he became wary. Crouching low to the ground, he crept around the side of cottage. In the shade of the redwoods that grew behind the house, he spied an indistinct gray shape on the ground.

But more, he noted that the bark on the trees was scarred and scratched. Some of the branches were broken, and the grass was torn up. It was obvious that a fight had taken place here!

With the barest of movements, the gray shape slowly turned a curly head to regard him with dull eyes. At the same time, an arm stretched out and gnarled fingers flexed. An old satyr sat painfully up. One of his horns had been snapped off, and blood and dirt matted his hairy face. He stared at Harrow, trying to focus his vision.

"They took her!" he muttered through blood-caked lips. "I tried to fight 'em, but they took her!"

Harrow moved closer to the satyr and studied him with concern. "Who took who?"

One of the satyr's blue eyes was nearly swollen shut, and he rubbed a fist over the other. "Griffins!" he answered, spitting dirt as he raised his fists. "I struck 'em, I did, and gave 'em what-for, but I couldn't stop 'em! They took Sarabet! My wife! Jus' flew off with her, they did!"

Harrow regarded the old satyr open admiration. Not many creatures would try to stand up to a griffin. But he'd seen no sign of griffins from the sky. "You must have been unconscious for quite a while," he said sympathetically.

"No matter," the satyr answered. "I know the direction they came from and the direction they went."

At this news, Harrow gave a low growl in his throat. "Show me."

The old satyr turned and pointed. "See those two tall poplar trees in the distance? They're good as markers to a pair of sharp eyes." He rose unsteadily to his feet and put one hand to the wound on his head. "I seen 'em coming. Straight off the horizon the pair of 'em flew, an' they passed right between those poplars. An' even when I was lyin' on the ground half-dead after they took Sarabet, I watched the direction they went. It was right back through 'em!"

Harrow bent even lower to stare in the direction the old Satyr indicated. He wished there was something more he could do for the poor fellow, but his claws weren't delicate enough for bandaging and medicines. "I have a score to settle with some griffins, myself," Harrow confided.

"Then don't worry none about me," the satyr answered. "Just go settle it. An' settle it for me, too. They said they'd kill Sarabet if I told anyone, but I figure one way or another they'll kill her if I don't."

"I'll bring your wife back if I can," Harrow said.

Marking the direction once more, Harrow rose into the sky and flew as swiftly as he could. With a captive, the griffins would fly in a straight line to their hiding place. If he was lucky, he might overtake them. If not, he'd keep a straight course even if it took him all the way to Angmar!

The sun continued to sink lower and lower in the west. In the east, darkness began to gather as night made its advance. Though he caught no sight of griffins in the sky, Harrow drove himself onward, ignoring the growing fatigue in his wings. No longer skimming the treetops, he flew at an altitude, relying on sharp vision and instinct.

Then, in the deep twilight just before full night, with the pale moon beginning to peek over the eastern horizon, he saw—the Ruins. That was the only name anyone ever called them by, for no one alive remembered their purpose, or their builder. Castle or Monastery or Something Else? The answer was lost in antiquity. Before Stormfire had led the Great Migration to Wyvernwood the Ruins had been—the Ruins.

Again, he recalled words that his father had spoken. *There are things in Wyvernwood older than we are.* The Ruins were proof of that. Many people believed they were haunted, so few ever went there.

Harrow didn't need to fly closer to know where Gaunt was hiding.

With his quest so near its end, he could finally admit his fatigue. Directly below, he spied a low hillock with few trees crowning its summit. With a sigh, he landed and wrapped himself in his wings. Once down, he couldn't see the Ruins. Too many hills and too much forest blocked his view. But he could sense that Gaunt was close, feel him as surely and as strongly as he felt the blood pumping through his own body, and he found a strange, inexplicable comfort in that.

Could Gaunt feel him near in the same way?

He gazed at the moon. It was past fullness, a waning moon, but the darkened half that rounded it out was still barely visible and more mysteriously beautiful to him somehow than the brighter half.

He was like that moon. Calm and tranquil, there was no war between his dark side and his brighter. He knew in his heart that it was wrong to kill, and yet he was going to kill Gaunt, and his heart didn't argue. Like the moon, his two natures co-existed at peace with each other.

Perhaps he'd gone mad. He found a certain irony to think that he had begun his day wrapped in his wings on a high mountaintop basking in sunlight, and now he was ending it wrapped in his wings on a low hilltop bathed in the light of the moon. His father would have appreciated that.

When this is over, maybe I'll try my hand at poetry.

The breeze blew harder as the moon moved toward zenith. The trees bent and swayed, and the silvery leaves rustled. Rested, Harrow spread his wings and took to the sky again, turning toward the Ruins. Against the black of night, he was little more than a shadow in the heavens. He climbed rapidly, gaining altitude, and then began a long, silent glide toward his target.

Even from some distance, as he began his approach, he could tell that something was different. The Ruins were no long in ruins. The encircling walls had been repaired and strengthened. The four towers, once crumbling, stood tall and formidable again. The courtyards were clear of debris. Massive new gates replaced the shattered old ones. The surrounding woods had been cut back, and a broad space cleared around the structure.

So Gaunt had built himself a fortress. To Harrow, it was further proof of the Griffin's perfidy. That kind of reconstruction took time. He had to give credit where it was due—Gaunt had planned well and long and hatched his schemes in secret.

But he had not planned alone!

Suddenly, Harrow saw the true depth of Gaunt's villainy. The calm he'd carried inside him from the hillock dissolved, and a red anger swept over him as he recalled three warships sailing down the Black-water, passing right beneath the great nest of Gorganar and Argulo, right through the Valley of Eight Winds. Aborting his approach, Harrow swooped high and circled the Ruins, noting details he should have observed sooner. The walls were constructed of smoothly hewn stone blocks, wedged and mortared and reinforced. The architecture revealed a skill and craftsmanship the Griffinkin could never have achieved on their own.

That was the work of Man!

To confirm his suspicions, the moon shifted just enough to reveal a narrow road running straight from the fortress through the woods—straight northward.

Yet, there were griffins at watch on the walls, and Griffins in the courtyards.

Gaunt had made some alliance with Angmar!

The realization sickened and enraged Harrow. Folding his wings, he dived out of the night toward the fortress with but one thought in his mind—to smash the abomination and kill Gaunt! He extended his claws as he rushed toward the nearest tower. The air screamed past his ears.

Atop the tower, a pair of griffin guards, alerted at the last instant by a shadow or the rush of wind, looked up. Their eyes snapped wide with surprise that turned instantly to terror. They cast their spears, and without waiting to see if they struck, the pair leaped from the parapet and spread their eagle's wings.

Harrow spread his own wings, braking on the air. For a moment, he seemed to hang directly above the tower as he exhaled a blast of fire. Heat and flame engulfed the tower. The pair of griffin guards screamed as they felt their feathers scorch and singe, and their screams were joined by others at their posts atop the other towers and upon the walls.

Harrow's momentum carried him past the fortress and out over the forest. He wheeled about for a second attack and let out a roar of anger. Though his blast had blackened the stone, the tower still stood!

He attacked again, strafing the largest courtyard. Griffins scrambled to get out of his path. Again his fire lit up the night. A wagon exploded. Barrels and crates blossomed into flame. Again, Harrow sailed out over the forest and turned. The destruction he'd caused was minimal and brought little satisfaction.

He'd do better this time!

But as he raced toward the walls again, a trio of griffins rose up to intercept him. Harrow smiled grimly. These three, at least, had found a measure of courage. He respected a Griffin's strength—no other creature could match them for that. But they couldn't match his speed or his aerial agility. With a roar, he charged right through them, using his leathery wingspan to sweep them from the sky.

A pair of tall gates loomed before him. Those, at least, were made of wood! He spat fire, and they ignited in a red, crackling flash!

He had no time to rejoice, though. A large rock whistled past his shoulder and struck the wall as he shot passed it. A second rock flashed by his ear. Twisting as he flew, Harrow looked over his shoulder. Yet another griffin with a bag of stones around his neck chased after him. Already he held a third missile in his lion's paw and prepared to throw.

Flying suddenly upward, Harrow soared in a wide loop and leveled out again behind his startled attacker. Opening his mouth wide, he drew a deep breath. The griffin screamed, dropped his stone, and dived in a panic for the shelter of some trees.

Harrow only laughed as he struck at the trees with his tail, scattering leaves and broken branches. Then he flew on. His war was with Gaunt, not with his pathetic underlings.

The burning gates fell off their hinges and crashed to the ground. Flame and sparks shot upward. Still, the damage Harrow had done disappointed him. Forgetting the walls for the moment, he glared at the towers again and spied an unshuttered window near the top of the tallest one. Immune to fire, he seized a large chunk of the burning gates, soared upward, and flung it through the opening. Instantly, the interior lit up with a wild, red flickering. Black smoke boiled out, and Harrow roared in triumph.

But new cries caught his attention, and these were not griffin-screams! A pair of minotaur children rushed across the courtyard toward the shattered gates. Behind them ran a Fomorian, a bear-cub, a she-satyr, and a trio of basilisks. They were risking everything to make their escape in the confusion.

A griffin wielding a whip charged out of one of the towers and chased after them. Remembering the injured old satyr he'd found earlier, Harrow roared. Even the escapees stopped in their tracks, and the whip-wielding griffin spun around too late. Black dragon claws closed tightly around him, crushing his eagle-wings.

Harrow tossed the griffin aside and turned to the escapees. "Hide in the forest!" he shouted, taking the moment to study the she-satyr, certain that she was the wife he'd promised to return home "Go quickly!"

They didn't need to be told again. Dodging and leaping over the burning pieces, they dashed through the open gate, and Harrow took to the sky to cover them until they reached the trees. When they were out of sight, he turned once more to press the fight.

Rising skyward, he circled the highest of the four towers, settled on top of it, and dug his claws into the structure. Pieces of mortar and stone chips came loose, but he only scowled. Whoever had built this place had built it well. Pausing, he shot a look around for something easier to destroy. In that moment, he noted the shape and nature of the four towers and the way the scarlet light of his flames reflected upon them.

Redclaw. He knew now what that meant.

When he was done with it, it would be the Ruins again.

Harrow, son of Stormfire, stretched his neck upward and blew a blast of fire that seemed to ignite the sky itself. For a moment the breeze seemed to stop as it met a wall of heat, and the silver shine of the moon on the nearest forest trees turned red.

It was his challenge to Gaunt.

And it was raw rage.

19

GAUNT SPRANG BACK FROM THE WINDOW barely in time. Burning debris came crashing through. A velvet tapestry took fire immediately. Flaming embers scattered over the floor and touched the pile of dry sticks and grass that made his bed. In an instant, that also burst into flame.

"Put it out! Put it out!" Gaunt cringed away from the flames. The largest piece of the debris blocked the door, making it impossible to escape.

Minhep seized a braided rug from the floor and tried to beat out the hottest flames, but the rug took fire as well. His underling, Callus, kicked and stomped at the edges of the bed with his bare paws. Burning sticks flew up, spreading more flames.

"It burns!" Gaunt shrieked. In terror, he dashed for the window again, gripped the sill with his front paws, and rose to stand on it. On the verge of leaping out into the night, he froze. Pain lanced through his right side as he tried to lift his wings. He still couldn't fly!

He was trapped!

"Put it out!" he cried again. Shrinking away from the window, he lunged toward the door, the only exit from the room, but the flames drove him back. Desperately, he whirled, seeking something with which to beat out the fire. But there was little of actual use in the room. The tapestry was already aflame, and Minhep wielded the only bit of carpet!

Callus stomped at the bed again. His eyes were alight with fear and desperation to match Gaunt's, and with a bit too much strength, he kicked a sizable section of it across the room. Minhep screamed and, dropping his bit of rug, threw himself into a safe corner as fiery sticks and burning grass showered around the griffin-leader.

Flinging up his left wing to shield himself, Gaunt turned away, saving his only good eye. But his exposed feathers began to curl and shrivel. "You fool! You good-for-nothing fool!" he shouted. But Callus was beyond any insult. He stared in horror at the fire, then dived for the window. Even as he shook embers from his wings, Gaunt caught the cowardly griffin by his hind legs. "Now, you're good for something!"

Callus let out a shrill scream as Gaunt swung him high and smashed him down on the nearest flames. "I told you to put the fire out!" Gaunt shouted. "And now you will!" Again and again, with merciless fury and all his fear-driven griffin's strength, he raised and swung Callus, using him as he would a blanket to beat out the fire.

Finally, when the last flames were out, he let go of a lifeless, smoldering body and sat back on his haunches to wipe his brow. "Sweaty work," he said to Minhep, who still cringed in his safe corner. Adjusting his eye-patch, Gaunt gazed around. There was as much blood as soot on the walls and floor. "I just saved your life, Minhep."

Beyond the window, the sky flashed with orange fire.

Gaunt leaped to his feet. At the same instant, the charred door smashed inward. Canaan, with a pair of griffins, stared across the threshold. Angmar's reluctant ambassador stepped daintily inside. "Are we having a good time in here?"

The griffin-leader snarled. "Curse Stormfire's black hatchling!"

"Indeed," Canaan agreed. "It looks like he nearly cooked you in your own bedchamber." He nudged Callus's corpse with a booted toe. "Good thing you had a fire extinguisher."

Trembling, Minhep rose to his feet. Even through the feathers on his face, he looked pale as he leaned on the wall for support. "I don't like your tone, Man!" he hissed as he held out his burned paws. He shot a look at Gaunt. "This pink-meat is laughing at us!"

Gaunt glared at his lieutenant. "Maybe he's just remembering a joke—the way you were yesterday, Minhep."

Heeding the subtle warning, Minhep fell silent and cowered back in his corner.

Canaan stepped over Callus's body, went to the window, and peered out. "I assume you've been watching the black Dragon from here?" he said. "Certainly, it's safer than down below." He turned to Gaunt, then swept his gaze around the charred and blood-spattered room. "Or maybe not." Forcing a smile, he shrugged and stared out the window again as Harrow went sweeping past on another attack run. He folded his arms across his chest, and without looking back, continued. "Personally, I think it's time we dealt with this small aggravation and taught the Dragons a lesson they sorely need to learn."

Gaunt growled. "What kind of lesson do you think you can teach the son of Stormfire, pink-meat? If he didn't fry you in your boots, he could step on you as if you were a bug and never notice the goop between his toes!"

The night beyond the window flashed red-orange again as Harrow blasted fire. A small squad of howling griffins zoomed by the window with smoldering tails and singed wings. A vibration shivered through the stones as the dragon struck the tower again.

Canaan spoke with open scorn. "The Age of Dragons is passing," he said, his voice hard and cold. "It's the Age of Man that's dawning, not the Age of Griffins. Maybe it's time you learned a lesson, yourself." Stepping over Callus, he crossed to the shattered door where the two griffin guards that had attended him still waited. "Follow me, your Majesty," he said with a mocking bow. "School is in session." He exited, beckoning for the pair of griffin guards to accompany him. They fell in without question or hesitation.

Minhep rose to his feet again. The fur was singed off his paws, and they were blistered. His expression betrayed his pain. "How can you tolerate . . . !"

"Shut up!" Gaunt hissed, holding up a hand to silence Minhep. He glanced at Callus on the floor, then at his lieutenant's hands. Minhep, at least, had fought the fire and stayed by his side. That deserved some reward. He softened his tone. "Later, maybe I'll let you eat Canaan. But first, let's see what he thinks he can teach us."

Gaunt hurried into the hallway, past numerous doors and down the long spiral staircase. Huffing and puffing, he struggled for breath as he descended and fought the wave of blackness that tried to engulf him. The wound in his side throbbed painfully, and he could feel the hot blood seeping through the bandage again. Fear had given him the strength he needed to beat the flames out, but now that the danger was passed he knew he'd overtaxed himself. He did his best to hide it, though.

A king could never show weakness—especially a Griffin King!

His step faltered as he passed his throne room, and for just a moment, he paused to lean on the wall. Then, someone touched his elbow and offered him support. He turned his head to meet Minhep's stare. Gaunt couldn't hide his surprise, nor his suspicion. "Through everything that happens, through all the abuse I heap upon you," he said, "Why do you stay at my side?"

Minhep scowled. "Because you're the son of Gorganar," he said fiercely, "and the grandson of Argulo, who brought us to Wyvern-wood. If I don't believe in you now, what else is there to believe in?"

"Believe in yourself!" Gaunt answered. "My father said before he died that we griffins were all cowards. Prove him wrong!"

Minhep held out his arm and allowed Gaunt to lean on it, and together they strode toward the door to the main courtyard. "But he wasn't wrong, was he?" Minhep said bitterly.

Gaunt didn't answer. His anger, as well as his pain, threatened to overwhelm him, but he wanted desperately to know what Canaan was up to. The pink-meat was already through the doors and outside with his two new lackeys. Gaunt reminded himself to find out later what Canaan had offered them to so command their loyalty.

"Move it into place!" he heard Canaan shouting as he hesitated on the threshold and gazed nervously out for any sign of Harrow. "Hurry! He's turning! He'll be back this way any moment!"

Canaan's two griffins, along with four others, wheeled a strange machine into place at one end of the courtyard. Gaunt hadn't even noticed it before, though there were two others nearby. As he watched, the six griffins turned the machine and, hauling together on a thick rope, cocked the giant catapult.

"Now, get up there!" Canaan ordered. "Make sure you draw him this way, as I told you!"

His two griffins spread their wings and flew upward just as Harrow came screaming over the far wall. Straight for the Dragon they flew as if to offer challenge, but just as Harrow drew breath to blast his cursed fire, they turned around.

Gaunt's good eye narrowed to a disbelieving slit. Canaan's griffins were offering themselves as bait!

Harrow followed them. Straight for the machine he unwittingly flew, and the pair of griffins folded their wings so suddenly they fairly crashed into the ground. At the machine, Canaan leaned on a lever. The catapult sprang up.

Gaunt expected some stone or some massive missile to fly from its cup. Instead, the catapult launched a shower of water and a heavy net whose corners and sides were weighted with stones. The net unfolded and unfolded again as it sailed upward.

Gaunt, with all his griffins, gave a shout of triumph as Stormfire's hatchling smashed into the net. Instantly, it entangled his wings and closed tightly around his body. Still, his momentum carried him beyond Redclaw's wall and out of sight, but the sound of his crash could be heard by all.

"What kind of lesson is this?" Gaunt shouted to Canaan from the relative safety of the doorway. "He'll burn through your net in no time!"

Canaan's griffins and the four that had assisted in positioning the catapult wasted no time; they flew into the air, over the wall, and after Harrow. Other griffins, following their lead, sprang out of hiding in the other towers or from the shadows of the walls to join them. They howled for blood, and their shrieking filled the night.

Leaving his machine, Canaan strode across the courtyard to stand before Gaunt. It was all Gaunt could manage to keep from clawing the arrogant grin off the man's face. "The net is thoroughly saturated," Canaan explained. "That adds to its weight, and it will prevent him from burning through it long enough for your griffins to club him senseless." His grin turned into a malicious smirk. "Or if you've a big enough log lying around, maybe you'd care to finish him off in the same stylish and innovative manner that you finished his father."

Minhep gave a growl and started toward Canaan, but Gaunt gripped his arm and pulled him back. "I don't want the hatchling killed," he said calmly. "At least, not yet. That would only enrage his brother and sister, and the rest of the Dragonkin, as well."

"You can't hold a Dragon for long," Minhep warned. "He may not be able to burn through the net, but he can burn anyone who comes near, whether the net is saturated or not, and the net will dry. If crashing to the ground at his best speed didn't break his neck, then better to kill him now while we can!"

Gaunt cuffed Minhep with the back of one paw. "No!" he shouted. "I want this one alive until I decide what to do with him!" He whirled toward Canaan, forcing the man to take a step back. "But I'll take your suggestion and improve on it. You'll see who is the teacher here!"

With newfound strength, setting aside his pain, he strode across the courtyard and out through the ruined gates. Canaan and Minhep hurried after him, and that gave him a gnarly satisfaction. He was the king of the griffins, and if there were any lessons to give, he would give them! Around the outside of the walls he went, guided by the enthusiastic cries of his subjects.

Only the twitching and thrashing of the black Dragon's tail gave any indication that he still lived. Under the weighted net he lay, and griffins swarmed over him. They beat him with their fists or with clubs, kicked him, taunted and clawed him. The sight disgusted even Gaunt; they were like insects that had brought down a giant, and they were enjoying their victory!

Still, it was his victory, too. "Go into the forest!" he commanded several of his guards. "Find a pair of stout trees and strip them bare. Make sure their ends are sharp when you bring them back! And be quick!"

Howling, four griffins sprang into the air and vanished into the dark woods.

"What are you up to?" Canaan demanded in a dark mood.

Gaunt ignored him. From the nearby woods came a snapping and cracking. Leaves shivered and timbers fell. Then came still more cracking, an unholy racket. Shortly, the four griffins returned. Between them, they carried two tall trees stripped bare of branch and bark and wickedly pointed. The white, wet wood gleamed in the moonlight

Gaunt shouted commands to the other griffins. "Stretch out his wings! Hold him down! Keep that net on him!" As the other griffins obeyed, turning Harrow onto his back and stretching his leathery wings wide, Gaunt turned to the four. "Now fly high!" he ordered. "And pin him to the ground! Drive your spears deep!"

"Maybe you're not a coward," Minhep dared to whisper over Gaunt's shoulder, "but you're a fool!"

In pairs the four spread their feathered wings and lifted their weapons. On the ground, the other griffins held the edges of the net down with all their might. They no longer howled and cheered, but they watched the four fly upward with an anxious, hungry gleam in their eyes.

The night became thick and silent. Even Gaunt held his breath.

The four hurled their monstrous spears. The white wood flashed down, impaling the black wings, tearing through them with a sickening sound, driving into the earth. Such agony drove Harrow to wakefulness. His head jerked up against the net, and he screamed. His claws raked, but the net held. Above him, the griffins hammered on the trees with their fists, using their great griffin strength to drive them even deeper, more securely into the ground.

The other griffins began to howl again. In a frenzy, they beat their chests and tore each others' feathers and fur. Harrow's suffering only encouraged them, and overhead, the four aerial griffins hammered the make-shift stakes yet again, pounding them with such force that the upper ends splintered and the sound drummed far into the forest.

"Make sure that net is kept wet," Gaunt told one of the guards. "And get some stakes on it, too, to hold it tight." He grabbed another griffin by the arm. "Four guards on him at all times. If he shakes his tail, I want to know about it!"

Careful to stay a safe distance back, Gaunt walked slowly around his captive. Harrow seemed to have lost consciousness, but the Griffin King didn't mind that. He wasn't interested in the dragon's agony. Only in his value.

"I've never been so close to a Dragon before," he confided as he rejoined Minhep near the wall. "Even defeated and helpless, this one has a certain frightening grace that I can admire." He put a hand to his side and felt a shiver of fear as his paw came away stained red. Why wasn't his wound healing faster? He had to take greater care. He grasped at Minhep's arm. "Help me to my throne room."

Together, they walked the outside perimeter of Redclaw's walls and reentered the courtyard through the ruined gates. Scattered fires lit their way—a burning wagon here, there a small shed, some crates and barrels. Nothing that couldn't be replaced or rebuilt.

Gaunt felt a swell of pride. Redclaw had withstood Harrow's attack admirably. The Griffinkin had their Stronghold!

"You know his siblings will hear of this," Minhep warned. "Few secrets can be kept for long in Wyvernwood."

Gaunt paused to catch his breath and to look upward at the open window of his bedchamber in Redclaw's tallest tower. For a moment he recalled how close he'd come to death in that small room. "I'm counting on it," he answered. "No doubt every bird and bug with wings that lives in this part of the woods is already on the way to tattle."

With Minhep's support, he made his way to his throne room and curled up on the blue velvet seat. His banner, he noticed, had been knocked off the wall, but for the moment he didn't care. He wanted only to rest. With his bedchamber wrecked, this was as good a place as any to sleep. He ran one paw over the jeweled arms, marveling at their dark sparkle as he sank down. His father had never had such a throne, nor his grandfather.

"I don't see the esteemed ambassador from Angmar," Gaunt said with a sudden low chuckle.

Minhep snarled and nodded. "I don't think he had the stomach for the Dragon's crucifixion."

Gaunt crossed his paws and laid his head on them as he gently folded his wings. His beautiful wings! He'd always been so proud of them. The feathers of his left wing were scorched and withered. It would take a long time for new ones to grow. It would be a long time before he could fly again. He missed that simple joy.

"I want you to send a message to Stronghold," he said to Minhep. "Tell them they can have Harrow back—in exchange for my brother."

He closed his one good eye for a moment. He felt so tired that he knew he must sleep soon. Looking up again, he noted Minhep's injured paws and remembered that a king should reward loyalty. "Then bandage your burns," he continued in a weary voice. "After that, I imagine you're hungry. Why don't you see if you can stomach the ambassador?"

Minhep gave him a blank look. Then his lieutenant grinned.

* * *

Fleer arrived first shortly before noon, his wings beating thunder as the sun shimmered on his emerald scales. The young Dragon let out a cry of rage as he cleared the trees and spied Harrow cruelly pinned to the earth. With little more than an angry glance at Redclaw, he landed beside Stormfire's fallen child.

A pair of bold griffins, still drunk on their night's victory over the black Dragon, launched themselves from Redclaw's massive walls. Murder gleamed in their eyes as they extended their claws.

Fleer responded without mercy. Spreading his wings and leaning protectively over Harrow, he exhaled a fiery breath. His flames engulfed the pair in mid-leap, and they fell like burning stars to the ground. Four more took flight from the walls even as the first two fell, but watching their comrades burn, they turned tail and retreated back to the stone barricade. Dozens of other griffins swarmed to the top of the wall. Howling, they reared up on their hind legs and pelted the green Dragon with stones.

Fleer ignored the barrage. In a savage fury, he seized the giant stake that pierced Harrow's left wing, and with uncharacteristic strength, he ripped it free. The sudden shock brought Harrow back to consciousness, and he screamed in pain. Fleer screamed, too. Lifting the tree trunk high above his head, he flung it at the assembly of griffins. At the same time, as it left his grip, he blasted fire. The wood exploded. A shower of burning splinters and fragments rained down upon the bulwark.

On the far side of the wall, some guileful griffin turned one of the great catapults. A loud *crack* sounded as he fired it. The net sailed through the air, spreading wide. Looking up, Fleer breathed fire again. Still, the net came on, unscathed, and the griffins gathering once more upon the walls to watch howled and cheered, sure of success. After all, the net had worked once already.

But Fleer was planted firmly on the ground. He answered their cries with his own and swept the net from the sky with one wing before it could entangle him. An instant later, another barrage of stones smashed against his scaled body. The griffins howled again. The emerald Dragon paid no attention. He turned instead to the second tree-stake pinning Harrow's right wing. Wrapping his front legs around it, he attempted to pull it free as he had the first.

The second stake, though, had been driven deeper. He strained as he tried and failed to lift it. Harrow screamed in agony, and yet another barrage of stones rained down upon them. Fleer extended one wing to shelter the suffering Dragon, then slammed his weight against the huge spike to loosen the earth's grip upon it.

From behind the wall came another loud *crack*. The remaining net sailed over the wall in a spray of water. Another desperate cheer went up from the bulwark. As Fleer worked to tear the second stake away and free Harrow's right wing, he turned his head and breathed fire. The net's heavy rope strands smoked, but didn't burn.

Then, before the treacherous snare entangled Fleer another fiery light appeared above the forest. With wings that crackled on the wind, the last Phoenix in the world dived out of the bright dawn. Her talons caught the net, and without slowing her dazzling flight, she carried it to the wall and dropped it. Griffins scattered into the air or leaped back into the courtyard, but a luckless trio found themselves enmeshed in the weighted net. Struggling and writhing, they tumbled off the wall, shattering their eagles' wings as they struck the ground.

Avoiding another hail of stones, Phoebe veered away from the fortress and assumed a watchful position near the forest's edge. Rage had transformed her. Beautiful she still was, but also dangerous, deadly. Her slender beak opened to reveal a throat full of flames as she shrieked a challenge.

The barrage of stones from Redclaw ceased. Bending all his strength to the remaining tree-stake, Fleer finally ripped it free. Again, Harrow screamed, and Fleer roared in triumph. Raising the tree trunk high, he flung it toward the griffins. Though it fell short, it struck the wall like a thunderclap. The vibration shivered through the stone, and mortar spilled from between the blocks in a gray cloud.

The first net still stretched tightly over Harrow was all that held Stormfire's firstborn down. Seizing the strands, Fleer ripped it to shreds and cast the pieces away.

Finally free, Harrow beat his ravaged wings against the ground and thrashed his tail as he struggled to rise, but the night's ordeal had sapped his strength. Fleer knelt down and cradled the black Dragon's head and made sympathetic purring sounds to calm him.

Behind them, the treetops suddenly bent and rustled. Two more allies, arriving late, skimmed the highest branches and emerged from the forest to join the fray. Black-scaled Sabu, huge and frightening in her anger, settled to the ground beside her injured son. Taking Fleer's place, she cradled and hugged Harrow and kissed his scaled face. Then, looking toward Redclaw and the few griffins still lining its wall, she blasted red fire until the stones were scorched and blackened.

His own anger unabated, Fleer spread his wings and rose into the air.

But a shout from Morkir stopped him. Settling to the ground beside Sabu, the young griffin drew labored breaths. The strain of swift flight from Stronghold showed plainly on his feathered face, and though his bandages were gone and his wounds healed, it was obvious that one scarred wing still pained him. Nevertheless, he had come with Sabu.

"This fight is mine now!" he said to Fleer. "Stay with Stormfire's son, and see that you protect his mother, as well."

Fleer landed again beside Morkir and stared in amazement at Sabu. "How can she be flying?" he whispered. "I thought her sickness . . . !"

"Strength of will," Morkir growled. "Her child was in danger!"

Folding his wings flat against his lion's back, Morkir limped across the clear space toward the fortress. Only a pair of griffins still remained atop the bulwark. As Morkir approached, they turned and fled, spreading their wings and sailing northward toward Angmar, abandoning Redclaw.

Morkir also spread his wings, but only to fly over the wall and into the courtyard where he landed again. Wounded griffins cowered in the morning shadows, their eyes wide with fear as they recognized Gorganar's younger son.

"Where is Gaunt?" he snarled.

One of the griffin guards rose shakily to his feet. Blood matted his fur, and one wing dragged on the ground. He said nothing, but raised one leg and pointed to the tallest of Redclaw's four towers.

Morkir snarled again, and turning his back on the injured guard, he strode toward the tower's stout doors. No one blocked his way or interfered with him. Pushing the doors open, he padded inside with claws at the ready.

"Gaunt!" he shouted. "Your beloved brother is here!"

His voice echoed through the corridors, but no answer came. Alert, he sniffed the air. Gaunt's odor was distinctive, familiar. Morkir followed his nose, pacing down a long hallway, coming to a pair of polished doors. Rising on his hind legs, he leaned on the doors, and they swung open.

His brother lay curled on the seat of an elaborate throne at the far end of the room. He didn't look up or move at all as Morkir advanced. But there was another who sat at Gaunt's feet and rested one bandaged paw on one of Gaunt's.

"You're too late," Minhep said. His voice was tired, yet it contained a veiled anger that bordered on hatred.

An unexpected chill passed through Morkir. He'd come hot-blooded, expecting the fight of his life, a re-match with the brother who'd betrayed and almost killed him. Creeping closer, he studied his brother's still form, the golden feathers tipped with white on his head and chest, the broad, powerful paws crossed as if in sleep. He stared at the patched eye, the singed wing, and the stained bandage.

A sticky red river beside the throne told the story. Still, he murmured, "How?"

Minhep rose to stand protectively over Gaunt. "He wouldn't take care of his wound," Minhep said bitterly. "During the night, so slowly I don't think he even noticed, he bled to death."

Morkir could scarcely believe it. "You were with him?"

Minhep snarled. "I was—at dinner."

The chill Morkir felt gave way to a strange numbness. He looked at Gaunt again, seemingly so at peace, asleep. The brother he had grown up with, loved once—dead. He gazed around the room, noting the fallen banner, the ostentatious throne, and the fireplace gone cold.

"You're king of the griffins now," Minhep said without enthusiasm.

Morkir shook his head as he turned away. His father gone, and his brother dead. His home in the Valley of Eight Winds—it was all gone. He gazed at the stone walls around him, felt the stone tiles cold beneath his paws. "You stayed with him—you rule." His throat was tight; he found it difficult to speak. "I don't belong here. I don't know where I belong—but it's not here."

Slowly, he walked out of the room and out of the tower. Only a few Griffins remained anywhere in the courtyard. Almost all of them appeared to be injured or wounded, but they struggled to their feet and tried their best to stand at attention. They were looking to him for leadership.

But he couldn't lead them. His world had changed too much.

He had changed too much.

Spreading his eagles' wings, he flew beyond Redclaw's wall to land beside Sabu. Harrow had recovered enough to stand with Fleer's help. It would be sometime before the black Dragon flew again. Everyone looked Morkir's way, but no one spoke, and the silence was almost painful.

Sabu broke it. Beckoning with the tip of one wing, she called to the last Phoenix. "Phoebe, fly home and let everyone know we're all right." She forced a smile as she looked at the rest. "A long walk in the woods will do us all good."

20

"FOLLOW THE HUMMINGBIRD!" Bumble shouted as the gates creaked open. Revitalized by the honeysuckle blossoms, he fluttered into the air, his wings blurring nearly to invisibility. "Speed is our only friend now!"

"Make sure you stick to the streets," Marian warned as they waited for the gap in the gates to widen enough to let her through. "I'm not made for flitting over rooftops!"

Bumble flew three swift circles about her horn and buzzed her left ear. "No time to discuss Marian's flaws and shortcomings!" he laughed. "Into adventure, I plunge! Into danger I lunge! Though I am small and slight, I never flee when I can fight! Hi-ho! Hi-ho!" With that, he darted between the widening gates.

I'm beginning to seriously worry about that Bumble-bird! Marian thought to herself as she sprang through the gap. A pair of sleepy-eyed guards just taking up their posts inside the gates stumbled backward, dropped their spears, and fell in the dust. "Sorry!" she said with automatic politeness. "Coming through!" Then, lowering her head, she raced on through the street before they got a good look at her.

Bumble buzzed past her other ear. "This way, slaggard Marian!" he cried, all excitement and energy. "I'm small, but I'm fast! Now hurry up and move your . . . !"

"I'm going to tie a knot in your beak," Marian swore as she chased after her tiny partner.

At such an early hour with the sun not yet quite risen, the streets were nearly empty, yet there were signs of life from inside some of the homes. The smells of breakfast odors seeped out from chimney tops; lamplight flared behind shuttered windows. A couple of dogs foraging for garbage at the mouth of an alley looked up with startled eyes and

223

began barking as she charged past. A cat waiting patiently on a doorstep to be let inside arched its back and howled.

"Stop, Marian!" Bumble cried, suddenly at her ear again. With implicit trust in the little hummingbird, Marian stopped. "Hide here from eyes of pointy men!" He guided her into the narrowest of allies, little more than a dark gap between two warehouses, then flew away again, the perfect scout.

A moment later, Marian heard the heavy footfalls of soldiers march- ing in unison. From her hiding place she watched them go by. Judging by their direction, they were on their way to the docks. The glow of their torches preceded them, filling the dusty street with amber light and glimmering on their tapered metal helmets and spears. *Pointy men*, she recalled Bumble calling them, and she couldn't resist a smile.

"All safe! All clear!" Bumble sang, returning once more to lead the way when the soldiers could no longer be heard.

Marian took off after him again, suddenly mindful of the sound her own hoofbeats made. More lights were appearing behind more of the windows. From inside one home, she heard singing. From inside another, a grumbling conversation. She glanced up at the sky, which was only a thin ribbon as she passed down a narrow street lined with white-stoned, two-story apartments. The blackness of night was giving way slowly. She saw no stars overhead, only a streak of deep purple marking the coming dawn.

As she darted into the next street, she nearly collided with a wagon. The ox that was pulling it shot her a disbelieving look as he lurched sideways to avoid her. The yoke around his neck strained and groaned, and the wagon creaked as it tipped precariously onto its two left wheels. The driver, barely half awake, gave an awkward cry as he rose on the buckboard and tried to catch his balance, but he tumbled into the dust. A trio of fat barrels pitched out of the back of the wagon and rolled in different directions.

"Un . . . ! Uni . . . ! Unicorn!" the ox stuttered. His voice was deep and rusty and hoarse, as if he hadn't used it in a very long time. "What . . . what are you . . . ?"

Glancing at the driver as he started to pick himself up, Marian quickly hushed the ox. "Don't ask!" she urged, calling back over her shoulder as she sped away. "Don't tell!"

Locking his tiny talons around the tip of her horn, Bumble returned to glare at her. "Don't ask? Don't tell? That's the stupidest advice I've ever heard in my life!"

Marian increased her speed, running for all she was worth to put distance between herself and the driver. Down a long stretch of roadway, she dashed, and around a corner, her mane flying, her heart hammering as loudly as her hoofbeats.

An aging shopkeeper getting an early start on his day froze as he swept the steps leading to his doorway. Jaw gaping, he stared as she went by, and gasped, "Oh, my . . . !"

Marian gazed upward again as she raced away from the shopkeeper. The buildings around her were so close that she couldn't spot the two tall towers that marked her destination, and the deep purple sky had segued to lavender and pink! "Which way, Bumble?" she shouted.

"Don't ask!" Bumble answered in a sarcastic tone, but he flew away from her horn, soaring above the rooftops. "One tower! Two tower!" he cried as he pointed with a wingtip. "And in the square! I see! I see!" Glancing down at Marian, he winked. "But I better not tell!" In a flash of green and white, he darted ahead.

Again, Marian chased after him.

The sky was rapidly brightening, and more of Jiwashek's citizens were awakening to begin their daily tasks. As she followed Bumble around another corner, a blacksmith paused over his bellows, then ran into the street as she passed to reassure himself of what he'd seen. A pair of round-faced children sitting on a doorstep sprang up excitedly and tried to run after her. In the next block, a woman with an armload of laundry froze in the middle of the street, then gave a shriek. Clothing went up in the air as she spun about and dashed out of the way, and Marian ran the next block with a pair of underwear over her horn before she paused to shake them off.

Bumble reappeared long enough to laugh. "Once more into the breeches!" he shouted gleefully. Then he was off again.

At the next intersection, four men on their way to the docks walked across her path. Over their heads they carried an upside-down rowboat that prevented them from seeing anything but their feet and the road immediately in front of them. Bumble dashed right past them and, without slowing her pace, Marian gathered her legs under herself and leaped the rowboat's hull. The four men continued on, completely unaware.

The two towers loomed suddenly over the nearest rooftops. The street broadened and the hard dust gave way to cobblestone paving. On opposite sides of the street, two men on tall ladders were busy making arches of garlands and ribbons. One looked down in surprise as she entered the street. For an instant, he teetered on his ladder, then fell backward with a yelp. His partner, alerted by the yell, squinted over the line of garland he was nailing to the side of a building. He seemed not to recognize Marian for a moment. Then, spitting out a mouthful of nails, he climbed slowly, carefully down, then turned and ran. His partner, scrambling up, ran after him.

All around the street, doors flung open and shutters flew back from windows. Men and women stared uncertainly from their thresholds while the children clustered around their legs gasped and pointed. Marian slowed to a canter, then to a walk. Looking from side to side, she tossed her white mane and flashed her tail.

Bumble landed on her forelock, and his voice was a bare whisper. "Why are they afraid of you?"

"Don't ask," she whispered back. "Don't tell." Then she shook her head. It was a poor joke, and Bumble didn't laugh. She felt the brave little bird's shivering. "I don't know," she answered.

But she did know. To them, she was something old, something from another time, a legend. None of these short-lived men or their man-children had ever seen her like. She represented the unknown to them, and if she remembered nothing else about Men, she remembered how they feared anything unknown or strange or different. All their hatreds, all their wars always boiled down to that.

She met the cold stare of a man who stood in his doorway with a knife. She eyed another who stood half out in the street with a hammer, but he fell back as she came closer. She smiled at a mother clutching her newborn to her breast in an open window.

The mother smiled shyly back and turned her child to look.

It seemed that not all of them feared her. Here and there, a few regarded her with a different look. An old eye twinkled with knowing wonder. A mouth curved upward with a smile and a look of awe. A child reached out between its father's legs with an obvious desire to touch her.

"Am I still dreaming?" Marian heard someone whisper. And from somewhere else on the other side of the street, ". . . escaped from the carnival!"

It reminded Marian of her purpose. Breaking into a canter again, she hurried on down the ever-widening street under arching garlands and past ribbon-adorned lamp posts, her hooves clip-clopping sharply on the cobbles. It was no mere street she found herself on, but some kind of gaily-decorated Processional. Wreathes hung upon the doorways; the balconies of upper-level apartments were festooned with ribbons and strings of beads. Bright banners flew from rooftop poles.

"Bumble," Marian said softly, "I think it's time you told me what you saw in the square."

"The carnival we came to find," Bumble answered. "But unless these Bumble-eyes have double-vision, or even triple-vision, it's a lot bigger than we thought. So many wagons and tents!"

At a sound behind them, Marian stopped and turned. Though they hung back a safe distance, some of the men had decided to follow. That didn't bode well, she thought. She considered driving them away, scattering them by charging into their midst, but that would only frighten an already nervous lot.

She glanced up at the sky. It would be dawn already over the Windy Sea and out by the docks and wharves, but the sun hadn't yet quite reached over the walls of Jiwashek where the streets were still full of gloomy shadows. Resuming her course up the Processional, she put the following crowd out of her mind and tried to focus her thoughts on Chernovog.

The street ended on the edge of a large square. Even Marian caught her breath as she gazed at the colorful tents and the brightly painted wagons assembled there. Pennants and banners fluttered in the morning breeze, and the tents themselves snapped and rustled. A confusion of scents and smells assaulted her senses as the bright hues dazzled her eyes. As the wind rippled over the tents, the colors seemed to dance and churn like water!

Bumble swayed lightly as he clung to her forelock. "I think I prefer lousewort," he muttered. "The effect is pretty much the same."

Marian walked past the first tents, sniffing the air as she went. So many tents and wagons made a maze of the square. "Fly ahead, Bumble," she said as she wrinkled her nose. "Search everywhere until you find Chernovog, then come back to me. But pace yourself. We won't find any honeysuckle vines here."

The little hummingbird fluttered his wings and disappeared between a pair of tents. Alone, Marian wandered along the perimeter of the carnival. There was something strange in the air, scents that puzzled her, that sparked vague memories and vague fears. The breeze bore a curious hint of age. She looked back over her shoulder, mindful of the crowd that had followed her right to the edge of the square, but they had stopped there, reluctant to pursue her further. She wondered why.

A little farther along, she found an old man bent over on his knees. With needle and thread he was hemming the tattered edge of a red-and-white-striped tent. She guessed that his eyes were very bad, for he bent very low and held his work close to his face. Marian quietly watched him for a moment, amused that he took no notice of her at all.

He seemed harmless, and she made up her mind to talk to him. "Excuse me," she said politely. "I'm looking for my friend. His name is Chernovog."

Taking a spare needle from between his lips, the old man struggled to rise. "Hey, see here, Missy! We're not open yet, and tickets won't go on sale until . . . !" Bad eyes or not, his snapped wide as he turned and saw her. "Oh, my! You're not a. . . . ! I mean, you're a . . . !" He clapped a hand to his mouth and stared white-faced. Then turning, running away as fast as his creaky old legs would carry him, he screamed, "Malleus! Oh, Malleus!"

Scowling, Marian cursed herself. She should have known better. They were afraid; they were always afraid. Hadn't she just nearly told Bumble so?

She poked her head under the edge of the tent the man had been working on and peeked inside. Racks and racks of kewpie dolls stared back at her, but they were grotesque little dolls, she thought, with bodies of hard clay or twisted cloth. Some had dark stones for eyes, and others had black buttons. They seemed to lack any sense of symmetry. An arm or a leg was always too long, or the fingers were out of proportion to the hands, or the head was too big, or the feet were turned backward.

Marian shuddered as she backed away. What kind of a child would play with such dolls? What kind of a person would make them?

But now, she was curious about what she'd find in the other tents. Walking slowly around the next one, she found the entrance and pushed through the canvas flaps. The faint morning light penetrating through the tent's colorfully striped roof lent the interior a surreal gloom. Ropes had been carefully strung to guide crowds around the only object inside—a large glass coffin in the center of the floor.

Marian came forward cautiously. Inside the coffin, on a bed of red satin, lay a young Fomorian female. Her gray-feathered hawk's wings were neatly folded beside her body, and her taloned feet were wired to stand straight up to show the sharpness of her claws. Man-like arms and delicate, manlike hands were placed over her small, downy breasts. Beautiful in repose, she might have looked as if she were only sleeping, but the eyes in her hawk's head had also been wired open to show that they were blue as any man's.

Half sickened, Marian wondered who she was and how she'd died. It seemed wrong that a creature so obviously made to soar the skies should lie sealed in a box, even a glass one. Even more wrong that she was on display in such a horrible manner for curious onlookers.

Angered and offended, Marian left the tent. There was nothing she could do for the poor Fomorian, but she could find the carnival's owner and give him a good piece of her mind! Carnival Fantastica, indeed! What kind of grisly entertainment did this place offer? Who would pay money to look at an unburied Fomorian?

Tired of skulking about, she determined just to confront the man responsible for such a shameful exhibition. Lifting her head high, she shouted his name. "Malleus!"

A gusting breeze tickled her nose, and she sneezed. Again came that strange confusion of scents and smells that she had experienced before. Sawdust and paint and canvas, but also snake-scent and lion-scent and spider-scent! And yes, she thought! Minotaur scent! Yet it wasn't Chernovog's! And still there were things she couldn't identify!

A carnival roustabout darted suddenly from between a couple of tents with a coiled rope in his hands. With a skillful flick of his wrist, he made a quick toss, and the thin loop sailed neatly over her horn.

"Give me a break!" Marian said in disgust as she shook the loop free. The roustabout hurriedly began to recoil his rope for another toss, but the last unicorn in the world was in no mood for games. Eyes flashing and mane flying, she charged straight for him. With a cry, the man dropped his rope and ran. Thinking he might lead her to Malleus, Marian gave chase.

As she followed him around the next tent, however, another rope sailed through the air. Alerted just in time by the soft sound it made as the second roustabout twirled it around his head, Marian stopped in her tracks. The coil sailed over her shoulder, missing. But this man, braver than the first one and more determined to catch her, ran at her from behind.

"Braver you might be, but not smarter!" Marian muttered as she kicked him with a hind leg. The roustabout screamed as he crashed through the wall of the tent behind him. Fabric ripped and threads snapped, and the entire side of the tent came down.

Marian stared past the writhing, kicking, entangled man, aghast at what the rising morning light revealed inside the tent. Such creatures were long extinct, and she had not set eyes on one in years! Yet, cruelly stuffed and mounted on a polished block of mahogany, posed so that it reared up and flashed its shining claws was—a Manticore!

The dawn's light flashed on the Manicure's golden lion's fur and on its spiked tail. From out of a thick and noble mane, a sad human face seemed to stare back with eyes that fixed right upon her.

Marian screamed in rage. This was a carnival of horrors!

Rearing and spinning about, she began to run. Yet another roustabout dashed out from between a pair of tents, not with a rope, but with a whip in his hand. A loud *crack!* sounded in her ear, and she felt the sting of his lash on her right cheek. But if he hoped to stop her or turn her aside, he failed miserably. She struck him with her shoulder, knocking him flat.

With blue eyes narrowed to angry slits, she focused on the minotaur-scent and ran on. A chorus of voices and shouts rose on her left. The entire carnival knew by now that she was here. Another rope sailed toward her. She dodged it easily. A trio of boy-children suddenly blocked her path. Rather than running, one of them cartwheeled and back-flipped straight for her, and springing high, he landed lightly on her back! She felt his strong knees on her shoulders. With one hand, he pulled and yanked at her mane while he tried to slip something over her head with his other hand.

Marian had no wish to hurt children, but she wouldn't be taken or stopped. Whirling sharply about, she unbalanced the boy-child, and threw him into the sloping side of a striped tent. Upside-down, he slid neatly along the canvas side and rolled to his feet unharmed as she raced on.

With every gust of breeze, the minotaur-scent grew stronger. She leaped a low wall of hay bales and an empty cart that blocked her way, dodged yet another roustabout that challenged her with a whip and a chair, then knocked down a tent when she cut a corner too closely.

"Free me!" a hissing voice called after her. "Have mercy!"

Marian whirled about and stopped. Half-exposed by the tent's collapse was an immense cage. A shadow moved inside it, and she crept closer. Slipping the tip of her horn under a fold of canvas, she dragged the rough cloth away and suddenly recoiled as spider-scent rose into the air, thickly repulsive.

The cage's occupant was black and hairy and nearly as large as Marian. Its eight legs twitched and probed and wandered over the thick bars and the wire interlacing that made its prison, and glittering, multi-faceted eyes stared with unblinking malice as powerful mandibles clacked. There was no webbing in the cage, for it was not a web-spinning spider, but the floor was littered with the desiccated corpses of the rats and rabbits someone had fed to it.

"I am Sinobarre!" the spider hissed again. "Free me! Are we not kindred, Unicorn? Like you, I am too beautiful to be caged!"

Marian took a step back. Then she hesitated. Her senses reeled in the presence of Sinobarre. The spider's scent swirled around her like a cloud, smothering all other scents as Marian looked at her. She knew without knowing how she knew that Sinobarre was old, older than anything in Wyvernwood, older than anything had a right to be, and dimly, as she moved closer to the cage, she wondered how Malleus had ever managed to capture such a creature.

Sinobarre waved her two front legs in languid fashion. "Come closer," she urged. "Find the lock and break it! Smash it! End my hated confinement so that I may devour my captor!"

Marian studied the cage, seeking a lock, but she saw none. Not even a door! It seemed as if the cage had been welded around Sinobarre.

"Free me!" Sinobarre whispered. "Find a way!"

Marian reared up. Perhaps if she crashed her hooves down with all her strength she might shred the wire and shatter the bars. Indeed, Sinobarre was beautiful and deserved her freedom. No creature so old and rare should be caged!

But the breeze gusted, and for just an instant, Sinobarre's scent weakened. As if waking suddenly from a dream, Marian danced back and shook her head. Sinobarre glared at her through the cage. "My pretty! My precious!" she hissed. Her mandibles made an unpleasant clacking. "Help me!"

Marian backed away. "You're too dangerous," she answered. "Maybe when I've found my friends and made them safe, I'll come back. But you'll be the last thing here I free!"

Before Sinobarre could say another word, Marian ran as fast as she could. The echoes of that spidery voice followed, but grew fainter as she got farther away, and she fought to clear the last remnants of the fog that filled her head. She knew she'd just had a narrow escape. Once freed, Signboard might have gone off to devour her captor—but she'd have strengthened herself first on a Unicorn's blood!

She sneezed delibertately, forcing the last of Sinobarre's scent from her nostrils, then sniffed the air again. Roustabouts and carnival workers were hunting her among the tents. She could smell them as well as hear their voices. She wondered briefly about Bumble. For the moment, she could only hope the little hummingbird was faring well.

Four rough-looking men appeared suddenly in the lane between the tents. They seemed almost surprised to find her. Stopping in their tracks, they stared wide-eyed and doubtful, but then they rushed forward dragging a heavy net.

"We got her this time!" the men yelled.

"Don't let her escape!"

But one of them just cackled. "Ten-to-one she makes fools of us all again!"

Marian ran straight at them again. Before they could cast their net, she snagged it with her horn and charged on. Two of the men found the net jerked out of their hands, but two held on only to lose their footing. Yelling and shouting, they found themselves dragged through the dust while their brighter or luckier comrades laughed.

After a short distance, Marian shook the net free. To her right, the lane between the tents broadened. She stopped and sniffed. The minotaur-scent came from that direction. Again, she sniffed. It wasn't Chernovog; she knew that youngster's scent too well.

Suddenly wary, she advanced at a walk. The lane ended abruptly in a semi-circle of three large wagons. Each had stout iron bars and was built of thick wood. They sat on massively large wheels. Nothing moved in any of the wagons. But they were all occupied.

The nearest wagon held a monstrously large snake. Its diamond-marked coils spread completely over the wagon's floor and pressed against the sides of its prison. It watched Marian with dull, red, nictating eyes, but didn't stir or show any interest in her presence.

The second wagon held an old lion. Its baggy golden hide hung loosely over muscles that had atrophied from lack of use, and its mane had grown gray and thin. It snored softly as Marian passed, and gave no sign of waking.

The third wagon sat in the shadow cast by one of the two tall towers, but it was from there the minotaur-scent came. A figure sat huddled pathetically in the farthest corner. Leaning against the bars, it hugged its legs to its chest and rested its horned head on its knees. It barely glanced up over folded arms as Marian pressed her nose to the bars.

"Who are you?" she whispered. Then, as he raised his head a little higher, she gasped. "Oh, by the Great Fires!"

The minotaur gave a startled and disbelieving look. Then on hands and knees, he lunged suddenly and grabbed the bars. "Marian?" he whispered, keeping his voice low. "Is that really you?"

Marian could barely believe her eyes. "Ranock!" she answered. "But you're dead! You burned in the fire!"

"Malleus's agents set that fire!" he told her. "I thought it was the storm. But they wanted a new freak—a minotaur—for this ghastly sideshow, and they caught me! They've been quietly snatching our people from Wyvernwood for years!"

Marian swallowed and looked around. Not all of these creatures came from Wyvernwood, but there wasn't time to think about that. She could still hear the voices of the roustabouts searching for her among the tents. It would be only a matter of moments before they found her again. Unlike Sinobarre's cage, the wagon had both a door and a lock. "Now they've got Chernovog, too!" she told Ranock. "I came to find him!"

Ranock shot to his feet. "My son?" He shook his bars until the wagon creaked on its wheels. "He must be on the far side of the carnival. "But Marian, there are dangers here you don't suspect! The owner is a sorcerer!" Finally awake, the old lion roared as it rose and began to pace its cage. The snake shifted subtly and flicked the air with its scarlet tongue.

"Nonsense!" Marian said. "I'm going to break you out of here, and we'll find Chernovog together. Then we're going home!" Rearing up, she kicked at the lock with her front hooves. The wagon rocked under the impact, but the iron lock held. She kicked at it a second time, and her hooves left deep scars in the hard oak, but the lock remained intact.

"Please, Marian, listen to me!" Ranock pleaded. "Forget about me for now. Find Chernovog and get him out of here! You don't know what this place is like!"

Marian made a third attempt. Rising up, she kicked the lock with all the force she could muster. Pain shivered up through her hoof, through her fetlock and into her leg and hip, but still the cursed lock refused to break!

A sharp, rattling whisper came from behind her. "Hey baby," it said, "let Daddy help."

Marian spun around to find the huge snake facing her with its flat snout pressed against the bars of its cage. Its red eyes were no longer dull; they burned with a crimson flame. A slender, forked tongue flicked out over the cage's floor and up one of the bars, then the snake spoke again.

"Daddy's had a lot of lonely nights and a lot of frustration to work off when no one was looking to quietly pit his handsome self against these bars and walls," the snake explained with a wink. To demonstrate, he began to expand his smooth coils until he nearly filled the cage. The wooden sides of the wagon made a soft groan before he relaxed again. "Some of the joints are no longer what they used to be—and I don't mean my joints. If you use those slender little legs to kick this crate in the right places, Daddy bets it'll fall for you just as quickly as he has." He gave her another red-eyed wink and flicked his tongue between the bars. "I like your spirit, baby. You've got spunk. Not to mention, the nicest pair of flanks I've seen in a long time."

Suspicion and doubt wrinkled Marian's brow. Sinobarre before had nearly fooled her. Now she found herself reluctant to trust another stranger. "That might free you," she said, "but how would it help me or Ranock?"

The snake winked both eyes. "I like you, baby," it answered. "You've got brains, as well as looks. You get Daddy out, and I'll snuggle right up to the Minotaur's cage, wrap myself nice and comfy tight all around it, and give it a little huggin' and squeezin', not to mention teasin' and pleasin'." It winked again as it pressed its face right up to the bars. "Trust me, prettikins, not much in this world can resist my embrace."

Marian paced uncertainly, and then with stubborn determination, she reared up and smashed her hooves yet again at the lock on Ranock's cage with the same useless result. At almost the same moment, the lion let out a savage roar, and Ranock shouted a warning. A rope sailed through the air as she turned; the loop slipped past her horn and over her neck. The roustabout that had sneaked up on her gave a shout of triumph as he yanked the loop tight.

It was a short-lived shout. In her panic, Marian gave a powerful toss of her head. The man kept his grip on the rope, but her effort was just enough to drag him a few steps closer to the snake's cage. He gave a choked scream of terror as a red, wet tongue shot out and coiled about his throat. Daddy's eyes lit up as he reeled the roustabout closer.

With another toss of her head, Marian jerked the rope from his hands. Ranock leaned through his bars and removed the loop from her neck. The roustabout's eyes were bulging. He clutched at the bizarre, strangling noose and drummed his heels against the sides of the wagon as the snake lifted him off the ground.

"Don't eat him!" Marian cried.

Daddy shook his head, and the roustabout danced like a rag doll in a child's grip. Then he relaxed his hold, and the poor man fell in a gasping heap. "Don't worry, baby," the snake said with a hideous grin. "The little fish Daddy always throws back. It's the big fish I want."

Ranock banged his bull's horns against his bars as he nodded. "Malleus won't come anywhere near Daddy," he affirmed. "Or many of his other captives. He leaves all the work to his lackeys and hirelings."

Marian considered, then made up her mind. She didn't bother attacking the lock on Daddy's cage, nor even the outer walls. Leaning forward on her front legs, she spun and kicked out with her rear legs, using all her strength to attack one of the wagon's wheels. The wagon rocked and creaked.

"Yesssssss!" Daddy hissed, sounding more snake-like than ever in his excitement. "Brainsss and beauty!"

She kicked again. The wheels were strong, made of quality wood like the rest of the wagon, but the spokes were slender. A third kick shattered one. The fourth kick shattered another, and the rim of the wheel gave a loud crack.

"Look out!" Ranock shouted.

"Jussst gorgeousssss!" Daddy cried as the wheel began to buckle. The axle splintered as the wagon's weight shifted, and Daddy threw all his own massive weight into the sagging corner. Then the wheel gave way completely. The wagon pitched sideways and crashed down. The steel bars drove through the roof, splintering it.

Daddy's head smashed through the weakened roof as he sprang up on his coils. Further unbalanced, another wheel shattered, and the wagon crashed completely over on its side. It's occupant slithered out with astonishing speed. Uncoiled and free, the snake was far larger and far more frightening than she had imagined. It rose above her, its tongue lashing with menace and its scarlet eyes burning as it looked down.

Marian jumped away, her heart racing, suddenly fearful as she found her back against Ranock's cage.

But then, the snake coiled up again, lay its head flat on the ground, and grinned at her. "Sorry if I scared you, honey-girl," he said, in control of his speech again. "Daddy just had to stretch a little." He closed both of his eyes and softened his voice. "If I had knees, I'd be down on 'em thanking you. If you ever need a favor . . ."

Marian stepped closer to the snake and lowered her head until her horn lightly touched his nose and her mane brushed against his cheek. "Just free Ranock," Marian answered. "And let the lion go, too. These cages are hateful and cruel!"

Ranock leaned against his bars as Daddy began to coil around his cage. "Go find my son!" he pleaded. "I'll catchup when I can!"

Marian hesitated, reluctant to leave Ranock behind. The carnival was a big place with a lot of confusing turns and dead-ends among all the tents. But with every new danger she encountered in this horror show, she worried about Chernovog more. And she was beginning to worry about Bumble, as well.

With her horn, she pointed to the westernmost of the two great towers. "You meet me there, Ranock," she instructed. "I'll get your boy, and then I'm going to spend a little time razing this low-rent neighborhood!"

The snake began slowly to tighten his coils and squeeze the wagon that held Ranock. "Sweetness, Daddy will be well ahead of you," he said, winking and putting on that weirdly scary grin once more. "The Carnival Fantastica is long overdue for my special brand of loving."

Marian lingered long enough to return the snake's wink with one of her own. Startled, Daddy's grin vanished, and his jaw gaped in astonishment. "You said you liked me, Daddy" Marian told him. "Well, the sentiment is mutual. You're definitely a cut above the other reptiles I've met."

His grin returned, and so did his wink. "Size is everything, Baby!"

Marian wasted no more time, but turned and raced off again. As she rounded the next tent, a pair of roustabouts blocked her path, but instead of trying to stop or capture her, they threw up their arms and, yelling, dived frantically over a couple of barrels to get out of her way. With a snap of her teeth, Marian caught one of the men by the seat of his pants and shook him forcefully before she dropped him again.

"Enough fun and games!" she said angrily as she placed one hoof on the center of his chest and pinned him down. "I'm looking for a mino-taur-child, and you're going to lead me to him!"

A sudden familiar hum in her right ear interrupted her. "Who needs pokey fat man?" Bumble cried. Perching on her horn, he shook his tail feathers and danced a little jig. "One ... two ... three ... four! Bumble found the minotaur!"

"Bumble!" Marian exclaimed. Forgetting the roustabout, she took her hoof off him and let him scramble away. "I was beginning to worry about you!"

The little hummingbird shrugged and puffed out his chest. "Cher-novog's inside a big red tent in the center of the square" he said, breathless with excitement. "But he's locked up in a cage, and the lock's so big I could make a nest in the keyhole!"

"Lead the way!" Marian urged. "I've had all the carnival-thrills I can stomach!" As if to emphasize her point, she kicked one of the overturned barrels into the side of the nearest tent, breaking one of its support poles. As the tent collapsed, she and Bumble took off.

The red tent stood exactly between the two great towers. Unlike the other tents, which were made of painted canvas, this one seemed to be made of silk. It shimmered in the sunlight and rippled in the breeze, stirring and moving more like strange water or blood than like fabric. A gust of wind caught the thin flap that covered the entrance and lifted it. Blackness filled the interior.

Marian stopped as she regarded the odd pavilion. "You sure he's in there?" she whispered.

Bumble perched on her horn again and tapped the side of his beak with a wingtip. "The nose knows," he answered.

Marian drew a deep breath then passed through the entrance. Soft carpets covered the floor, and the air was heavy with jasmine and sandalwood. Yet, through that miasma she detected other scents. One of them was quite familiar. In the darkness, she walked unerringly to Chernovog's cage.

The young minotaur rose to his feet and gripped the bars. "Who's there?" he asked softly. A minotaur's vision was not nearly so acute as hers was, nor was their sense of smell so developed.

"I've come to take you home, Chernovog," she told the boy. "And after I get you out of this cage, I've got a wonderful surprise for you."

Chernovog pressed his face to the bars and stared outward with large brown eyes. He was quite a good-looking boy, actually, muscular for his age with reddish-brown hide and soft, well-shaped ears and a black nose. His horns were just beginning to grow, but they'd been polished and filed to perfect points—by his captor, Marian imagined.

The boy gasped. "Marian?"

"Bumble's with me, too," she answered as she studied the cage. "He's the one that found you. He's been a real hero."

Because Chernovog was smaller, his cage was also smaller. The lock, while huge to the little hummingbird, was no different from the locks on the other cages and wagons. His cage, however, did not set on wheels, but on a low wooden platform. No matter, nothing was going to stop her from cracking it open.

"Crouch down in the far corner and cover your head," she instructed. "This might get rough."

Bumble fluttered up into the air as Chernovog obeyed. "We're rough! We're tough! We're the dynamic duo!"

Rearing up, Marian crashed her hooves against the cage's wooden door. She didn't aim for the lock this time, but for the door itself. Again and again, she struck out. The door shivered, weakened. Turning about, she kicked it with her hind legs.

Bumble flew around her head, encouraging her. "Kick it again! Kick it again! Harder! Harder!"

Marian did just that. Her hooves and her shins began to ache, and the pavilion filled with a noisy racket as her hooves thundered on the wood and her breathing became harsh. Again, she kicked out, and this time she was rewarded with a sharp crack and a shower of wood splinters.

"Rah, rah roar! We're kicking down the door!" Bumble chanted "Rah, rah, rass! And then we'll kick some . . . !"

"Bumble!" Marian snorted as she dealt the door another kick. "Don't make me remind you that I'm a lady!"

Once more, summoning all her strength she lashed out with her rear hooves. The impact vibrated up through her shins, even into her hips. She gave a cry of pain, but the door shattered. Bits of wood exploded in all directions.

Chernovog yelped, but instantly leaped up. "Let me!" he shouted. Though his legs were hairless and man-like, he had strong bovine hooves of his own. He aimed a kick at the inside of the broken door, shattering another section of it.

"Get back!" Marian ordered. She kicked out again, ignoring the pain that radiated through her hindquarters.

"My turn!" Bumble cried, desperate to get in on the fun. Darting straight at the door, he stopped abruptly, hesitated, then dealt the wood a tiny whack with one taloned foot before he flashed away again.

"No, it's my turn!" Chernovog shouted. Lowering his bull's head, he ran at the door. With a loud crash, the boards broke. Fragments and splinters and wooden chunks flew outward, and Chernovog pitched headlong through the wreckage, hit the ground hard, and lay still.

Then, with a toothy grin, he looked up. "That was the most fun I've had in a long time," he said.

Marian limped over to him. With every step, pain lanced through her right rear leg, and her left felt only a little stronger. But she'd found Chernovog, freed him, and her heart swelled with joy. She nuzzled his ear with her nose, then licked the side of his face. "Let's go home," she said.

From somewhere in the darkness, a deep and eerily calm voice spoke. "The only home you're going to is a new cage."

Marian looked slowly around, but saw nothing. "Malleus," she said, matching his calm. "I wondered when you'd crawl out from under your rock."

Chernovog scrambled to Marian's side and placed one hand on her withers. She could feel his fear and trembling as he whispered in her ear. "He's a sorcerer!"

"You've caused a lot of trouble, Unicorn," Malleus continued, seemingly invisible. "But you'll make up for it when I make you my star attraction."

Unafraid, Marian snorted in disdain. "You must have quite a fantasy life," she answered. "We're walking out of here—over you would be preferable."

A pair of tall torches driven deep into the ground near the entrance flared to sudden life. In robes of black silk, Malleus posed between them with his arms outflung to block the way. Startled, Marian forgot herself and backed up a step.

"See?" Chernovog whispered as his fingers tightened nervously in her mane.

Marian gritted her teeth. Lowering her head, she pointed her horn at Malleus and began walking forward with the minotaur-boy clinging close. "I've seen fire," she said bitterly. "Fire like you can't even imagine."

Emboldened by Marian's tone, Chernovog swallowed his fear. "Yeah!" he cried. "Take your torches and shove 'em up your nose! I'm through dancing for you!" With that, he let go of Marian and charged straight at his captor.

Malleus muttered strange words as he flung out his right arm. Chernovog fell, entangled in some kind of ribbon that seemed to materialize around him. He writhed on the ground until Malleus stepped over him and put a booted foot on one of the boy's horns to hold him still. "Behave yourself," he ordered. "It would be a shame to harm such a wonderful little performer."

"It won't be a shame at all when I harm you!" Marian replied as she lunged forward.

Malleus muttered words again and gestured toward the ground. Smoke erupted around him. At nearly the same instant, the pair of torches went out, plunging the pavilion into darkness again.

Leaping over Chernovog, she dived through the smoke. Pain stabbed through her legs, and she stumbled as she landed, fell and rolled over on her side. Still, she rose quickly to her feet and peered around. Even a unicorn's eyes took a moment to adjust to sudden darkness.

In that moment, she felt her first tremor of doubt. Was it possible that Malleus really was a sorcerer?

Torches ignited again, a different pair this time in a different part of the tent. She turned toward a wide platform in the deepest corner of the interior. It was obviously some kind of stage. Malleus grinned and reached into his left sleeve. With a curt bow, he pulled out a red flower. His tone was oily and mocking as he said, "May I offer you a rose, my beauty?"

"Chow time!" Bumble dived out of the upper darkness where he'd been hiding and biding his time. But the lure of dinner was too much. Beak-first, he plunged into the scarlet petals.

Almost instantly, he rose up again, sputtering and spitting and shaking his head. "Fake!" he cried. Darting to Marian, he landed on her horn and glared at Malleus. "It's a fake! You're a fake!"

Malleus squinted and raised a hand to shield his eyes from the torchlight as he stared toward Marian. "Your tiny sidekick has found me out," he admitted. "It's all prestidigitation, but it fools the rubes. They're all hungry for the slightest taste of magic." He reached into his sleeve again. "Want to see a card trick?" Bending a deck between his thumb and forefinger, he fanned the individual cards, then tossed them upward. As they fluttered down again, they exploded into small, bright puffs of flame.

"Oh, but you've seen fire." He shrugged apologetically. "Maybe this will impress you." He made a fist, and when he opened his hand again a silver flask rested on his palm. Marian rolled her eyes, but she watched curiously as he unstoppered the flask, raised it to his lips, and blew gently across the opening. "Come closer," he said softly. "Come closer, my pretty Unicorn."

Marian took a tentative step forward. The flickering torchlight gleamed on the silver flask. It was attractive, dazzling. She'd never quite seen anything so beautiful. Malleus blew across it again. The perfume it contained was sweetly delicate, familiar and enticing. She breathed deeply.

It smelled of Sinobarre—hypnotic, irresistible.

"Come closer," Malleus whispered. His voice was low, rich, and compelling.

She recoiled, shook her head, and stamped the carpeted floor. The perfume crawled up her nose, suddenly cloying. She struggled to resist, to call for help. "Bumble!" she rasped. "The flask!"

No more than a blur, the little hummingbird flew through the gloom and knocked the vessel from Malleus's hand. Cursing, he leaped away. Again, a column of smoke swallowed him, and he disappeared.

Sinobarre's compelling scent still mingled with the incense, but without Malleus' seductive voice whispering to her, her will was her own again. Fighting the pain in her legs, she ran back to Chernovog.

"I can't get loose!" he told her, struggling in his bonds.

The ribbon that had seemed to materialize out of nothingness proved to be a bola. She recalled how Malleus had flung his arm out toward Chernovog, using the concealment of darkness to disguise his trick. Using her teeth, she tried to untangle him from the strands.

Malleus called to her, unseen from another part of the pavilion. "Did you think this was over, my lovely?"

Marian stared into the darkness again, wondering how he performed that particular trick—but sure it was a trick. "There's only one snake in this carnival that can address me that way, and you're not him."

Using her teeth to seize Chernovog's collar, she dragged the minotaur-boy toward the entrance. But the pain in her legs was so acute, and she made slow progress. Growing desperate, she began to cry, but she refused to quit.

"Relax." Malleus spoke from the darkness again. "Stop struggling, and let me be your friend."

Sinobarre's scent still wafted in the air. Not even the incense could weaken or disguise it. Marian sobbed as she felt its effect creeping into her brain again. Now she knew how a common carnival owner had managed to capture so many wondrous creatures. He'd simply talked them into surrender, enticed them into their cages!

"I want to be your little bird's friend, too," Malleus continued. "He'll make an amusing sideshow."

Clenching her jaws, refusing to release her hold on Chernovog, Marian fought the perfume and took another backward step, but her right leg suddenly failed her, and she sat awkwardly down on her haunches. "I . . . won't . . . give . . . up!" she cried. Rising, she seized Chernovog's collar again. She hadn't come all this way from Wyvernwood to lose the boy now. But her brain felt full of ice and fog. With no sense of direction left, she could only hope she was moving toward the entrance. Then, she felt the brush of silk against her flanks. Another step, and she was outside. Bright sunshine stabbed her eyes. She breathed deeply of fresh air.

Yet the battle wasn't over. Malleus appeared in the entrance, his face angry, his gaze maniacal. A number of tough-looking roustabouts also stood around, and farther away, she spied soldiers, men in armor with weapons. There seemed to be some fighting among the tents!

Malleus drew a long-bladed knife from his robe. "If I can't have you, no one will!" he shouted. "I'll slit both your throats!"

As he lunged at Marian, Ranock charged around the red pavilion. A startled roustabout, caught off-guard, went flying through the air as the minotaur-father lifted him and flung him aside. Wide-eyed, Malleus turned to face an unexpected new foe. But Ranock lowered his head, pounded forward, and knocked the would-be sorcerer flat.

"Papa!" Chernovog wrestled with his bonds as he struggled to sit up. The look on his face was joyful, confused, disbelieving, all at the same time.

Ranock stopped in his tracks, forgetting Malleus. "Chernovog!" He ran to his boy's side, threw himself down on his knees and seized the ribbons that bound his son. With a roar, he strained and snapped the strands. Father and son flung their arms around each other. "Thank you!" Ranock murmured, looking to Marian. "Thank you!"

Malleus rolled over and started to sit up. A green blur hit him in the eye. He screamed and rolled the other way. Again the green blur hit him, this time in the ear.

A roustabout crept toward Marian with a rake. She spun toward him, lowering her horn, and he danced back. Her anger surged again as she stared down two more. While her attention was diverted, one of the workers grabbed Malleus by his shoulders and dragged him to safety.

More soldiers raced up the lane between the tents, helmets glinting in the sunlight and their blue capes flashing. Joining the roustabouts, they ringed Marian and her friends. Some of their spear-points were bloodied, and that made Marian even angrier. The only possible foe they could have been fighting among the tents was Daddy and any of the other prisoners he'd managed to free.

Clutching his son to his side with one arm, Ranock swung a strand of the bola around and around his head to keep the soldiers and roustabouts back. The air whistled and roared with the sound of its spinning, and the weighted ball at its end made a formidable weapon. Yet Marian knew it wouldn't keep a spear at bay. She moved closer to Ranock, determined to protect him and his son at any cost. Bumble joined her, landing in her forelock.

A shadow passed suddenly overhead, eclipsing the sun, and a wind swept across the carnival. A powerful blast of flame reddened the sky. Every eye turned upward. A soldier screamed and threw down his spear. The roustabouts fled.

High atop one of the great towers, a Dragon spread immense gray wings and wrapped his tail around the slender structure. For a frightening moment, he glared at the scene below, and then he lifted his head skyward and gave a terrible roar.

Bumble screamed with glee and jumped up and down. "Ronaldo!"

One at a time, the soldiers backed away, unable to take their eyes from the creature perched upon the tower. Marian doubted any of them had ever seen a Dragon before. Their expressions were mixtures of wonder and terror, disbelief—and, strangely, hope.

Always over the next hill or in the next valley, Marian thought as she watched their slow and careful retreat, *we all hope that maybe there's just a drop of magic left somewhere.* She glanced from the soldiers to Malleus, who still lay on the ground. What a sad, pathetic figure he looked as he watched the Dragon.

Ronaldo breathed another great cloud of fire. Springing from the top of the tower, he soared through the cloud's burning heart and circled the second tower. Gracefully, almost serenely, he gyred downward in slow circles. The soldiers continued to back away, clearing a space for the Dragon to land.

Marian limped over to Malleus, and he gazed fearfully up as she stood above him. "Find another line of work," she told him coldly. "If you ever come to Wyvernwood again, or if I ever hear that you've captured another poor creature for your sideshows, I and my friends will find you. I swear it." She leaned closer, pressing the tip of her horn on his chest. "And when I do, you'll wish I'd fed you to Sinobarre."

She turned to Ronaldo as the Dragon touched down and folded his wings. Lowering his huge head close to hers, he gave her a shy look and blinked his eyes. "I'm sorry," he said.

Marian interrupted him. "Don't you ever apologize!" she said sternly. Then she limped closer and nuzzled his cheek. "My dear friend, I'm just glad to see you."

Bumble flew a circle around Marian's horn and perched on Ronaldo's nose. "Bumble's glad, too!" he sang. "Hooray for Ronaldo for scaring away the pointy-men!"

Arm in arm, Ranock and Chernovog came over. Chernovog put out a hand and patted Ronaldo's leathery cheek, then let go of his father and hugged the gray dragon. Ronaldo purred ever so softly. "Marian's fond of saying there's no magic left in the world," he said to Ranock. "But finding you alive and well puts the lie to that. Beatrice will be so happy."

"Oh, my gosh!" Chernovog exclaimed. He turned to his father. "You don't know—I have a baby brother!"

Beaming, Ranock knelt down, hugged his son again, and rumpled his hair. "There's probably not a cigar to be bought in this town," he said over Chernovog's shoulder to the others.

"For which some of us are very grateful," Marian said. She gazed around. Someone was missing. "Where did Malleus go?"

Ronaldo raised up enough to point with one of his foreclaws. "After your dire little threat, he slunk off between those tents. My guess is, he's headed for the docks as fast and as silently as he can go."

Ranock pursed his lips thoughtfully, then covered his son's ears with both hands so he couldn't overhear. "I wonder if he'll run into Daddy?"

"I like Daddy," Marian answered. "I wouldn't want to see him choke on a piece of bad meat."

Without warning, another shadow dimmed the sunlight. Then another. And another.

"I forgot to mention," Ronaldo said as everyone looked up. "I brought company. You might say they're on a goodwill tour."

Gleaming in the bright sunlight, Chan perched on the tower where Ronaldo had first landed. He fanned his massive wings, lashed the air with his tail, and blew one blast of fire. His sister, Luna, pale and ivory as the moon itself, perched on the other tower, a figure of dignified but dangerous calm. Above them flew a host of other Dragons. They circled the square and the city or perched on the walls that surrounded Jiwashek.

Goodwill tour, indeed.

A clearer message had never been written in any language.

21

RONALDO CARRIED MARIAN IN HIS CLAWS as gently as he could while Bumble huddled in the Gray Dragon's left ear. With ropes made from the carnival's tent riggings, and following Chan's advice, Ranock harnessed Chernovog to the white Dragon orphan, Snow-song, and then himself to silver Paraclion.

Luna wore a lopsided grin as she watched and shook her head. "First Chan and his man-child. And now this. Maybe we'd better start making saddles and bridles."

At her side, red Tiamat wore a sterner, disapproving look. "I would never allow it."

Following Chan, they rose one after another, into the bright sky and headed northward. In the streets below, Jiwashek's citizens turned out to watch them depart. Most stared in fear or sullen resentment. Only a few braved the animosity of their neighbors and dared to wave goodbye.

"I don't think we made many friends down there," Ronaldo said to Marian as he soared over the city walls.

Marian thought of Daddy and the old lion. After things had calmed down, she'd asked Ronaldo to look for them, but they'd disappeared as completely as Malleus. For Daddy, that probably meant to the sea, and for the lion, to the mountains south of the city. She wished them both well. "If we made only one friend," she answered, "it's one more than we had before we came."

"Never underestimate the value of a friend," Bumble sang in the Gray Dragon's ear.

Chan listened to their brief conversations with a wan smile as he flew near them. Yet, his mood was pensive. A more unlikely trio he couldn't have picked for the kind of adventure they'd just shared—a hermit artist, a reclusive Unicorn who was the last of her kind in the world, and a nearly brainless hummingbird who clearly wasn't quite as brainless as he seemed!

He thought that he knew them. Yet, he wondered if he really knew them at all. Though they hardly seemed aware of it, each of the three had changed.

He suspected the same was true of Ranock and his son, Chernovog. There was a similar look in their bovine eyes, something as hard as it was joyful, a look that was very un-minotaur. Father and son, for all the dangers they had faced, had seen things few others of their kind had before. Gazing askance at them, he marveled at how easily they rode upon the backs of Dragons, faces to the wind, calmly, as if it were perfectly natural.

Chan wondered if they would be content again with the rustic life of Whispering Hills. Ranock might once more find his place there; he had Beatrice for his wife, and a new son he hadn't even seen. But what of Chernovog? Youth could be so restless.

The city of Jiwashek disappeared in the southern distance, and the rolling hills that surrounded it began to flatten into the broad, grassy plains of Degarm. To Chan, it was an alien landscape, and the more he let his gaze roam over it, the more it disconcerted him. There had never been a time in his life when he hadn't been surrounded by trees, when he hadn't heard the music of their rustling leaves and smelled their rich earthiness. Even when he flew, Wyvernwood had always been beneath him. Even on the white-sand shore of the Windy Sea the forest was always at his back.

Still, he had to admit there was a warped kind of beauty to Degarm's open expanses. The way the wind rippled over the grass, the way the narrow streams and rivers could be seen for miles, like veins on the skin of Father Earth—these were sights he knew he'd never forget.

"You look like you have the weight of the world on your shoulders, Brother."

Luna flew up close beside him. "You should feel triumphant! We've turned back an invasion and demonstrated to Degarm how unwise it would be to provoke us. I think our father would be proud."

Chan snorted. "A handful of poorly equipped soldiers angry because their city had been attacked," he reminded her. "Hardly a battle to write songs about. As for demonstrating anything to Degarm..." he shrugged as he beat his wings and stared straight ahead. "Only time will tell. Men can be foolish and hard-headed."

"You're a pessimist!" she teased, brushing the tip of her wing against his, causing him to veer to one side.

He righted himself and caught up with his sister again. "A realist," he insisted as he employed the same playful trick to knock her off course. It was a game they'd played since childhood, and it gave him a briefly satisfying comfort to play it again. "With pessimistic tendencies," he added.

Would Stormfire be proud?

It seemed there had hardly been time to grieve for his father. Chan hadn't told anyone, but in quiet moments he still listened for Stormfire's voice. Sometimes he even thought he heard it. And whenever a tall shadow fell upon the ground, almost reflexively he looked back half-expecting to see his father. The smell of the smoke from the funeral pyre yet lingered in his nostrils; when he closed his eyes he still saw those bright, consuming flames.

"Look!"

Marian's unexpected outcry startled Chan from his reverie. He glanced at her, then followed the direction of her gaze as she strained her neck to see over Ronaldo's cupped paws. They were just passing over the small woodland where they had met the Gray Dragon as he was about to fly to Jiwashek. There was a story there that Chan knew he hadn't yet heard, but neither Marian nor the hummingbird or Ronaldo, himself, seemed inclined to talk about it.

He knew, however, that something important had happened there. Bears and wolves and bobcats and rabbits and squirrels, indeed it seemed every creature in the little forest, were waiting at its edge, and in the grassland surrounding it, and even in the dusty road to watch the Dragonkin go by. Hawks and robins rose up into the air side by side for a closer look. Even bats, who usually shunned the daylight, defied their nature and took to the air.

It was an amazing sight!

"Hello!" Bumble cried as he waved a wingtip. "Hello to all our friends below! So long, and thanks for all the flowers!"

A golden eagle flew suddenly up from the forest edge and paced alongside Ronaldo. As he flew, he turned his head toward Marian.

"Elvis sent me with a question, milady," he said as the wind rushed through his feathers. "What did you find over the next hill, or in the next valley?"

Marian gave the eagle a long, thoughtful look. Then, ever so carefully, she rose to stand in Ronaldo's paws. Her mane and tail blew wildly in the wind as suddenly she laughed. Every Dragon, every bird and creature in the sky looked her way. "Magic!" she cried. "Tell him—I found magic!"

The eagle closed its dark eyes and nodded. When he opened them again they glittered with happiness. "He'll be pleased," the eagle answered. "But I know he'd want me to tell you this, that we found it, too. One day, it just came walking into our homes, and we are all transformed." Dipping a wing, he flew a sweeping circle and headed back to the woodland.

"Good-bye!" Bumble shouted, waving as the all the other birds and bats began to fall away. "Good-bye to all our friends in the sky!" He flew from Ronaldo's ear and nestled in Marian's mane as she settled down in the Dragon's clutch again. "Bumble is afraid," he said to the last Unicorn in the world, and his little voice trembled. "My Bumble-brain is small, and I may soon forget my friends below!"

"I don't think you'll forget," Marian answered gently. "But if you want, I'll tell you stories everyday to remind you."

Without slowing his flight, Ronaldo twisted his neck and turned his gray head around. "I'll paint pictures and make drawings," he promised. "Just for you. And since you don't have a home, you can live with me."

Bumble snuggled deeper in Marian's mane and sighed. "Never underestimate the value of friends!"

Ronaldo, Marian, and Bumble became quiet again, and Chan looked around for his sister. She had fallen back to take up a position beside Tiamat among the rest of the Dragonkin. As he watched, she played the same trick on the ruby Dragon that she had just played on him, sending Tiamat spinning earthward. Never in real danger, he recovered himself and swooped upward to overtake her again. Then, with a powerful beat of his wings, he surged right behind her and nipped the tip of her tail.

Chan laughed softly to himself, and his mood improved a little until, near the setting of the sun, they passed over the city of Karlass.

Though the central and southwestern corners of the city were mostly untouched, flames had consumed the docks and riverfronts and most of the northern sections. A tall tower and a high, encircling wall near the center of the city stood scorched and blackened by smoke and heat, and a long and jagged crack split one side of the stone tower, testifying to the fire's intensity.

Yet, not all of its citizens had fled the destruction, and already some small rebuilding efforts seemed to be underway. Men with hammers and shovels, wheel barrows and handcarts were working to clear the wreckage. Already the framework for a new wharf had been erected on the coastal side.

Shirtless and soot-covered men paused at their labors to glare upward as the Dragonkin flew by. Chan didn't have to see their faces to sense their sullen animosity. They blamed Wyvernwood for allowing the Angmar ships to sail down the Blackwater and attack them from behind, and there was no reasoning with them. An enemy had wounded them, and it would take a long time for that wound to heal.

He led the Dragonkin across the Blackwater. Wyvernwood spread out before him, dark and mysterious in the deepening twilight, and he breathed deeply of the forest fragrances, glad to taste familiar air again. The motion of the treetops in the wind seemed to sweep his worries away as he turned toward the Whispering Hills. Ranock and his son would be eager for home, and there, Jake also waited. Chan found himself surprisingly eager to see the boy.

The hills rose in the distance, and on a sudden impulse, he called out. "Ronaldo!"

The Gray Dragon gazed at Chan and glided closer with a questioning look in his eyes.

"This is your home," Chan said, meeting Ronaldo's curious gaze. "Yours and Marian's and Bumble's, and you're the heroes of the day. Take the lead and guide us in."

Ronaldo swallowed and looked straight ahead. "I'm not worthy of any honors," he answered. "It's better that a child of Stormfire leads us."

Marian scowled and rose on swollen knees in Ronaldo's palms. "Oh, give us a break!" she snapped. "Don't make me get up and kick your gray behind!"

Bumble flew back to his former perch in Ronaldo's ear. "Kick him again! Kick him again! Harder! Harder!" he chanted as he launched a rapid series of harmless kicks at Ronaldo's earlobe with his tiny feet. Then, leaning deeper into the Dragon's ear, he called, "Lighten up, you big lug!"

Chan gave Ronaldo a long, scrutinizing look as he remembered the first time his father took him, as a child, to meet the great artist in his Whispering Hills home. The memory was still vivid, poignant, because it was one of the few times he had ever spent alone with his father. Yet, it was Ronaldo who stood out in that memory. Even then, he had been a legend among the Dragonkin.

"I know what bothers you, Master," Chan said. When Ronaldo started to protest, Chan shook his head and continued. "My father said you were a master. Master Ronaldo, he called you. I've seen your paintings, myself, and I know you for what you are. But you see yourself as something less because you are gray. Yet look behind you, Master." Chan's voice was insistent, even commanding. "Look!"

Slowly, Ronaldo turned his great head to look over one shoulder, and Chan looked with him at the score of Dragons in the darkening sky that followed.

"A complete palette has many colors, Master," Chan continued. "We are ruby red, sapphire blue, green as an emerald, silver and gold, white and ivory and black as night. But don't you see, Master?" He hesitated, looking for some response from the greatest artist of the Dragonkin. When Ronaldo failed to speak up, Chan pressed his point. "As night comes on, none of those colors matter. You can't tell now who is red, who is gold, or who is black. But it doesn't matter. All that really matters is the fire in our hearts, and that we are Dragons!"

"And make no mistake, my dear friend," Marian added quietly. "A long night is coming. The Dragonkin and all of Wyvernwood are going to need you.

Ronaldo was quiet for a long moment as he fixed his gaze on the forest below. "There's much of your father in you, Child of Stormfire," he said finally as he lifted his head to meet Chan's gaze. "Very well, then. Just this once, I'll take the lead."

The moon was just beginning to spill its frosty light over the trees when they reached the hill where Beatrice lived. There wasn't room for all the Dragons to land together, so many of them scattered throughout the nearby forest. Ronaldo led Chan, Snowsong, and

Paraclion right down to the minotaur-wife's front yard where they also found Ramoses waiting.

Lamplight shone warmly in the windows of the farmhouse. The front door slammed open almost at once. Jake rushed out first, followed by Beatrice with Coniff in one arm, and Granny Scylla chasing after.

"Chernovog!" Beatrice cried as she spotted her son on Snowsong's neck. "Oh, blessed earth and stars! My boy is back!" She looked to Ronaldo with moist eyes, and then to all the Dragons. "Thank you! Thank you all!"

On Paraclion's neck, Ranock silently bent to untie the knots around his waist and legs. No one, not even Chernovog, said anything as the silver Dragon lowered his head, and the minotaur slid to the ground.

Granny Scylla noticed him first. Her eyes widened and her jaw gaped. Then she slipped to the grassy earth in a faint.

Beatrice gave a small cry as she balanced Baby Coniff and knelt down beside Granny, but the old minotaur woman was already awake again, though unable quite to find her voice. She pointed a gnarly finger toward the shadows around Snowsong.

Slowly, Beatrice turned her head. With a grin on his face, her husband stepped into the pale light that spilled from the windows. "Hello, Beatrice," he said simply.

Beatrice clapped a hand to her mouth. Then, she began to weep, softly at first, then in great wracking sobs. Ranock ran to her. Throwing his arms around her, he showered kisses on her bovine face and stroked her soft, brown cheeks.

"Isn't anyone going to help me down?" Chernovog shouted in mild annoyance as he struggled with his own knotted ropes.

Jake didn't wait to be asked. With a grin at Chan, he hurried to the minotaur-boy's aid and with deft fingers made short work of the bonds. Without a word of thanks, Chernovog sprang from Paraclion's neck, somersaulted in the air over Jake, and ran to join his family.

Jake looked somewhat surprised. "He's a gymnast?" he asked, raising one eyebrow dubiously.

"Not exactly," Marian answered as Ronaldo leaned forward and gently set her down. She tested her sore legs, stretching them and taking a few ginger steps. "Chernovog is a bull-dancer. Quite a good one, too, when you can get him to perform." She smiled suddenly and trembled as she watched the family on the lawn. Even Granny Scylla had thrown herself into the hugging and kissing and crying and head patting. "Everything we went through," she said almost to herself, "that makes it all worth it."

Ronaldo turned to Chan. It had been a very long flight, and his gray face betrayed his fatigue. In fact, everyone was quite exhausted. "Look for the three of us in Stronghold soon," Ronaldo said wearily. "I think we'd like to pay our respects to your father."

"One! Two! Three!" Bumble said, flying from Ronaldo's ear to perch on Marian's horn. "Ronaldo, Marian, and me!"

Chan watched the three of them depart into the darkness as they headed for Ronaldo's cave on the far side of the hill. A strange feeling of contentment suddenly flooded through him. He was tired, and his wings ached, but more than anything he wanted to fly again, to feel the wind in his face and to sail the star-speckled night.

Jake sidled up to him and touched his scaled leg. "Are you all right?" he whispered.

Chan looked down at the man-boy. "How would you like to go for another ride?"

Jake's eyes lit up, and he made a grab for the ropes that lay on the ground, the same ones that Ranock and Chernovog had used before. Without another word, Chan lowered his head. Jake sprang into place and tied himself securely.

"Rest," Chan said to the other Dragons. "We'll head for home tomorrow."

Ramoses stepped closer. At Chan's request, the old Dragon had stayed behind while he led the others farther into Degarm. The ancient knowledge, leadership, and wisdom he possessed were too valuable to risk. Now, however, he clearly had something on his mind. "There's room in the sky for two of us, Chan," Ramoses said.

Jake answered before Chan could, politely making it plain that he didn't intend to be left behind. "We couldn't ask for better company!"

Laughing, Chan leaped into the sky and Ramoses followed after. With Jake whooping and yelling, he skimmed low above the trees, startling birds in their nests and sending a family of deer racing deeper into the woods. Overhead, a flock of geese filled the night with honking to greet them as they passed.

Farther to the north, a ring of fire shimmered in the darkness, then faded. A moment later, another took its place. It also faded, only to be replaced by yet another. Against the starlight, two dim shapes could be seen flying in loops and circles, swooping high and gliding low, sometimes chasing one another. Exhaling fire, one of the shapes suddenly sailed backward in a tight loop. Flames crackled in the darkness, seeming to follow until both ends met.

"Who's that?" Jake called from his seat on Chan's neck.

"Unless I miss my guess," Chan answered with a low chuckle as he watched the display, "that's Luna and Tiamat."

"It's almost like they're dancing!" Jake shouted.

"In a sense, they are." Chan wondered how he could feel so at peace. So much had happened. So much had changed. Marian had been right when she said a long night was coming on. Yet, with this boy on his back and his forest home below, none of it seemed to matter tonight. Especially as he watched his sister in the distance. He smiled as he explained. "They're on their mating flight."

He looked over his shoulder. Ramoses was watching Luna and Tiamat, too. He wore a look of quiet pride, and his eyes shimmered with the moonlight with a soft wetness that hinted of tears.

"In the face of war," Chan said to the old dragon, "life goes on."

"Some lives go on," Ramoses answered grimly. "A pair of hawks brought news from the coast today. It's what I wanted to tell you. Thursis has fallen to Angmar."

Chan squeezed his eyes shut as he felt a flash of anger. Thursis, the island paradise off the coast of Wyvernwood, where the Mer-folk made their homes! The Mers would surely have escaped. Most of them, anyway. "Go back and tell the others," Chan told Ramoses as he changed his course and flew eastward. "Make sure they're welcomed on our shores and beaches."

The Windy Sea was not very far away. Alone, but for Jake, Chan flew into the moonlight. His fatigue no longer mattered. Ramoses's news had shattered the brief peace he'd felt. He didn't expect to find the Mers this far south, but he felt a need to stand upon the white sand and gaze upon the tossing water.

"You're going to need me, you know." Jake leaned down until he lay flat against Chan's scaled neck, and he slipped his arms wide as if to hug the Dragon. "And Trevor and Markam and Ariel, and even little Pear."

"I know," Chan answered as they approached the shoreline. "The Dragonkin are big and powerful, even fierce when we must be. But there are things about your people we don't understand. You'll have to teach me."

Jake slapped his right hand against Chan's neck. "Don't call them *my people*," he said sharply. "I'm where I belong. I've already chosen my side." Sitting up again, he pointed into the wind. "Look!"

Neither of them said anymore. Far out upon the Windy Sea, illuminated by the glimmering moon, two great navies raced across the waves—Angmar from the north and Degarm from the south. Water fell like diamonds from the oars that drove them forward, and the heart-pounding throb of master-drums echoed through the night.

Chan landed on the shore to watch the inevitable clash.

It began with flaming arrows streaking both ways through the darkness. Such pitiful little sparks compared to the fire a dragon could make. But it was fire enough. Rigging began to burn, and ships began to blaze. Over the beat of the master-drums came screams. One ship rammed another. Oars shattered, wood splintered and timbers cracked like thunder. The sea, itself, seemed to catch fire, and smoke rose like a thick fog that drifted slowly, inexorably toward Wyvernwood.

The long night had begun.

Epilogue

CURLED IN THE CROOK OF HIS MOTHER'S ARM, little Puck purred and looked to the stars beyond the mouth of the cave. Rono had moved too high in the heavens for him to see, but through the naked limbs of the black trees bright Oculo shone with a pure, silvery fire and just below it, he spied red-glowing Brakkar.

In his imagination, the silvery star was Luna, though Luna was not really silver. Brakkar was red-scaled Tiamat chasing her across the sky in their wedding flight.

"Is that the end of the story?" he asked with a yawn when his mother fell quiet.

Marina smiled and rubbed her child's head, scratching him lightly between the ears the way he liked best. "Oh no, my Puck," she answered softly. "That's just the beginning. But it's enough for tonight. Autumn's almost passed, and winter is coming. We have to save a few stories for the cold nights ahead."

"But Mama!" Puck protested. "You know so many stories. Tell me more! Tell me now!"

It was black outside the cave. The hour was late, and the air had grown cold. Yet, she remained by the door and stared outward, tired and wistful. When the wind blew there was still music in the bare branches, in the creaking of the limbs and the groaning of the old trunks. And when she listened carefully there was singing, too, and sometimes a faint drumming.

This time of year the ghosts of Wyvernwood were a restless lot. She told her tales, not just for Puck, but for them, and always with her door open. They liked to be remembered.

"It's bedtime for you, little one," Marina said, hushing Puck's squirming protests. "Go and wash your face, and in a few moments I'll come tuck in your covers."

Puck stopped purring. With a pouty look, he rose and stomped back into the cave. Before he headed for his bed, though, he stopped by the fireplace, gazed into the flames and then turned again. The firelight danced on his thin golden scales and on his immature wings as he tried to flex them. "Thank you, Mama," he said quietly. "But next time I want to hear about the three Dragons."

Marina tilted her head as she regarded her beautiful Dragon-child. "The three Dragons?" she said. "Harrow, Chan, and Luna?"

Puck shook his head. Moving past the fire to the wall, he ran one paw over a shelf of books. There were many shelves, but he could only reach so high, and he craned his neck back to let his gaze roam over the rows and rows of bound volumes above his head. "No, not them," he answered. He pointed to the highest shelf where the many tomes that made up the *Book of Stormfire* rested. Though he couldn't reach them, he knew where they were. "I want to hear about the Glass Dragon, the Diamond Dragon, and the Herd of all Dragons."

"The Heart of all Dragons," Marina corrected.

"Will you tell it tomorrow night?" Puck persisted.

Marina smiled. "Yes, my little love," she promised. "If you don't wear me out tomorrow, and if you go to bed now."

Puck looked thoughtful for a moment, then ran forward, threw his arms around her and gave her a kiss. As Marina watched him run off to bed, she touched the place where his lips had brushed her. It wouldn't be much longer, she knew, before he'd feel too big to kiss his mother anymore. That made each one she received now a treasure.

The wind howled suddenly and gusted through the mouth of the cave, causing the flames in the fireplace to flicker and dance. "Go away, Gaunt," she whispered. "There's no place for you here by my fire."

The wind withdrew, and the howling ceased. The fireplace burned calm and steady once again.

Closing her eyes, Marina listened to the sounds of the forest and inhaled the autumn earthiness that filled the night. She wasn't really so old as she had told Puck at the beginning of the story, and he knew that, too, but it made the tellings so much more vivid when they both pretended, and wasn't any opening better than *Once upon a time?*

She hadn't met Stormfire, but she knew him through Ramoses' books, which now were her books, and she had read them every one. She knew him, too, from all the stories and tales she'd heard at Luna's knee or stretched out on her arm, as Puck stretched out on hers.

Marina smiled at that memory. She missed her grandmother so much it hurt sometimes.

But Luna was never far away. She dwelled close by with all the other ghosts in Wyvernwood. Sometimes, she even came to visit. Marina could feel her out there now, breathing ghost-fire on the cold night air.

"Goodnight, Grandmother," she murmured. "Goodnight."

Rising slowly, she folded her arms upon her chest and stared out across the forest and across the Whispering Hills. There was no reason to feel lonely. She was never alone. She had Puck, and she had her memories, and there were others out there—not ghosts—like her. Others that had not forsaken the woodlands. Sometimes they came to visit, too.

But not tonight. And probably not tomorrow night. Winter was coming, and there was no better way to pass the winter than curled up beside your own fire in your own cave or burrow or nest among all the things and small treasurers you held so dear.

The wind blew again, and at the bottom of the hill something moved among the moonshadows and the trees. A flash of white, Marina thought, and a hint of a golden horn. It regarded her briefly from the edge of the forest, then moved on and vanished.

"Goodnight, Marian," she whispered. "And you, too, Bumble."

She cast one final glance at the stars. *Always remember*, she told herself. *There are still dreams to dream and stars to be wished upon.* She sighed as Oculo glimmered above. Though it was late, and it wasn't really the first star she'd seen that night, she still made a wish. She wished for peace.

Then Marina stepped back inside the caveand gently closed the ancient tiger oak door.